Blood Royal

ALEXANDRE DUMAS

Blood Royal

— OR —

The Son of Milady

Book Four of the Musketeers Cycle:
The Conclusion of *Twenty Years After*

EDITED AND TRANSLATED
BY LAWRENCE ELLSWORTH

PEGASUS BOOKS
NEW YORK LONDON

Blood Royal

Pegasus Books, Ltd.
148 West 37th Street, 13th Fl.
New York, NY 10018

Blood Royal, by Alexandre Dumas, Translated by Lawrence Ellsworth
Translation and Original Material Copyright 2020 © by Lawrence Schick

First Pegasus Books cloth edition November 2020

Interior design by Sabrina Plomitallo-González, Pegasus Books

Library of Congress Cataloging-in-Publication Data is available.

ISBN: 978-1-64313-570-0

10   9   8   7   6   5   4   3   2   1

Printed in the United States of America
Distributed by Simon & Schuster
www.pegasusbooks.com

CONTENTS

Introduction

by Lawrence Ellsworth

Dumas and His Musketeers

As a successful playwright, Dumas was well-known in Paris by 1840, and had tasted celebrity, but his 1844 novel *The Three Musketeers* was a global phenomenon. His fame was suddenly worldwide, readers clamored for a sequel, and Dumas gave it to them in 1845 with *Twenty Years After,* a sprawling historical drama bigger even than *The Three Musketeers*—too large, in fact, for single-volume publication except in oversized editions or with tiny type between narrow margins.

The sequel was also unexpected in that it didn't pick up right where *Musketeers* had left off (Dumas saved that approach for *The Red Sphinx*), but instead carried d'Artagnan and his comrades from youth into maturity— *Twenty Years After,* as the title promised. For Dumas had much bigger plans for his best-beloved characters than just giving them further adventures. By that time he was himself over forty, and wanted to show how his four varying archetypal heroes came to grips with the challenges of aging and the complexities of responsibility, while still finding ways to be true to themselves and their codes of honor and morality. To do this he worked out the plan of his four musketeers' entire lives from the 1620s through the late 1660s, interweaving, clashing, separating, and rejoining, defining them through what today we call long character arcs. And he involved them with a huge ensemble cast of secondary characters historical and fictional whose lives intertwined with theirs. He plotted a grand tale that would run to over a million words through the course of two giant sequels, the enormous *Twenty Years After* and the even more titanic *Le Vicomte de Bragelonne.*

This grand tale appeared in serial form, chapter after chapter, in Parisian periodicals from 1845 to 1850, and then was collected into books that were nearly always published in multiple volumes—especially in translation, where the sequels appeared in anywhere from four to eight parts.

Your current editor has decided the saga divides most comfortably into six volumes, with *Twenty Years After* split in half; this book, *Blood Royal,* is the second volume of what Dumas originally published as *Twenty Years After.*

What Has Gone Before

It is 1648, and France has changed since the time of *The Three Musketeers:* King Louis XIII has died, and his son, Louis XIV, is still a minor, so Anne of Austria rules as queen regent. Cardinal Richelieu, the great prime minister of the previous reign, died shortly before his king, and has been replaced by his Italian-born protégé, Cardinal Mazarin, whose relationship with Queen Anne is so close that it's rumored they are secretly married. Mazarin has continued Richelieu's policy of centralizing political control under the monarchy, which has alienated the parliament and the nobility, and of demanding high taxes to support the seemingly endless war with Spain, which has angered the populace. The result is burgeoning unrest, an ill-organized and intermittent civil war against the crown that history knows as the Fronde.

D'Artagnan is still Lieutenant of the King's Musketeers, a post he has held for almost twenty years, increasingly acting as de facto commander as his captain, Tréville, has aged, though without receiving the captain's rank and rewards. Long in harness, his horizons narrowed by a career in military service, he's grown sour and wry, but the flames of the Fronde rouse him from his long hibernation. The civil unrest means Mazarin needs more than mere soldiers, he needs covert agents with initiative who can wield both wits and swords—which is d'Artagnan's specialty.

So, the cardinal offers d'Artagnan a special mission, holding out the promise of his long-awaited captaincy, on condition that first the Gascon find his three former comrades in adventure and recruit them as well. Enlisting the mighty Porthos is easy, for though he's become a wealthy man of leisure, what he really longs for is the dignity of a noble title, which

Mazarin can provide. But sly Aramis has joined the Church and become an abbot, a rising star of the Jesuit order, and claims no further interest in politics or intrigue, while the noble Athos has retired to a modest country estate where he is raising a young ward, Raoul de Bragelonne—and he, too, declines to return to the service of the crown. Seemingly, the aid of Porthos will have to be enough.

But d'Artagnan has the feeling there's something his old friends aren't telling him, and his instincts are right: Athos and Aramis have joined "the Princes," the faction of the nobility on the side of the Frondeurs who are opposed to Mazarin and the queen. Among the Princes, there is one rebellious Prince of the Blood whom Mazarin fears over all the others, the Duc de Beaufort, whom he's already imprisoned outside Paris in the Château de Vincennes. The duke is heavily guarded, but Athos and Aramis have a plan to liberate him, having planted Athos's trusty manservant Grimaud among the warden's guards. Meanwhile, Cardinal Richelieu's old agent, the Comte de Rochefort, is freed from his incarceration by d'Artagnan's former lackey Planchet, now himself a Frondeur. With Rochefort's help, Athos, Aramis, and Grimaud succeed in getting Beaufort out and over the wall of Vincennes, and all gallop away on waiting horses.

Mazarin frantically assigns d'Artagnan his first mission: recapture the Duc de Beaufort! Summoning all his old energy and determination, unaware that he's also chasing his two former comrades, d'Artagnan takes Porthos and they ride hell-for-leather through the night to overtake the fleeing duke. But their attempt to recapture the prince is forestalled by Athos and Aramis, who fight d'Artagnan and Porthos to a standstill. D'Artagnan, bitter, is forced to admit defeat and has to return to Mazarin to confess his failure, but first he sets up a parley in Paris between the old friends so they can come to terms upon their now-evident conflict and opposition.

It takes two increasingly friendly meetings, but the four musketeers overcome their differences and agree that, though they fight for opposing sides, they will never fight each other again, and the old bonds of comradeship are reaffirmed. Meanwhile, Athos has other business in Paris, taking Raoul to visit the fascinating Duchesse de Chevreuse, that perennial conspirer against the authorities and, twenty years before, the lover of Aramis—and not just Aramis, for it's revealed that Raoul is actually the secret son of Athos and the duchess. The lad is now old enough to take up arms in the war against Spain, so his parents, their relationship still unknown to him, arrange for him to serve the Prince de Condé, the leading French general of the time.

Raoul rides off to war, finding friendship and adventure along the way: friendship in the person of the young Comte de Guiche, also riding to join Condé, and adventure in a skirmish with the Spanish, in which Raoul and de Guiche capture a prisoner whose information is key to the prince's victory at the Battle of Lens. They also encounter another young man on the road, a sinister monk with a foreign accent who brutally murders a wounded man they'd rescued from the skirmish, and then flees toward Paris.

But not before Grimaud, who'd been sent to accompany Raoul, realizes the monk's true identity: he is Mordaunt, the now-adult son of Milady de Winter, the murderess whom the musketeers had hired an executioner to slay at the end of *The Three Musketeers.* The wounded man Mordaunt had murdered was that same executioner, and now Mordaunt is bound for Paris to seek revenge on those who'd hired him.

Mordaunt also has an official reason to travel to Paris, as he's been sent by Oliver Cromwell, the leader of the Parliamentary rebels in England, as an envoy to Mazarin on a mission to persuade the cardinal to send no French aid to King Charles I, whom Cromwell is on the verge of defeating. However, the English Baron Winter, Mordaunt's hated uncle who had conspired with the musketeers at the execution of his mother, has come to Paris on behalf of King Charles with the opposite mission. Mordaunt reaches Mazarin first and Winter's plea for aid is refused—and Mordaunt recognizes Winter and begins to shadow him.

Winter, desperate for any help for Charles, remembers the four musketeers. D'Artagnan and Porthos are in the service of Mazarin and out of reach, but Winter finds Athos and Aramis and brings them to a meeting with Charles's wife Queen Henriette, who's fled the chaos of the English Civil War and is living in poverty at the Louvre. Touched by the pleas of the forlorn yet hopeful queen-in-exile, Athos and Aramis agree to return to England with Winter and do what they can to support King Charles in his final battles.

Athos and Aramis prepare to follow Winter back to England, but the three are themselves pursued by Mordaunt, who is now on their trail. As they take a ship from Boulogne, they are threatened from the shore by Mordaunt, who promises to hunt them down and have his revenge—in England, where d'Artagnan and Porthos will soon be journeying as well, on a mission of their own from Mazarin.

To England—And Back to France

Which brings us to *Blood Royal,* and the conclusion of this chapter of the Musketeers Cycle.

In this volume we see the shape of a new d'Artagnan start to emerge, as he faces his shortcomings in *Twenty Years After* and begins to adapt to the many-layered challenges of maturity. It helps that, though d'Artagnan has always been bold and clever, he has another core attribute that now comes to the fore: he is persistent. He tries new ideas, different approaches. And over the course of the story, he faces the reality that to prevail in this new world of complexity and compromise, he must grapple with moral ambiguity. To defeat his new enemies, he must adapt to their dubious methods— and sometimes even adopt them himself.

It is a considerable irony that d'Artagnan will be repeatedly forestalled by the much-younger Mordaunt, who comes out of the past of *The Three Musketeers* to embody the strengths of audacity and cunning that were once d'Artagnan's hallmarks. Mordaunt, burning with the fire of vengeance, has usurped and corrupted those youthful strengths, and the older d'Artagnan is no match for him until he finally pulls his former team back together. To weld that team into a unit and wield it as a weapon, he must give up his exclusive reliance on the forthright methods of youth and add to them the tools of maturity: foresight, compromise, dissimulation, and even manipulation of his own allies. He will have to become a true leader of men, leading not just by example but also by persuasion, influencing others by understanding their motivations. Once he accepts this, the team can be re-formed, and they can defeat the specter of their past.

That accomplished, the musketeers must then wrestle with an even greater threat, the eternal nemesis of youthful heroism—*politics*. As we'll see, though still and always a man of action when action is called for, d'Artagnan grows and evolves to become that which he once despised: a politician.

And politics is a skill he will need as the saga continues into the future, for when Louis XIV comes into his power, d'Artagnan will have to learn to navigate the treacherous perils of the Court of the Sun King. Here in *Blood Royal* Dumas introduces the themes and characters that will be central to the story to follow, in the four final volumes of the Musketeers Cycle. Here we meet Raoul de Bragelonne, the son of Athos and heir to the traditions of chivalry; young Louis XIV, king in principle but not yet in practice, who will embody the new regime of absolute monarchy; and Louise de La Vallière, whom both Raoul and Louis will love in a romance that will prove a defining metaphor for the new era. There's little romance in *Blood Royal*, a lack Dumas admittedly regretted, but it firmly establishes the context for the affairs of the heart that will drive the adventures to come, in which love, politics, and power play essential roles in the great drama Dumas mounts on the stage of history.

A Note on the Translation

The public appetite for a sequel to *The Three Musketeers* was so great that the chapters comprising *Blood Royal* were rushed into book publication before the serial had even finished running in *Le Siècle*. The first (and unauthorized) edition, published in Brussels in early 1845, was cobbled together by collecting the installments published in Paris, so the sources of the original French version of the tale are a jumble. Where there were inconsistencies, this translator usually relied on the Pléiade version of *Twenty Years After* edited by Gilbert Sigaux in 1962, as well as the edition compiled and annotated by Charles Samaran that same year for Éditions Garnier.

Historical Character Note

The first time a notable character from history is mentioned in the text, their name is marked with an asterisk.* A brief paragraph describing that person appears in the Historical Characters appendix at the end of the book.

Blood Royal

I

The *Te Deum* for the Victory at Lens

The commotion in Paris that Queen Henriette* had noticed was caused by news of the victory at Lens, brought by the Duc de Châtillon on behalf of Monsieur le Prince. The duke, who'd had such a noble share in the triumph, was also charged with hanging twenty-two flags in the vault of Notre-Dame, banners captured from the Lorrainers and Spaniards.

This news was decisive in resolving the conflict with parliament in favor of the Royal Court. All the taxes that had been decreed, and which the Parliament had opposed, were immediately ratified to sustain the honor of France during the ongoing battle with its enemies. The country had experienced nothing but defeats since the Battle of Nördlingen, and parliament had had a fine time mocking Mazarin* for the promised victories that never occurred, but now victory was in hand at last, and a great victory, too: everyone regarded it as a double triumph for the Court, giving it the upper hand over enemies both domestic and foreign, so that the young King Louis XIV,* upon hearing the news, declared, "Ah, gentlemen of the Parliament, what do you have to say now?"

Hearing that, Queen Anne* had hugged to her heart her royal child, whose hauteur accorded so well with her own. A council was called that very evening, summoning Maréchal de La Meilleraie and Monsieur de Villeroy because they were Cardinalists, Chavigny* and Séguier because they hated parliament, and Guitaut* and Comminges* because they were devoted to the queen. None of this council's decisions were made public, except that on the following Sunday there would be a *Te Deum* sung at Notre-Dame in honor of the victory at Lens.

That Sunday, the Parisians awoke with joy: at that time a *Te Deum* was a grand affair, not yet made routine by overuse, and it was widely hailed.

The sun, which seemed a willing partner in the festivities, had risen radiant, gilding the somber towers of the city, its streets already teeming with immense crowds; even the darkest alleys had taken on a festive air, and along the quays streamed long lines of citizens, workers, women, and children moving toward Notre-Dame, like fish in a river ascending toward its source. The shops were deserted, the houses closed up; everyone wanted to see the young king, his royal mother, and the famous Cardinal Mazarin, whom they hated so much they couldn't do without him.

Freedom of speech reigned among the surging crowds; every shade of opinion was loudly expressed, and rang out like a call to riot, just as the thousand bells of the churches of Paris rang out the *Te Deum.* The citizens of Paris made their own rules that day and ensured that nothing dampened the cries of hatred or stilled the flow of slander.

At eight in the morning, the Regiment of the Queen's Guards, commanded by Guitaut and seconded by his nephew, Comminges, had marched, to the sound of drums and trumpets, from the Palais Royal to Notre-Dame, a maneuver which the Parisians had watched with their habitual admiration of military music and bright uniforms.

Friquet was part of the crowd, dressed in his best, able to attend thanks to a temporary swelling caused by jamming a huge number of cherry pits into the side of his mouth, which had persuaded Bazin to give him the day off. Bazin had refused at first, for the beadle was in a lousy mood, first due to the departure of Aramis,* who had left without telling him where he was going, and then from having to serve at a mass in honor of a victory that didn't accord with his opinions—Bazin, we recall, was a Frondeur. If there was some way by which, despite the dignity of his position, the beadle could absent himself as easily as the choirboy, Bazin would certainly have made the same request of the archbishop the choirboy had made of him. Thus, he had refused Friquet at first, but the boy's cheek continued to swell, so for the honor and reputation of the choir, which couldn't be compromised by such a deformity, he had finally given in, muttering to himself.

Outside the church door, Friquet had spat out the cherry pits and sent toward the oblivious Bazin one of those supremely rude gestures that demonstrate the superiority of the Parisian gamin to all other guttersnipes. As for his tavern job, he had naturally avoided that by saying he'd be serving at the mass at Notre-Dame. Friquet was thus free, and as we mentioned, dressed in his very best, capped by a remarkable ornament, one of those bulbous bonnets worn during the period between the cap of the Middle Ages and the brimmed hat of the reign of Louis XIII.* His mother had made this grotesque headgear for him, and either from whim or from a lack of uniform fabric, had sewn it from an assortment of colors, so that this paragon of 17th-century haberdashery was yellow and green on one side and red and white on the other. This made Friquet, who had always loved bright colors, all the more proud and triumphant.

After leaving Bazin, Friquet ran toward the Palais Royal. He arrived just as the regiment of guards was marching out, and as he hadn't come for any reason other than to see the sights and enjoy the music, he took a position marching at the head of the column, beating a tattoo with two wooden slats. From the tambour he passed on to the trumpet, which he imitated with his mouth in a way that was the envy of his fellow amateurs of musical imposture.

This amusement lasted from the Barrière des Sergents all the way to Place Notre-Dame, and Friquet thoroughly enjoyed it. But then the regiment halted, and the companies deployed along the streets in the heart of the Île de la Cité, from the end of Rue Saint-Christophe almost to Rue Cocatrix, where Broussel* lived. Then Friquet, remembering he'd not yet had breakfast, considered where best to acquire this important meal, and after thinking for a moment, decided to let Councilor Broussel pick up the tab.

Following this impulse, he ran till he was out of breath, and was soon knocking loudly at the councilor's door. His mother, Broussel's aging maid-servant, opened and said, "What are you doing here, lad, and why aren't you at Notre-Dame?"

"I was there, Mother Nanette," said Friquet, "but I saw things going on that Master Broussel should be warned about, so with the permission of Monsieur Bazin—you know him, Bazin the beadle, right?—I've come to speak to Monsieur Broussel."

"And what do you want to say, you monkey, to Monsieur Broussel?"

"I'll tell him that personally."

"Well, you can't, because he's working."

"Then I'll wait," said Friquet, pleased, because that suited how he intended to spend the time.

And he ran quickly up the stairs, with Dame Nanette following slowly behind him. "But what do you want with Monsieur Broussel?" she called.

"I want to tell him," shouted Friquet at the top of his lungs, "that there's a whole regiment of guards coming this way! And since everybody says the Court is angry with him, I've come to warn him to look out!"

Broussel heard the young prankster's cries and, charmed by this display of zeal, came down to the first floor from where he'd been working up above. "What's this about a regiment of guards, my friend?" he said. "You simpleton, you'll start a panic. Don't you know it's their custom to march this way, and that the regiment always lines the streets where the king is to pass?"

Friquet pretended to be surprised, and said, turning his new hat between his hands, "Well, of course you'd know that, Monsieur Broussel, because you know everything. But I didn't know it, I swear to God, and thought I was bringing you important news. Please don't be angry with me, Monsieur Broussel."

"On the contrary, my dear lad, your zeal pleases me. Dame Nanette, see if you can find those apricots Madame de Longueville* sent us yesterday from Noisy, and give a half dozen to your son with a crust of fresh bread."

"Ah, thank you, Monsieur Broussel!" said Friquet. "I like apricots a lot."

Broussel went to find his wife and ask for his own breakfast. He stopped at the window; the street was completely deserted, but in the distance could be heard, like the rush of an incoming tide, the waves of sound that were rising from the crowds around Notre-Dame.

This sound redoubled when d'Artagnan* arrived at the head of a company of musketeers to take up a position at the doors of Notre-Dame. He'd invited Porthos* to join him and take the opportunity to see the ceremony, and Porthos, in full court dress and mounted on his finest horse, was playing the part of an honorary musketeer, as d'Artagnan had so often done. The company's sergeant, a veteran of the wars with Spain, had recognized his old companion Porthos, and was regaling his subordinates with tales of the deeds of this giant, a champion of the King's Musketeers under old Captain Tréville.* The company, therefore, had welcomed him with pride.

At ten o'clock, the cannon of the Louvre announced the king's departure. A movement like that of the trees bending before a windstorm swept along the ranks of the crowd, stirring behind the rigid hedge of the muskets of the guards. At last the king appeared in a gilded carriage with his mother the queen. This was followed by ten other carriages containing the ladies of honor, the officers of the royal house, and the other members of the Court.

"*Vive le roi!*" came the cheers from every side.

The young king gravely brought his head to the carriage door, made a face that might have been approval, and bowed slightly, which made the crowd cheer all the louder.

The procession advanced slowly, taking almost half an hour to advance from the Louvre to Place Notre-Dame. Arriving there, the Court moved group by group into the vast and somber vault of the church, and the divine service began.

As the procession was arriving, a coach bearing the arms of Comminges left the line of carriages waiting to disembark their courtiers and turned slowly down Rue Saint-Christophe, now entirely deserted. Once parked around the corner, four guards and an officer went into the heavy coach and closed all the shutters, leaving only the one in front slightly open so the officer could look out toward Rue Cocatrix, as if waiting for someone to arrive.

Everyone was occupied with the ceremony, so no one paid any attention to the coach or the careful precautions of those within. Friquet, the only one nosy enough to spot them, had climbed up onto a house opposite Notre-Dame, where he savored his apricots as he watched the arrival of the king, the queen, and Cardinal Mazarin, and heard the mass as well as if he'd been taking part in it.

Toward the end of the service, the queen, seeing that Comminges was standing near at hand awaiting confirmation of the order she'd given before they left the Louvre, said to him in a low voice, "Go, Comminges—and may God go with you!"

Comminges went at once, leaving the church and turning down Rue Saint-Christophe. Friquet, who noticed this handsome officer marching with two guards behind him, amused himself by following along, as the ceremony had ended and the king had reentered his carriage.

As soon as the officer in the coach saw Comminges arrive at the end of Rue Cocatrix, he spoke an order to the driver, who put the vehicle into motion and drove it to Broussel's door. Comminges began knocking on that door just as the coach arrived.

Friquet came up behind Comminges as he was knocking on the door. "What are you doing here, monkey?" asked Comminges.

"I'm waiting to go into Councilor Broussel's house, Monsieur l'Officier," Friquet said, in that obsequious tone the Parisian gamin can adopt at need.

"Does he live here?" Comminges asked.

"Yes, Monsieur."

"On what floor?"

"All of them," said Friquet. "The whole house is his."

"But where is he usually found?"

"He works on the second floor but comes down to the first for his meals. Right now, he must be eating, since it's noon."

"Good," said Comminges. Just then the door opened. The officer questioned the servant, learning that Broussel was at home and dining. Comminges followed the servant up the stairs, and Friquet went up behind Comminges.

Broussel was seated at the table with his family, his wife across from him, his two daughters by his side, and at the end of the table was his son, Louvières,* whom we already met on the day of the councilor's accident, from which he was now fully recovered. The good man, restored to full health, was enjoying the apricots sent by Madame de Longueville.

Comminges, who had stopped the servant by grabbing his arm as he was about to open the door and announce him, opened the door himself and was face-to-face with this family tableau.

At the sight of the officer Broussel felt uneasy, but as the officer bowed politely, he rose and did the same.

Despite this polite exchange, the women looked anxious, while Louvières, turning pale, waited impatiently for the officer to explain himself.

"Monsieur," said Comminges, "I'm the bearer of an order from the king."

"Very well, Monsieur," Broussel replied. "Where is this order?" And he extended his hand.

"I am commissioned to detain you, Monsieur," said Comminges, in the same polite tone, "and if you'll take my word for that, it will save you the trouble of reading this long letter. Please follow me."

If a thunderbolt had fallen among those good people, so peacefully gathered, it couldn't have had a more terrible effect. Broussel backed away, trembling. It was a terrible thing at that time to be imprisoned by direct order of the king. Louvières made a movement toward his sword, which hung on a chair in the corner, but a look from Broussel, who was determined not to lose his head, stopped him. Madame Broussel, separated from her husband by the width of the table, burst into tears, and the two young daughters embraced their father.

"Come, Monsieur, make haste," said Comminges. "We must obey the king."

"Monsieur," said Broussel, "I'm in poor health and in no condition to give myself up—I need some time."

"Impossible," replied Comminges. "It's a formal order and must be executed at once."

"Impossible?" said Louvières. "Monsieur, be careful you don't drive us to desperate measures."

"Impossible!" screeched a voice from the rear of the room.

Comminges turned to see Dame Nanette, broomstick in hand and eyes aflame with anger.

"My good Nanette, calm down," said Broussel, "I beg you."

"Me, calm down while they arrest my master, the supporter, the liberator, the father of the people! Oh, right! You know me better than that! You," she said to Comminges, "get out of here!"

Comminges smiled. "Come, Monsieur," he said, turning to Broussel, "silence this noisy woman and follow me."

"Silence me! Me!" said Nanette. "It will take more than just you to do that, my king's pretty coxcomb. You'll see." And Dame Nanette rushed to the window, opened it, and shouted in a voice so piercing it could be heard in the Place Notre-Dame, "Help! *Help*! They're arresting my master! They're arresting Councilor Broussel! Help!"

"Monsieur," said Comminges, "make up your mind: will you obey, or do you intend rebellion against the king?"

"I obey, I obey, Monsieur," cried Broussel, trying to disengage himself from his clinging daughters, and from his son, who wanted to help him escape.

"In that case," said Comminges, "make this old crone shut up."

"Oh! Crone, is it?" said Nanette. And, clinging to the bars of the window, she began to scream even louder, "Help! Help! Help for Master Broussel, who's being arrested for defending the people! Help!"

Comminges grabbed the maidservant by the arm and tried to drag her from the window, but another voice, issuing falsetto from the ground floor below, took up the cry: "Murder! Fire! Assassination! They're slaughtering Monsieur Broussel!"

It was Friquet. Dame Nanette, encouraged by his support, joined loudly in chorus.

Already a few curious heads were appearing at neighboring windows. People, attracted to the end of the street, came around the corner at a run, individuals, groups, and then a whole crowd. They saw the coach but didn't understand what it meant. Friquet leapt from the staircase to the top of the vehicle. "They're trying to arrest Monsieur Broussel!" he cried. "There are guards in the coach, and an officer upstairs!"

The crowd began to shout and approach the coach and horses. The two guards who'd stayed in the street went inside to assist Comminges, while those in the coach came out and blocked the doorway with crossed halberds.

"Do you see them?" cried Friquet. "Look! Here they are!"

The driver turned and gave Friquet a blow with his whip that made him howl in pain. "*Agh!* You devil's coachman! You want a fight? Just wait!" And he jumped back to the staircase, from which he peppered the driver with whatever projectiles came to hand.

Despite the guards' aggressive response, or perhaps because of it, the crowd began to close in on the coach. The guards struck out with the flats of their halberds, and the rebels were driven back. However, the tumult continued to increase, and soon the street was overflowing as the mob came from every direction, and people began to invade the space between the coach and the formidable pole arms of the guards. The soldiers, compressed as by living walls, seemed about to be crushed against the wheels and side of the vehicle. The cry, "In the king's name!" repeated twenty times over by the officer, just seemed to make the mob angrier—until a young cavalier, hearing the king's name invoked, and seeing uniformed soldiers being mistreated, rushed into the fray with his sword in his hand, bringing unexpected aid to the guards.

This young man, fifteen or sixteen years old, was pale with anger. Like the guards, he dismounted, put his back against the shaft of the coach, made a rampart of his horse, drew his pistols from the saddle holsters, thrust them through his belt, then drew his sword and began to use it like a man who knows how.

For several minutes, the young man on his own fended off the attacks of the crowd. But then the mob saw Comminges come out, pushing Broussel before him.

"Smash the coach!" cried the crowd.

"Help! Help!" cried the old woman.

"Murder! Murder!" cried Friquet, as he continued to pepper the guards with everything he could find.

"In the king's name!" cried Comminges.

"The next one who tries something is dead!" cried Raoul de Bragelonne,* who, feeling himself pressed, especially by a giant of a man who looked ready to crush him, pricked him with the point of his sword, and the giant, feeling himself wounded, recoiled with a howl.

For it was indeed Raoul, who, returning from Blois after five days' absence, as he'd promised the Comte de La Fère, had wished to have a look at the ceremony, and was thus in the streets that led to Notre-Dame. Arriving in the neighborhood of Rue Cocatrix, he'd found himself swept along by the huge crowd—and hearing the words, *In the king's name*, he'd recalled that Athos* had told him, "Serve the king," and he'd rushed into the fight to defend the royal guards.

Comminges basically threw Broussel into the carriage and tumbled in after him. At that moment an arquebus was fired, the ball perforated Comminges's hat, and went on to break a guard's arm. Comminges looked up and saw, behind the powder smoke, the menacing figure of Louvières at the second-floor window. "Very well, Monsieur," Comminges called, "you'll be hearing from me about this."

"As you'll hear from me, Monsieur," Louvières said, "and we'll see who speaks the loudest."

Friquet and Nanette were still screaming; the shouts, the sound of the shot, the smell of gunpowder, always so intoxicating, all these had their effect. "Kill the officer! Kill him!" the crowd cried. And they surged forward.

"One more step," shouted Comminges, knocking open the shutters so everyone could see into the carriage, and placing the point of his sword on Broussel's chest, "one more step, and I kill the prisoner. I was ordered to bring him in dead or alive, and I'll bring him in dead if I have to."

There was a terrible cry from above, as Broussel's wife and daughters held out their hands in supplication to the people. And the people realized that this officer, so pale but seemingly so resolute, would do as he said, so they continued to threaten, but drew back a bit.

Comminges had the wounded guard get into the coach with him, and ordered the others to shut the door. "To the palace," he called to the driver, who was more dead than alive.

The coachman whipped up his animals, who forced their way through the crowd. But upon reaching the quay they could go no further; the coach was upset, and the horses carried away by the crowd. Raoul, still on foot, as he'd never had time or space to remount his horse, gave up striking with the flat of his blade and began using the point. But this last resort only infuriated the mob. Weapons began to appear in the crowd, a musket barrel here, a rapier blade there; shots rang out, a sound that only added to the excitement, and projectiles rained down from the windows above. The crowd's voice rose to that roar heard only in a true riot, and faces showed expressions seen only on days of bloody conflict. Shouts of "*À mort!* Kill the guards! Throw the officer in the Seine!" could be heard even above the clamor of the crowd. Raoul, his hat crushed, his face bloody, felt that not just his strength, but his very reason began to abandon him. His vision clouded with a reddish mist, and through this fog he saw a hundred arms reaching out to menace him, ready to seize him when he fell.

In the overturned coach, Comminges tore his hair in rage. The guards couldn't help him, as they could barely defend themselves. It was all over: coach, horses, guards, officer, maybe even the prisoner, all seemed likely to be torn to pieces—when suddenly a voice well-known to Raoul rang out, and a familiar sword shone in the air. The crowd separated and reeled back as an officer of the King's Musketeers, striking and slashing left and right, ran to Raoul and took him in his arms just as he was about to fall.

"*Sangdieu!*" the officer cried. "Have they murdered him? If so, woe unto them!" And he turned, bristling with such fury, menace, and force that even the angriest rebels recoiled, some retreating right into the Seine.

"Monsieur d'Artagnan," Raoul murmured.

"Yes, God's blood! In person, and fortunately for you it seems, my young friend. This way! Over here!" he called, leaping back into the saddle and waving his sword to the rest of his musketeers, who were just catching up. "Come on, drive this rabble back! Muskets at the ready! Present arms! Prepare to fire! Ready. . ."

At this order the populace withdrew so suddenly that d'Artagnan couldn't restrain a burst of Homeric laughter.

"Thank you, d'Artagnan," said Comminges, protruding half out the door of the overturned coach. "And thank you, my young gentleman. Your name? For I must tell the queen."

Raoul was about to respond, when d'Artagnan leaned down and said in his ear, "Keep quiet, and let me do the talking." Then, turning to Comminges, he said, "No time for that now, Comminges. Get out of this coach if you can, and let's find you another."

"Another? What other?"

"*Pardieu*, the first one that comes along! They'll be happy, I'm sure, to lend their carriage to the service of the king."

"Well, I don't know," said Comminges.

"Let's move, or in five minutes that rabble will be back with swords and muskets. You'll be killed and your prisoner set free. Come on. Ah, here comes a carriage now."

Then, leaning back toward Raoul, d'Artagnan whispered, "No matter what, don't mention your name." The young man looked at him in astonishment.

"Very well, we'll go then," said Comminges. "But if the crowd comes back, open fire."

"No, by no means," replied d'Artagnan. "On the contrary, nobody make a move. A shot fired today would be dearly paid for tomorrow."

Comminges took his four guards and the same number of musketeers and ran to the approaching carriage. He made the passengers get out and brought the carriage to the overturned coach. But when Broussel was to be transferred from the broken vehicle to the new one, the people, who saw the man they called their liberator, uttered angry screams and rushed forward anew.

"Go," said d'Artagnan. "I'm sending ten musketeers with you; I'll keep twenty to hold back the crowd. Go, and don't lose a moment. Ten men for Monsieur de Comminges!"

Ten men separated from the troop, surrounded the new carriage, and departed at a gallop.

At the departure of the carriage the cries redoubled; ten thousand people crowded the quays, thronging the Pont Neuf and the nearby streets.

A few shots rang out. A musketeer was wounded. "Forward," cried d'Artagnan, pushed to the limit and gnawing his mustache.

And with his twenty men he charged the entire crowd, who fell back in terror. Only one man stood fast, holding an arquebus. "Ah!" said the man. "It's you, the one who tried to trample the councilor! Now we'll see." And he lowered his arquebus on d'Artagnan, who approached at the gallop.

D'Artagnan leaned low on his horse's neck as the young man fired, so the ball only cut the plume from his hat.

The furious horse hurtled into the reckless young man, who'd tried single-handed to stop a tempest, and threw him against a wall. While his musketeers continued their charge, d'Artagnan reined in his horse and raised his sword over the man he'd knocked down.

"Wait!" cried Raoul, who recognized the young man from Rue Cocatrix. "Spare him, Monsieur—that's Broussel's son."

D'Artagnan lowered his sword. "Ah, you're his son?" he said. "That changes things."

"Monsieur, I surrender," said Louvières, holding out his smoking arquebus.

"Not at all! Surrender? *Mordieu*, on the contrary, run for it, and quickly! If you're captured, you'll hang."

The young man didn't wait to be told twice. He ducked under the horse's neck and disappeared around the corner of Rue Guénégaud.

"*Ma foi,*" d'Artagnan said to Raoul, "it was high time to stop me, because he was a dead man otherwise, and if I'd killed him and then learned who he was, I'd have regretted it."

"Please, Monsieur," said Raoul, "allow me, after thanking you for saving that poor lad, to thank you for saving me. I was as good as dead when you arrived."

"Hush, my young friend, save your breath till you recover." Then, drawing from a saddle bag a canteen of Spanish wine, he said, "Drink two sips of this."

Raoul drank, then tried to renew his thanks. "Dear lad," d'Artagnan said, "we'll talk about this later." Then, seeing that his musketeers had swept the crowd away from the Pont Neuf to the Quai Saint-Michel and were returning, he waved his sword to signal haste.

The musketeers arrived at the trot, but at the same time, the ten troopers who'd been sent as escort with Comminges reappeared at the end of the quay. "*Holà!*" called d'Artagnan. "What's happened?"

"Eh, Monsieur," said the sergeant, "that carriage is broken down as well. It's like a curse or something."

D'Artagnan shrugged his shoulders. "Incompetence," he said. "Why couldn't they choose a decent carriage? If you set out to arrest a Broussel, you need a carriage strong enough to carry a thousand."

"What are our orders, Lieutenant?"

"Take the detachment and escort them home."

"But you're going off alone?"

"I am. Do you think I'm in need of an escort?"

"Well . . ."

"Get going."

The musketeers departed, leaving Raoul with d'Artagnan, who said to him, "Now, are you hurt?"

"Yes, Monsieur, they cracked my head good."

"Your head? Let's take a look," d'Artagnan said, lifting Raoul's hat. "Ow, look at that bump."

"Yes, I think they hit me with a flower pot."

"The rabble!" said d'Artagnan. "But you're wearing spurs—were you on horseback?"

"Yes, I dismounted to defend Monsieur de Comminges, and then my horse disappeared. But wait, here it comes."

In fact, at that moment Raoul's horse came galloping along, ridden by Friquet, who was waving his hat of four colors and crying, "Broussel! Broussel!"

"Hold on! Pull up, you young rascal," d'Artagnan cried. "Bring that horse over here."

Friquet heard him but pretended not to, trying to continue on his way. D'Artagnan thought about running after him, but didn't want to leave Raoul, so he just pulled out a pistol and cocked it. Friquet had a sharp eye and a keen ear; he saw what d'Artagnan was up to and stopped the horse short. "Ah, it's you, Monsieur," he said, riding up to d'Artagnan. "I'm very glad to see you."

D'Artagnan looked at Friquet and recognized him as the gamin of the Rue de la Calandre. "Ah, it's you, little jester," he said. "Come here."

"Why yes, it's me, Monsieur l'Officier," Friquet said innocently.

"Have you found a new calling? Are you no longer a choirboy or a potboy? Are you a horse thief now?"

"Oh, Monsieur, how can you say that?" said Friquet. "I was looking for the gentleman who owns this horse, a young cavalier as brave as Caesar. . . ." He then pretended to see Raoul for the first time. "Why, if I'm not mistaken, here he is! Monsieur, you remember me, don't you?"

Raoul put his hand into his pouch.

"What do you think you're doing?" said d'Artagnan.

"Giving ten livres to a brave young lad," Raoul replied, pulling a pistole from his pocket.

"Ten whacks on the head is more like it," said d'Artagnan. "Get going, jester! And don't forget I know where you live."

Friquet, who hadn't expected to get off so easy, dismounted and disappeared up the Rue Dauphine. Raoul regained his horse, and at a walking pace, d'Artagnan guarding the young man as if he were his own son, they made their way to Rue Tiquetonne.

Along the way they could hear tumult in the distance and were given threatening looks, but the appearance of this officer, so upright and martial, and the sight of the well-worn sword in his determined grip, kept trouble at bay, and no serious attempts were made to interfere with the two cavaliers. They arrived without incident at the Hôtel de La Chevrette.

There, the lovely Madeleine reported to d'Artagnan that Planchet had returned accompanied by Mousqueton, who had heroically borne the extraction of the musket ball and was as well as could be expected given his condition. D'Artagnan asked her to call Planchet, but though Planchet was summoned, he didn't appear—he was gone. "In that case, some wine!" said d'Artagnan.

Once the wine had been brought, and d'Artagnan was alone with Raoul, he looked Raoul straight in the eye and said, "You're quite pleased with yourself, aren't you?"

"But yes," said Raoul. "It seems to me I did my duty. Didn't I defend the king?"

"And who told you to defend the king?"

"Why, the Comte de La Fère himself."

"Right, he said the king. But today you didn't defend the king, you defended Mazarin, which isn't the same thing at all."

"But, Monsieur . . ."

"You have blundered, young man, and mixed yourself up in things that don't concern you."

"But you yourself . . ."

"Oh, me! That's another thing entirely. I had to follow the orders of my commander. Hear me well: your commander is Monsieur le Prince, and you have no other. But today you had the ridiculous idea of assisting Mazarin, and helping him to arrest Broussel, of all things! Don't breathe a word of this to anyone. Why, the Comte de La Fère would be furious."

"You think the Comte de La Fère would be angry with me?"

"Think so? I'm sure of it! If it wasn't for that I'd thank you, for you certainly worked hard on our behalf. So, I'll scold you in his place—and believe me, the storm of my reproof is a lot milder than his would be. Anyway," d'Artagnan added, "I'm just exercising the responsibilities your guardian placed on me in his absence."

"I don't understand, Monsieur," Raoul said.

D'Artagnan got up, went to his desk, picked up a letter and presented it to Raoul.

Raoul finished reading the letter and looked up in dismay. "My God!" he said, his handsome eyes moist with tears. "Has Monsieur le Comte left Paris without even seeing me?"

"He left four days ago," d'Artagnan said.

"But his letter implies he runs the risk of death."

"What, *him*—in danger of death? Hardly. He's traveling on business and will return soon enough. In the meantime, I hope you're not reluctant to accept me as your acting guardian."

"Oh, no, Monsieur d'Artagnan!" Raoul said. "You're such a brave gentleman, and Monsieur le Comte loves you!"

"Then, by God, you should love me as well! I promise not to torment you more than you deserve, my young friend, on the condition that you remain a Frondeur—and a dedicated Frondeur, at that."

"But may I continue to see Madame de Chevreuse?"*

"*Mordieu*, I should think so! And the coadjutor* as well, and Madame de Longueville, and even good Councilor Broussel, whom you so foolishly helped to arrest. If you see him, apologize at once, and kiss him on both cheeks."

"All right, Monsieur, I'll obey you, though I don't understand you."

"It's not necessary for you to understand me," said d'Artagnan, turning toward the door as it opened. "And now here comes Monsieur du Vallon with his fine clothes all torn."

"Yes," said Porthos, dripping with sweat and covered in dust, "but in exchange I tore a lot of others' skin. *Peste!* The rabble actually tried to take away my sword. It's an uprising, I tell you," the giant continued, dusting himself serenely. "But I knocked over a good twenty of them with the pommel of Balizarde here. A little wine, if you please, d'Artagnan."

"Oh, it's an uprising, I quite agree with you," said the Gascon, filling Porthos's glass to the brim. "But once you've had a sip, I'd like your opinion on something."

Porthos drank the wine in a single swallow, sucked his mustache, put down the glass, and said, "On what?"

"You see before you," d'Artagnan replied, "one Monsieur de Bragelonne, who did everything he could to assist at the arrest of Broussel, and whom I prevented from defending Monsieur de Comminges only with the greatest of difficulty."

"*Peste!*" said Porthos. "And his guardian? What would he say if he learned of this?"

"You see?" d'Artagnan said to Raoul. "Be a Frondeur, my young friend, and take my word in everything as if I were the count." Then, turning to his companion, he said, "Are you coming, Porthos?"

"Where to?" asked Porthos, pouring himself another glass of wine.

"To pay our compliments to the cardinal."

Porthos swallowed the second glass with the same tranquility he had the first, picked up his hat, and followed d'Artagnan.

As for Raoul, he stayed behind and tried to sort out the confusing things he'd been told, remaining in his chamber, at d'Artagnan's request, until all the commotion in the streets had died down.

II

The Beggar of Saint-Eustache

D'Artagnan's delay in reporting to the Palais Royal was entirely calculated; it had given Comminges time to arrive before him, and to inform the cardinal of the valuable services which he, d'Artagnan, and his friend had performed that morning on the queen's behalf. So, they were well received by Mazarin, who paid them many compliments, and told them they were more than halfway to the goals they desired, that is, d'Artagnan to his captaincy and Porthos to his barony.

D'Artagnan would rather have had money than compliments, for he knew that Mazarin promised more often than he paid off. He regarded the cardinal's promises as mists and smoke but tried to appear satisfied while in the presence of Porthos, whom he didn't want to discourage.

While the two friends were with the cardinal, the queen sent for him. The cardinal thought he saw a way to increase the zeal of his two champions by procuring for them the queen's personal thanks, so he beckoned them to follow him. D'Artagnan and Porthos protested, displaying their torn and soiled garments, but the cardinal shook his head. "These outfits," he said, "are better than those of the courtiers you'll find around the queen, for these are the uniforms of war." D'Artagnan and Porthos obeyed.

The court of Anne of Austria was crowded and joyfully loud, for, after having won a victory over the Spanish, they'd won another victory over the people. Broussel had been taken out of Paris without resistance and by this hour should be in the prison at Saint-Germain. Blancmesnil, who'd been arrested at that same time as Broussel, but without noise or difficulty, was already incarcerated in the Château de Vincennes.

Comminges was near the queen, who was asking him about the details of his expedition, and everyone was listening to his account when he saw d'Artagnan and Porthos at the door, entering behind the cardinal. "Ah, Madame," he said, rushing over to d'Artagnan, "here's someone who can tell you better than I, for he was my savior. If not for him, at this moment my body would probably be getting caught in the fish-nets at Saint-Cloud, for the mob was about to throw me into the river. Speak, d'Artagnan, speak."

He just bowed. Since he was a Lieutenant of the Musketeers, d'Artagnan had found himself in the same room as the queen a hundred times before, but she'd never spoken with him.

"Well, Monsieur, after having rendered me such a service, you remain silent?" Anne of Austria said.

"Madame," d'Artagnan replied, "I have nothing to say other than that my life is in Your Majesty's service, and I'll be happy on the day I lose it for her."

"I know that, Monsieur, I know that," the queen said, "and have for a long time. So, I'm delighted to have an opportunity to make a public show of my esteem and gratitude."

"Allow me, Madame," said d'Artagnan, "to share some of that with my friend, a former musketeer of the company of Tréville, as I was"—he emphasized these words—"and who has performed wonders."

"Monsieur's name?" the queen asked.

"In the musketeers," d'Artagnan said, "he was known as Porthos"—the queen started—"but his real name is the Chevalier du Vallon."

"De Bracieux de Pierrefonds," added Porthos.

"These names are too numerous for me to remember them all—and I prefer to remember only the first," the queen said graciously.

Porthos bowed. D'Artagnan took two steps back.

Just then the coadjutor was announced. There was a cry of surprise from the royal assembly. Though the coadjutor had preached at the morning's mass, it was known that he leaned strongly toward the Fronde; Mazarin, in asking the Archbishop of Paris to have his nephew conduct a victory mass, had evidently intended to bestow upon Monsieur de Retz one of those underhanded Italian blows of which he was so fond.

In fact, upon leaving Notre-Dame, the coadjutor had learned what was going on. Though friendly with the leading Frondeurs, he wasn't in so deep that he couldn't retreat if the Court offered him the right incentives; for him, the office of coadjutor was just a means to an end. Monsieur de Retz wanted to be an archbishop like his uncle, or a cardinal like Mazarin, and the people's faction could hardly award him those royal favors. He'd come to the palace to compliment the queen on the victory at Lens, and how his compliments were received would determine whether he would side for or against the Court. So, the coadjutor entered, and at his appearance, the entire Court, giddy with triumph, turned in curiosity to hear what he had to say.

Now the coadjutor, by himself, almost had more wit than all those gathered there prepared to mock him. His speech was so eloquent and proper that those who were ready to ridicule him could find no fault to seize upon. He concluded by placing all his weak and unworthy powers at the feet of Her Majesty.

The queen appeared, while it lasted, to enjoy the coadjutor's address, but when it ended with that expression of devotion—the only phrase that provided any pretext for mockery—she turned away from him toward her favorites with a look that said that now he was fair game. At once the court wits began pretending surprise and mystification. Nogent-Bautru, the Court's leading clown, declared that the queen must be thrilled to have the support of the Church, though it came when she no longer needed it.

Everyone started to laugh.

The Comte de Villeroy said that he didn't see how anyone could have been anxious for a moment when the Court had as a defender against parliament and the mob one such as the coadjutor, who with a word could raise an army of curates, beadles, and choirboys.

The Maréchal de La Meilleraie added that, if it came to blows, the coadjutor should join in, though it would be a shame they wouldn't be able to recognize him in the mêlée by a red cardinal's hat, the way Henri IV had been known by his white plume at the Battle of Ivry.

Coadjuteur de Gondy remained calm and serene before this storm, which he could turn about and make deadly to his mockers. The queen then asked him if he had anything to add to the fine speech he'd just made.

"Yes, Madame," said the coadjutor. "Victories are fine things, but I must beg you to think twice before throwing the kingdom into civil war."

The queen turned her back and the laughter resumed.

The coadjutor bowed and left the chamber, after sending the cardinal, who was watching him, one of those looks that everyone knew declared them mortal enemies. This look was so sharp that it went right to Mazarin's heart, and he, sensing that it was a declaration of war, grabbed d'Artagnan by the arm and said, "When the time comes, you'll recognize that man, won't you? The one who just went out."

"Yes, Monseigneur," d'Artagnan said. Then, turning to Porthos, he added. "The devil! I don't like quarrels with men of the Church."

Meanwhile, Gondy made his way out of the palace, bestowing blessings as he went, and savoring the pleasure of making his enemies' servants fall on their knees. "Oh," he muttered, passing through the palace gate, "what an ungrateful court—a perfidious court—a cowardly court! Tomorrow they'll be laughing in a different tone."

But while the courtiers at the Palais Royal outdid each other in transports of joy to entertain and exalt the queen, Mazarin, who was a man of sense, and who, moreover, had the foresight that comes from fear, wasted no time in vain and dangerous distractions: he left right behind the coadjutor, secured his account books, locked up his gold, and with workers he trusted, contrived new secret caches in the walls.

On returning home, the coadjutor learned that a young man had arrived after his departure and now awaited him; he asked for the young man's name and started with pleasure when he heard it was Louvières. He rushed to his office, where Broussel's son was in fact waiting for him, still furious and bloodstained from his fight with the king's guards. The only precaution he'd taken before coming to the archbishopric had been to leave his arquebus with a friend.

The coadjutor went up to him and held out his hand. But the young man looked searchingly at him, as if trying to plumb the depths of his heart. "My dear Monsieur Louvières," said the coadjutor, "please believe that I am personally moved by the tragedy that's come upon you."

"Is that true? Do you mean it sincerely?" asked Louvières.

"From the bottom of my heart," Gondy said.

"In that case, Monseigneur, the time for words has passed, and the hour for action has come. Monseigneur, if you will it, within three days my father will be out of prison, and within six months you will be a cardinal."

The coadjutor flinched.

"Oh, let's speak frankly!" said Louvières. "Let's put all our cards on the table. One doesn't hand out thirty thousand crowns in alms, as you've done in the past six months, from pure Christian charity—no one is that good. You are ambitious: you're a man of genius, and you want your worth to be recognized. As for what I feel, I hate the Court, and at this moment my sole desire is for vengeance. Give us the clergy and the working poor, I'll bring you the bourgeoisie and the Parliament, and with these four elements, Paris will be ours within a week. And then believe me, Monsieur le Coadjuteur, the Court will give us out of fear what they won't give out of benevolence."

The coadjutor looked at Louvières with his piercing gaze, and said, "But, Monsieur Louvières, don't you know that what you're proposing is nothing less than civil war?"

"You've been preparing for that for a long time, Monseigneur, so that should be welcome to you."

"Regardless," said the coadjutor, "you understand that what you propose requires reflection?"

"How much time are you asking for?"

"Twelve hours, Monsieur. Is that too long?"

"It's noon; I'll be back here at midnight."

"If I haven't returned by then, wait for me."

"Good! At midnight then, Monseigneur."

"At midnight, my dear Monsieur Louvières."

Left alone, Gondy summoned all the curates with whom he was in contact. Two hours later, he had assembled the thirty priests whose parishes were the most populous, and thus the most contentious, in Paris. Gondy related the insults he'd suffered at the Palais Royal, and the mockeries of Bautru, the Comte de Villeroy, and the Maréchal de La Meilleraie. The curates asked him what was to be done.

"It's very simple," the coadjutor said. "You are the conscience of the people. Well! You must undermine the culture of respect and fear of kings. Tell your congregations that the queen is a tyrant, and repeat, forcefully so that everyone knows, that all the evils France suffers come from Mazarin, her lover and her corrupter. Begin this work today, this very hour, and within three days I hope to see results. Now, if any of you have useful advice to give me, stay behind and I'll be pleased to listen."

After the others had left three priests remained, the curates of Saint-Merri, of Saint-Sulpice, and of Saint-Eustache. "You think you have better ways to help me than your colleagues?" Gondy asked.

"We hope so," the curates replied.

"Come, let's start with you, priest of the parish of Saint-Merri."

"Monseigneur, I have in my parish a man who might be of great service to you."

"Who is this man?"

"A merchant of the Rue des Lombards who has great influence over the local tradesmen."

"What is he called?"

"He's named Planchet; he started a riot all by himself about six weeks ago, but afterward, since they were out to hang him, he's disappeared."

"And can you find him again?"

"I hope so. I haven't heard that he was arrested, and since I'm his wife's confessor, if she knows where he is, I'll know too."

"Very well, Monsieur le Curé, seek out this man, and if you find him, bring him to me."

"At what time, Monseigneur?"

"At six o'clock, if you can."

"I'll bring him to see you at six o'clock, Monseigneur."

"Go then, my dear Curate, and God go with you!"

The curate departed.

"And you, Monsieur?" Gondy said, turning to the Curate of Saint-Sulpice.

"I, Monseigneur," said the latter, "know a man who's done great things for one of the popular princes. He'd make an excellent rebel captain, and I can place him at your disposal."

"What do they call this man?"

"Monsieur le Comte de Rochefort."*

"Yes, I know him too—but unfortunately he isn't in Paris."

"Monseigneur, he's in Rue Cassette."

"Since when?"

"Since about three days ago."

"Why hasn't he come to see me?"

"They told him . . . Monseigneur will pardon me . . . ?"

"Of course. Speak."

"He heard Monseigneur was negotiating with the Court."

Gondy bit his lips. "He was mistaken. Bring him to me at eight o'clock, Monsieur le Curé, and may God bless you as I bless you!"

The second curate bowed and departed.

"It's your turn, Monsieur," said the coadjutor, turning to the remaining curate. "Do you have something to offer me as good as those two?"

"Better, Monseigneur."

"The devil! Take care not to exaggerate; the one offered me a merchant, the other a count. Do you offer me a prince, then?"

"Monseigneur, I offer you a beggar."

"Indeed!" said Gondy, reflecting. "You're right, Monsieur le Curé—I could use someone who could rouse that legion of the poor who choke the streets of Paris, who could make them shout out loud enough for all France to hear that it was Mazarin who reduced them to beggary."

"I have just the man."

"Bravo! And who is this man?"

"A simple beggar, as I said, Monseigneur, who for some years has asked alms by dispensing holy water on the steps of the Church of Saint-Eustache."

"And you say he has influence over his fellow beggars?"

"Is Monseigneur aware that begging is an organized occupation, a sort of association of those of no association, to which each contributes a share and reports to a chief?"

"Yes, I'd heard that," replied the coadjutor.

"Well! This man I offer you is one of their syndics."

"And what do you know of this man?"

"Nothing, Monseigneur, other than that he seems to me tormented by remorse."

"What makes you think that?"

"On the twenty-eighth of each month he has me say a mass for the rest of the soul of a person who died a violent death; just yesterday I said this mass again."

"What do you call him?"

"Maillard—but I don't think that's his real name."

"And do you think that right now we'd find him at his post?"

"Certainly."

"Let's go see your beggar, Monsieur le Curé—and if he's all you say he is, then you're right, it's you who's brought me the real treasure."

Gondy dressed as a cavalier, wearing a large felt hat with a red plume, a long sword at his belt, and spurs buckled on his boots, then enveloped himself in a large cloak and followed the curate.

The coadjutor and his companion traversed the streets between the archbishopric and the Church of Saint-Eustache, taking careful note of the temper of the populace. The people were aroused, but like a swarm of bees uncertain of where to settle, and if no leadership was found for them, their buzzing would simply fade and die.

Upon arriving at the Rue des Prouvaires, the curate pointed toward the square before the church. "There," he said, "see him, he's at his post."

Gondy looked and saw a poor man sitting on a cheap chair and leaning against a balustrade. He had a small bucket next to him and held a holy water sprinkler in his hand. "Does he have that spot by special privilege?" Gondy asked.

"No, Monseigneur," said the curate, "he made a deal with his predecessor for the position of holy water dispenser."

"A deal?"

"Yes, these positions are bought and sold. I believe he paid a hundred pistoles for it."

"So, this rascal is rich?"

"Some of these men die leaving behind twenty or thirty thousand crowns—or more."

"Huh!" said Gondy, laughing. "I didn't know my alms were such a good investment."

Meanwhile they were advancing into the square; when the curate and the coadjutor reached the base of the church stair, the beggar rose and lifted his aspergillum. He was a man of between sixty-five and seventy, small and portly, with gray hair and light eyes. His face was stamped with the struggle between two opposing principles, an evil nature constrained by sheer force of will, perhaps through repentance.

On seeing the cavalier who accompanied the curate, he started slightly and stared, surprised. The curate and the coadjutor touched the holy water sprinkler with their fingertips and made the sign of the cross, and the coadjutor dropped a silver coin into the open hat sitting on the ground.

"Maillard," said the curate, "we've come, monsieur and I, to speak with you for a moment."

"With me!" said the beggar. "This is quite an honor for a poor holy water dispenser." The man's voice was accented with a tone of irony he couldn't quite suppress, and which astonished the coadjutor.

The curate, apparently accustomed to this tone, went on, "Yes, we wanted to get your opinion on the events of the day, and what you're hearing from people going in and out of the church."

The beggar shook his head. "These are sad times, Monsieur le Curé, and as always, the poor people have the worst of it. As for what's being said, everyone is dissatisfied, and everyone complains, but when you say everybody, you say nobody."

"Explain yourself, my friend," said the coadjutor.

"I say that all these cries, all these complaints and curses, are nothing but wind and thunder, and without a leader to steer the storm, no lightning will strike."

"My friend," said Gondy, "you seem like a clever fellow. If we had a little civil war, would you be inclined to place at the disposal of its leader, if we find one, the personal power and influence you have over your comrades?"

"Yes, Monsieur, provided this war was blessed by the Church, and thus could lead me to my goal, which is the remission of my sins."

"This war will not only be blessed by the Church, it will be led by it. As for the remission of your sins, we'll have on our side the Archbishop of Paris, who has all the powers of the Court of Rome, and even Monsieur le Coadjuteur, who can grant plenary indulgences; we could recommend you to him."

"Consider, Maillard," said the curate, "that I've vouched for you to monsieur, who is a powerful lord, so in a way I'm responsible for you."

"I know, Monsieur le Curé, that you've always been very good to me," said the beggar, "so I'm inclined to serve you."

"And do you think your influence with your colleagues is as great as Monsieur le Curé tells me it is?" asked Gondy.

"They hold me in a certain esteem," said the beggar with pride. "They'll do whatever I ask of them, and wherever I go, they'll follow."

"And do you think you could find for me fifty reliable and energetic men ready for a brawl, and able to shout, 'Down with Mazarin!' loud enough to bring down the walls of the Palais Royal as was done at Jericho?"

"I think," said the beggar, "we could undertake to do things even more difficult and significant than that."

"Ah!" said Gondy. "Could you undertake to build a dozen barricades overnight?"

"I could undertake to build fifty of them, and to defend them, when the time comes."

"*Pardieu*," said Gondy, "you speak with an assurance that pleases me, and since Monsieur le Curé vouches for you . . ."

"I do," said the curate.

"Here's a purse containing five hundred pistoles in gold. Make all your arrangements and tell me where I can meet you this evening at ten o'clock."

"It would have to be a high place, from which we can see every quarter of Paris."

"Would you like me to have a word with the vicar of Saint-Jacques-la-Boucherie? He could let you up into the tower," said the curate.

"Perfect," said the beggar.

"Then till this evening, at ten o'clock," said the coadjutor. "And if I'm satisfied with you, you'll have another purse of five hundred pistoles."

The beggar's eyes shone with a gleam of greed, quickly suppressed. "Until tonight, Monsieur," he said. "Everything will be ready." He took his chair, pail, and aspergillum and stored them in the church, dipped some holy water from the basin as if he had no confidence in his own, and went on his way.

III

The Tower of Saint-Jacques-la-Boucherie

By a quarter to six, Monsieur de Gondy had made all his arrangements and had returned to the archbishop's palace. At six o'clock the Curate of Saint-Merri was announced. The coadjutor noticed that he was followed by another man. "Come in," he said.

The curate entered, with Planchet right behind him. "Monseigneur," said the Curate of Saint-Merri, "this is the person whom I had the honor to tell you about."

Planchet bowed with the air of a man familiar with genteel houses.

"Are you disposed to serve the cause of the people?" Gondy asked.

"I certainly am," said Planchet. "I'm a Frondeur to the soul. I stand before you, Monseigneur, a man condemned to be hanged."

"For doing what?"

"From the hands of Mazarin's officials, I liberated a noble lord whom they were escorting back to the Bastille, where he'd languished for five years."

"His name?"

"Oh, Monseigneur knows him well! It was the Comte de Rochefort."

"Ah! Yes indeed!" said the coadjutor. "I've heard talk of this affair—you raised the whole quarter, I was told."

"Very nearly," said Planchet, with a satisfied air.

"And your situation is . . . ?"

"Confectioner, Rue des Lombards."

"Explain to me how it happens that, coming from such a gentle occupation, you have such warlike inclinations?"

"How is it that Monseigneur, a man of the Church, receives me now dressed as a cavalier, with a sword at his side and spurs on his boots?"

"*Ma foi*! Not bad!" said Gondy, laughing. "But you know I've always had warlike inclinations despite my clerical calling."

"Well, Monseigneur, before I was a confectioner, I spent three years as a sergeant in the Piedmont Regiment, and before that for eighteen months I was lackey to Monsieur d'Artagnan."

"The Lieutenant of Musketeers?" Gondy asked.

"The same, Monseigneur."

"But who's said to be loyal to Mazarin?"

"Uh . . ." stammered Planchet.

"What are you trying to say?"

"Nothing, Monseigneur. Monsieur d'Artagnan is in the service, so Monsieur d'Artagnan obeys Mazarin, who pays him, just as we bourgeois Frondeurs attack Mazarin, who robs us."

"You're a smart fellow, my friend, but are you reliable?"

"I think Monsieur le Curé can vouch for that," said Planchet.

"Indeed, but I'd prefer to hear it from your own mouth."

"You can count on me, Monseigneur, if it's a matter of inciting a riot in the streets."

"That's exactly what this is. How many men do you think you could assemble in a night?"

"Two hundred muskets and five hundred halberds."

"If we had just one man in each quarter who could do the same, by tomorrow we'd have a mighty army."

"That's so."

"Would you be willing to follow the orders of the Comte de Rochefort?"

"I'd follow him into hell—which is no small statement, considering I think he's capable of getting there."

"Bravo!"

"What sign shall we use to distinguish friend from enemy?"

"Have every Frondeur wear a knot of straw in his hat."

"Good. I'll spread the word."

"Do you need money?"

"Money never hurts, Monseigneur—if we don't have any, we'll do without, but if we have some, things will go better and faster."

Gondy went to a coffer and pulled out a sack. "Here are five hundred pistoles," he said. "If the action goes well, count on receiving a similar sum tomorrow."

"I'll give Monseigneur a faithful accounting of how it's spent," said Planchet, tucking the sack under his arm.

"If it's an accountant you want to follow, I recommend the cardinal to you."

"Nevertheless, it's in good hands."

Planchet went out, but the curate stayed behind for a moment. "Are you satisfied, Monseigneur?" he said.

"Yes, he seems like a dependable rascal."

"He'll deliver even more than he promises."

"If so, he's a wonder."

And the curate left to rejoin Planchet, who was waiting for him on the stairs.

Ten minutes later the Curate of Saint-Sulpice was announced. As soon as the door to Gondy's office was opened a man rushed in—the Comte de Rochefort. "So, it *is* you, my dear Count!" said Gondy, holding out his hand.

"Have you finally decided you're with us, Monseigneur?" asked Rochefort.

"I always was," said Gondy.

"Then we won't mention it again—if you say so, I believe you. We're going to invite Mazarin to a ball."

"Well . . . I hope so."

"And when shall the dancing begin?"

"The invitations were sent out tonight," said the coadjutor, "but the violins won't begin to play until tomorrow."

"You can count on me, plus fifty soldiers promised me by the Chevalier d'Humières whenever I need them."

"Fifty soldiers?"

"Yes, he's raising recruits that he'll lend to me; when the dance is over, I'll find a way to replace any losses."

"Very good, my dear Rochefort—but that's not all."

"What else is there?" asked Rochefort, smiling.

"Monsieur de Beaufort,* what is he doing?"

"He's in the Vendômois, where he's waiting until I write and tell him it's time to return to Paris."

"Write to him; it's time."

"Then you're sure about this business?"

"Yes, but he should hurry: once the people of Paris are in revolt, we'll have ten princes who want to place themselves at their head. If he's late, he'll find someone else in his place."

"Can I tell him that comes straight from you?"

"Yes, absolutely."

"And can I tell him he can count on your support?"

"Completely."

"And you'll put him in charge?"

"Of the war, yes—but as to policy . . ."

"You know that's not his strong suit."

"He must allow me to bargain for my cardinal's hat as I think best."

"Why do you want one?"

"Since I must wear a hat that isn't a helmet," said Gondy, "I at least want it to be red."

"There's no need to argue about shapes and colors," said Rochefort with a laugh. "I'll answer for his consent."

"You'll write to him tonight?"

"I'll do better than that—I'll send a messenger."

"How long will it take him to get here?"

"Five days."

"Let him come. He'll find things have changed."

"So I hope."

"I'll answer for it."

"What now?"

"Go assemble your fifty men and stand ready."

"For what?"

"For anything."

"Is there a rallying sign?"

"A straw knot on the hat."

"Very good. Adieu, Monseigneur."

"Adieu, my dear Rochefort."

"Ah, Mazarin! Mazarin!" said Rochefort, trailed by his curate, who hadn't been able to get a word into the conversation. "Now you'll see if I'm too old to be a man of action!"

It was half past nine, and it took a half hour to go from the archbishopric to the tower of Saint-Jacques-la-Boucherie.[1] The coadjutor noticed a light glimmering in one of the highest windows of the tower. "Good," he said, "our syndic is at his post."

He knocked, and they opened the door for him. The vicar himself led him up, lighting the way to the top of the tower; arriving there, he opened a small door, set the lantern in a corner so the coadjutor could find it upon leaving, and went back down. Though the key was in the door, the coadjutor knocked.

"Enter," came a voice the coadjutor recognized as that of the beggar.

Gondy entered, and indeed there was the holy water dispenser of the Saint-Eustache square, reclining on a sort of pallet. Upon seeing the coadjutor come in, he rose. Ten o'clock sounded. "Well!" said Gondy. "Have you kept your word?"

"Not exactly," said the beggar.

"What do you mean?"

"You asked me for five hundred men, yes?"

"Yes—well?"

"Well! I will have two thousand."

"That's no boast?"

"Would you like proof?"

"I would."

Three candles were burning, each in front of a different window, one facing the Île de la Cité, the second toward the Palais Royal, the third toward Rue Saint-Denis. The man went silently to each of these candles and, one by one, blew them out. The coadjutor found himself in darkness, the room lit only by the uncertain rays of a moon lost among the clouds, edging their dark masses with silver. "What did you do?" the coadjutor asked.

"I've given the signal."

"To do what?"

"To raise the barricades."

"Ah!"

"When you leave here you'll see my men at work. Take care not to break your legs by tripping over a chain or falling into a trench."

"Good! Here's a sum equal to what you received before. Now remember that you're a leader and stay away from drink."

"For the last twenty years I've drunk nothing but water."

The man took the purse from the coadjutor, who could hear him handling it and feeling the coins within. "Ah ha!" Gondy said to himself. "You are a greedy rascal, after all."

The beggar sighed and put the purse down. "Will I never change?" he said. "Will I never be able to set aside the man I was? What vanity! What misery!"

"But you'll take it, won't you?"

"Yes, though I swear a vow before you now that whatever remains afterward will be spent in pious works." His face was pale and drawn like that of a man who has fought an inner battle.

"Strange man!" Gondy murmured. He picked up his hat, but turning to go he saw the beggar between him and the door.

His first thought was that the man meant him some harm—but the beggar only clasped his hands and fell to his knees. "Monseigneur," he said, "before you leave, give me your blessing, I pray you."

"Monseigneur?" Gondy said. "My friend, you've mistaken me for someone else."

"No, Monseigneur, I take you for who you are, that is, Monsieur le Coadjuteur. I knew you at first glance."

Gondy smiled. "And you want my blessing?" he said.

"Yes. I need it."

The beggar said these words in a tone of humility so great and of repentance so profound, that Gondy extended his hand and gave him his blessing with all the unction at his command. "Now there is communion between us," said the coadjutor. "I have blessed you, and you are sacred to me, as I am to you. Come, have you committed any crime for which human justice pursues you, and from which I can protect you?"

The beggar shook his head. "My crime, Monseigneur, is not a matter for human justice, and you can only help me by freely blessing me as you have."

"Come, be frank with me," said the coadjutor. "You haven't always followed your current calling?"

"No, Monseigneur, only for the last six years."

"What did you do before that?"

"I was in the Bastille."

"And before you were in the Bastille?"

"I will tell you, Monseigneur, on the day you hear my confession."

"Very well. Remember that at whatever hour of the day you choose to present yourself, I'll be ready to give you absolution."

"Thank you, Monseigneur," the beggar said in a low voice, "but I'm not yet ready to receive it."

"Very well. Adieu, then."

"Adieu, Monseigneur," said the beggar, opening the door and bowing before the prelate. The coadjutor picked up the lantern and went down the stairs, leaving the supplicant to himself.

IV

The Riot

It was about eleven o'clock at night. Gondy had scarcely gone a hundred steps along the streets of Paris when he saw that strange changes were underway. The whole city seemed inhabited by specters, silent shadows that could be seen flitting down the streets, or dragging and overturning carts, while others dug trenches deep enough to swallow entire companies of cavalry. All these energetic figures toiled away busily, like demons performing some unknown labor. These were the beggars of the Court of Miracles,[2] the agents of the holy water dispenser of Saint-Eustache, preparing the barricades for the following day.[3]

Gondy regarded these men of the darkness, these nocturnal laborers, with a certain terror; he wondered if, having summoned these unclean creatures from their lairs, he would have the power to compel them to return there. When one of these figures neared him, he was moved to make the sign of the cross.

He reached Rue Saint-Honoré and went along it toward the Rue de la Ferronnerie. There, the situation changed: merchants were going from shop to shop, closing shutters and locking doors, opening them only long enough to admit men trying to conceal what they were carrying—shopkeepers bringing spare weapons to lend to those who had none.

One individual went from door to door, bending under a stack of swords, arquebuses, muskets, and weapons of every kind, which he deposited as he went along. As he passed near a lantern, the coadjutor recognized Planchet.

The coadjutor returned to the river by the Rue de la Monnaie; along the quays, groups of citizens in cloaks of black or gray, depending on whether they were of the upper or lower bourgeoisie, stood waiting, while isolated individuals passed from one group to another. All these gray or black cloaks bulged out behind with the point of a sword, or in front with an arquebus or musket.

On arriving at the Pont Neuf, the coadjutor found that the bridge was guarded. A man approached him and asked, "Who are you? I don't recognize you as one of us."

"Then you fail to recognize your friends, my dear Monsieur Louvières," said the coadjutor, raising his hat. Louvières saw who it was and bowed.

Gondy crossed the river and turned toward the Tour de Nesle.[4] There, he saw a long line of people filing past the city wall. One might have taken them for a procession of phantoms, for they were all enveloped in white cloaks. At a certain point, these men seemed to vanish one after another. Gondy drew closer and watched them disappear into the earth from the first to the last. The final phantom looked up as if to make sure that he and his companions weren't observed, and saw Gondy watching from the shadows. This phantom marched right up to him and put a pistol to his head. "*Holà*, Monsieur de Rochefort," said Gondy with a laugh. "Let's not get too playful with the firearms."

Rochefort recognized the voice. "Ah! Is it you, Monseigneur?" he said.

"Myself. What are these people doing entering the bowels of the earth?"

"They're my fifty recruits from the Chevalier d'Humières, who are wearing white cloaks as they're destined for the light horse."

"Where are they going?"

"We're assembling in the underground studio of a sculptor friend of mine, going in through the trap door where they bring in the slabs of marble."

"Fine," said Gondy. And he shook hands with Rochefort, who followed his men down and closed the trap door behind him.

The coadjutor returned home. It was one o'clock in the morning. He opened his window and leaned out to listen.

An uncanny ferment, unprecedented, unknown, sounded from the city. One could hear echoing down the streets, dark and hollow, something strange and terrible. From time to time a rumbling like a distant storm or rising swell could be heard, but there was nothing clear, nothing distinct, nothing intelligible about it. It was like that mysterious and subterranean growling said to precede earthquakes.

The work of preparing for revolt lasted all night. The next day Paris, upon awakening, seemed to tremble at her own appearance. It was like a city under siege. Armed men stood at the barricades, their eyes menacing, their muskets at the ready; passwords, slogans, interrogations, and arrests were what passersby encountered in every block. Those with plumed hats and gilded swords were stopped and made to cry out, "Long live Broussel! Down with Mazarin!"—and any who resisted this ceremony were booed, spat upon, and even beaten. No one was killed as yet, but the desire to do so was evident.

The barricades had been pushed almost to the Palais Royal. From the Rue des Bons-Enfants to Rue de la Ferronnerie, from Rue Saint-Thomas-du-Louvre to the Pont Neuf, from Rue Richelieu to the Saint-Honoré gate, there were more than ten thousand men under arms, the most forward of whom called challenges to the impassive sentinels of the regiment of guards placed in defensive positions around the Palais Royal, the gates of which were closed behind them, which made their situation precarious. In between the barricades there circulated, in bands of a hundred or more, ragged and desperate men bearing banners that read, *Behold the misery of the people!* Wherever these folk passed, shouts and frantic cries went up—and there were many such bands roaming the streets.

Upon arising, Anne of Austria and Mazarin were astonished when they were informed that the city, which had been tranquil the evening before, now trembled with fever and emotion; neither of them would believe the reports until they witnessed it with their own eyes and ears. An outer window was opened for them: they saw, they heard, and were convinced.

Mazarin shrugged his shoulders and pretended to dismiss this fever of the populace, but he paled visibly, and, at the first opportunity, rushed to his study, where he shut himself up with his gold and jewels, running his hands over the finest of his diamonds. As for the queen, furious and left to her own devices, she summoned Maréchal de La Meilleraie[5] and ordered him to take as many men as he pleased and go find out the meaning of this nonsense.

The marshal was both adventurous and arrogant, displaying that disdain for the commoners typical of men of the sword. He took a hundred and fifty men and tried to march out by the Louvre bridge, but he encountered Rochefort with his fifty light horse, supported by over fifteen hundred men on foot. There was no way to force such a barrier, and the marshal didn't even try, falling back to the quay.

But at the Pont Neuf he found Louvières and his bourgeois. This time the marshal tried to charge, but was met by a volley of musketry, while stones fell like hail from the windows. He left three men there.

The marshal beat a retreat toward the quarter of Les Halles, but there he encountered Planchet and his halberdiers. The halberds were leveled menacingly toward him; he tried to make headway against these gray-cloaked opponents, but the gray-cloaks stood their ground. The marshal retreated toward Rue Saint-Honoré, leaving four guards who'd been killed behind.

On Rue Saint-Honoré he encountered the barricades built by the beggar of Saint-Eustache. They were guarded, not only by armed men, but also by women and children. Master Friquet, owner of a pistol and a sword given him by Louvières, had organized a band of rascals like himself, and if nothing else they made a lot of noise.

The marshal thought these defenses less well guarded than the others and tried to force them. He ordered twenty men to dismount and storm the first barricade, while he and the rest of the mounted troop protected the assailants. The twenty men marched right up to the obstacle, but from behind the beams, through the cart wheels, from the windows on either side, came a terrible fusillade. At the sound of this musketry, Planchet's halberdiers appeared at the corner of the Cemetery of the Innocents, while Louvières's bourgeois came up the Rue de la Monnaie.

The Maréchal de La Meilleraie was taken between two fires. But the marshal was brave, and resolved to die where he stood. His men gave back blow for blow and screams of pain began to rise from the crowd. The guards, better trained, dealt out more damage, but the citizens so outnumbered them they began to drop beneath a veritable hurricane of iron. Casualties fell so fast it was almost like Rocroi or Lérida. Fontrailles, the marshal's aide-de-camp, had his arm broken, and his horse took a ball in the neck, the pain of which drove it nearly mad and made it impossible to control.

It was at this climactic moment, when even the bravest felt a thrill of fear and a cold sweat, that the crowd opened up toward the Rue de l'Arbre-Sec, shouting, "*Vive le Coadjuteur!*" Gondy appeared, in a surplice and hood of chainmail, and walked serenely into the midst of the fusillade, distributing blessings left and right as calmly as if he were conducting the Procession of Corpus Christi.

Everyone fell on their knees.

The marshal recognized Gondy and rushed up to him. "Get me out of here, in the name of heaven," he said, "or I and all my men are going to lose our skins."

There was such a clamor that in the midst of it not even thunder could have been heard. Gondy raised his hand to demand silence. Everyone fell quiet. "My children," he said, "this is the Maréchal de La Meilleraie, whose actions you have misunderstood. He intends, upon returning to the Louvre, to ask the queen in your name for the release of our Broussel. You agree to this, don't you, Marshal?" added Gondy, turning to La Meilleraie.

"*Morbleu!*" the latter cried. "Agree to it? I should think so! I never hoped to get off so cheaply."

"He gives you his word as a gentleman," said Gondy.

The marshal raised his hand in sign of assent.

"Long live the coadjutor!" the crowd shouted. Some even added, "Long live the marshal!" But then everyone returned to the refrain: "Down with Mazarin!"

The crowd drew back. The Rue Saint-Honoré was the shortest route, so the barricades were opened, and the marshal and his remaining troops retreated, led by Friquet and his rascals, some pretending to beat on drums while others imitated trumpets.

It was almost a triumphal march—except that the barricades closed again behind them. The marshal gnawed on his knuckles.

Meanwhile, as we've said, Mazarin was in his study, putting his affairs in order. He had sent for d'Artagnan, but in all the tumult he didn't expect to see him, since d'Artagnan wasn't on duty. But after about ten minutes the lieutenant appeared in the doorway, followed by his inseparable Porthos.

"Ah! Come in, come in, Monsieur d'Artagnan," cried the cardinal, "and be welcome, your friend as well. But what is going on in this damned Paris?"

"What's going on, Monseigneur? Nothing good," said d'Artagnan, shaking his head. "The city is in open revolt, and just now, as I was crossing Rue Montorgueil with your servant Monsieur du Vallon, in spite of my uniform—or maybe because of my uniform—they tried to get us to shout, 'Long live Broussel!' And can I tell you, Monseigneur, what else they wanted us to shout?"

"Tell me."

"'Down with Mazarin!' And, *ma foi,* that was the more popular cry."

Mazarin smiled, but became very pale. "And did you shout it?" he said.

"My faith, no," said d'Artagnan. "I was not in good voice, and Monsieur du Vallon, who has a cold, also refused to shout. Then, Monseigneur . . ."

"Then what?" asked Mazarin.

"Take a look at my hat and my cloak." And d'Artagnan showed him four bullet holes in his cloak and two in his hat. As for Porthos's clothing, a halberd had slashed open the side of his doublet, and a pistol shot had cut short his plume.

"*Diavolo!*" said the cardinal thoughtfully, regarding the two friends with genuine admiration. "Even I would have shouted it."

At that moment the tumult seemed to grow nearer. Mazarin wiped his forehead and looked around. He wanted to go to the window but didn't dare. "See what's going on, Monsieur d'Artagnan," he said.

D'Artagnan went to the window with his usual nonchalance. "Oh ho!" he said. "What have we here? Maréchal de La Meileraie is returning without his hat, Fontrailles has his arm in a sling, I see wounded guards, horses covered in blood . . . but wait! What are the sentries doing? They're presenting arms and preparing to fire!"

"They've been ordered to fire upon the people," said Mazarin, "if the people approach the Palais Royal."

"But if they fire, all is lost!" cried d'Artagnan.

"We still have the gates."

"The gates! They'll have those down inside of five minutes, torn right from their hinges! Don't shoot, *mordieu*!" d'Artagnan cried, opening the window.

Despite this desperate cry, which, in all the clamor, hadn't even been heard, three or four musket shots sounded out, and in reply there was a terrible fusillade. They heard the patter of musket balls on the façade of the Palais Royal, and one passed under d'Artagnan's arm and shattered a mirror, at which Porthos glanced complacently. "*Ohimé!*" cried the cardinal. "My Venetian glass!"

"Oh, Monseigneur," said d'Artagnan, quietly closing the window, "don't bother weeping now, it's not worth it, since inside of an hour, in all likelihood, there won't be a single mirror still intact in the Palais Royal, whether Venetian or Parisian."

"But what should we do, then?" said the cardinal, trembling.

"Why, *morbleu*! You'd better give them Broussel, since that's what they demand. What the devil do you want with a Councilor of Parliament anyway? He's not good for anything."

"And you, Monsieur du Vallon, is that your advice? What would you do?"

"I'd give up Broussel," said Porthos.

"Come, come, Messieurs," cried Mazarin, "I must speak of this matter to the queen."

At the end of the corridor he paused. "I can count on you, can't I, Messieurs?" he said.

"We don't give our loyalty twice," said d'Artagnan. "We're committed to you and will follow your orders."

"Good!" said Mazarin. "Wait here in this office." And turning aside, he went into the salon by a different door.

V

The Riot Becomes a Revolt

The office in which d'Artagnan and Porthos were waiting was separated from the queen's salon by nothing but tapestry doors. This thin partition made it possible to hear everything that was passing within, while the gap between the curtains, narrow though it was, made it possible to see. The queen stood in the center of her salon, pale with anger, but her self-control was so great that, but for her pallor, one would have said she was quite undisturbed. Behind her were Comminges, Villequier, and Guitaut, while beyond them were her lords and ladies.

In front of her, Chancellor Séguier—the same man who, twenty years before, had so persecuted her—recounted how his carriage had been upset, how he'd been pursued into the Hôtel d'O, and how that house had been immediately invaded, plundered, and devastated. Luckily, he'd had time to get into a closet behind a tapestry, where an old woman had hidden him and his brother the Bishop of Meaux. But the danger had been so real, as madmen searched the house shouting threats, that the chancellor had believed his hour had come, and he'd confessed himself to his brother, so he'd be prepared for death if discovered. Fortunately, that hadn't happened, and the mob, believing he'd gotten out by some back door, marched off and gave him a chance to escape. He'd disguised himself by dressing in some of the Marquis d'O's clothes and had left the hôtel, stepping over the bodies of an officer and two guards who had died defending the door to the street.

During this account, Mazarin had come in, quietly glided over next to the queen and listened. "And so?" the queen asked the chancellor once he'd finished. "What do you have to say about this?"

"I think the situation is very serious, Madame."

"But what advice do you have for me?"

"There is a course I would propose to Your Majesty, but I dare not."

"Oh, be daring, Monsieur," said the queen with a bitter smile. "You have dared other things."

The chancellor reddened and stammered out a few words.

"This has nothing to do with the past, just the present," said the queen. "You said you have some advice to give me. What is it?"

"Madame," said the chancellor, hesitating, "it would be to release Broussel."

The queen, already pale, turned even paler, and her face contorted. "Release Broussel!" she said. "Never!"

At that moment steps were heard in the antechamber, and without being announced, the Maréchal de La Meilleraie appeared on the threshold. "Ah! There you are, Marshal!" Queen Anne cried joyfully. "You've taught that rabble to see reason, I hope?"

"Madame," said the marshal, "I've left three men dead on the Pont Neuf, four at Les Halles, six at the corner of the Rue de l'Arbre-Sec, and another two at the gates of the palace, fifteen in all. I have ten or twelve wounded. My hat is I know not where, carried away by a bullet, and in all probability, I'd be with my head if it wasn't for Monsieur le Coadjuteur, who came and got me out of that mess."

"Ah!" said the queen. "I would have been surprised not to find that bow-legged hound mixed up in this."

"Madame," said La Meilleraie with a laugh, "don't speak ill of him in front of me, I beg, for the service he's done me is still too recent."

"Very well," said the queen, "be grateful to him all you like, but that doesn't bind me. You're safe and sound, and to me that's what matters. Your safe return is very welcome to us."

"Yes, Madame—but I've been allowed to return on one condition, which is that I convey to you the will of the people."

"Their will!" said Anne of Austria, frowning furiously. "Oh, Monsieur le Maréchal, you must have found yourself in great danger indeed to accept so strange a mission!" These words were pronounced with an accent of irony that didn't escape the marshal.

"Your pardon, Madame," said the marshal. "I'm not a diplomat, I'm a man of war, so perhaps I don't weigh my words well; I should have said the desire of the people, and not their will. As to the reply with which you honored me, I believe you were implying that I was afraid."

The queen smiled.

"Well! Yes, Madame, I was afraid. This is only the third time in my life it's happened, though I've been in a dozen pitched battles and I don't know how many fights and skirmishes; yes, I was afraid, and I'd rather be here facing Your Majesty, no matter how threatening your smile, than facing those demons from hell who chased me back here, and who come from I know not where."

"Bravo!" said d'Artagnan quietly to Porthos. "Well answered."

"Well, then!" said the queen, biting her lips, while the courtiers looked on in astonishment. "What is this desire of my people?"

"To release Broussel, Madame," said the marshal.

"Never!" said the queen. "Never!"

"Your Majesty commands," said La Meilleraie, bowing and taking a step back.

"Where are you going, Marshal?" said the queen.

"I go to take Your Majesty's response to those who await it."

"Stay here, Marshal—I don't wish to appear to be parleying with rebels."

"Madame, I have given my word," said the marshal.

"Which means what?"

"That unless you arrest me, I'm compelled to return to them."

Anne of Austria's eyes flashed like lightning. "Oh! If it comes to that, Monsieur," she said, "I've arrested greater men than you. Guitaut!"

Mazarin hastened forward. "Madame," he said, "if I might dare to offer some advice . . ."

"If it's also to release Broussel, Monsieur, you may dispense with it."

"No," said Mazarin, "though that advice might be as good as any."

"What is it, then?"

"It's to call for Monsieur le Coadjuteur."

"The coadjutor!" cried the queen. "That miserable troublemaker! He's the one who's behind the entire revolt."

"All the more reason," said Mazarin. "If he did it, he can undo it."

"And here's the opportunity," said Comminges, who was near a window and looking out, "because there he is, giving blessings in the square outside the Palais Royal."

The queen rushed to the window. "It's true!" she said. "Look at him, the great hypocrite!"

"What I see is that everyone kneels to him although he's just a coadjutor," said Mazarin, "while if I were out there they'd tear me to pieces, even though I'm a cardinal. I persist, then, in my *desire*"—Mazarin emphasized the word—"that Your Majesty receive the coadjutor."

"Why not just say it's your *will*?" replied the queen in a low voice.

Mazarin just bowed.

The queen stood thoughtfully for a moment. Then, raising her head, she said, "Monsieur le Maréchal, go find the coadjutor and bring him to me."

"And what shall I say to the people?" asked the marshal.

"To have patience," said Anne of Austria, "as I've had!"

In the voice of the proud Spaniard there was an accent so imperious that the marshal refrained from a reply; he bowed and went out.

D'Artagnan turned toward Porthos and said, "How do you think this will end?"

"We'll see soon enough," said Porthos, calm as ever.

Meanwhile Anne of Austria went to Comminges and spoke to him in a whisper.

Mazarin, uneasy, glanced toward where he knew d'Artagnan and Porthos were.

The other advisors exchanged words in low voices.

The door reopened, and the marshal reappeared, followed by the coadjutor. "Here, Madame," said the marshal, "is Monsieur de Gondy, who hastens to comply with Your Majesty's orders."

The queen took a couple of steps toward him and stopped, cold and stern as a statue, her lips curled in disdain.

Gondy bowed respectfully.

"Well, Monsieur," said the queen, "what's the meaning of this riot?"

"It's no longer just a riot, Madame," the coadjutor replied, "it's a revolt."

"The revolt is on the part of those who think my people *can* revolt!" cried Anne, unable to contain herself before the coadjutor, whom she seemed to regard as the one responsible for the disturbance. "Those who incite such unrest may dignify it with the name of revolt, but just wait—the authority of the king will soon restore order."

"Is it to tell me that, Madame," Gondy replied coldly, "that Your Majesty has admitted me to the honor of her presence?"

"No, my dear Coadjutor," said Mazarin, "it's to ask your advice in the unfortunate situation in which we find ourselves."

"Can it be true," said Gondy, feigning astonishment, "that Her Majesty has summoned me to ask for my advice?"

"Yes," said the queen. "I wish it."

The coadjutor bowed. "Then Her Majesty desires . . ."

"That you tell her what you would do in her place," Mazarin hastened to reply.

The coadjutor looked at the queen, who signified her assent. "In Her Majesty's place," Gondy said coldly, "I wouldn't hesitate: I'd release Broussel."

"And if I don't release him," the queen snapped, "what do you think will happen?"

"I think Paris will be rubble by tomorrow," said the marshal.

"I didn't ask you," said the queen drily, without even turning around, "I asked Monsieur de Gondy."

"If it's me Her Majesty is asking," replied the coadjutor in the same tone, "I would say that I'm of the same opinion as the marshal."

The blood mounted to the queen's face, and her beautiful blue eyes seemed ready to start from her head; her rosy lips, compared by all the poets of the time to flowers in bloom, turned pale and trembled in rage. She very nearly frightened even Mazarin, accustomed as he was to her furies. "Release Broussel!" she finally spat, with a frightful smile. "Fine advice, *ma foi*! It's obvious it comes from a priest!"

Gondy stood firm. The insults of this day seemed to have no more effect on him than the mockeries of the day before—but hatred and desire for revenge were glowing like burning coals in the bottom of his heart. He looked coldly at the queen, who nudged Mazarin to get him to add something.

Mazarin, as usual, thought a great deal but said little. "Hmm," he said, "good, friendly advice. I, too, would release Monsieur Broussel, dead or alive, and that would be an end to it."

"If you release him dead, everything will be at an end, Monseigneur, though perhaps not in the way you mean," said Gondy.

"Did I say dead or alive?" replied Mazarin. "It's just a manner of speaking. You know I'm not as good with French, spoken or written, as you are, Monsieur le Coadjuteur."

"Here's a real Council of State," said d'Artagnan to Porthos, "but we've had better than this at La Rochelle, with Athos and Aramis."

"At the Saint-Gervais bastion," said Porthos.

"There, and elsewhere."

The coadjutor allowed the brief shower of sarcasm to pass, and then replied, still in his calm tone, "Madame, if Your Majesty doesn't appreciate the advice I submit to her, doubtless it's because she has better advice to follow; I know too well the wisdom of the queen and her advisors to expect that they'll leave the city for long in a state so troubled that it might lead to revolution."

"So, in your opinion," replied the royal Spaniard with a sneer, biting her lips in anger, "the riot of yesterday, which is a revolt today, may tomorrow become a revolution?"

"Yes, Madame," the coadjutor said gravely.

"To hear you tell it, Monsieur, the people have no self-restraint."

"It's a bad year for kings," said Gondy, shaking his head. "Look at England, Madame."

"Yes, but fortunately we have no Oliver Cromwell* in France," the queen replied.

"Who knows?" said Gondy. "Such men are like lightning, unexpected till they strike."

Everyone shuddered, and there was a moment of silence.

Meanwhile, the queen had both hands resting on her chest, and one could see that she was trying to steady her own heartbeat.

"Porthos," murmured d'Artagnan, "take note of this priest."

"All right, I see him," said Porthos. "Well?"

"Well! There stands a man."

Porthos looked at d'Artagnan with surprise; it was obvious he didn't quite understand what his friend was telling him.

"Your Majesty intends to take such measures as suits herself," continued the coadjutor, pitilessly. "But I predict their nature will be such as to only infuriate the rebels even further."

"In that case you, Monsieur le Coadjuteur, who have such influence over them, and who are our friend," said the queen ironically, "will calm them by giving them your blessings."

"Perhaps it will be too late," said Gondy, still icy, "and perhaps I will have no more influence—whereas by releasing Broussel, Your Majesty removes the excuse for rebellion, and gains the right to cruelly punish any recurrences of revolt."

"Do I not have that right already?" cried the queen.

"If you have it—use it," Gondy replied.

"*Peste!*" said d'Artagnan to Porthos. "That's the sort of character I like. If only *he* were my minister, and I were his officer, instead of my being attached to Mazarin. Ah, *mordieu!* What great things we would do!"

"Yes," said Porthos.

The queen, with a gesture, dismissed her Court, except for Mazarin. Gondy bowed and began to withdraw with the others, but the queen said, "Remain, Monsieur."

"Good," Gondy said to himself, "she's going to yield."

"She's going to have him killed," said d'Artagnan to Porthos. "But if she does, I won't be the one to do it. I swear to God that on the contrary, if anyone comes to attack him, I'll fall on them myself."

"Me too," said Porthos.

"Good!" murmured Mazarin, taking a seat. "Now we'll see something new."

The queen watched her people go, following them out with her eyes. When the last one had closed the door, she turned. One could see what efforts she was making to contain her anger; she fanned herself, inhaled some perfume, and walked up and down. Mazarin remained seated, apparently thinking. Gondy, who'd begun to get uneasy, scanned the tapestries and curtains, tapped the cuirass he wore under his long robe, and checked from time to time to make sure the good Spanish dagger he also had under his robe was easy to get at.

"Now," said the queen, pausing at last, "now we are alone, repeat your advice, Monsieur le Coadjuteur."

"Here it is, Madame: to feign reflection, and then publicly acknowledge having made a mistake, a mark of a strong government; then let Broussel out of prison and return him to the people."

"Oh!" cried Anne of Austria. "To humiliate me so! Am I not the queen? Are those howling rabble my subjects or not? Have I no friends, no guards? Ah! By Our Lady, as Queen Catherine used to say," she continued, her voice rising, "before I'll give up this insolent Broussel, I'll strangle him with my own hands!"

And she shook her clenched fists at Gondy, who at that moment she hated at least as much as she hated Broussel.

Gondy remained motionless; not a muscle on his face even twitched—but his icy glance crossed like a sword with the furious gaze of the queen.

"There stands a dead man, if there was still someone like Vitry[6] at Court, and he came in at this moment," said the Gascon. "But before he could reach this good prelate, I'd kill such a Vitry on the spot! And Cardinal Mazarin would be infinitely grateful to me."

"Hush!" said Porthos. "Listen."

"Madame!" cried the cardinal, drawing Anne of Austria back. "Madame, what are you doing?" Then he added in Spanish, "Anne, are you crazy? You're fighting with a churchman—you, a queen! Don't you see that you have before you, in the person of this priest, all the people of Paris, whom it's dangerous to insult, especially now, since if he wills it, he could have your crown within the hour! Another day, another time, you will stand firm and strong, but this is not that time. Today you will flatter and cajole, not quarrel like a fishwife."

At the first words of this speech d'Artagnan had taken Porthos by the arm and squeezed it gradually tighter, only letting go when Mazarin was through. "Porthos," he whispered, "never mention in Mazarin's hearing that I understand Spanish, or I'm a dead man, and so are you."

"Fine," said Porthos.

This sharp reprimand, marked by the eloquence characteristic of Mazarin when he spoke Italian or Spanish, and which he completely lacked in French, was spoken with such an impassive expression on his face that Gondy, skilled at reading people though he was, thought Mazarin was just warning her to be more moderate.

The queen, thus sharply rebuked, quickly turned milder; she let the fire in her eyes die down, her flush paled away, and she swallowed the angry words on her lips. She sat down, dropped her arms to her sides, and said, in a voice edged with tears, "Pardon me, Monsieur le Coadjuteur, and blame my outburst on my suffering. I'm a woman, and subject to the weaknesses of my sex; I'm terrified of civil war, but as a queen accustomed to obedience, I can't abide contradiction."

"Madame," said Gondy with a bow, "Your Majesty would be wrong to reject my sincere advice. Your Majesty has only submissive and respectful subjects. It's not the queen the people oppose, they just want Broussel, that's all. If Your Majesty releases Broussel, they'll be only too happy to live under Your Majesty's laws," Gondy added, smiling.

At the words, *It's not the queen the people oppose,* Mazarin thought the coadjutor was going to mention their oft-repeated cry of "Down with Mazarin!" He was grateful when Gondy didn't, and said, with an imploring expression and in his silkiest voice, "Madame, do believe the coadjutor, who's one of our most able politicians. The first available cardinal's hat seems made to order for him."

"Ah!" Gondy said to himself. "I see how badly you need me, you cunning rogue!"

"And what will he promise us," whispered d'Artagnan, "on the day they want us to kill Gondy? *Peste,* if he gives out red hats so easily, get ready, Porthos, as we're each going to ask for a regiment tomorrow. *Corbleu!* If the civil war only lasts a year, I'll get them to revive the Sword of the Constable for me!"

"And for me?" said Porthos.

"For you? I'll see that you get the marshal's baton of Monsieur de La Meilleraie, since it looks like he's going to be out of favor."

"So, Monsieur," said the queen, "you seriously fear a popular uprising?"

"To be serious, Madame—I do," said Gondy, astonished at how little progress he was making. "When a flood breaks through a dike, it can cause terrible damage."

"And I," said the queen, "think that in that case, we must build new dikes. I will consider; you may go."

Gondy looked at Mazarin in astonishment. Mazarin approached the queen to speak to her. Just then a terrible tumult erupted outside the gates of the Palais Royal. Gondy smiled, the queen's eyes kindled, and Mazarin paled. "Now what?" he said.

At that moment Comminges rushed into the salon. "Pardon, Madame," he said to the queen as he entered, "but the people have crushed the sentries against the gates and are starting to force them open. What are your orders?"

"Listen, Madame," said Gondy.

The roar of waves, the crash of thunder, the rumblings of a volcano were nothing compared to the tempest of cries that now arose.

"What are my orders?" said the queen.

"Yes, time is short."

"How many men do you have in the Palais Royal?"

"Six hundred."

"Put a hundred men around the king, and with the rest sweep away this rabble."

"Madame," said Mazarin, "what are you doing?"

"Go!" said the queen.

With the passive obedience of a soldier, Comminges left.

Just then a horrible, grinding crash was heard, as one of the gates gave way.

"Ah, Madame!" said Mazarin. "You're going to ruin us all—you, me, and the king."

Anne of Austria, at this cry of fear from the depths of the cardinal's soul, at last grew afraid as well, and called back Comminges.

"It's too late!" said Mazarin, tearing his hair. "It's too late!"

The other gate fell, and they could hear the people howling with glee. D'Artagnan drew his sword and gestured to Porthos to do the same.

"Save the queen!" cried Mazarin to the coadjutor.

Gondy rushed to the window and opened it; he recognized Louvières at the head of a mob of maybe three or four thousand men.

"Not another step!" he shouted. "The queen will sign!"

"What are you saying?" cried the queen.

"The truth, Madame," said Mazarin, presenting her with a pen and paper. And he added, "Sign it, Anne, please—I beg of you."

The queen collapsed on a chair, but took the pen and signed.

Contained by Louvières, the people had paused, but the terrible growl of their anger continued.

Above her signature, the queen wrote, "The Concierge of the Prison of Saint-Germain is to set Councilor Broussel at liberty."

The coadjutor, who devoured her every movement with his eyes, grabbed the paper as soon as she was done, returned to the window and waved it, saying, "This is the order!"

All Paris seemed to draw breath, and then cry out in joy, "Long live Broussel! Long live the coadjutor!"

"Long live the queen!" said the coadjutor. But few took up the cry. And perhaps the coadjutor only made it to emphasize to Anne of Austria her weakness.

"And now that you have what you came for, Monsieur de Gondy," she said, "go."

"When the queen needs me," said the coadjutor, bowing, "Her Majesty knows that I'm at her service."

The queen nodded, and Gondy withdrew.

"Ah! Cursed priest!" cried Anne of Austria, shaking her fist toward the door, which had scarcely closed. "One day I'll make you drink from the poisoned draught you poured out for me today."

Mazarin tried to approach her. "Begone!" she said. "You are no man!" And she went out.

"It's you who are no woman," murmured Mazarin.

Then, after a moment's thought, he remembered that d'Artagnan and Porthos were at hand and must have heard everything. He frowned, went to the tapestry door and opened it—but the chamber beyond was empty.

At the queen's final words, d'Artagnan had grabbed Porthos by the arm and dragged him out to the gallery. In his turn, Mazarin came out to the gallery, where he found the two friends walking up and down. Mazarin said, "Why did you leave the antechamber, Monsieur d'Artagnan?"

"Because the queen ordered everyone to leave," said d'Artagnan, "and I thought that order included us as well as the others."

"Then you've been here for . . ."

"For about a quarter of an hour," said d'Artagnan, giving Porthos a look telling him not to contradict him.

Mazarin noticed this look and was convinced that d'Artagnan had seen and heard everything, but was grateful for the falsehood. "Decidedly, Monsieur d'Artagnan," he said, "you're the man I've been looking for, and you can count on me to be your friend." Then, gracing the two friends with his most charming smile, he returned quietly to his study, for with the departure of Gondy, the tumult had ceased as if by magic.

VI

Misfortune Aids the Memory

Anne had stormed off to her private chapel. "What!" she cried, flailing her beautiful arms. "The people saw Monsieur de Condé, the First Prince of the Blood,* arrested by my mother-in-law, Marie de Médicis; they saw my mother-in-law, their former regent, driven out by Cardinal Richelieu;* they saw Monsieur de Vendôme, the son of Henri IV, imprisoned in Vincennes; they said nothing while all these great persons were threatened, insulted, and imprisoned—but they rise up for Broussel! Jesus, what is the point of royalty?"

Anne had touched on the burning question of the day. The people had said nothing for the princes, but they'd arisen for Broussel. It was because he was a commoner, and in defending Broussel, the people instinctively knew they defended themselves.

Meanwhile, Mazarin was pacing back and forth in his study, glancing from time to time at the splintered shards of his Venetian mirror. "Eh!" he said. "It's sad to have to yield this way, but bah! We'll have our revenge. What does one Broussel matter, more or less? He's just a symbol, not a faction."

Mazarin, able politician though he was, had got it wrong this time: Broussel was more than just a symbol.

The next morning, when Broussel made his entry into Paris in a splendid carriage, with his son Louvières beside him and Friquet riding up behind, all the armed citizens rushed to see him pass. The cries of "*Vive Broussel! Long live our father!*" arose on all sides, and sounded like impending death to Mazarin; the reports of the cardinal's many spies brought nothing but bad news, which made the minister grow anxious and the queen grow very quiet. Her Majesty appeared to be nerving herself up to some great resolve, which only made the cardinal more worried. For he knew that proud princess and feared the resolve of Anne of Austria.

The coadjutor had returned to parliament more of a monarch than the king, queen, and cardinal put together; on his advice, an edict of parliament had invited the citizens to lay down their arms and demolish the barricades. Of course, they knew that the people could re-arm themselves in an hour and the barricades could be rebuilt overnight.

Planchet returned to his shop. The victory was as good as an amnesty, and he had no more fear of being hanged. He was convinced that if an attempt was made to arrest him, the people would rise up for him as they had for Broussel.

Rochefort returned his troop of light horse to the Chevalier d'Humières; at the roll call two were found missing, but the chevalier, who was a Frondeur at heart, refused all offers of indemnity.

The beggar had resumed his post in the plaza outside Saint-Eustache, once more distributing his holy water with one hand while asking for alms with the other—and no one suspected those hands of having pried at the foundation stones of the edifice of royalty.

Louvières was satisfied and proud; he'd taken his revenge upon Mazarin, whom he detested, he'd been instrumental in getting his father released from prison, his name was now repeated in terror at the Palais Royal, and he said with a laugh when the councilor was once more among his family, "Do you think, Father, that if I asked the queen for the command of a regiment that now she'd give it to me?"

D'Artagnan took advantage of the moment of calm to send off Raoul, whom he'd had difficulty in keeping indoors during the riot, when he'd been eager to draw his sword for one side or the other. The lad had been stubborn about it until d'Artagnan had invoked the name of the Comte de La Fère. Raoul first paid a visit to Madame de Chevreuse, and then departed to rejoin the army.

Rochefort alone was sorry the affair was over—he'd sent to the Duc de Beaufort to come to Paris, and the duke would arrive to find the city tranquil. He went to the coadjutor to ask if he thought the prince should be met on the road and turned around; Gondy thought for a moment, and then said, "Let him come anyway."

"Then it's not over yet?" Rochefort asked.

"Over! My dear Count, it's barely begun."

"What makes you think that?"

"My understanding of the queen's heart: she won't stand for being beaten."

"Is she preparing something?"

"I hope so."

"But what do you know?"

"I know that she wrote to Monsieur le Prince to return from the army in haste."

"Oh ho!" Rochefort said. "You're right, we must encourage Monsieur de Beaufort to come."

That very evening, word went around that the Prince de Condé had arrived. There was nothing strange about this, but the news made a great impression. Madame de Longueville, it was said, had been indiscreet, repeating some confidences made to her by Monsieur le Prince, whom gossip accused of having for his sister a tenderness beyond the bounds of fraternal friendship. These secrets involved some sinister plans on the part of the queen.

On the evening of the Prince de Condé's arrival, some of the more radical high-ranking citizens, aldermen and ward captains, got together and said, "Why shouldn't we take charge of the king and install him in the Hôtel de Ville? It's a mistake to leave him to be raised by our enemies, who fill his head with bad advice. Now if the coadjutor was his mentor, he'd absorb more tolerant principles, and learn to love the people."

That night was busy with furtive activity, and the morning saw the return of the gray and black cloaks, the bands of beggars, and patrols of armed merchants.

The queen had spent the night in private conference with Monsieur le Prince, who had been admitted to her chapel at midnight and had stayed there until five in the morning. Then the queen went to the cardinal's study. She'd been up all night, but he was already awake and at work. He was writing a reply to Cromwell, six days having already passed of the ten he'd asked Mordaunt to wait. "I may have kept him waiting," he said to himself, "but Cromwell knows something of revolutions, and will understand."

As he reread with satisfaction the first paragraph of his letter, a scratching came from the door of the passage that led to the queen's chambers. Anne of Austria was the only one who'd use that door, so the cardinal got up to open it.

The queen hadn't yet dressed, but undress suited her, for, like Diane de Poitiers and Ninon de Lenclos,[7] Anne of Austria had the gift of looking beautiful in every condition—and that was never more true than on this morning, when her eyes were radiant with an inner joy.

"What is it, Madame?" asked Mazarin, inwardly anxious. "You seem bursting with pride."

"Yes, Giulio," she said, "pride and happiness, for I've found the means to slay the hydra."

"Then you are a great politician, my Queen," said Mazarin. "Tell me of this means." And he slid the unfinished letter under another sheet.

"You've heard they want to take the king from us?" said the queen.

"Yes—and hang me while they're at it!"

"They shall not have the king."

"And they certainly won't hang me, *benone*."

"Listen: I myself will spirit my son away, and you with us. It will change the face of things overnight—but I want it done without warning, unknown in advance to anyone but you, me, and a third person."

"And who is this third person?"

"Monsieur le Prince."

"So, he's arrived, as I'd heard?"

"Last night."

"And you've seen him?"

"I just left him."

"He's ready to assist this project?"

"It was his idea."

"And Paris?"

"We starve the city and force it at length to surrender."

"The proposal isn't without grandeur, but you may have overlooked something."

"What?"

"The fact that it's impossible."

"Nonsense. Nothing is impossible."

"In theory."

"And in execution! How much money do we have?"

"A little," said Mazarin, trembling for fear that Anne of Austria might empty his purse.

"How many troops?"

"Five or six thousand."

"And have we no courage?"

"Plenty of that."

"Then we'll do it, and easily. Oh, can't you see it, Giulio? Paris, wretched Paris, awakening in the morning to find king and queen gone, the city surrounded, besieged, starving, with no one to turn to but that stupid parliament and their bow-legged coadjutor!"

"Yes, very pretty—it's a lovely dream. I just don't see any way of making it a reality."

"I'll find a way!"

"You're talking about war, *civil* war: furious, relentless, and implacable."

"Oh, yes, it's war, all right" said Anne of Austria. "I want to reduce this rebellious city to ashes; I want to extinguish the fire with blood; I want to punish their crimes with a terrible example. Paris! I hate it. I detest it!"

"Gently, Anne; how bloodthirsty you are! Take care, these aren't the days of Malatesta and Castruccio Castracani,[8] who plunged all Italy into bloody strife. You'll get yourself decapitated, my sweet Queen, and that would be a shame."

"You laugh."

"I laugh very little at war, especially against an entire nation. Look at your brother-in-law Charles I*—he's in a bad way, very bad."

"We're in France. And I am Spanish."

"All the worse for us, *per Bacco*. I'd like it better if you were French, and me too, for that matter. They wouldn't hate us so much."

"However—do you approve of my plan?"

"Yes, if I could see how it was possible."

"It is, I'll answer for it. Get ready to depart."

"Me! I'm always ready to depart—only, you know, I never actually go. And this time is probably no different than the others."

"Well, if I go, will you go with me?"

"I'll try."

"You're killing me with your fears, Giulio. What is it you're afraid of?"

"A lot of things."

"Such as?"

Mazarin's expression, which had been mocking, turned somber. "Anne," he said, "you're a woman, and as a woman you can insult men as you please, sure you can do so with impunity. You accuse me of being afraid—but I'm not as fearful as you, for I wasn't planning to run. Whose downfall does the mob cry out for? Who is it they want to hang—you or me? Nonetheless, I stand up to the storm—not with bravado, that's not my style—but I hold out. Yet you call me afraid. Imitate me: less noise, more effect. You make loud declarations, but nothing comes of them. And now you talk about fleeing!" Mazarin shrugged, took the queen's hand and led her to the window. "Look!"

"Well?" said the queen, blinded by obstinacy.

"Well, what do you see from this window? Those are, unless I'm mistaken, your subjects out there wearing cuirasses and helmets and armed with good muskets, like in the days of the Catholic League—and they're staring right at this window. If you lifted the curtain a bit, you'd be recognized. Now, look out this other window: what do you see? Armed Parisians just outside your gates. You'd see the same thing from any other window in this palace: your gates are guarded, as are your postern doors, your sally ports, even the vents of your cellars. I say to you what La Ramée told Monsieur de Beaufort: unless you're a bird or a mouse, you cannot get out."

"But Beaufort got out, didn't he?"

"Do you plan to get out the same way he did?"

"Then . . . I'm a prisoner?"

"*Parbleu!* Isn't that what I just proved to you?" And Mazarin sat down and quietly went back to work on his letter, picking up from where he'd been interrupted.

Anne, flushed and trembling with anger and humiliation, left the study, slamming the door hard behind her. Mazarin didn't even turn his head.

Returning to her chambers, the queen threw herself into an armchair and began to cry. Then she was struck by a sudden idea. "I am saved!" she said, arising. "Of course! Yes, I know a man who can get us out of Paris, a man I've forgotten for far too long." Alight with joy, she said, "Ingrate that I am, for twenty years I've forgotten this man, whom I should have made a Marshal of France. My mother-in-law lavished gold, titles, and caresses on Concini, who plotted against her; the king my husband made Vitry a Marshal of France for assassinating Concini; but I, I left in obscurity and misery that noble d'Artagnan, who saved me." She rushed to a table, where she found paper and ink, and began to write.

VII

The Interview

That morning d'Artagnan was in Porthos's room, still asleep. Sharing a room was a habit the two old friends had resumed since the disturbances had begun. Their swords were under their pillows, and their pistols were on a table near at hand. D'Artagnan was dreaming that the sky was covered by a great glowing cloud, and from this cloud fell a rain of gold that he was catching in his hat. Porthos, meanwhile, was dreaming that his carriage's door panel wasn't large enough to contain the coat of arms he was having painted on it.

They were awakened at seven o'clock by a valet wearing no livery who brought a letter for d'Artagnan. "From whom?" asked the Gascon.

"From the queen," replied the valet.

"Hey!" said Porthos, rising on his bed. "What does it say?"

D'Artagnan asked the valet to wait in the next room, and as soon as the door was closed he leapt from his bed and quickly read the letter, while Porthos watched with wide eyes, not daring another question.

"Friend Porthos," said d'Artagnan, handing him the letter, "here's your title of baron and my promotion to captain. Read it and see if I'm wrong."

Porthos reached out, took the letter, and read in a trembling voice, "'The queen wishes to speak with Monsieur d'Artagnan, who is to follow the bearer of this letter.' Well!" said Porthos. "I see nothing here out of the ordinary."

"Whereas I see much that is extraordinary," said d'Artagnan. "If I'm summoned, it's because there's going to be trouble. Consider what upheaval must have taken place in the mind of the queen to make her suddenly remember me after twenty years."

"You're right," said Porthos.

"Sharpen your sword, Baron, load your pistols, and ready your horses, as I foresee big news by tomorrow. And keep this quiet!"

"*Ah çà!* But are you sure this isn't some kind of a trap to get rid of us?" said Porthos, always worried that others might feel threatened by his future greatness.

"If it's a trap, rest assured, I'll smell it," said d'Artagnan. "Mazarin may be an Italian, but I'm a Gascon." And d'Artagnan dressed himself in less than a minute.

As Porthos, still in bed, reached for his cloak, there came another knock at the door. "Come in," said d'Artagnan.

A second valet entered and handed d'Artagnan a second letter, saying, "On the behalf of His Eminence Cardinal Mazarin."

D'Artagnan looked at Porthos. "This is awkward," said Porthos. "Who do you answer first?"

"No, it's perfect," d'Artagnan said. "His Eminence summons me to an appointment in half an hour."

"Good."

"*Mon ami,*" said d'Artagnan, turning to the valet, "tell His Eminence that in half an hour I'll be at his command."

The valet bowed and went out. "It's lucky he didn't see the other valet," d'Artagnan said.

"Then you don't think the two have sent to you for the same meeting?"

"I not only don't think so, I'm certain of it."

"Then go, d'Artagnan, and quickly! The queen is waiting for you—and after the queen, the cardinal. And after the cardinal, me!"

D'Artagnan called back Anne of Austria's valet. "I'm ready, friend," he said. "Lead on."

The valet took him by way of the Rue des Petits-Champs, where, turning left, he led him through a small door into a garden adjacent to Rue Richelieu, where they entered a secret staircase that brought d'Artagnan to the queen's chapel.

A certain unexpected emotion made the lieutenant's heart beat faster. He no longer had the blind confidence of youth, and experience had taught him the gravity of involvement in events like this. He understood the power of princes and the majesty of kings, and the insignificance of his family and fortune in comparison. Once he would have approached Anne of Austria as a young man going to pay his respects to a lady; but now he went to her as a humble soldier does to a commander.

A slight noise broke the silence of the chapel, and d'Artagnan started as a white hand drew back a tapestry—a hand white in color and beautiful in shape, a royal hand he recognized and once had kissed.

The queen entered. "It's you, Monsieur d'Artagnan," she said, regarding the officer with a look of affectionate melancholy, "it's you—I know you well. Look at me, I am the queen—do you recognize me?"

"No, Madame," replied d'Artagnan.

"But don't you recall," continued Anne of Austria, in that sweet tone she could adopt when it pleased her to do so, "how a queen once needed a brave and devoted young cavalier, and found that cavalier, and who, though he might have believed that she'd forgotten him, kept him in a place in the bottom of her heart?"

"No, Madame, I don't recall that," said the musketeer.

"So much the worse, Monsieur," said Anne of Austria, "so much the worse, at least for the queen, for that queen once again has need of that bravery and devotion."

"What!" said d'Artagnan. "The queen, surrounded as she is by servants so devoted, by counselors so wise, by men so mighty in merit and position, deigns to cast her eyes on an obscure soldier!"

Anne understood this veiled reproach, but she was more moved than angered by it. The Gascon gentleman's patient and unselfish service had long been an unacknowledged humiliation for her, and she was outdone by his generosity. "Everything you say about those around me, Monsieur d'Artagnan, may perhaps be true," said the queen, "but you are the only one I can trust. I know you serve the cardinal, but serve me as well, and I will make your fortune. Come, would you do for me today what the cavalier you don't recall once did for his queen?"

"I am at the orders of Your Majesty," said d'Artagnan.

The queen reflected for a moment on the circumspect attitude of the musketeer. "Perhaps you prefer ease and repose?" she said.

"I wouldn't know, Madame—I've never had any."

"Do you have any comrades?"

"I had three: two have left Paris and gone I know not where. Only one is still with me—but he's one of those who knew, I think, the cavalier of whom Your Majesty has done me the honor to speak."

"Very well," said the queen. "You and your friend are worth an army."

"What must I do, Madame?"

"Come back at five o'clock and I'll tell you—but in the meantime, Monsieur, don't tell a living soul about that rendezvous."

"No, Madame."

"Swear it by Christ."

"Madame, I never lie once I've given my word; if I say no, I mean no."

The queen, though astonished by such language, so different from what she heard from her courtiers, took it as a sign of the zeal d'Artagnan would apply to the accomplishment of her plan. It was an occasional artifice of the Gascon's to hide his deep subtlety under a guise of brusque loyalty. "The queen has no further orders for the moment?" he said.

"No, Monsieur," replied Anne of Austria, "and you may retire until the time I've appointed."

D'Artagnan bowed and went out. "The devil!" he said once he'd passed through the door. "There seems to be a great need for me around here."

Then, as the half hour had passed, he went across the gallery and knocked on the cardinal's door. Bernouin* let him in. "I've come at your orders, Monseigneur," d'Artagnan said to the cardinal. As was his custom, he took a quick glance around the room, noticing that Mazarin had a sealed letter before him—but it was placed facedown on the desk, so it was impossible to see to whom it was addressed.

"You've just come from the queen?" said Mazarin, looking directly at d'Artagnan.

"Me, Monseigneur? Who told you that?"

"No one—but I know it."

"I am sorry to tell Monseigneur he is mistaken," the Gascon replied shamelessly, in accord with the promise he'd just made to Anne of Austria.

"I was at the door of the antechamber and saw you coming from the end of the gallery."

"That's because I was brought in by the secret staircase."

"Why was that?"

"I don't know; there may have been some mistake."

Mazarin knew how hard it was to get d'Artagnan to talk when he didn't want to, so he decided to set aside for later the mystery of whatever the Gascon was hiding. "Let's discuss my affairs," said the cardinal, "since you won't tell me anything about yours."

D'Artagnan bowed.

"Do you like traveling?" asked the cardinal.

"I've spent my life on the high roads."

"There's nothing to keep you here in Paris?"

"Nothing but the orders of my superior."

"Good. Here's a letter that must be delivered to a certain address."

"An address, Monseigneur? But it has none."

And in fact, the side opposite the seal was blank.

"That's because it's a double envelope," said Mazarin.

"I understand—I must open the outer one only after I've arrived at a given place."

"Exactly. Take it and go. You have a friend, Monsieur du Vallon, whom I like very much—take him as well."

"The devil!" d'Artagnan said to himself. "He knows we overheard his conversation yesterday, and he wants to get us out of Paris."

"You hesitate?" asked Mazarin.

"No, Monseigneur, I leave at once. There's only one thing I request . . ."

"What's that? Speak."

"It's that Your Eminence should go to the queen."

"When?"

"Right away."

"To do what?"

"Just to say this: 'I have sent Monsieur d'Artagnan somewhere and asked him to leave immediately.'"

"So, I see," said Mazarin, "that you have met with the queen."

"I had the honor to tell Your Eminence that it was possible there'd been some mistake."

"What does that mean?" Mazarin asked.

"Shall I renew my request of His Eminence?"

"Very well, I'll go. Await me here." Mazarin checked carefully to make sure none of the keys had been left in the strongbox locks and went out.

Ten minutes elapsed, during which d'Artagnan did everything he could to try to read the address of the inner envelope through the fabric of the outer, to no avail.

Mazarin returned, pale and deeply preoccupied, and sat at his desk. D'Artagnan examined his expression as closely as he had the dispatch, but the envelope of the cardinal's face was as impenetrable as the envelope of the letter. "Uh-oh," the Gascon said to himself, "he looks angry. Is it toward me? He's considering—is he thinking of clapping me in the Bastille? Good luck, Monseigneur! At the first order you issue to do so, I'll strangle you and turn Frondeur. They'll carry me in triumph like Monsieur Broussel, and Athos will proclaim me the French Brutus. That would be funny."

The Gascon, with his ever-active imagination, had already carried his hypothetical situation to its end. However, Mazarin gave no such order, but on the contrary said, in a cajoling tone, "You were quite right, my dear Monsieur d'Artagnan, you cannot leave us so soon."

"Ah!" said d'Artagnan.

"Return to me that dispatch, if you please."

D'Artagnan obeyed. Mazarin assured himself the seal was still intact. "I'll need you this evening," he said. "Come back in eight hours."

"In eight hours, Monseigneur," said d'Artagnan, "I have an appointment that I cannot fail to keep."

"Don't worry about that," said Mazarin, "it's all the same business."

Good! thought d'Artagnan. *I suspected as much.*

"Return then at five o'clock and bring with you that dear Monsieur du Vallon—only leave him in the antechamber, as I'll want to speak to you alone."

D'Artagnan bowed, saying to himself, "The same order from both, at the same hour and the same place, the Palais Royal—I get it. Ah, now here's a secret Monsieur de Gondy would pay a hundred thousand livres for."

"You have a concern?" said Mazarin anxiously.

"Yes, I was wondering if we should come armed or not."

"Armed? To the teeth!" said Mazarin.

"Very well, Monseigneur, we shall be."

D'Artagnan bowed, went out, and hurried back to his friend to report on the interview, including Mazarin's flattery and promises, which made Porthos very happy.

VIII

The Escape

When d'Artagnan returned at five in the evening, the Palais Royal, despite the signs of agitation in the city, presented a cheerful appearance. This wasn't surprising: the queen had given up Broussel and Blancmesnil to the people, so the queen had nothing more to fear, as the people had nothing more to ask. But inside her emotions were still overwrought, a disturbance that would take some time to dissipate, as after an ocean storm it sometimes takes several days for the swell to subside.

There had been a grand formal dinner, the pretext for which had been the return of the victor of Lens. The princes and princesses had all been invited, and their carriages had crowded the courtyard since midday. After dinner, there was to be gaming in the queen's apartments.

Anne of Austria was charming that day, graceful and witty, and had never been seen in better humor. The joy of vengeance to come shone in her eyes and on her lips.

As soon as they rose from the dinner table, Mazarin slipped away. D'Artagnan was already awaiting him in the antechamber. The cardinal arrived chuckling, took d'Artagnan by the hand and drew him into his study. "My dear Monsieur d'Artagnan," said the minister, sitting down, "I will show you the greatest mark of confidence a minister can give an officer."

D'Artagnan bowed. "I hope," he said, "that Monseigneur grants it to me without hesitation, and in the conviction that I'm worthy of it."

"The worthiest of all, *mon cher ami*, since it's to you that I give it."

"Well," said d'Artagnan, "I must admit, Monseigneur, that I've been waiting so long to hear that, I hope you'll speak quickly and delay no longer."

"This evening, my dear Monsieur d'Artagnan," replied Mazarin, "you're going to have the security of the entire state in your hands." He paused.

"Please explain, Monseigneur. I'm waiting."

"The queen has decided to take the king on a short trip to Saint-Germain."[9]

"Ah!" said d'Artagnan. "What you mean is, the queen has decided to leave Paris."

"A feminine caprice—you understand."

"Oh, I understand very well," d'Artagnan said.

"That was why she sent for you this morning and asked you to return at five o'clock."

"So much for going to all that trouble to have me swear not to mention the appointment to anyone!" murmured d'Artagnan. "Ah, the women! Even when they're queens, they're still women."

"Do you disapprove of this little sojourn, my dear Monsieur d'Artagnan?" asked Mazarin anxiously.

"Me, Monseigneur?" said d'Artagnan. "Why do you ask?"

"You shrugged your shoulders."

"That's just my habit when talking to myself, Monseigneur."

"Then you approve of this journey?"

"I neither approve nor disapprove, Monseigneur—I follow orders."

"Good—because you're the one I've chosen to get the king and queen safely to Saint-Germain."

"A double deceit," d'Artagnan said to himself.

"So, you see," continued Mazarin, trying to penetrate d'Artagnan's impassivity, "that as I said, the security of the State will be in your hands."

"Yes, Monseigneur, and I feel all the responsibility of such a charge."

"You accept, though?"

"I always accept."

"You think the thing is possible?"

"Everything is possible."

"Will you be attacked on the way?"

"It seems likely."

"How will you handle that?"

"I'll ride through the attackers."

"What if you can't get through them?"

"If I can't go through them, I'll go over them."

"And you'll bring the king and queen safe and sound to Saint-Germain?"

"Yes."

"On your life?"

"On my life."

"You're a true hero, *mon cher!*" said Mazarin, looking admiringly at the musketeer.

D'Artagnan smiled.

"And me?" said Mazarin after a moment of silence, looking fixedly at d'Artagnan.

"What about you, Monseigneur?"

"What if I want to go along?"

"That . . . would make it harder."

"How so?"

"Your Eminence might be recognized."

"Even wearing this disguise?" And he lifted a cloak from an armchair, under which was a complete cavalier's outfit of pearl gray and garnet with silver lace.

"If Your Eminence is disguised, the matter is easier."

"Ah!" said Mazarin with a sigh of relief.

"But it means that Your Eminence must do what he said he'd have done the other day in our situation."

"What do I have to do?"

"Shout, 'Down with Mazarin!'"

"I can shout that."

"In French, in *good* French, Monseigneur, taking care with the accent. They killed six thousand Angevins in Italy because they spoke bad Italian. Be careful so the French don't take their revenge for the Sicilian Vespers."[10]

"I'll do my best."

"There are a lot of armed men in the streets," continued d'Artagnan. "Are you sure no one else knows about the queen's plan?"

Mazarin reflected.

"It would be a pretty risky affair if this matter fell into the hands of a traitor, Monseigneur. The trip you propose would provide an opportunity for the worst sort of mischief."

Mazarin shuddered—was that an implied threat?—but then considered that a man who planned treachery wouldn't say so. "No," he said briskly. "I don't rely on just anybody, and the proof is that I've chosen you to escort me."

"You're not going with the queen?"

"No," said Mazarin.

"You plan to go after the queen does?"

"No," Mazarin said again.

"Oh ho!" said d'Artagnan, who was beginning to understand.

"Yes, I have my own plans," the cardinal continued. "If I go with the queen, I double her danger; if I follow the queen, I double my own. Besides, the Court, once saved, might forget about me—the great can be so ungrateful."

"That's true," said d'Artagnan, glancing in spite of himself at the queen's diamond ring on Mazarin's finger.

Mazarin noticed this look and gently turned the ring's stone inside. "I wish, then," said Mazarin with his handsome smile, "to keep them from being ungrateful to me."

"It's just Christian charity not to lead one's neighbor into temptation," said d'Artagnan.

"And that's exactly why I want to leave ahead of the others," said Mazarin.

D'Artagnan smiled; he was the sort of man who could appreciate the Italian's trick. Mazarin saw him smile and took advantage of the moment. "Then you'll undertake to get me out of Paris first, my dear Monsieur d'Artagnan?"

"That's no easy task, Monseigneur!" said d'Artagnan, resuming his serious air.

"But," Mazarin said, looking at him attentively, "you made no such objections regarding the king and the queen."

"The king and the queen are my queen and my king, Monseigneur," the musketeer replied. "My life is theirs; I belong to them. What they ask of me, I do—without objection."

"That's fair," Mazarin said quietly. "As your life isn't mine, then, I must buy it from you, no?" And with a heavy sigh, he began to rotate the ring's diamond back out.

D'Artagnan smiled. These two men had one thing in common: cleverness. If on top of that they'd only had courage in common, they would have done great things together.

"You understand then," said Mazarin, "that if I ask this service of you, it's with the intention to be grateful for it."

"Does Monseigneur have only the intention?" asked d'Artagnan.

"Here," said Mazarin, pulling the ring from his finger. "Here, my dear Monsieur d'Artagnan, is a diamond that once belonged to you; it's only right that it should return. I beg of you, take it."

D'Artagnan didn't put Mazarin to the trouble of insisting; he took it, inspected the stone to make sure it was the same, recognized the purity of its water, and placed it on his finger with profound pleasure.

"I was . . . very attached to it," said Mazarin, giving it a last look. "But no matter, I'm very pleased to give it to you."

"And I, Monseigneur, am very pleased to receive it," said d'Artagnan. "Come, let's talk about your little affair. You want to leave before everyone else?"

"Yes, I do."

"At what time?"

"At ten o'clock?"

"And the queen, when does she leave?"

"At midnight."

"Then it's possible—I'll get you out first, leave you outside the gates, and return to bring her."

"Wonderful, but how can I get safely out of Paris?"

"Oh, as to that, leave it to me."

"You're in charge; bring as large an escort as you like."

D'Artagnan shook his head.

"But surely that's the safest way," said Mazarin.

"Maybe for you, Monseigneur, but not for the queen."

Mazarin bit his lip. "Then how will we manage things?" he said.

"You must let me manage them, Monseigneur."

"Hrm!" said Mazarin.

"You must put me in full command of this exercise."

"Yes, but . . ."

"Or find somebody else," said d'Artagnan, turning to go.

"Eh?" Mazarin said to himself. "I think he's leaving with my diamond."
He called him back, in a cajoling voice: "Monsieur d'Artagnan, my dear
Monsieur d'Artagnan."

"Monseigneur?"

"You'll answer for whatever happens?"

"I guarantee nothing—but I'll do my best."

"Your best?"

"Yes."

"Well, then! We must trust in that."

"At last," d'Artagnan said to himself.

"Then you'll come back at half past nine?"

"Will I find Your Eminence ready?"

"Entirely ready."

"Then we're agreed. Now, Monseigneur, will you take me to see the
queen?"

"To what end?"

"I'd like to get Her Majesty's orders from her directly."

"She's directed me to give them to you."

"She might have forgotten something."

"You have to see her?"

"It's indispensable, Monseigneur."

Mazarin hesitated a moment, but d'Artagnan remained implacable.

"Let's go, then," said Mazarin. "I'll take you to see her, but don't say a word about our conversation."

"What was said between us regards only us, Monseigneur," said d'Artagnan.

"You swear to say nothing?"

"I never swear, Monseigneur. I say *yes* or I say *no,* and as I'm a gentleman, I keep my word."

"All right, I see I must trust you completely."

"Believe me, Monseigneur, that's the best possible course."

"Come," said Mazarin. He conducted d'Artagnan to the queen's chapel and told him to wait there.

D'Artagnan didn't have to wait long. Five minutes later the queen came into the chapel, still in her full regalia. Dressed thus she was still beautiful and seemed no older than thirty-five.

"Ah, Monsieur d'Artagnan," she said, with a gracious smile. "I'm glad you insisted on seeing me."

"I beg Her Majesty's pardon," said d'Artagan, "but I thought it best to receive Madame's orders directly."

"You know what they concern?"

"Yes, Madame."

"And you accept this mission I entrust to you?"

"Gratefully."

"Very good. Be here at midnight."

"I'll be here."

"Monsieur d'Artagnan," said the queen, "I know your honest loyalty too well to speak to you now of my gratitude, but I swear to you I will not forget this second service as I did the first."

"I don't know what any of that means; Her Majesty is entitled to decide what to forget, and what to remember." And d'Artagnan bowed.

"Go, Monsieur," said the queen with her most charming smile. "Go, and return at midnight."

She gestured in farewell, and d'Artagnan withdrew; but as he retired he glanced at the way the queen had come in, and at the foot of the tapestry he saw the tip of a velvet shoe. "So," he said to himself, "Mazarin eavesdropped to see if I'd betray him. Truly, this Italian puppet doesn't deserve the service of an honorable man."

D'Artagnan was nonetheless punctual with his appointment, and at half past nine he entered the cardinal's antechamber. Bernouin was waiting and showed him in to the study. He found the cardinal dressed as a cavalier; that kind of attire suited him, as we've said, and he wore it elegantly, though he was very pale and trembling slightly.

"Just you?" said Mazarin.

"Yes, Monseigneur."

"And the good Monsieur du Vallon, will he be joining us?"

"Yes, Monseigneur, he's waiting at the carriage."

"Where's that?"

"At the Palais Royal's garden gate."

"Then we're going in a carriage?"

"Yes, Monseigneur."

"And with no other escort but you two?"

"Isn't that enough? One of us would suffice!"

"In truth, my dear Monsieur d'Artagnan, you terrify me with your nonchalance," said Mazarin.

"I'd have thought, on the contrary, that it would inspire confidence."

"And Bernouin, am I not taking him?"

"There's no room for him; he can follow with the others and rejoin Your Eminence later."

"All right," said Mazarin, "since I must do everything just the way you want."

"Monseigneur, there's still time to call it off, and Your Eminence is perfectly free to do so," said d'Artagnan.

"No, no," said Mazarin, "let's be on our way."

And they went down by the secret staircase, Mazarin holding onto the arm of d'Artagnan, who could feel him trembling.

They crossed the courtyards of the Palais Royal, where a few carriages awaiting guests were still lingering, reached the garden, and found the little door. Mazarin tried to unlock it with a key he drew from his pocket, but his hand trembled so much he couldn't find the keyhole. "Let me," said d'Artagnan. Mazarin gave him the key; d'Artagnan opened the door and put the key into his own pocket. He expected to need it when he returned.

Beyond was the carriage, its footboard lowered and door open; Mousqueton stood at the door, with Porthos on the rear seat. "Get in, Monseigneur," said d'Artagnan. Mazarin didn't wait to be told twice; he leapt into the vehicle.

D'Artagnan got in behind Mazarin, Mousqueton closed the door, and then climbed with many a groan up onto the carriage's rear step. He had made some objections about coming along on the pretext that he was still suffering from his wound, but d'Artagnan had said to him, "Stay if you like, my dear Monsieur Mouston, but I warn you that tonight, Paris will burn." After that, Mousqueton had stopped complaining, and declared he was ready to follow his master and Monsieur d'Artagnan to the ends of the world.

The carriage set off at a steady trot, though not so fast as to imply that its passengers were in a hurry. The cardinal wiped his forehead with a handkerchief and looked around. He had Porthos on his left and d'Artagnan on his right, each guarding a door and serving as a rampart. Facing them, on the front seat, were two pairs of pistols, one before Porthos and the other before d'Artagnan. Both men held their swords beside them.

A hundred paces from the Palais Royal the carriage was stopped by a people's patrol. "Who goes there?" said the leader.

"Mazarin!" replied d'Artagnan, laughing.

The cardinal felt the hair rise on his head.

This joke seemed like a good one to the citizens, who, seeing a carriage without arms or escort, didn't think to believe the response could be a reality. "*Bon voyage!*" they cried. And they let the carriage pass.

"Ha!" said d'Artagnan. "How did Monseigneur like my answer?"

"Oh, you're quite the wit," said Mazarin, sweating.

"By the way," said Porthos, "I got that one."

In the middle of the Rue des Petits-Champs, the carriage was stopped by a second patrol. "Who goes there?" called the patrol's leader.

"Prepare yourself, Monseigneur," said d'Artagnan. Mazarin sank down so deeply between his two guardians that he disappeared completely.

"Who goes there?" the voice repeated impatiently.

D'Artagnan saw that they were making ready to seize the horses' heads; he leaned halfway out the carriage door and called, "Hey, Planchet!"

The leader approached. It was indeed Planchet—d'Artagnan had recognized his former lackey's voice.

"Why, Monsieur!" said Planchet. "Is that you?"

"*Mon Dieu,* yes, old friend. Our dear Porthos has just taken a sword-wound, and I'm bearing him back to his country house at Saint-Cloud."

"Really?" Planchet said.

"Porthos, friend Porthos, if you can still talk," said d'Artagnan, "say a few words to our good Planchet."

"Planchet, my friend," said Porthos with a groan, "I feel awful; if you meet a doctor, please send him along after me."

"Oh! Great God, what a terrible thing!" said Planchet. "How did this happen?"

"I'll tell you that," said Mousqueton, while Porthos gave a great groan.

"Make way, Planchet, or he won't make it," said d'Artagnan in a low voice. "He took it through the lungs."

Planchet shook his head with the air of a man who says, *In that case, it's all over.* Then, turning to his men, he said, "Let them pass—they're friends."

The carriage resumed its ride, and Mazarin, who'd been holding his breath, dared to exhale. "*Bricconi!*" he murmured.

A few paces short of Porte Saint-Honoré they encountered a third troop, this one composed of ragged men who looked more like bandits than anything else. They were the men of the beggar of Saint-Eustache.

"Beware, Porthos!" said d'Artagnan. Porthos reached for his pistols.

"What is it?" said Mazarin.

"Monseigneur, I think we've fallen into bad company."

A man carrying a sort of scythe came to the door; it was the beggars' chief himself. "Who goes there?" he asked.

"Dolt! Don't you recognized the carriage of Monsieur le Prince?" said d'Artagnan.

"Prince or not," said the beggar, "open up! It's our duty to guard the gate, and no one passes who we don't know."

"What should we do?" asked Porthos.

"*Pardieu!* We go on," said d'Artagnan.

"Go on? But how?" said Mazarin.

"Through them or over them. Coachman, at the gallop!"

The driver raised his whip. "Not one step further," said the beggar who seemed to be the leader, "or I'll hamstring your horses."

"*Peste!* That would be a shame," said Porthos. "Those horses cost me a hundred pistoles."

"I'll pay you two hundred," said Mazarin in a low voice.

"Sure," said d'Artagnan, "but after they hamstring the horses, they'll hack off our heads."

"There's one on my side," hissed Porthos. "Should I kill him?"

"Do it—with your fist, if you can. No shooting unless we have to."

"I can do that," said Porthos.

"Come have a look, then," called d'Artagnan to the man with the scythe, meanwhile picking up one of his pistols by the barrel, so he could strike with the butt. The man approached. D'Artagnan, to gain room to move, leaned halfway out the door, into the light of a lantern. His eyes met those of the beggar, who seemed to recognize the musketeer, for he suddenly turned pale—and d'Artagnan seemed to recognize him, for a visible shudder ran through him.

"Monsieur d'Artagnan!" the man gasped, recoiling a step. Then he shouted, "It's Monsieur d'Artagnan! Let them pass!"

D'Artagnan might have replied to this, but a sound came like that of a sledge-hammer striking an ox on the head; it was Porthos felling his man.

D'Artagnan turned to see the poor man lying four paces from the carriage. "Whip on! Whip on!" he cried to the driver. "Now! Belly to the ground!"

The coachman cracked his whip over the horses, and the noble animals leapt forward. Cries came as men were thrown aside. There was a double jolt as the wheels passed over a body.

Then there was a moment of quiet as the carriage passed through the gate. "To the Cours-la-Reine!"[11] d'Artagnan called to the driver. Then, turning to Mazarin, he said, "Now, Monseigneur, you may say five *Paters* and five *Aves* to thank God for your deliverance—you are free, and you are safe!"

Mazarin's only reply was a sort of groan. He didn't believe in miracles.

Five minutes later the carriage stopped, having arrived at the Cours-la-Reine. "Is Monseigneur satisfied with his escort?" asked the musketeer.

"Enchanted, Monsieur," said Mazarin, risking a look out one of the doors. "Now do the same for the queen."

"That will be less difficult," said d'Artagnan, jumping to the ground. "Monsieur du Vallon, I commend His Eminence to your care."

"Rest easy," said Porthos, extending his hand.

D'Artagnan took Porthos's hand and shook it. "Ouch!" said Porthos.

D'Artagnan looked at his friend in astonishment. "What's wrong?"

"I think I sprained my wrist," said Porthos.

"Why the devil did you hit him? Didn't you hear my man?"

"I had to do it, he was aiming his pistol. But you, how did you get rid of your man?"

"Oh!" said d'Artagnan. "Mine was no man."

"What was he, then?"

"He was . . . a specter."

"And . . . ?"

"And so, I conjured him away."

Without further explanation, d'Artagnan took his pistols from the front seat, thrust them through his belt, wrapped himself in his cloak, and then, not wishing to return through the same gate they'd come out, made his way toward Porte Richelieu.

IX

The Carriage of Monsieur le Coadjuteur

Instead of reentering the city by Porte Saint-Honoré, d'Artagnan, who had a little time, rode around and returned through Porte Richelieu. There citizen guards stopped him for inspection, and, when they saw he was a musketeer with his feathered hat and embroidered cloak, they surrounded him and insisted that he shout, "Down with Mazarin!" At first, he considered refusing, but then he remembered what mission he had ahead of him, and cried out so enthusiastically that the citizens were satisfied.

He rode in along the Rue de Richelieu, considering how he would get the queen out in her turn, which he certainly couldn't do in a coach displaying the Arms of France, when he spotted a carriage standing at the gate of Madame de Guéménée's mansion, and was struck by an idea. "Ah, *pardieu,*" he said, "it would be poetic justice." He approached the carriage until he could see what arms were painted on the door and whose livery was worn by the coachman—an examination made all the easier as the driver was asleep, snoring on his seat.

"No doubt about it: this is Monsieur le Coadjuteur's carriage," he said. "Upon my word, I begin to believe we may have Providence on our side."

He climbed quietly into the carriage, found the silk cord the passengers used to communicate with the coachman, tugged on it and called, "To the Palais Royal!"

The driver awakened with a start, and drove off toward the given destination, without the least suspicion that the order had come from anyone but his master. The Swiss Guards at the gate almost barred their entry, but the sight of the magnificent vehicle persuaded them the visit must be one of importance, so they let the carriage pass, and it stopped beneath the portico. Only then did the coachman notice the carriage had no lackeys on the rear step. He thought the coadjutor must have given them other orders, so he jumped down from his seat to open the door.

D'Artagnan leapt out of the carriage, and as the coachman, frightened at not seeing his master, took a step back, the musketeer grabbed him by the collar with his left hand and clapped a pistol to his head with the right. "Say one word and you're dead," said d'Artagnan.

The coachman saw by the expression on his captor's face that he'd fallen into a trap, and he froze, gaping and wide-eyed.

Two musketeers were crossing the courtyard; d'Artagnan called them over by name. "Monsieur de Bellière," he said to one of them, "do me the favor of taking this brave man's reins, climbing up onto his seat, and driving the carriage to the door of the private staircase. Await me there, on a matter of the greatest importance and in the king's service." The musketeer, who knew his lieutenant would never joke about a matter of the king's service, obeyed without saying a word, though the order seemed strange to him.

Then, turning to the second musketeer, he said, "Monsieur du Verger, help me conduct this man to a safe place." The musketeer, thinking his lieutenant must have just arrested some disguised rebel prince, bowed, drew his sword, and indicated he was ready.

D'Artagnan went up the stairs, followed by his prisoner and the other musketeer, crossed the vestibule, and entered Mazarin's antechamber. Bernouin was there, waiting impatiently for news of his master. "Is all well, Monsieur?" he asked.

"Extremely well, my dear Monsieur Bernouin. But here, if you please, is a man who needs to be put someplace for safekeeping."

"Where would that be, Monsieur?"

"Wherever you like, provided the place has shutters with a padlock and a door that locks with a key."

"That we have, Monsieur," said Bernouin. And he led the poor coachman into a small counting-room that had iron bars across the window and resembled a prison cell. "Now, *mon ami*," said d'Artagnan, "I invite you to remove your hat and cloak and lend them to me."

The coachman, as might be imagined, made no resistance—besides, he was so stunned by events that he staggered and stammered like a drunk. D'Artagnan put the hat and cloak under Bernouin's arm, and said, "Now, Monsieur du Verger, stay in here with this fellow until Monsieur Bernouin returns to let you out. This sentry duty may be long and not very amusing, I know—but it's on the king's service," he added gravely.

"As you command, Lieutenant," replied the musketeer, who could see he was involved in serious matters.

"By the way," said d'Artagnan, "if this man tries to shout or get away, run him through."

The musketeer made a formal salute.

D'Artagnan went out, taking Bernouin with him. Midnight was sounding. "Take me to the queen's chapel," d'Artagnan said. "Inform her that I'm there, and then take that bundle there—the one with the loaded carbine—down and put it on the seat of the carriage waiting at the bottom of the private staircase."

Bernouin conducted d'Artagnan into the chapel, where he sat down, thoughtfully. Everything seemed in order at the Palais Royal as usual. By ten o'clock all the evening's guests had retired; those that were to flee with the Court had been given the secret password and told to make their way to the Cours-la-Reine between midnight and one o'clock.

At ten o'clock, Anne of Austria had gone in to see the king. They had already put Monsieur, his brother,[12] to bed, and young Louis, who was still up, was enacting a battle with some lead soldiers, a game he greatly enjoyed. Two children of honor were playing with him. "La Porte,"[*] said the queen, "it's time for His Majesty to go to bed."

The king asked to stay up, as he wasn't ready for sleep, but the queen insisted. "Don't you plan to go at six in the morning to bathe at Conflans? That was your own idea, as I recall."

"You're right, Madame," said the king, "and I'm ready to retire to my room as soon as you kiss me goodnight. La Porte, give the candlestick to the Chevalier de Coislin." The queen rested her lips on the pale royal forehead which the august child offered with all the gravity of etiquette.

"Fall asleep quickly, Louis," said the queen, "because you're getting up early."

"I'll do my best to obey you, Madame," said young Louis, "though I don't really feel sleepy."

"La Porte," whispered Anne of Austria, "find some very boring book to read to His Majesty, but don't undress."

The king retired, accompanied by the young Chevalier de Coislin as candle-bearer; the other child of honor went off to his room.

Then the queen returned to her own apartments. Her women, that is to say Madame de Brégy, Mademoiselle de Beaumont, Madame de Motteville, and her sister Socratine, so called due to her wisdom, had just brought into the dressing room the remains of the dinner, upon which the queen supped, as was customary.

The queen then gave her final orders, spoke about a dinner for her the following day hosted by the Marquis de Villequier, designated those to be honored by dining with her, and announced that on the day after that she would pay a visit to Val-de-Grâce,[13] where she intended to make her devotions. She then told Béringhen, her premier *valet de chambre*, to accompany her.

The ladies having finished their supper, the queen pretended to be very tired and went into her bedchamber. Madame de Motteville, who was on duty that evening, followed her in and helped her undress. The queen got into bed, spoke to her affectionately for a few minutes, and then dismissed her.

It was at that moment that d'Artagnan was entering the Palais Royal courtyard with the coadjutor's coach. Just after that, the carriages of the ladies of honor drove out, and the gate was shut behind them.

Midnight sounded. Five minutes later, Bernouin knocked at the queen's door, coming through the secret passage from the cardinal's study. Anne of Austria opened the door herself. She was already dressed, that is, she'd put on her stockings and wrapped herself in a long robe. "Is that you, Bernouin?" she asked, "And is Monsieur d'Artagnan there?"

"Yes, Madame, in your chapel, where he's waiting until Your Majesty is ready."

"I'm ready. Go and tell La Porte to awaken and dress the king, and from there go to the Maréchal de Villeroy and ask him to come to me."

Bernouin bowed and went out. The queen went to her chapel, which was lit by a single Venetian lamp. There she found d'Artagnan waiting for her.

"It's you?" she said to him.

"Yes, Madame."

"You're ready?"

"Quite ready."

"And the cardinal?"

"Got out without injury. He awaits Your Majesty at the Cours-la-Reine."

"But in what carriage will we go?"

"I've arranged everything; a carriage is waiting for Your Majesty below."

"Let's go to the king."

D'Artagnan bowed and followed the queen. Young Louis was already dressed in everything but his shoes and his doublet. He allowed himself to be dressed despite his astonishment, and showered La Porte with questions, who just told him, "Sire, this is by the queen's orders." The royal bedcovers were thrown back, exposing sheets so worn there were holes in some places—evidence of Mazarin's shameful stinginess.

The queen came in, while d'Artagnan remained on the threshold. The child, seeing the queen, escaped from La Porte's hold and ran to her. The queen beckoned d'Artagnan to approach. D'Artagnan obeyed, removing his hat.

"My son," said Anne of Austria, pointing to the musketeer, who stood calm and upright, "here is Monsieur d'Artagnan, who is as brave as one of those noble knights whose stories you love so much when my ladies read them to you. Remember his name and take a good look at him so you will recognize him again, for tonight he renders us a great service."

The young king regarded the officer with his proud gaze and repeated, "Monsieur d'Artagnan?"

"That's him, my son."

The young king slowly raised his boyish hand and extended it to the musketeer, who fell to one knee and kissed it. "Monsieur d'Artagnan," Louis repeated, nodding. "It is well, Madame."

At that moment they heard an approaching clamor. "What's that?" said the queen.

"Uh-oh," d'Artagnan said, cocking his intelligent head. "It's the sound of the people, aroused."

"We must flee!" said the queen.

"Your Majesty has granted to me the direction of this affair—and I say we must stay until we know what this noise means."

"Monsieur d'Artagnan!"

"I'll answer for everything."

Nothing is more contagious than confidence. The queen, herself strong and brave, responded to those virtues in others. "So be it," she said. "I rely on you."

"Will Her Majesty permit me to give orders in her name?"

"Give your orders, Monsieur."

"What is it the people want?" asked the king.

"We'll soon know, Sire," said d'Artagnan. And he quickly left the room.

The tumult grew, until it seemed to envelop the entire Palais Royal. Cries came from within, the meaning of which was unclear—but there was evidently some commotion and unrest. The king, half dressed, the queen, and La Porte all remained just as they were, listening and waiting.

Comminges, who was on guard duty that night at the Palais Royal, rushed in; he reported that he had about two hundred men in the courtyards and the stables, and placed them at the queen's disposal. "Well?" Anne of Austria asked as d'Artagnan reappeared. "What's going on?"

"A rumor has spread that the queen has left the Palais Royal, taking the king with her, and the people demand proof to the contrary, or they threaten to demolish the palace."

"Oh! This time, it's too much," said the queen. "I'll prove to them that I haven't gone."

D'Artagnan saw, from the queen's face, that she was going to order some violent retaliation. He approached her and whispered, "Does Your Majesty have full confidence in me?"

His voice made her tremble. "Yes, Monsieur—full confidence," she said.

"Will the queen deign to follow my advice?"

"Speak."

"Would Your Majesty be so kind as to dismiss Monsieur de Comminges, and have him order his troops to withdraw into the guardhouse and stables?"

Comminges gave d'Artagnan that envious look with which every courtier regards a new favorite.

"Did you hear, Comminges?" said the queen.

D'Artagnan turned to Comminges, and with his usual shrewdness recognized the man's unease. "Monsieur de Comminges," he said, "pardon me, but we're both servants of the queen, aren't we? It's my turn to be useful to her; don't be envious of my moment."

Comminges bowed stiffly and went. *And thus*, thought d'Artagnan, *I've managed to make myself another enemy.*

"Now," said the queen, addressing d'Artagnan, "what's to be done? For as you can hear, instead of decreasing, the noise is growing louder."

"Madame," d'Artagnan replied, "if the people want to see the king, they should see him."

"What do you mean, they should see him—and where? On the balcony?"

"Not there, Madame, but here in bed, asleep."

"Oh, Your Majesty, Monsieur d'Artagnan is absolutely right!" said La Porte.

The queen thought for a moment, and then smiled like a woman to whom duplicity is no stranger. "We'll do it," she murmured.

"Monsieur La Porte," said d'Artagnan, "go out through the palace gates and announce to the people that if they would be satisfied, in five minutes they will not only see the king but see him in his bed—however, add that the king is asleep, and the queen begs that they remain silent so as not to awaken him."

"You mean everyone, not just a delegation of a few persons?"

"Everyone, Madame."

"But think about it, this will take all night."

"It will take a quarter of an hour. Trust me on this, Madame—believe me, the people are like big children who just need to hear some calm words. At the sight of the sleeping king, they will be silent, sweet, and gentle as lambs."

"Go, La Porte," said the queen.

The young king approached his mother. "Why do we have to do what these people ask?" he said.

"Because we must, my son," said Anne of Austria.

"But then, if I must do what they tell me, am I still the king?"

The queen said nothing.

"Sire," said d'Artagnan, "will Your Majesty permit me to ask him a question?"

Louis XIV turned, astonished that someone should address him uninvited. The queen took hold of his hand. ". . . Yes, Monsieur," he said.

"Does Your Majesty remember playing in the park at Fontainebleau, or in the courtyards at Versailles, when suddenly the sky clouded over and there came the sound of thunder?"

"Yes, of course."

"Well! That thunder, no matter how much Your Majesty wished to continue to play, said to you, 'Sire, you must go inside.'"

"No doubt, Monsieur—but I was always told that the sound of thunder was the voice of God."

"Well, Sire," said d'Artagnan, "if you listen to the voice of the people, you'll hear that it sounds a lot like thunder."

In fact, at that moment a terrible rumble was borne in on the night breeze.

Then suddenly it stopped.

"There, Sire," said d'Artagnan, "they just told the people that you are asleep. And by that you see that you are still the king."

The queen looked with astonishment at this strange man whose courage was equal to the bravest, and whose subtle and clever wits were the equal of anyone's.

La Porte came in. "Well, La Porte?" the queen asked.

"Madame," he replied, "Monsieur d'Artagnan's prediction was justified—they've calmed down as if by magic. We're going to open the doors to them, and in five minutes they'll be here."

"La Porte," said the queen, "if you substituted one of your sons for the king, that would give us time to escape."

"If Your Majesty so commands," said La Porte. "My sons, like myself, are at the queen's service."

"No," said d'Artagnan. "If just one of them knew His Majesty by sight and detected the trick, all would be lost."

"You're right, Monsieur—always right," said Anne of Austria. "La Porte, put the king to bed."

La Porte put the king, dressed as he was, into bed, and pulled the sheet up to his shoulders. The queen bent over him and kissed him on the forehead. "Pretend to be asleep, Louis," she said.

"All right," said the king, "but I don't want any of those people to touch me."

"Sire, I'm right here," said d'Artagnan, "and I say to you that if any one of them is so presumptuous, he'll pay with his life."

"Now, what should we do?" asked the queen. "I hear them coming."

"Monsieur La Porte, go to meet them, and remind them to stay silent. Madame, wait there by the door. I'll be at the king's bedside, prepared to die for him."

La Porte went out, the queen stood by the tapestry door, and d'Artagnan slipped behind the bed, hidden by its curtains.

Then came the plodding march of a multitude of men; the queen raised the tapestry herself, finger to her lips.

When they saw the queen, the citizens stopped in respect. "Come in, Messieurs, come in," said the queen.

Then the people hesitated, as if ashamed. They'd expected resistance; they'd expected to be opposed; they'd expected to have to force the gates and overwhelm the guards—but the gates had been opened for them, and the king, seemingly, had no one to guard him but his mother.

The men in front stammered and tried to back up. "Come in, Messieurs," said La Porte, "since the queen permits it."

One man, bolder than the others, ventured beyond the threshold and advanced on tiptoe. The others imitated him, and the room fell silent, as if these men were nothing but the most humble and devoted courtiers. Outside the door could be seen the heads of those who, unable to fit, stood on tiptoe to peer in. D'Artagnan saw everything through a gap he'd made in the curtains—and he recognized the man who entered first as Planchet.

"Monsieur," the queen said to him, regarding him as the leader of that band, "you wished to see the king, and I wished to show him to you myself. Approach, look at him, and say if this looks like people who are trying to escape."

"It . . . it doesn't," said Planchet, rather astonished at receiving such an honor.

"Then you must tell my good and loyal Parisians," replied Anne of Austria, with a smile that didn't fool d'Artagnan in the slightest, "that you have seen the king abed and asleep, and the queen prepared to go to bed in her turn."

"I'll tell them, Madame, and all those with me will tell them as well, but . . ."

"But what?" asked Anne of Austria.

"I hope Your Majesty will forgive me," said Planchet, "but is that really the king I see lying there?"

Anne of Austria trembled. "If there is anyone among you who knows the king," she said, "let him come forth and state whether this is truly His Majesty."

A man wrapped in a cloak, draped to hide his face, came in, approached the bed, and took a long look. D'Artagnan thought the man might intend harm, and put his hand to his sword, but the cloak slipped slightly, and d'Artagnan recognized the coadjutor. "It is indeed the king," the man said in a muffled voice. "God bless His Majesty!"

"Yes," answered Planchet, in a stage whisper, "yes, God bless His Majesty!"

And all those men, who had come in furious, went from anger to sympathy, and murmured blessings on the royal child. "Now," said Planchet, "let's thank the queen, my friends, and depart."

Everyone bowed, and then one by one they quietly went out the way they'd come in. Planchet, the first to enter, was the last to leave. The queen stopped him. "What is your name, my friend?" she asked.

Planchet turned, astonished by this question. "Yes," said the queen. "I'm as honored to have received you this evening as if you were a prince, and I desire to know your name."

Oh, yes, thought Planchet, *so you can treat me the way you treat the princes!*

D'Artagnan shuddered at the idea that Planchet, seduced like the raven of the fable, might say his name, and that the queen, hearing his name, might learn that Planchet belonged to him.

"Madame," Planchet respectfully replied, "I'm called Dulaurier,[14] at your service."

"Thank you, Monsieur Dulaurier," said the queen. "And what do you do?"

"Madame, I'm a draper in the Rue des Bourdonnais."

"That's all I wanted to know," said the queen. "Much obliged, my dear Monsieur Dulaurier. You'll be hearing from me."

"Well, now," murmured d'Artagnan behind his curtain, "clearly Master Planchet is no fool, and learned his lessons in a good school."

The door dropped, and the various actors of this strange scene stood for a moment in tableau without saying a word, the queen standing by the door, d'Artagnan half out of his hiding place, and the king raised up on one elbow and ready to fall back again at the least noise that indicated the return of the mob—but instead of approaching, the noise grew more and more distant, and finally disappeared altogether.

The queen exhaled slowly; d'Artagnan mopped his damp forehead; the king slid out of bed, saying, "Let's leave."

Just then La Porte reappeared. "Well?" asked the queen.

"Well, Madame," replied the valet, "I followed them to the gates, where they announced to everyone that they'd seen the king, and the queen had spoken to them, so they all went away proud and happy."

"Oh, the wretches!" murmured the queen. "They'll pay dearly for their insolence, this I promise!" Then, turning to d'Artagnan, she said, "Monsieur, this evening you've given me the best advice I've ever received. To continue, what should we do now?"

"Monsieur La Porte, finish dressing His Majesty," said d'Artagnan.

"Then we can go now?" asked the queen.

"Whenever Your Majesty likes. She has only to go down the secret staircase, where she will find me at the door."

"Go, Monsieur," said the queen. "I shall follow."

D'Artagnan went down, where he found the carriage waiting, with the musketeer on the driver's seat. D'Artagnan picked up the package he'd directed Bernouin to put in the carriage, which included the hat and cloak of Monsieur de Gondy's coachman. He wrapped the cloak around his shoulders and put the hat on his head.

The musketeer de Bellière got down from the driver's seat. "Monsieur," said d'Artagnan, "I'm sending you to set free your companion, who's guarding the coachman. Then I want you to mount up and ride to Rue Tiquetonne, the Hôtel de La Chevrette, where you'll find my horse and that of Monsieur du Vallon. Saddle and equip them as if for war, then lead them out of Paris and bring them to us in the Cours-la-Reine. If you can't find us at the Cours-la-Reine, then continue on to Saint-Germain. In the king's service!"

The musketeer put his hand to his hat in salute and departed to fulfill his orders. D'Artagnan climbed up on the driver's seat. He had a brace of pistols in his belt, a carbine at his feet, and his naked sword on the seat behind him.

The queen appeared, followed by the king and his younger brother, the Duc d'Anjou. "The coadjutor's carriage!" she cried, recoiling a step.

"Yes, Madame," said d'Artagnan, "but it's all right, because I'm driving it."

The queen stifled a cry of surprise and entered the carriage. The king and Monsieur followed and sat down beside her. "Come, La Porte," said the queen.

"What, Madame!" said the valet de chambre. "How can I ride in the same carriage as Your Majesties?"

"This isn't a matter of royal etiquette, but of saving the king. Get in, La Porte!"

La Porte obeyed.

"Pull down the shades," said d'Artagnan.

"But won't that look suspicious, Monsieur?" asked the queen.

"Rest easy, Your Majesty. I have my responses ready," said d'Artagnan.

The shades were pulled down, and they set off at a gallop along the Rue de Richelieu. On arriving at the gate, the leader of the citizen guards came out with a lantern in his hand, followed by a dozen men. D'Artagnan made a sign for him to approach. "Do you recognize this carriage?" he said to the sergeant.

"No," the man replied.

"Take a look at the arms on its door."

The sergeant brought his lantern near the door panel. "The arms of Monsieur le Coadjuteur!" he said.

"Hush! He's receiving the favors of Madame de Guéménée."

The sergeant began to laugh. "Open the gate," he called, "I know who this is." Then, approaching the door and speaking through the shades, he said, "You're a lucky man, Monseigneur!"

"Not so loud!" said d'Artagnan. "Do you want to get me in trouble?"

The gate creaked on its hinges, and d'Artagnan, seeing the way opened, whipped up the horses and departed at a trot.

Five minutes later they arrived where the cardinal's carriage was waiting. "Mousqueton," called d'Artagnan, "come open the door of Her Majesty's coach."

"It's him," said Porthos.

"On the driver's seat!" cried Mazarin.

"Of the coadjutor's carriage!" said the queen.

"*Corpo di Dio,* Monsieur d'Artagnan!" said Mazarin. "You are worth your weight in gold!"

X

In Which d'Artagnan and Porthos Gain the One 219 and the Other 211 Golden Louis by Selling Straw

Mazarin wanted to leave at once for Saint-Germain, but the queen declared she would wait for the others who were expected to join them. But she invited the cardinal to take La Porte's place in her vehicle. The cardinal accepted and crossed from one carriage to the other.

There was a reason that the rumor had spread that the king was to leave Paris in the night: ten or twelve persons had been in on the secret since six o'clock in the evening, and no matter how discreet they might be, they hadn't been able to give their orders for departure without the word getting out. Besides, each of these persons had one or two other close associates, family or dear friends, and as no one believed that the queen intended to leave Paris without plans for taking her revenge, they had warned their friends and relations, and the rumor of the departure had spread like wildfire through the streets of the city.

The first carriage to arrive after that of the queen was that of Monsieur le Prince, containing the Prince de Condé, Madame la Princesse, and Madame the Princess Dowager.[15] The latter two had been awakened in the middle of the night and had no idea of what was happening.

The second carriage contained Monsieur le Duc d'Orléans, Madame la Duchesse, la Grande Mademoiselle,[16] and the Abbé de La Rivière, the prince's inseparable favorite and intimate counselor.

The third carriage to arrive contained Monsieur de Longueville and the Prince de Conti,* brother-in-law and brother of Monsieur le Prince. They got out, approached the carriage of the king and the queen, and paid their respects to Their Majesties. The queen looked across into their carriage, the door of which stood open, and saw that it was empty. "But where then is Madame de Longueville?" she asked.

"Indeed, where's my sister?" asked Monsieur le Prince.

"Madame de Longueville is ill, Madame," the duke responded, "and charged me with conveying her apologies to Your Majesty."

Anne glanced quickly at Mazarin, who responded with an almost-imperceptible shake of the head. "What do you think?" the queen asked.

"I think she's a hostage for the Parisians," replied the cardinal.

"Why didn't she come?" asked Monsieur le Prince in a low voice to his brother.

"Hush!" Conti replied. "No doubt she has her reasons."

"She's betraying us," murmured the prince.

"She's saving us," said Conti.

Other vehicles arrived in a rush. Maréchal de La Meilleraie, Maréchal de Villeroy, Guitaut, Comminges, and Villequier all came in convoy. The two musketeers arrived leading the horses of d'Artagnan and Porthos, who got into their saddles. Porthos's coachman replaced d'Artagnan on the seat of the royal carriage, and Mousqueton replaced the coachman, standing up in the seat and driving erect for reasons best known to himself, like Achilles's driver Automedon.

The queen, though occupied with a thousand details, sought for d'Artagnan, but the Gascon, with his usual prudence, had already disappeared into the crowd. "Let's make up the vanguard," he said to Porthos, "and find ourselves some decent lodgings at Saint-Germain, as no one will think to do it for us. I feel rather fatigued."

"I'm about ready to fall off my horse," said Porthos, "and there wasn't even a proper battle. Really, the Parisians are such fools."

"Isn't it rather that we were very clever?" said d'Artagnan.

"Maybe."

"And how is your wrist doing?"

"Better. But do you think we've won them this time?"

"What?"

"You, your promotion, and me, my title?"

"Faith! Yes, I'd just about bet on it. Besides, if this time they forget, I'll make sure they remember."

"I think I can hear the voice of the queen," said Porthos. "She's asking to ride on horseback."

"Yes, she might like that, but . . ."

"But what?"

"But the cardinal won't want it. Messieurs," d'Artagnan continued, addressing the two musketeers, "ride escort on the queen's carriage, staying right next to the doors. We're going ahead to prepare lodgings."

And d'Artagnan spurred off toward Saint-Germain, accompanied by Porthos.

"On our way, Messieurs! Let's go!" said the queen. And the royal carriage set out, followed by the other carriages and more than fifty mounted cavaliers.

They arrived at Saint-Germain without accident. Upon descending from her carriage, the queen found Monsieur le Prince waiting at the step, uncovered and offering his hand. "It will be a rude awakening for the Parisians!" said Anne of Austria, radiant.

"It means war," said the prince.

"Well! It's war, then. Don't we have on our side the victor of Rocroi, of Nördlingen, and of Lens?" The prince bowed in token of thanks.

It was three o'clock in the morning. The queen was the first to enter the château, and then everyone followed her; about two hundred people had joined in the escape.

"Messieurs," said the queen, laughing, "find lodging in the château where you will—it's vast, and there's plenty of room, but as we couldn't warn them we were coming, I'm afraid there are only three beds: one for the king, one for me . . ."

"And one for Mazarin," said Monsieur le Prince in an undertone.

"And me, am I supposed to sleep on the floor?" asked Gaston d'Orléans* with a worried smile.

"Not at all, Monseigneur," said Mazarin. "The third bed is destined for Your Highness."

"But what of you?" asked the prince.

"Oh, I won't go to bed," said Mazarin. "I have work to do."

Gaston was shown to the room where he could find the third bed, without worrying about where his wife and daughter might stay.

"Yes, well, I'm certainly going to bed," said d'Artagnan. "Come with me, Porthos."

Porthos followed d'Artagnan with the profound confidence he had in the wits of his friend. As they walked across the château courtyard, Porthos looked with surprise at d'Artagnan, who was calculating something on his fingers. "Four hundred at a pistole apiece makes four hundred pistoles."

"Yes, that makes four hundred pistoles," said Porthos. "But *what* makes these four hundred pistoles?"

"A single pistole isn't enough," continued d'Artagnan. "It's worth a full *louis*."[17]

"What's worth a louis?"

"Four hundred, at a louis each, makes four hundred louis."

"Four hundred?" said Porthos.

"Yes, there are two hundred of them, and it takes at least two per person, thus two per person makes four hundred."

"But four hundred what?"

"Listen," said d'Artagnan. And as there were all sorts of people around watching in amazement as the Court arrived, he finished his sentence with a whisper in Porthos's ear.

"I understand," said Porthos, "My faith, I understand perfectly! Two hundred louis for each of us sounds lovely—but what will the Court say?"

"They can say what they like. Besides, how will they know we were behind it?"

"But who will take charge of the distribution?"

"Mousqueton's here, isn't he?"

"In my livery!" said Porthos. "Which will be recognized."

"He can turn his coat inside out."

"You're right, as always, my friend," said Porthos. "Where the devil do you get all these ideas from?" D'Artagnan smiled.

The two friends turned up the first street they came to, Porthos knocking on the doors on the right, while d'Artagnan took the doors on the left. "Straw!" they called. "We need straw."

"Monsieur, we don't have any," replied the first man to open to d'Artagnan. "You should ask the fodder merchant."

"And where do I find this fodder merchant?"

"Behind the large gate at the end of the street."

"On the right or the left?"

"The left."

"And are there any other such merchants in Saint-Germain?"

"There's the innkeeper of the Crowned Mutton, and Gros-Louis the farmer."

"Where do they live?"

"Rue des Ursulines."

"Both of them?"

"Yes."

"Excellent!"

The two friends got directions as clear and exact for the second and third addresses as they had for the first, and then d'Artagnan went to the fodder merchant's and bargained with him for a hundred and fifty bundles of straw, which he bought for the sum of three pistoles. He then went to the innkeeper, where he found that Porthos had just purchased two hundred bundles for about the same price. They got a final one hundred and eighty from Gros-Louis the farmer, which brought their total to four hundred and thirty bundles of straw.

At the Château de Saint-Germain, there were none.

All this trading took no more than half an hour. Mousqueton, duly briefed, was made the figurehead of the commercial venture. He was advised to not to let a single bundle of straw get out of his hands for less than a louis, which meant they were counting on him to bring in four hundred thirty louis. Mousqueton nodded his head and shrugged, not quite understanding the nature of the enterprise.

D'Artagnan, carrying three bundles of straw, returned to the château, where everyone, weary and shivering with cold, looked on in envy at the king, the queen, and Monsieur in their beds. The musketeer's entry into the great hall carrying an armload of straw produced a general reaction of laughter, until d'Artagnan, who didn't seem to notice he was an object of derision, began with deliberation and cheer to form his straw into a comfortable sleeping pallet, at which everyone else regarded him with sudden envy.

"Straw?" they cried. "A pallet of straw! Where can *we* get hold of some straw?"

"I can show you," said Porthos. And he led the nobles to Mousqueton, who generously distributed his straw at a louis a bundle. They thought it a bit expensive, but when one is desperate for a good night's sleep, who wouldn't pay two or three louis for such a luxury?

D'Artagnan sold his bed to an eager customer, got some more straw, and did the same thing again ten times over—and since he was supposed to have bought his straw like the others, he pocketed about thirty louis in less than an hour. By five in the morning straw was going for three louis a bundle, but there was no more to be had.

D'Artagnan had taken care to set four bundles aside for himself. He put into his pocket the key of the closet where he'd hidden them, and then, accompanied by Porthos, went back to Mousqueton, who, shrewdly and like the worthy steward that he was, turned over four hundred and thirty louis to them, keeping an extra hundred for himself. Mousqueton, who knew nothing of what was going on in the château, couldn't understand how it had never occurred to him before to go into the straw-selling business.

D'Artagnan collected the coins in his hat, and on the way back, split them with Porthos. Each ended up with two hundred and fifteen louis. Only then did Porthos realize he'd kept no straw for himself. He returned to Mousqueton, but he'd sold the straw down to the last bundle.

Porthos went back to d'Artagnan, whom he found making, with his four bundles of straw, a bed so soft, luxurious, and well-padded that the king himself might have envied it, if he hadn't had a bed of his own. D'Artagnan refused to sell his glorious bed to Porthos at any price—but for four louis, paid in advance, he did agree to share it.

D'Artagnan placed his sword at his head, his pistols at his side, covered himself in his cloak, propped his hat on his head, and stretched out voluptuously upon the crackling straw. He was already sinking into the sweet dreams that came after collecting two hundred and nineteen *louis* in an hour[18] when a voice rang out in the great hall, making him jump. "Monsieur d'Artagnan!" it cried. "Monsieur d'Artagnan!"

"Over here!" said Porthos, who knew that if d'Artagnan was called away, he'd have the entire bed to himself.

D'Artagnan raised himself on one elbow as an officer approached. "Are you Monsieur d'Artagnan?" he said.

"Yes, Monsieur. What do you want from me?"

"I've been sent to find you."

"On whose behalf?"

"That of His Eminence."

"Tell His Eminence that I'm going to sleep, and I advise him as a friend to do the same."

"His Eminence hasn't gone to bed and isn't planning to. He requests you to come at once."

"Plague take this Mazarin, who doesn't know how to sleep!" murmured d'Artagnan. "What does he want? Is it to promote me to captain? In that case, I'll forgive him."

And the musketeer got up, muttering, took his sword, pistols, hat, and cloak, and then followed the officer, leaving Porthos in sole possession of the bed, arranging himself as d'Artagnan had.

"Monsieur d'Artagnan," said the cardinal, upon seeing the man he'd so untimely summoned, "I haven't forgotten how zealously you've served me, and I'll give you a proof of that."

Well! thought d'Artagnan. *This certainly sounds promising.* He said, "Oh, Monseigneur . . . !"

Mazarin was watching the musketeer and had seen his face flush. He said, "Monsieur d'Artagnan, do you really desire to be a captain?"

"Yes, Monseigneur."

"And does your friend still wish to be a baron?"

"At this very moment, Monseigneur, he's dreaming that he already is!"

"Then," said Mazarin, drawing from a satchel the letter he'd shown d'Artagnan previously, "take this dispatch and carry it to England."

D'Artagnan looked at the envelope; it still had no address. He said, "Can I know to whom I should deliver it?"

"You'll know when you arrive in London, because that's when you'll open the outer envelope."

"And what are my instructions?"

"To obey in every respect the one to whom this letter is addressed."

D'Artagnan was about to ask further questions when Mazarin added, "You will travel by way of Boulogne. There, at the English Arms, you'll find a young gentleman named Monsieur Mordaunt."

"Very well, Monseigneur—and what shall I do with this gentleman?"

"Follow him wherever he takes you."

D'Artagnan looked at the cardinal in astonishment.

"You have your instructions," said Mazarin. "Now go."

"Go! That's easy to say," d'Artagnan replied, "but to go takes money, and I don't have any."

"Really?" said Mazarin, scratching his ear. "You say you don't have any money?"

"None, Monseigneur."

"What about that diamond I gave you last night?"

"I treasure that as a memento of Your Eminence."

Mazarin sighed.

"It's expensive to live in England, Monseigneur, especially as an envoy extraordinaire."

"Not so!" said Mazarin. "It's a simple and sober country, never more so than since the revolution. But no matter." He opened a drawer and drew out a purse. "What do you say to a thousand crowns?"

D'Artagnan pushed out his lower lip in disapproval. "I say, Monseigneur, that it isn't much, since I won't be traveling alone."

"I'm counting on it," replied Mazarin. "That worthy gentleman Monsieur du Vallon must accompany you, my dear Monsieur D'Artagnan—there's no man in France I esteem more than he."

"Then, Monseigneur," said d'Artagnan, indicating the purse that Mazarin still held, "in consideration of your esteem for him . . ."

"Indeed! In consideration of that, I'll add two hundred crowns more."

"Miser!" d'Artagnan murmured, then added aloud, "But upon our return, at least, we can count on Monsieur Porthos receiving his baronetcy and I my promotion?"

"Faith of a Mazarin!"

I don't put much stock in that oath, d'Artagnan thought to himself, then said, "May I pay my respects to Her Majesty the Queen?"

"Her Majesty is asleep," Mazarin replied briskly, "and you must leave without delay. Go, Monsieur."

"One more word, Monseigneur: if they're fighting in the place where I'm going, shall I fight?"

"You will follow the orders of the person I've sent you to."

"Very well, Monseigneur," said d'Artagnan, extending his hand for the purse, "then I'll leave my respects with you."

D'Artagnan carefully placed the purse in his largest pocket, and then turned to the officer who'd brought him and said, "Monsieur, will you go awaken Monsieur du Vallon on the orders of His Eminence, and tell him I await him at the stables?"

The officer immediately set off with an eagerness in which d'Artagnan thought he detected some self-interest.

Porthos had finally made himself completely comfortable on his bed and had begun his usual vigorous snoring when he was awakened by a tap on the shoulder. He thought it was d'Artagnan returning and didn't move.

"On the orders of the cardinal," said the officer.

"Eh?" said Porthos, opening his eyes wide. "What did you say?"

"I say that His Eminence sends you to England, and Monsieur d'Artagnan awaits you at the stables."

Porthos gave a deep sigh, got up and took his sword, pistols, hat, and cloak, and left after a final regretful look at the bed in which he'd hoped to sleep so well.

He had scarcely turned his back before the officer had taken his place and was barely out the door before his successor began to snore. Which was only natural, because of the entire Court, only the king, the queen, and Monseigneur Gaston d'Orléans had a better bed than he.

XI

A Warning from Aramis

D'Artagnan had gone straight to the stables. Day was just dawning; he recognized his horse and that of Porthos tied to the manger, but it was empty. He felt pity for the poor animals and went toward a corner of the stable where he saw a few wisps of straw. But upon sweeping up this straw with his foot, hit boot connected with a round body, which, doubtless touched in a sensitive place, cried out, rose to its knees, and rubbed its eyes. It was Mousqueton who, having no straw for himself, had borrowed the hay from the horses. "Mousqueton!" said d'Artagnan. "Come on, we're leaving."

Mousqueton, recognizing the voice of his master's friend, hastened to rise, accidentally dropping some of the extra coins he'd raked off from selling the straw. "Oh ho!" said d'Artagnan, picking up a louis and sniffing it. "This gold has a funny odor—it smells like straw!"

Mousqueton blushed so openly and seemed so embarrassed that the Gascon laughed and said to him, "Porthos might be angry, my dear Monsieur Mousqueton, but as for me, I pardon you. Just remember that this gold must serve as a balm for your wound as we ride, for we must travel!"

Mousqueton pretended to smile, quickly saddled his master's mount, and then climbed on his own without too much wincing. Meanwhile Porthos arrived in a sullen mood, and was surprised to find d'Artagnan resigned, and Mousqueton almost happy. "Ah çà," he said, "have we got your promotion and my barony?"

"We're on our way to secure the brevet and patent," said d'Artagnan, "and on our return Mazarin will sign them."

"And where are we going?" asked Porthos.

"To Paris, first of all," d'Artagnan replied. "I want to settle some business there."

"Then let's go to Paris," said Porthos.

And they set off for Paris.

When they reached the gates, they were surprised by the menacing aspect of the capital. Around a shattered carriage a crowd was crying threats and insults, holding the passengers who'd tried to flee as prisoners. These were an old man and two women.

However, when d'Artagnan and Porthos demanded entry, the people fawned upon them, assuming they were deserters from the royalist party had come to join the citizens' faction. "What's the king doing?" they asked.

"He's sleeping."

"And the Spaniard?"

"She's dreaming."

"And that cursed Italian?"

"He's watching. So, stand firm—for if they've fled, it's because they must have a plan," said d'Artagnan. "But since, at the end of the day, you're the strongest, never fear women and old men, and stay true to your cause."

The people felt better upon hearing this, and released the ladies, who thanked d'Artagnan with an eloquent look. "And now, onward!" said d'Artagnan.

They continued on their way, crossing barricades, passing chains, and answering questions. In the square outside the Palais Royal, d'Artagnan saw a sergeant who was drilling five or six hundred citizens. It was Planchet, employing his experience in the Piedmont Regiment for the benefit of the urban militia. As d'Artagnan passed, he recognized his former master. "*Bonjour*, Monsieur d'Artagnan!" said Planchet proudly.

"Bonjour, Monsieur Dulaurier," d'Artagnan replied.

Planchet stopped short, staring wide-eyed at d'Artagnan. The first rank of militia, seeing him stop, did the same, and each successive rank followed suit. "These bourgeois are just ridiculous," d'Artagnan said to Porthos as they continued on their way.

Five minutes later they dismounted at the Hôtel de La Chevrette. The lovely Madeleine rushed out to greet d'Artagnan. "My dear Madame

Turquaine," said d'Artagnan, "if you have any money, bury it fast; if you have any jewelry, hide it even faster; if you have any debtors, call in your debts; and if you have any creditors, by no means pay them."

"Why's that?" asked Madeleine.

"Because Paris will soon be rubble and as ruined as old Babylon, of which you might have heard tell."

"And that's the moment you choose to leave me?"

"That very moment," said d'Artagnan.

"And where are you going?"

"Ah! If you could tell me that, you'd be doing me a real service."

"Oh, *mon Dieu! Mon Dieu!*"

D'Artagnan gestured to his hostess to spare him her laments, as they were useless and unnecessary, and asked, "Have any letters come for me?"

"There's only this one that just arrived." And she gave the letter to d'Artagnan.

"From Athos!" cried d'Artagnan, recognizing his friend's firm and formal handwriting.

"Ah!" said Porthos. "Let's see what he has to say."

D'Artagnan opened the letter and read:

> *Dear d'Artagnan, and my dear du Vallon—my friends, this may be the last time you hear from me. Aramis is distressed, but God, our courage, and the memory of your friendship support us. Take care of Raoul. Certain written instructions have been left at Blois, and if you haven't heard from us within two and a half months, please take note of them. Embrace the viscount with all the heart you have for your devoted friend,*
>
> *ATHOS*

"I am going to take this to heart," said d'Artagnan, "and embrace Raoul when I can, since he's on our probable route. And if he has the misfortune to lose our poor Athos, from that moment on he becomes my son."

"And I will make him my sole heir," said Porthos. "But look, on the back Athos added a postscript: *And if, on your way, you meet a Monsieur Mordaunt, defy him. I can say no more in a letter.*"

"Monsieur Mordaunt!" said d'Artagnan in surprise.

"Monsieur Mordaunt, right," said Porthos, "we'll remember that. But see here, there's another postscript, this one from Aramis."

"Indeed," said d'Artagnan. And he read: "*We're keeping our location a secret, dear friends, because knowing your fraternal devotion, you'd come to die with us.*"

"*Sacrebleu!*" interrupted Porthos, in an angry explosion that made Mousqueton jump across the yard. "Are they really in danger of death?"

D'Artagnan continued, "*Athos entrusts you with Raoul, and I bequeath you a vengeance. If you find yourself within arm's-reach of a certain Mordaunt, tell Porthos to take him into a corner and twist his head from his neck. I dare say no more in a letter. –ARAMIS.*"

"Is that all?" said Porthos. "'Tis easily done."

"On the contrary," said d'Artagnan somberly, "it's quite impossible."

"And why is that?"

"It's this very Monsieur Mordaunt whom we're supposed to meet in Boulogne and who is supposed to escort us to England."

"Well, then! Suppose that instead of going to join Monsieur Mordaunt, we go to join our friends?" said Porthos, shaking a fist that would frighten an army.

"I considered that," said d'Artagnan, "but this letter has neither date nor address."

"That's true," said Porthos, frowning. And he began striding up and down like a wild man, gesticulating and sometimes half-drawing his sword.

As for d'Artagnan, he stood rooted in place like a man afflicted with uncertainty, dismay painted all over his face. "Oh, this is bad," he said. "Athos insults us by wanting to die by himself. This is awful."

Mousqueton, seeing these two great men in despair, sat down in another corner and burst into tears.

"Come," said d'Artagnan, "this is getting us nowhere. Let's go, find Raoul and embrace him, and see if he's heard any news from Athos."

"Now there's a good idea," growled Porthos. "In truth, d'Artagnan, I just don't know how one man can have so many ideas. Let's go embrace Raoul."

"I wouldn't give a *denier* for the life of anyone who'd cross my master at this moment," muttered Mousqueton.

They mounted their horses and set out. On arriving in Rue Saint-Denis, they encountered a great crowd of people. Monsieur de Beaufort had just arrived from the Vendômois, and the coadjutor was presenting him to the Parisians, who were beside themselves with joy. With the arrival of the Duc de Beaufort, they regarded themselves as invincible.

The two friends turned down a side street to avoid the prince and thereby reached the Saint-Denis barrier. "Is it true," the guards asked the two cavaliers, "that Monsieur de Beaufort has arrived in Paris?"

"It couldn't be more true," said d'Artagnan, "and the proof is that he's sent us out to meet Monsieur de Vendôme, his father, who's coming in his turn."

"Long live Monsieur de Beaufort!" cried the guards. And they parted respectfully to allow the envoys of the great prince to pass.

Once beyond the barrier, they raced up the road like riders to whom fatigue and discouragement were unknown. Their horses fairly flew, and all along the way they spoke of Athos and Aramis.

Mousqueton was suffering terrible torments, but he consoled himself with the thought that his masters had sufferings of their own. Indeed, he'd come to regard d'Artagnan as his second master, and obeyed him if anything more promptly than he did Porthos.

The army's camp was between Saint-Omer and Lambres, so the two friends made a detour thereto, and informed the general staff of the escape of the king and the queen, the details of which had remained a secret until then. They found Raoul near his tent, lying on a bale of hay from which his horse was tearing a few scraps. The young man had red eyes and seemed dejected; the Maréchal de Grammont* and the Comte de Guiche* had returned to Paris, leaving the poor lad on his own. After a few moments Raoul looked up and saw the two cavaliers looking down at him; he recognized them and ran to them with open arms. "Oh! It's you, dear friends!" he cried. "Were you coming to get me? Are you taking me with you? Have you brought any news of my guardian?"

"Have you no news yourself?" d'Artagnan asked the young man.

"Alas! None, Monsieur, and in truth I don't know what's become of him. I'm so worried I could almost cry." And indeed, two fat tears rolled down the young man's tanned cheeks.

Porthos turned his head to conceal the feelings in his own heart. "The devil!" said d'Artagnan, more upset than he'd been in a long time. "Don't despair, my friend—if you haven't received any letters from the count, we at least have had . . . er . . . one. . . ."

"Really?" cried Raoul.

"And a very reassuring one, too," said d'Artagnan, seeing what joy this news brought the young man.

"Do you have it?" asked Raoul.

"Yes—or anyway, I had it," said d'Artagnan, pretending to search his clothes. "Wait, it was right here in my pocket. He spoke of his return, didn't he, Porthos?" Gascon though he was, d'Artagnan didn't want to bear the entire burden of this falsehood.

"Yes," said Porthos, coughing.

"Oh, give it to me!" said the young man.

"Sure, you can read the whole thing. Oh, wait, it's gone! There's a hole in my pocket!"

"What a shame, Monsieur Raoul," said Mousqueton. "The letter was really very comforting. These gentlemen read it to me, and I wept with joy."

"So at least, Monsieur d'Artagnan, you know where he is?" asked Raoul, half reassured.

"Well, of course I know where he is," said d'Artagnan, "but it's a secret."

"Not from me, I hope."

"No, not from you . . . so I'll tell you where he is."

Porthos looked at d'Artagnan with eyes wide in astonishment.

D'Artagnan muttered, "Where the devil can I say he's gone so Raoul won't try to follow him?"

"Well? Where is he, Monsieur?" asked Raoul in his soft, hopeful voice.

"He's . . . in Constantinople!"

"Among the Turks!" cried Raoul in dismay. "Good God! What are you telling me?"

"Why, what are you afraid of?" said d'Artagnan. "Bah! What are the Turks to men like the Comte de La Fère and the Abbé d'Herblay?"

"Oh, so his friend is with him?" said Raoul. "That reassures me a little."

"This d'Artagnan has the Devil's own wit!" said Porthos to himself, amazed by his friend's cunning.

"Now," said d'Artagnan, eager to change the subject, "Here are fifty pistoles Monsieur le Comte sent by the same courier. I assume by now you must be out of money, and this will be welcome."

"I still have twenty pistoles, Monsieur."

"Never turn down money. Take these, and then you'll have seventy."

"And if you want any more . . ." said Porthos, putting his hand to his pocket.

"Thank you," said Raoul, blushing. "A thousand thanks, Monsieur."

At that moment, Olivain ambled up. "By the way," said d'Artagnan, loud enough so the lackey could hear, "are you satisfied with Olivain?"

"Yes, mostly."

Olivain pretended not to have heard and went into the tent.

"You have complaints about this buffoon?"

"He's a glutton."

"Oh, Monsieur!" said Olivain, reappearing at this accusation.

"He's a petty thief."

"Oh, now, Monsieur!"

"And worst of all, he's a coward."

"Ah, Monsieur, you dishonor me!" said Olivain.

"Peste!" said d'Artagnan. "Understand, Master Olivain, that people like us aren't served by cowards. Steal from your master, eat his rations and drink his wine, but, *cap de Diou,* don't be cowardly, or I'll cut off your ears! Look at Monsieur Mousqueton, ask him to show you the honorable wounds he's taken, and see the dignity his habitual bravery has stamped upon his face."

Mousqueton was in seventh heaven at this praise, and would have embraced d'Artagnan if he'd dared, while promising himself to die for him at the first opportunity.

"Send this dolt home, Raoul," said d'Artagnan, "for if he's a coward, someday he'll dishonor himself—and you."

"Monsieur says I'm a coward," cried Olivain, "because the other day he wanted to fight with a cornet of the Grammont Regiment, and I refused to accompany him."

"Monsieur Olivain, a lackey must never be disobedient," said d'Artagnan sternly. Then, drawing him aside, he added, "If your master was in the wrong, then here's a crown for you. But if he's ever insulted and you don't get cut into quarters defending him, I'll cut out your tongue and ruin your looks. Remember that well."

Olivain bowed and put the crown in his pocket.

"And now, friend Raoul, we must depart, Monsieur du Vallon and I, on our mission as ambassadors," said d'Artagnan. "I can't tell you more than that, because I don't know myself, but if you need anything, write to Madame Madeleine Turquaine, à la Chevrette, Rue Tiquetonne, and draw on her funds as you would on a banker—but gently, as her vault is not so well furnished as that of Monsieur d'Émery."

And then, having embraced his temporary ward, he passed him over to the mighty arms of Porthos, who hugged him right off the ground and held him suspended against the noble heart of the formidable giant. "Come," said d'Artagnan, "let's be on our way."

They set out again for Boulogne, where they arrived toward evening, their horses soaked with sweat and white with foam. Ten paces from where they paused before entering the town was a young man dressed in black who seemed to be waiting for someone, and whose eyes were fixed upon them from the moment they appeared.

D'Artagnan approached him, and seeing that his gaze never dropped, said, "See here, friend, I don't like being stared at."

"Monsieur," said the young man, ignoring d'Artagnan's remark, "you come from Paris, don't you?"

D'Artagnan thought he must just be a curious fellow looking for news from the capital. "I do, Monsieur," he replied, in a milder tone.

"Are you planning to stay at the English Arms?"

"Yes, Monsieur."

"Are you charged with a mission from His Eminence Cardinal Mazarin?"

"Yes, Monsieur."

"In that case," said the young man, "you're looking for me. I am Monsieur Mordaunt."

"Ah ha!" said d'Artagnan in a low voice. "He's the one Athos told us to distrust."

"Oh ho!" whispered Porthos. "And the one Aramis wants me to strangle."

And they both looked attentively at the young man, who mistook the meaning of their gaze. "Do you doubt my word?" he said. "If so, I can provide you with proof."

"Not at all, Monsieur," said d'Artagnan, "and we place ourselves at your disposal."

"In that case, Messieurs, we'll leave without delay," said Mordaunt, "for it's the last day of the period the cardinal asked me to wait. Our vessel is ready, and if you hadn't come, I was going to leave without you, for General Oliver Cromwell* must be waiting impatiently for my return."

"Ah," said d'Artagnan, "so it's to General Cromwell that we're dispatched."

"Don't you bear a letter for him?" asked the young man.

"I have a letter inside a double envelope that I'm supposed to open once we reach London—but since you tell me to whom it's addressed, there's no point in waiting until then." D'Artagnan tore open the outer envelope, revealing a letter addressed, "*To Monsieur Oliver Cromwell, General of the Armies of the English Nation.*"

"Ah!" said d'Artagnan. "A singular commission!"

"Who is this Oliver Cromwell?" asked Porthos in a low voice.

"A former brewer," d'Artagnan replied.

"Does Mazarin want to speculate in beer as we did in straw?" asked Porthos.

"Come, Messieurs," said Mordaunt impatiently. "Let's go."

"What?" said Porthos. "Without dinner? Can't Monsieur Cromwell wait a little longer?"

"Yes, but I . . ." said Mordaunt.

"Yes, but you?" said Porthos. "What?"

"I am in haste!"

"Hasten, then," said Porthos. "That's nothing to do with me. I intend to dine with or without your permission."

The young man's mild gaze suddenly inflamed, and he seemed about to reply angrily, but he restrained himself.

"Monsieur," said d'Artagnan, "please excuse a pair of hungry travelers. Besides, our dinner won't delay you much, and we must take care of our horses. Walk on down to the port, we'll eat a few bites, and be there at almost the same time you will."

"Whatever you like, Messieurs, so long as we go," said Mordaunt.

"All right . . . this time," murmured Porthos.

"The name of the vessel?" asked d'Artagnan.

"The *Standard.*"

"Very well. We'll be on board inside half an hour." And the pair pricked up their horses, spurring on to the English Arms.

"What do you think of this young man?" asked d'Artagnan as they rode.

"I think I don't like him one little bit," said Porthos, "and I have a strong inclination to follow Aramis's advice."

"Take care, my dear Porthos, this man is an envoy of General Cromwell, and Cromwell won't receive us very well if we report that we've wrung his agent's neck."

"Just the same," said Porthos, "I've always felt that Aramis was a man who gave excellent advice."

"Listen," said d'Artagnan, "when our embassy is over . . ."

"What then?"

"If he escorts us back to France . . ."

"Well?"

"Well! Then we'll see."

The two friends arrived at the English Arms, where they dined with good appetite, and then went straight to the port. A brig was ready to set sail, on the deck of which they recognized Mordaunt, who was pacing up and down impatiently.

"It's amazing," said d'Artagnan, as the longboat ferried them out to the *Standard*, "how much this young man resembles someone I once knew, but I can't say who." They hove to at the ladder, and a moment later they were aboard. But the embarkation of the horses took longer than that of the men, and the brig couldn't weigh anchor until eight in the evening. Then the young man, stamping with impatience, ordered them to raise every sail.

Porthos, exhausted by three sleepless nights and a horseback ride of seventy leagues, retired to his cabin and slept.

D'Artagnan, overcoming his repugnance to Mordaunt, walked with him on deck and engaged him with a hundred stories to try to draw him out.

Mousqueton was seasick.

XII

"Like Judas, for the Love of Gold,
the Faithless Scot his Monarch Sold"

And now, as the *Standard* sails, not for London, where d'Artagnan and Porthos thought they were going, but to Durham, where letters Mordaunt had received from England during his stay in Boulogne had ordered him to go, our readers must leave them and follow us to the royalist camp, located on the banks of the Tyne near the city of Newcastle.

It's here, between two rivers, on the frontier of Scotland but the soil of England, that the tents of a small army are spread. It is midnight. Men who can be recognized as Highlanders by their bare legs, their short skirts, their colorful plaids, and the feathers on their bonnets, keep a casual watch. The moon, gliding between large clouds, illuminates through the gaps the sentries' muskets and outlines the walls, roofs, and towers of Newcastle, the town that Charles I has just turned over to the parliamentary forces,[19] along with Oxford and Newark, which had held out for him in hope of a negotiated peace.

At one end of the camp, beside a sprawling canvas pavilion full of Scottish officers holding a council presided over by their chief, the old Earl of Leven, a man, dressed as a cavalier, sleeps on the grass, his hand on his sword.

Fifteen paces beyond, another cavalier chats with a Scottish sentry, and though foreign, his grasp of the English language is good enough to enable him to understand the soldier's thick Perth dialect.

As one o'clock struck in the town of Newcastle, the sleeper awoke, and after going through all the gestures of one who's awakened from a deep sleep, he looked around him, and finding himself alone, got up and went to pass by the cavalier who was talking to the sentry. That cavalier must have finished his conversation, for after a moment he took his leave of the sentry and followed the awakened cavalier.

In the shade of a tent pitched near the path, the first cavalier awaited the second. "Well, *mon cher ami?*" he said, in the purest French as it was spoken between Rouen and Tours.

"Well, my friend, there's no time to lose if we're going to warn the king."

"What's going on?"

"It would take too long to tell you, and besides, you're about to hear it anyway. Another word wasted here, and all may be lost. We must go find Milord de Winter."

And the pair made their way toward the other end of the camp—but as the camp was no more than five hundred paces square, they soon reached the tent of the man they were looking for.

"Is your master asleep, Tony?" said one of the cavaliers in English to a servant lying under the outer awning that served as an antechamber.

"No, Monsieur le Comte," replied the footman, "or if so it hasn't been for long, since after leaving the king he was pacing back and forth for a good two hours, and the noise of his footsteps only quit about ten minutes ago. Anyway," said the servant, lifting the door of the tent, "you can see for yourself."

In fact, Winter was seated before an opening in the canvas like a window, which allowed the entry of the night air, and through which with melancholy eyes he watched the moon as it sailed lost among the dark clouds.

The two friends approached Lord Winter who, head leaning on his hand, gazed up into the sky, oblivious to their arrival until he felt a hand on his shoulder. Then he turned, recognized Athos and Aramis, and extended his hand. "Have you noticed," he said, "how the moon tonight is tinged with blood?"

"No, it seemed normal to me," said Athos.

"Look, Chevalier and Count," said Winter.

"I confess," said Aramis, "that like the Comte de La Fère, I see nothing unusual about it."

"Milord," said Athos, "in a position as precarious as ours, it's the earth we should study, and not the heavens. Have you considered the Scots, and are you quite sure of them?"

"The Scots?" asked Winter. "Which Scots?"

"Eh? Why, our Scots, *pardieu!*" said Athos. "Those to whom the king is entrusted—the Scots of the Earl of Leven."

"No," said Lord Winter. Then he added, "Are you telling me that you can't see the reddish tint that spreads across the sky?"

"Not at all," said Athos and Aramis.

"Tell me," continued Winter, obsessed with his idea, "isn't it said in France that, the night before he was assassinated, King Henri IV, who was playing chess with Bassompierre, saw bloodstains on the chessboard?"

"Yes," said Athos, "I heard the late marshal say so myself."

"That's it," Winter murmured, "and the next day Henri IV was dead."

"But how can Henri IV's vision matter to you, Milord?" asked Aramis.

"It can't, Messieurs, and indeed it's madness to speak of such things, when your arrival at my tent at this hour tells me you must bring news of importance."

"Yes, Milord," said Athos. "I would like to speak to the king."

"To the king? But the king is asleep."

"I have some very important matters to place before him."

"Can't these matters wait until tomorrow?"

"He must hear them immediately, and even now it may be too late."

"Then follow me, Messieurs," said Winter.

The baron's tent was next to the royal pavilion, and a corridor of canvas connected the two. This corridor was guarded, not by a sentry, but by a confidential valet of Charles I, so that in urgent need the king could send immediately for his devoted guardian Winter. "These gentlemen are with me," Winter said. The valet bowed and let them pass.

Within, on a camp bed, dressed in his black doublet and long boots, with his belt loosened and his hat beside him, King Charles had succumbed to sleep. The men approached, and Athos, who was in the lead, considered for a moment in silence that noble visage, so pale, framed by his long black hair, damp with the sweat of a troubled sleep, around eyes that seemed swollen with fatigue.

Athos gave a deep sigh, and the king's sleep was so shallow this awakened him. He opened his eyes, raised himself on one elbow, and said, "Ah, is that you, Comte de La Fère?"

"Yes, Sire," replied Athos.

"You didn't come to watch me sleep—you have news."

"Alas, Sire!" said Athos. "Your Majesty has guessed right."

"And the news is bad, isn't it?" said the king, smiling sadly.

"Yes, Sire."

"No matter, the messenger is welcome, and you can never enter my presence without bringing me pleasure. You, whose devotion transcends nation and misfortune, who are sent to me by Henriette—whatever news you have to bring me, relate it with confidence."

"Sire, Monsieur Cromwell arrived tonight in Newcastle."

"Ah!" said the king. "Has he come to fight me?"

"No, Sire—he's come to buy you."

"What are you saying?"

"I'm saying, Sire, that the Scottish army is owed four hundred thousand pounds sterling."

"Their back pay? Yes, I know; for nearly a year my brave and loyal Scots have been fighting for honor."

Athos smiled. "Well, Sire, though honor is a fine thing, they've grown tired of being paid with it, and tonight they've sold you for two hundred thousand pounds, in other words, half of what they're due."

"Impossible!" cried the king. "The Scots, to sell their king for two hundred thousand pounds?"

"The Jews sold their God for thirty silver pieces."

"And who is the Judas who's made this infamous deal?"

"The Earl of Leven."

"Are you sure of that, Monsieur?"

"I heard it with my own ears."

The king breathed a deep sigh, as if his heart were breaking, and took his head in his hands. "Oh, the Scots, the Scots!" he said. "The Scots, whom I called my own! The Scots, whom I trusted, when I could have gone to Oxford! The Scots, my compatriots! The Scots, my brothers! . . . But are you entirely sure, Monsieur?"

"I lay behind the Earl of Leven's tent, where I lifted the canvas, and saw and heard everything."

"And when will this odious bargain be completed?"

"Today, this very morning. As Your Majesty can see, there's no time to lose."

"But since I've been sold out, what should I do?"

"Cross over the Tyne to reach Scotland, and join up there with Lord Montrose, who will never sell you."

"And what would I do in Scotland? Wage war on my country from beyond its borders? Such a war is unworthy of a king."

"The example of Robert the Bruce is there as a precedent, Sire."

"No, no! I've fought for too long; if they've really sold me, then let me be betrayed, and let the eternal shame of their treason fall upon them."

"Sire," said Athos, "perhaps that's what a king should do, but not a husband and a father. I have come at the urging of your wife and your daughter, and in their names, and in the names of the other two children you have in London, I say to you: Live, Sire. God wills it!"

The king got up, tightened his belt, buckled on his sword, mopped his glistening brow with a handkerchief, and said, "Well, what is to be done?"

"Sire, is there in your army a regiment you can count on?"

"Winter," said the king, "do you trust in the loyalty of yours?"

"Sire, they are only men, and men have shown themselves to be very weak or very wicked. As for their loyalty, I'd trust my own life to them, but I hesitate to entrust that of Your Majesty."

"Well!" said Athos. "We may not be a regiment, but we are three devoted men. We'll do. Let Your Majesty mount his horse and place himself between us. We'll cross the Tyne, reach Scotland, and we'll be safe."

"Is that your advice, Winter?" asked the king.

"Yes, Sire."

"And yours, Monsieur d'Herblay?"

"Yes, Sire."

"Then let it be done. Winter, give the orders."

Winter went out, while the king finished dressing. The first rays of daylight were filtering into the tent when Winter returned. "Everything is ready, Sire," he said.

"And us?" asked Athos.

"Grimaud and Blaisois have your horses saddled."

"In that case," said Athos, "let's lose not a moment more, and go."

"Let's go," said the king.

"Sire," said Aramis, "does Your Majesty need to warn his friends first?"

"My friends?" said Charles I, shaking his head sadly. "I have none here but the three of you: a friend of twenty years who's never forgotten me, and two friends of a week whom I'll never forget. Come, Messieurs— let's go."

The king went out of his tent and found his horse was ready for him. It was a dun-colored charger he'd been riding for three years and of which he was very fond. The horse, seeing him, neighed with pleasure. "Ah!" said the king. "I spoke unfairly—here's someone who, if not a friend, is at least a creature who loves me. You'll be faithful to me, won't you, Arthus?"

As if he'd understood these words, the horse brought its snuffling nose near the king's face, and happily showed its white teeth. "Yes, yes," said the king, stroking him, "yes, you're good, Arthus, and I'm very pleased with you."

And then, with that deftness that made the king one of the best horsemen in Europe, Charles swung himself into the saddle, and said, turning toward Athos, Aramis, and Winter, "Well, then, Messieurs—I await you."

But Athos stood motionless, his eyes fixed beyond, and pointed toward a dark line along the banks of the Tyne that extended for twice the length of the camp. "What is that line?" Athos said, for the last long shadows of night struggling with the first rays of the day prevented him from seeing clearly. "What is that line? I didn't see it yesterday."

"It's probably just mist rising from the river," said the king.

"Sire, that's something more solid than steam."

"In fact, I see something like a reddish rampart," said Winter.

"It's the enemy, advancing from Newcastle to envelop us," cried Athos.

"The enemy!" said the king.

"Yes, the enemy. It's too late. Look, look! In that sunbeam, there, toward the town, do you see the shining breastplates of the Ironsides?" (That's what they called the cuirassiers that Cromwell had made his guards.)

"Ah!" said the king. "Now we'll see if it's true that my Scots have betrayed me."

"What are you going to do?" said Athos.

"Give them the order to charge and break through those miserable rebels." And the king, spurring his horse, dashed off to the tent of the Earl of Leven.

"After him," said Athos.

"Let's go," said Aramis.

"But is the king wounded?" said Winter dazedly. "I see spots of blood on the ground."

He pricked up to follow the two friends, but Athos stopped him. "Go and assemble your regiment," he said. "I'm afraid we're going to need it very soon."

Winter reined aside, and the two friends continued on their way. Within seconds the king had arrived at the pavilion of the general in chief of the Scottish army. He jumped down and went in. The general was surrounded by his officers. "The king!" they cried, rising and staring at each other in surprise.

Charles stood before them, his hat on his head, his brows furrowed, whipping his boot with his riding crop. "Yes, Gentlemen," he said, "the king, in person. The king, who comes to ask you for an explanation of what's going on."

"What's the matter, Sire?" asked the Earl of Leven.

"The matter, Milord," said the king, letting himself get carried away by anger, "is that General Cromwell arrived last night in Newcastle, and that you knew and didn't warn me; that the enemy has left the city and blocked the passage of the Tyne, and that your sentinels must have seen this movement, but you didn't alert me; that you have, through an infamous bargain, sold me to the Parliament for two hundred thousand pounds sterling—but at least there I've been warned. That is what's the matter, Gentlemen—now excuse or explain yourselves, for I hereby accuse you."

"Sire," stammered the Earl of Leven, "Your Majesty must have been deceived by some false report."

"I have seen with my own eyes the enemy's army arrayed between me and Scotland," said Charles, "and I can very nearly say I heard with my own ears the details of the bargain."

The Scottish leaders looked at each other, frowning and coughing. "Sire," murmured the Earl of Leven, head bowed down with shame, "Sire, we're ready to give you every proof of our loyalty."

"I ask only one," said the king. "Put the army into line of battle and march on the enemy."

"That cannot be, Sire," said the earl.

"What? It cannot be! And what prevents it from happening?" cried Charles I.

"Your Majesty is well aware there's a state of truce between us and the English army," the earl replied.

"If there's a truce, the English army broke it when they left the city, against the article that kept them there. Now, I say to you, pass with me through that army and back into Scotland, for if you don't, then . . . Well! Choose the shameful name by which you'll be known to all men henceforth—as either cowards or traitors!"

The Scots' eyes flamed, and as often happens on such occasions, they instantly went from being ashamed to being reckless. Two clan chiefs stepped forward, to either side of the king, and one said, "Promises? That's right—we promised to deliver Scotland and England from the one who's been draining them of blood and gold for twenty-five years. And we'll keep that promise. King Charles Stuart, you are our prisoner."

And they both reached out to seize the king, but before they could touch him they both fell, one knocked out and the other dead. Athos had clouted one with the pommel of his pistol, and Aramis had run the other through with his sword.

Then, as the Earl of Leven and the other chiefs recoiled from this unexpected attack, which seemed to fall from heaven to steal away one they'd already considered captured, Athos and Aramis pulled the king out of that tent of treachery, into which he'd so imprudently ventured, and, leaping on their horses, galloped back to the royal pavilion. On their way they saw Winter at the head of his regiment, and the king beckoned him to follow.

XIII

The Avenger

The four entered the king's tent; they had no plan and had to make one quickly. The king dropped onto a camp chair. "I am lost," he said.

"No, Sire," replied Athos, "you are only betrayed."

The king gave a deep sigh. "Betrayed, betrayed by the Scots, among whom I was born, and whom I always preferred to the English. Oh, the wretches!"

"Sire," said Athos, "this is not the hour for recriminations, but the moment to show that you are a king and a gentleman. Rise, Sire, rise! For you have at least three men who, you may rest assured, will not betray you. Ah, if only they were five!" he murmured, thinking of d'Artagnan and Porthos.

"What do you have in mind?" asked Charles, rising.

"I think, Sire, we have only one chance. Milord de Winter answers for his regiment, or nearly so—we won't quibble over words. He must place himself at the head of his troops, while we stand beside Your Majesty, and together we'll cut our way through Cromwell's army and reach Scotland."

"As another precaution," said Aramis, "if one of us would wear the king's clothing and ride his horse, he might be pursued while the king gets through."

"That's good advice," said Athos, "and if His Majesty wishes to honor one of us with that role, we would be very grateful to him."

"What do you think, Winter?" said the king, regarding with admiration these two men whose only thought was to take his perils upon themselves.

"I think, Sire, that if there's a way to save Your Majesty, it's what Monsieur d'Herblay just proposed. I therefore humbly beg Your Majesty to choose quickly, as we have no time to lose."

"But if I accept, it's death, or at least prison, for the one who takes my place."

"It's the honor of having saved one's king!" cried Winter.

The king looked at his old friend with tears in his eyes, and then detached the ribbon of the Order of Saint-Esprit,[20] which he was wearing in honor of the two Frenchmen, and hung it around Winter's neck, who fell to his knees to receive this fatal mark of the esteem and confidence of his sovereign.

"That's only right," said Athos. "He has served far longer than we have."

The king heard that and turned with eyes damp with tears. "Wait a moment, Messieurs," he said, "I also have a ribbon for each of you." And he went to a wardrobe containing his private effects and drew out two Orders of the Garter.[21]

"Such orders are not for us," said Athos.

"And why not, Monsieur?" asked Charles.

"These orders are for the royal, or nearly so, and we are simple gentlemen."

"If all the thrones of the world passed before me in review, I'd find no greater souls than yours," said the king. "You don't do yourselves justice, Messieurs, so I'm here to do it for you. On your knees, Count."

Athos knelt, the king passed the order's ribbon around his neck from left to right, as was traditional, and raised his sword, but instead of the usual words—*I dub you a knight; be brave, faithful, and loyal*—he said, "You *are* brave, faithful, and loyal; I dub you a knight, Monsieur le Comte."

Then turning to Aramis, he said, "Now for you, Monsieur le Chevalier." And he performed the same ceremony with the same words, while Winter, helped by his squire, removed and donned Charles's shining cuirass, so he might more easily be mistaken for the king.

When Charles was finished with Athos and Aramis, both were embraced by Winter, who, in the face of such devotion, had recovered all his courage. "Sire," he said, "we're ready."

The king looked at the three gentlemen. "Then we really must flee?"

"In every country in the world, Sire," said Athos, "fleeing through an army is called charging."

"Then I shall die with the sword in my hand," said Charles. "Monsieur le Comte, Monsieur le Chevalier, if ever I am king . . ."

"You have already honored us above the deserts of simple gentlemen, so the gratitude is all ours. But let's lose no more time, for we've already lost enough."

The king shook each man's hand for the final time, exchanged his hat with Winter's, and went out.

Winter's regiment was drawn up on a little rise that dominated the center of the camp. The king, followed by the three friends, went straight to them.

The Scottish camp seemed to be awake at last; the men had left their tents and assumed ranks as if for battle. "Look," said the king. "Maybe they've repented and are ready to march."

"If they've repented, Sire, they'll follow us," said Athos.

"Good!" said the king. "What do we do next?"

"Observe the enemy army," said Athos. They turned their eyes toward the line that, at the day's dawning, they'd taken for fog, and which the first rays of the sun now clearly delineated as an army arrayed for battle. The air was as clear and crystalline as it usually was at that hour of the morning. One could easily distinguish the various regiments, their standards, and even their horses and the colors of their uniforms.

Then on a low crest ahead of the enemy line a man appeared, short and stout, amid a group of officers. He pointed a telescope toward the king and his small group. "Does Your Majesty recognize that man?" asked Aramis.

Charles smiled. "That man is Cromwell," he said.

"Then lower the brim of your hat, Sire, so he doesn't notice our little substitution."

"Ah!" said Athos. "We've lost a lot of time."

"Then give the order, and let's go," said the king.

"Will you give it, Sire?" asked Athos.

"Not me, I'm just a lieutenant general here," said the king.

"Listen then, Milord de Winter," said Athos. "Give us a little room, if you will, Sire—what we have to say doesn't concern Your Majesty."

The king smiled and stepped away.

"This is what I propose," continued Athos. "Divide your regiment into two squadrons. Put yourself at the head of the first, and His Majesty and us with the second. If nothing bars our passage, we'll charge together to force the enemy line and throw ourselves into the Tyne, which we'll cross by fording or swimming. On the other hand, if we encounter an obstacle on the way, you and your troops will take the lead and fight to the last man, while we continue on with the king. Once we've reached the banks of the river, your squadron will have done its duty, and the rest is up to us."

"To horse!" said Winter.

"To horse!" said Athos. "Everything is decided."

"Then forward, Gentlemen!" said the king. "Let us charge to the old French cry of '*Montjoie and Saint-Denis!*' The cries of England have been too tainted by traitors."

They mounted, the king on Winter's horse, and Winter on the king's. Then Winter took the lead position of the first squadron, while the king, with Athos to his right and Aramis to his left, assumed the lead of the second.

The entire Scottish army watched these preparations without moving and with the silence of shame. A few chiefs could be seen stepping out of the ranks and breaking their swords. "Come, that's some consolation," said the king. "They're not all traitors."

Then Winter's voice rang out, crying, "Forward!" The first squadron moved out, and the second followed, riding down from the rise.

A regiment of cuirassiers nearly equal in numbers to theirs formed in front of the crest ahead and charged toward them. The king pointed them out to Athos and Aramis. "This contingency is planned for, Sire," said Athos. "If Winter's men do their duty, this maneuver will save us rather than doom us."

And then they heard, above the galloping and neighing of the horses, the voice of Winter crying, "Draw your sabers!" The sabers flashed from their scabbards like lightning.

"Come, Gentlemen!" cried the king in his turn, intoxicated by the sound and fury. "Gentlemen, draw your sabers!"

But to this command, despite the example of the king, only Athos and Aramis obeyed. "We are betrayed," said the king in a low voice.

"Not so fast," said Athos. "Maybe they didn't recognize Your Majesty's voice and are waiting for their commander's orders."

"Haven't they heard the voice of their colonel? But look!" cried the king, stopping his horse short with a shock, and grabbing the bridle of Athos's horse.

"Ah! Cowards! Wretches! Traitors!" shouted Winter, while his men, leaving their ranks, scattered across the fields. Only about fifteen men remained around him, awaiting the charge of Cromwell's cuirassiers.

"Let's die with them!" said the king.

"Forward!" said Athos and Aramis. "To death!"

"To me, all faithful hearts!" cried Winter. The two friends heard him and set off at the gallop.

"No quarter!" came a cry in French, replying to Winter, at the sound of which he trembled. "No mercy!" came the voice, and Winter turned pale and froze.

The voice was that of a cavalier mounted on a magnificent black horse, and who charged, in his zeal, ten paces ahead of the rest of the English regiment. "It's him!" murmured Winter, staring, his sword hanging limp in his hand.

"The king! The king!" cried several voices, fooled by Winter's disguise. "Take him alive!"

"That's not the king!" cried the cavalier. "Don't be deceived! It's Milord Winter, and not the king. Because you *aren't* the king, are you, Uncle?"

At the same time, Mordaunt, for it was he, pointed the barrel of a pistol at Winter and fired. The ball penetrated the chest of the older gentleman, who fell back from his saddle and into the arms of Athos, gasping, "The avenger!"

"Remember my mother!" snarled Mordaunt as he passed in a rush, carried on by his horse's furious charge.

"You wretch!" cried Aramis, aiming his pistol at point blank range as he passed, but only the priming went off and the shot misfired.

At that moment the entire regiment fell upon the few men around Winter, and the two Frenchmen were surrounded in the press. Athos, after ascertaining that Winter was dead, dropped the body and drew his sword, shouting, "Come, Aramis—for the honor of France!" And the two Englishmen closest to the two friends fell instantly, mortally wounded.

With an angry roar thirty blades flashed above their heads. Suddenly a man burst from the English ranks, leaped upon Athos with arms of iron, snatched away his sword, and held him in place, whispering in his ear, "Silence—Place Royale! To yield to me is no surrender."

A giant had likewise taken hold of Aramis, who struggled in vain to escape his grip. "Place Royale," said the giant, looking Aramis in the eye.

Aramis nodded his head, as Athos turned around. "D'Art . . . !" cried Athos, as the Gascon clapped a hand over his mouth.

"I surrender," said Aramis, handing his sword to Porthos.

"Shoot them! Shoot!" cried Mordaunt, returning to the group around the two men.

"Shoot them? Why?" said the English colonel. "Everyone has surrendered."

"He's the son of Milady," said Athos to d'Artagnan.

"I recognized him."

"It's the murdering monk," said Porthos to Aramis.

"I know."

At the same time the ranks began to open. D'Artagnan took Athos's horse by its reins, while Porthos took those of Aramis, and they began to lead their prisoners from the battlefield. This opened a space around the spot where Winter's body had fallen. With the instincts of hatred, Mordaunt had found him, and looked down from his horse with a hideous smile. Athos, as calmly as ever, put his hand to the pistol in his saddle holster. "What are you doing?" said d'Artagnan.

"Let me kill him."

"Don't make a move or say a single word that shows you know who he is, or all four of us are lost." Then, turning to the young man, he called, "Fine prizes, friend Mordaunt! Monsieur du Vallon and I have each got one—Knights of the Garter, no less!"

"But how could that be?" cried Mordaunt, looking at Athos and Aramis with blood in his eyes. "Aren't they Frenchmen?"

"I know nothing about it. Are you French, Monsieur?" d'Artagnan asked Athos.

"I am," Athos replied gravely.

"Well, my dear Monsieur, you are the prisoner of a compatriot."

"But what about the king?" said Athos in dismay. "The king?"

D'Artagnan gripped his prisoner's hand tightly, and said, "The king? We have him."

"Yes," said Aramis, "by disgraceful treachery."

Porthos gripped his friend's wrist so hard he nearly crushed it, and said, "Well, Monsieur, war is won as much by finesse as by force: look!"

In fact, at that moment the squadron that was to have protected Charles during his escape was advancing slowly toward the English regiment, surrounding the king, who was marching alone on foot in an empty space in their center. The monarch seemed calm, but one could see it took an effort to appear that way: sweat beaded his forehead, and he wiped his temples and mouth with a handkerchief that came away from his lips with bloodstains.

"Behold Nebuchadnezzar!"[22] cried one of Cromwell's cuirassiers, an old Puritan whose eyes blazed at the sight of the one they called the tyrant.

"Who are you calling Nebuchadnezzar?" said Mordaunt with a dreadful smile. "No, that's King Charles I, that good King Charles who strips his subjects of their estates."

Charles raised his eyes to look at the man who spoke with such insolence but didn't recognize him. Yet the calm and serene majesty of his face made

Mordaunt look away. "Good morning, Messieurs," said the king to the two gentlemen he saw in the hands of d'Artagnan and Porthos. "It's an ill day, but that's no fault of yours, thank God! Where's my old friend Winter?"

The two gentlemen turned their heads and remained silent.

"He's gone to meet Strafford!" said Mordaunt harshly.

Charles started—the demon had struck home. The death of Strafford was his eternal remorse, the shadow of his days and the ghost that haunted his nights.

The king looked down and found a corpse at his feet. It was that of Lord Winter. Charles didn't speak a word or shed a tear, only grew more pallid. He fell to one knee, raised Winter's head, and kissed him on the brow, then took the ribbon of the Order of Saint-Esprit from Winter's neck and placed it solemnly on his chest.

"De Winter is dead, then?" asked d'Artagnan quietly, his eyes fixed on the cadaver.

"Yes," said Athos, "and at the hands of his nephew."

"Ah, well! There goes the first of us," murmured d'Artagnan. "May he rest in peace; he was a brave man."

"Charles Stuart," said the colonel of the English regiment, advancing toward the king, who had just regained his royal regalia, "will you surrender yourself to us?"

"Colonel Tomlinson," said Charles, "the king does not surrender, though the man must yield to force."

"Your sword."

The king took his sword and broke it across his knee.

At that moment a horse without a rider, dripping with foam, eyes red and nostrils wide, galloped up and, recognizing its master, stopped and neighed with joy; it was Arthus.

The king smiled, caressed him with his hand, and jumped lightly into the saddle. "Come, Gentlemen," he said, "take me where you will." Then, turning quickly, he said, "Wait, I thought I saw Lord Winter stir. If he lives, by whatever you hold sacred, don't abandon this noble gentleman."

"Oh, don't worry about him, King Charles!" said Mordaunt. "The ball pierced his heart."

"Don't breathe a word, don't move a muscle, don't even risk a glance at me or Porthos," said d'Artagnan to Athos and Aramis, "for Milady isn't dead—her soul lives on in this demon's body!"

And the detachment moved off toward the town, bearing its royal prisoner—but halfway there, an aide-de-camp from General Cromwell brought Colonel Tomlinson an order to escort the king to Holdenby Castle.[23]

At the same time couriers were dispatched in all directions to announce to England and all Europe that King Charles Stuart was the prisoner of General Oliver Cromwell.

XIV

Oliver Cromwell

"Are you going to the general?" Mordaunt asked d'Artagnan and Porthos. "You know he said to report to him after the action."

"First we'll put our prisoners in a safe place," d'Artagnan said to Mordaunt. "Do you know, Monsieur, that these gentlemen are worth fifteen hundred pistoles each?"

"Don't worry," said Mordaunt, unable to keep the malice and ferocity out of the look he gave the prisoners, "my cavalrymen will guard them, and guard them well—I'll answer for it."

"I'll guard them even better myself," replied d'Artagnan. "Besides, all we need is either a strong chamber with sentries, or their simple word that they won't try to escape. I'll attend to this, and then we'll have the honor of presenting ourselves to the general and asking him for letters to His Eminence."

"Are you planning to leave soon?" asked Mordaunt.

"Our mission is complete, and there's nothing to keep us in England but the good pleasure of the great man to whom we were sent."

The young man bit his lips, then leaned over and said into his sergeant's ear, "You are to follow these men, and not lose sight of them. Once you discover where the prisoners are lodged, return to meet me at the city's main gate."

The sergeant nodded his obedience. Then, instead of following the bulk of the prisoners, who were being marched into the town, Mordaunt took himself to the crest from which Cromwell had watched the battle, and where he'd set up his tent. Cromwell had left orders that no one should be allowed to enter, but the sentry, who recognized Mordaunt as one of the general's closest confidants, thought the order didn't apply to the young man.

As Mordaunt lifted the canvas of the door, he saw Cromwell seated at a table, his head in his hands and his back toward him. If Cromwell heard the noise Mordaunt made in entering, he didn't turn.

Mordaunt stayed standing by the door. After a while, Cromwell raised his heavy head and, as if instinctively feeling that someone was there, turned around. Seeing the young man, he snapped, "I said I wanted to be alone!"

"I didn't think the order included me, Sir," said Mordaunt. "However, if you command it, I'll leave."

"Oh, it's you, Mordaunt!" said Cromwell, shrugging off, as if by force of will, the mantle of gloom that had shrouded him. "Since you're here, you might as well stay."

"I came to congratulate you."

"Congratulate me? On what?"

"On the capture of Charles Stuart. Now you are the master of England."

"I was much more so two hours ago," said Cromwell.

"How's that, General?"

"Then England needed me to take the tyrant—but now the tyrant is taken. Have you seen him?"

"Yes, Sir," said Mordaunt.

"What was his attitude?"

Mordaunt hesitated, but the truth seemed to escape from his lips. "Calm and dignified," he said.

"Did he say anything?"

"Just a few words of farewell to his friends."

"To his friends!" murmured Cromwell. "He still has friends, then?" Aloud he added, "Did he defend himself?"

"No, Sir—he was abandoned by everyone but three or four friends. Defense was impossible."

"To whom did he surrender his sword?"

"He didn't surrender it, he broke it."

"A fine gesture. But instead of breaking it, he'd have done better to wield it well."

There was a moment's silence. Then Cromwell, looking closely at Mordaunt, said, "The colonel of the regiment that was to escort King Charles—he was killed, was he not?"

"Yes, Sir."

"By whom?"

"By me."

"What was his name?"

"Lord Winter."

"Your uncle?" cried Cromwell.

"My uncle!" replied Mordaunt. "Traitors to England are no family of mine."

Cromwell looked at the young man thoughtfully for a moment, then said, with that deep melancholy so well portrayed by Shakespeare, "Mordaunt, you are a fearsome servant."

"When the Lord commands, there is no arguing with his orders," said Mordaunt. "Abraham raised his knife over Isaac, and Isaac was his son."

"Yes," said Cromwell, "but the Lord then forbade the sacrifice."

"I looked around me," said Mordaunt, "and I saw neither goat nor kid caught in the thickets of the field."

Cromwell inclined his head. "You are mighty even among the strong," he said. "And how did our Frenchmen conduct themselves?"

"Like men of courage, Sir," said Mordaunt.

"Yes, they would," said Cromwell, musing. "The French are good fighters. In fact, through my telescope, it seems to me I saw them in the front ranks."

"That's where they were," said Mordaunt.

"Behind you, however," said Cromwell.

"That wasn't their fault, it was the fault of their horses."

There was another moment of silence, then Cromwell asked, "And the Scots?"

"They kept their word," said Mordaunt, "and didn't move a step."

"Miserable wretches!" murmured Cromwell.

"Their officers ask to see you, Sir."

"I don't have the time. Have they been paid?"

"Tonight."

"Let them go, then—let them return to their mountains where they can hide their shame, if their mountains are high enough for that. I have no more business with them, nor they with me. And now you may go, Mordaunt."

"Before I go, Sir" said Mordaunt, "I have a few questions to ask you, Milord, and a request to make."

"Of me?"

Mordaunt bowed. "I come to you, my hero, my protector, my father, to ask you this: Master, are you satisfied with me?"

Cromwell looked at him in astonishment. "Yes," he said, "since I've known you, you've done, not just your duty, but more than your duty. You've been a loyal friend, a capable negotiator, and a fine soldier."

"Do you recall, Sir, that I was the one who first had the idea of bargaining with the Scots to give up their king?"

"Yes, that thought did come from you, it's true. I had not yet reached that level of contempt for mankind."

"Was I a good envoy to France?"

"Yes, you got everything from Mazarin that I asked for."

"Have I always fought zealously for your interests and your glory?"

"Too zealously, perhaps—which is what I reproached you for just now. But where are you going with all these questions?"

"To tell you, Milord, that the moment has come when you can reward all my services with one word."

"Ah!" said Cromwell, with a slight shrug of disdain. "True, I'd forgotten that every service deserves its reward, that you have served me, and that I've not yet rewarded you."

"Sir, I can be justly rewarded this instant, beyond even what I'd wished."

"How so?"

"The price is here and almost in my hands."

"And what is this price?" asked Cromwell. "Do you want gold? Position? A governorship?"

"Sir, will you grant me my request?"

"Let's hear what it is first."

"Sir, when you've said to me, 'You must carry out an order,' have I ever said, 'First let's hear the order'?"

"Your request might be impossible to fulfill."

"When you had a desire and charged me with fulfilling it, did I ever reply, 'That's impossible'?"

"But a request couched in such exacting terms . . ."

"Oh, rest assured, Sir," said Mordaunt in a tone of sincerity, "it won't ruin you."

"Well, then," said Cromwell, "I promise to grant your request insofar as it's within my power. Ask."

"We took two notable prisoners this morning, Sir," Mordaunt replied. "I ask you to give them to me."

"Have they offered a substantial ransom?" said Cromwell.

"On the contrary, Sir, I don't think they're at all wealthy."

"Are they friends of yours, then?"

"Yes, Sir, that's it," cried Mordaunt. "They're friends of mine, dear, dear friends, and I'd give my life for them."

"Fine, Mordaunt," said Cromwell, happy to have his good opinion of the young man restored. "Fine, I give them to you. I don't even need to know who they are; do as you please."

"Thank you, sir," cried Mordaunt, "thank you! My life is now yours, and even if I lose it I'll still be indebted to you. Thank you, you've paid me magnificently for my services." He threw himself at Cromwell's feet, and, despite the efforts of the Puritan general to prevent him, who didn't want or pretended not to want this almost royal homage, he took Cromwell's hand and kissed it.

"What!" said Cromwell, rising and making him stop. "No other reward? No money? No promotion?"

"You've given me all that I desire, Milord, and I'll never ask for more." And Mordaunt rushed from the general's tent with the joy in his heart shining from his eyes.

Cromwell watched him go. "Killed his own uncle!" he muttered thoughtfully. "Alas! What kind of men are my servants? It may be that this one, who asks for nothing, or seems to, asks a higher price in the sight of God than those who ask for the wealth of a province, or to steal the bread of the unfortunate. No one serves me for nothing; even Charles, my prisoner, still has friends. I? I have none." And with a sigh, he resumed the reverie that Mordaunt had interrupted.

XV

Gentlemen

While Mordaunt made his way to Cromwell's tent, d'Artagnan and Porthos conducted their prisoners back to the house that had been assigned to them as lodging in Newcastle. Mordaunt's brief aside with his sergeant hadn't escaped the Gascon, so he'd warned Athos and Aramis to take every precaution. Consequently, the pair had marched along in silence, keeping near their ostensible captors, while wrapped in their own thoughts.

If ever a man was astonished, it was Mousqueton when he saw from the doorway the approach of the four friends, followed by the sergeant with almost a dozen men. He rubbed his eyes, unable to believe in the sight of Athos and Aramis, but finally he was forced to give in to the evidence. He was about to explode into questions and exclamations when a look from Porthos silenced him without argument. Mousqueton stepped back from the doorway but continued to stare, dismayed by the way the four friends didn't seem to recognize each other.

The house to which d'Artagnan and Porthos had brought Athos and Aramis was where they'd been staying since the day before, when Cromwell had assigned it to them. It was on the corner of a street, had a small garden, and a stable around the corner on the side. The windows on the ground floor were barred, as is often the case in small provincial towns, making it somewhat resemble a prison.

The two friends ordered Mousqueton to take their horses to the stable, then paused on the threshold of the door to let their prisoners enter first. "Why aren't we going in with them?" said Porthos.

"Because first," replied d'Artagnan, "we must see what this sergeant and the men who came with him want from us."

The sergeant and his men were taking up a position in the small garden. D'Artagnan asked them what they wanted and why there were posted there. "We were ordered to help you guard your prisoners," said the sergeant.

Nothing could be said against that; on the contrary, it had to be regarded as a sort of favor, an attention for which one should show gratitude. D'Artagnan thanked the sergeant and give him a crown with which to drink to the health of General Cromwell. The sergeant replied that Puritans didn't drink, but still put the crown in his pocket.

"Ah, d'Artagnan!" said Porthos when he returned. "What a terrible day!"

"What do you mean, Porthos? How can you complain about a day on which we found our friends?"

"Yes, but consider the circumstances!"

"It's true that our current situation is a trifle embarrassing," said d'Artagnan, "but no matter, let's go inside and see if we can clear things up a little."

"It's a complete mess," said Porthos, "and now I understand why Aramis recommended I strangle that dreadful Mordaunt."

"Be silent!" said d'Artagnan. "Don't say that name."

"But I'm speaking French, and those soldiers speak English," said Porthos.

D'Artagnan gaped at Porthos with the awe of a man of reason in the presence of a prodigy. Then, as Porthos just stared back with a look of incomprehension, d'Artagnan pushed him toward the house and said, "Let's go in."

Porthos entered first, followed by d'Artagnan, who carefully closed the door before embracing his two friends. Athos was stricken with sorrow. Aramis looked at Porthos and d'Artagnan without saying a word, but his look was so expressive that d'Artagnan understood it. "You wonder how it is we come to be here, eh? *Mon Dieu*, that should be easy to guess: Mazarin ordered us to carry a letter to General Cromwell."

"But how is it you come in the company of Mordaunt?" said Athos. "Mordaunt, whom I warned you against, d'Artagnan."

"And whom I advised you to strangle, Porthos," said Aramis.

"Mazarin again," said d'Artagnan. "Cromwell had sent him to Mazarin, and Mazarin sent us to return with him to Cromwell. Fate seems to have taken a hand in this."

"Yes, you're right, d'Artagnan—fate which divides us, and then ruins us. So, Aramis, let's say no more about it and prepare ourselves to submit to fate."

"God's blood!" d'Artagnan swore. "On the contrary, we're going to talk about it, because we agreed once and for all that we would always support each other, even if we were on different sides."

"Very different indeed," said Athos with a sour smile. "For here I must ask you, which side do you serve? Ah, d'Artagnan, you see what serving that wretch Mazarin has gotten you? Do you know what crime you were guilty of today? Of the capture of the king—of his humiliation—of his death."

"Oh!" said Porthos "Do you really think that?"

"You exaggerate, Athos," said d'Artagnan. "They won't go that far."

"Won't they, by God? On the contrary. Why does someone arrest their king? If you wish to respect him as a master, you don't buy him like a slave. Do you think it was to restore him to the throne that Cromwell paid two hundred thousand pounds for him? Friends, they mean to kill him, you can be sure of that at the very least. It's better to behead a king than to beat and belabor him."

"That may be possible, I won't argue," said d'Artagnan. "But what does that have to do with us? I'm here because I'm a soldier, and I serve my commander, from whom I draw my pay. I swore an oath to obey, and so I obey. But you, who have sworn no oath, why are you here, and what cause do you serve?"

"The most sacred cause in the world," said Athos. "that of chivalry, royalty, and religion. A friend, a wife, and a daughter did us the honor to ask for our help. We served them as best as our feeble means allowed, and God will measure our intentions rather than our abilities. You see things differently, d'Artagnan, and though I don't turn away from you, I do blame you for it."

"Oh?" said d'Artagnan. "And what's it to me if Monsieur Cromwell, who's English, wants to rebel against his king, who's Scottish? I'm French, I am, and none of these things concern me. Why hold me responsible for them?"

"That's right," said Porthos.

"Because all gentlemen are brothers; because you are gentlemen; because the kings of all nations are the first among gentlemen; because the peasants, like blind, ungrateful beasts, take pleasure in tearing down their betters—and it's you, d'Artagnan, a man of the old aristocracy, a man of good name, a nobleman of the sword, it's you who helped deliver a king into the lowly hands of brewers, tailors, and carters! Oh, d'Artagnan—as a soldier perhaps you did your duty, but as a gentleman, I say you have failed."

D'Artagnan, chewing on a straw, felt ill at ease and didn't answer. He looked away from Athos, only to meet the eyes of Aramis.

"And you, Porthos," continued the count, as if to avoid further embarrassing d'Artagnan, "you, the warmest heart, the best friend, the finest soldier I know; you, whose greatness of soul makes you worthy enough to have been born at the foot of a throne, as will someday be recognized by an intelligent king; you, my dear Porthos, a gentleman by manners, by taste, and by boldness—you are as guilty as d'Artagnan."

Porthos blushed, with pleasure rather than shame, but nonetheless bowed his head as if humiliated, and said, "Yes, yes, I'm sure you're right, my dear Count."

Athos rose. "Come," he said, approaching d'Artagnan and offering his hand, "come, don't be dismayed, my dear son, for everything I've said to you, I've said it if not in the voice, then at least with the heart of a father. It would have been easier, believe me, just to thank you for saving my life, without revealing a word of my feelings."

"No doubt, Athos," said d'Artagnan, clasping his hand, "but the kind of feelings you have in that great heart are like those of no one else. Who could imagine that a reasonable man would leave France, his home, and his ward, a charming young man whom we visited in camp—to go where? To try to rescue a rotten and worm-eaten monarchy ready to collapse any day like an old barracks. The feelings you speak of are noble and high, certainly, but so high they're superhuman."

"Whatever they may be, d'Artagnan," replied Athos, without falling into the trap his Gascon friend had set by alluding to his paternal affection for Raoul, "whatever they may be, you know very well in the bottom of your heart that they're right—but it is wrong of me to dispute so with my master. I'm your prisoner, d'Artagnan, and you may treat me as such."

"Ah, *pardieu!*" said d'Artagnan. "You're well aware that you won't be my prisoner for long."

"No," said Aramis, "they will doubtless treat us like those who were taken at Philiphaugh."[24]

"And how were they treated?" asked d'Artagnan.

"Half of them were hanged, and the other half were shot," said Aramis.

"Indeed?" said d'Artagnan. "Well, I'm telling you now that as long as there's a drop of blood in my veins, you'll be neither hanged nor shot. *Sang-Diou!* Let them come! Athos, do you see this door?"

"Yes. Well?"

"Well! You can use this door whenever you please—and as soon as you do, you and Aramis are as free as air."

"Now there I recognize my brave d'Artagnan," replied Athos, "but you're not the power that holds us—that door is guarded, d'Artagnan, as you're well aware."

"Oh, you'll get through," said Porthos. "What's there to stop you? Ten men at the most."

"That would be nothing for the four of us, but it's too much for just us two. No, divided as we are now, we're doomed. You've already seen the example, on the high road to Vendômois, where d'Artagnan, though brave, and Porthos, though valiant and strong, were defeated. And now, for Aramis and me, it's our turn. That never happened when we four were united, but now, well, let us die as de Winter died. As for me, I declare I refuse to flee unless we all four go together."

"Impossible," said d'Artagnan. "We're here under Mazarin's orders."

"I know it, and I won't press you further. My arguments have been useless; they must have been bad arguments, since they haven't persuaded minds as fair as yours."

"Besides, even if we'd succeeded," said Aramis, "we'd just have compromised our two fine friends d'Artagnan and Porthos. Rest easy, Messieurs— we'll honor you by dying well. As for me, I'm proud to stand up before the bullets, or even go to the rope with you, Athos, for you've never seemed to me so great as you do today."

D'Artagnan said nothing, but after chewing his straw down to a nub, he gnawed his fingers. Finally, he said, "Do you really think they want to kill you? And why? Who would have an interest in your death? Besides, you're *our* prisoners."

"Fool, triple fool!" said Aramis. "I thought you said you knew Mordaunt? Well, I exchanged just a single glance with him, and by that look I knew we were condemned."

"As a matter of fact, I'm sorry I didn't strangle him as you advised, Aramis," said Porthos.

"Bah! Don't talk to me about Mordaunt!" snapped d'Artagnan. "That insect! Cap de Diou! If he buzzes too close to me, I'll crush him. There's no reason to flee, because, I swear to you, you're as safe here as you were twenty years ago, when Athos was in Rue Férou and Aramis in Rue de Vaugirard."

"Enough," said Athos, pointing out one of the two barred windows that admitted light into the room. "You'll know soon enough whether you can hold us, because here he comes now."

"Who?"

"Mordaunt."

In fact, looking where Athos had indicated, d'Artagnan saw a cavalier approaching at a gallop. It was indeed Mordaunt.

D'Artagnan darted to the door. Porthos began to follow him, but d'Artagnan said, "Wait here. Don't come out until you hear me drum my fingers on the door."

XVI

"The Lord Our Savior!"

When Mordaunt arrived before the house, he saw d'Artagnan at the doorway, and the soldiers sprawled out in the garden next to their weapons. "Hey!" he called, out of breath from his swift ride. "Are the prisoners still there?"

"Yes, Sir," said the sergeant, rising quickly along with his men, who, like him, raised hands to hats in sudden salutes.

"Good. Four men are to take them right away to my quarters."

Four men prepared themselves.

"What's your pleasure?" said d'Artagnan in that mocking air with which our readers are familiar. "What's all this, if you please?"

"What it is, Monsieur," said Mordaunt, "is that I've ordered four men to take charge of the prisoners taken this morning and escort them to my quarters."

"And why is that?" asked d'Artagnan. "You'll pardon my curiosity, but you can understand my desire to be educated on the subject."

"Because these prisoners are mine now," replied Mordaunt haughtily, "and I can dispose of them as I like."

"Permit me, my young gentleman, to point out that you're in error," said d'Artagnan. "The custom is that prisoners go to those who took them, and not to those who watched them taken. You could have taken Milord de Winter, who was your uncle, or so they say, but you preferred to kill him. Well, Monsieur de Vallon and I could have killed these two gentlemen, but we preferred to take them. Everyone to his taste."

Mordaunt went white to his lips.

D'Artagnan realized that things were about to get out of hand and drummed the march of the guards on the door. Porthos emerged and stood just outside the door, his giant frame filling the doorway. The significance of this move wasn't lost on Mordaunt. "Monsieur," said he, anger starting to rise, "to resist is useless, as these prisoners have been given to me just now by the general in chief, my illustrious patron, Oliver Cromwell."

These words struck d'Artagnan like a thunderbolt. He flushed to his temples, a cloud passed before his eyes, and as he comprehended the young man's fierce hopes, his hand dropped instinctively toward the hilt of his sword.

As for Porthos, he watched d'Artagnan to match his own actions to the Gascon's. This look from Porthos worried rather than reassured d'Artagnan, who was beginning to be sorry he'd deployed the brute force of Porthos into a matter it now seemed to him had to be handled by a ruse. "Violence can't solve this," he said to himself. "D'Artagnan, *mon ami,* you must prove to this young serpent that you are not only stronger than he, but smarter as well."

"Ah!" he said aloud, making a deep bow. "Why didn't you say that before, Monsieur Mordaunt? You come on behalf of Oliver Cromwell, the most illustrious captain of our times?"

"I just left him, Monsieur, this very minute," said Mordaunt, dismounting and giving his horse to one of his soldiers.

"You should have said so immediately, *mon cher* Monsieur!" continued d'Artagnan. "All England is at the command of Monsieur Cromwell, and since you demand the prisoners in his name, I bow to you, Monsieur, and say to you, take them."

Mordaunt advanced, radiant, while Porthos, devastated, looked at d'Artagnan in a profound stupor, and opened his mouth as if to speak. But d'Artagnan kicked Porthos, who then understood that his friend was playing a game.

Mordaunt mounted the doorstep and then, hat in hand, prepared to pass between the two friends, while gesturing to his four men to follow him. "But, begging your pardon," said d'Artagnan with his most charming smile, while resting his hand on the young man's shoulder, "if the illustrious

General Oliver Cromwell has disposed of these prisoners in your favor, you no doubt have a writ that orders such a disposition."

Mordaunt stopped short.

"If you can show me such a letter, even the least little note, that attests you come in his name, then give me that scrap so I will have at least some pretext for handing over my compatriots. Otherwise, you understand, though I'm sure General Cromwell wishes them no harm, it would have an improper appearance."

Mordaunt drew back, feeling the blow, and glowered fiercely at d'Artagnan, but the latter just maintained the most friendly and amiable expression ever seen on any face. "When I tell you something, Monsieur," said Mordaunt, "will you insult me by doubting it?"

"I!" exclaimed d'Artagnan. "I, to doubt what you say? God forbid, my dear Monsieur Mordaunt. On the contrary, I regard you as a worthy and accomplished gentleman—to all appearances. But come, Sir, will you speak frankly with me?" continued d'Artagnan, all sincerity.

"Speak, Monsieur," said Mordaunt.

"Monsieur du Vallon, who is rich, has an income of forty thousand livres a year, and has no further need of money—so I don't speak for him, only myself."

"Go on, Monsieur."

"But as for me, I'm not wealthy. In Gascony, that's no dishonor, no one is—even Henri IV, of glorious memory, who was King of the Gascons, as His Majesty Philip IV is king of all Spain, even he never had a penny in his pocket."

"Get to it, Monsieur," said Mordaunt. "I think I see where you're going, and if that's the hold up, that difficulty can be overcome."

"Ah! I knew all along," said d'Artagnan, "that you were a man of intelligence. Well, here's the point, the spot where the saddle rubs, as we Frenchmen say: I'm a soldier of fortune, nothing more; I have only what my sword gets for me, which is usually more blows than bank-notes. Now, upon taking this morning two Frenchmen who appear to be of high rank, two

Knights of the Garter, no less, I said to myself, 'My fortune is made.' I say two, because under the circumstances, Monsieur du Vallon, who is wealthy, always yields his prisoners to me."

Mordaunt, completely taken in by d'Artagnan's charm offensive, smiled like a man who is in on the joke, and wryly replied, "I'll have you your order within the hour, Monsieur, and two thousand pistoles to go with it—but meanwhile, let me take these men with me."

"What does a half-hour delay matter to someone like you?" said d'Artagnan. "No, I'm an orderly man, Monsieur, and I like things done properly."

"You know, Sir, that I could take them by force," replied Mordaunt. "I command here."

"Ah, Monsieur," said d'Artagnan, smiling agreeably, "it's clear that, though Monsieur du Vallon and I have had the honor of traveling in your company, you do not know us. We are veteran gentlemen of the sword, and quite capable, we two, of killing you and your eight men. Before God, Monsieur Mordaunt, don't be obstinate, because when you persist I persist, and I can get terribly stubborn. And Monsieur here," continued d'Artagnan, indicating Porthos, "is even more stubborn and difficult than I am—and besides, we were sent by Cardinal Mazarin, who represents the King of France. Which means that we represent the king and the cardinal, and are therefore, in our capacity as ambassadors, quite inviolable—a thing that Oliver Cromwell, who is a great politician in addition to a great general, certainly understands. Ask him for the written order. What does that cost you, my dear Monsieur Mordaunt?"

"Yes, a written order," said Porthos, who began to understand d'Artagnan's intentions. "That's all we're asking for."

However inclined Mordaunt might be to use force, he had to recognize that the reasons d'Artagnan had given him were good ones. Besides, d'Artagnan's reputation was impressive, and since what he'd seen that morning had only reinforced that reputation, he paused to reflect. Also, ignorant as he was of the friendship between the four Frenchmen, his suspicions were settled by the very convincing motive of the ransom money. So, he decided to go get the requested order, and to return with the promised two thousand pistoles into the bargain.

Mordaunt remounted his horse, and, after ordering the sergeant to remain on guard, turned and rode off.

"Good!" muttered d'Artagnan. "It'll take a quarter of an hour to reach the general's tent, and another quarter-hour to return, which is more time than we need."

Then, turning to Porthos without the slightest change in his expression, so that anyone watching might think he was just continuing the same conversation, he said, "Friend Porthos, listen closely. First of all, not a word to our friends of what you just heard—there's no need for them to know of the service we just rendered them."

"All right, I understand," said Porthos.

"Go to the stable, where you'll find Mousqueton. Saddle the horses, load the pistols into their holsters, bring the horses out, and lead them down the street and around the corner. Then just mount and wait—the rest is up to me."

Porthos made no remarks, just obeyed with that sublime confidence he had in his friend. "I go," he said, "only, could I pass through the room where our friends are?"

"No, that's unnecessary."

"Fine! Just do me the favor to collect my purse, which I left on the mantel."

"No problem."

Porthos walked calmly and quietly toward the stable, passing among the soldiers who, Frenchman though he was, couldn't help but admire his great stature and mighty limbs. At the corner of the street he met Mousqueton, whom he took with him.

Then d'Artagnan went inside, whistling a little air he'd begun while watching Porthos leave. "My dear Athos," he said, "I've been considering your arguments, and I'm entirely convinced. I regret getting involved in this business. Mazarin is a wretch, just as you say, so I've decided to escape with you.

No time for talk, prepare yourselves; your swords are there in the corner, and don't forget them, as they're tools which, under the circumstances, may prove useful. Which reminds me to get Porthos his purse—ah, here it is!"

D'Artagnan put the purse into his pocket as his two friends gaped at him in amazement. "Well, what are you staring at?" he asked. "I was blind, but now I see, thanks to Athos. Come over here."

His friends approached. "Do you see that street?" said d'Artagnan, pointing. "That's where the horses will be. You're just going to go out the door, turn left, jump on the horses, and that's all there is to it. Just wait until you hear me call out the signal, which will be, 'The Lord Our Savior!'"

"But you, d'Artagnan—give us your word that you're coming with us," said Athos.

"Before God, I swear it!"

"All right," said Aramis. "At the cry of, 'The Lord Our Savior,' we go out, knock over anyone who gets in our way, run to our horses, jump in the saddle, and spur off. Right?"

"As rain!"

"You see, Aramis," said Athos, "I always tell you d'Artagnan is the best of us."

"Fine," said d'Artagnan, "but while you pay me compliments, I'll get on with it. Adieu."

"And you'll be right behind us, won't you?"

"I hope so. Now don't forget the signal: 'The Lord Our Savior!'" And he went back out wearing the same calm demeanor as when he'd entered, whistling the tune he'd interrupted.

The soldiers dozed or played cards, while two in a corner badly sang the psalm, "By the waters of Babylon." D'Artagnan called to the sergeant, "*Mon cher* Sir, Monsieur Mordaunt has asked me to attend on General Cromwell. Please take good care of the prisoners."

The sergeant shrugged to indicate that he didn't understand French. D'Artagnan tried to make him understand by gestures and sign language what he wanted to convey, and the sergeant nodded to indicate everything was fine.

D'Artagnan went around to the stable, where he found all five horses saddled, his own among them. "Each of you take an extra horse," he said to Porthos and Mousqueton, "and lead it around to the left to where Athos and Aramis can see you from their window."

"Then will they come out?" said Porthos.

"In a moment."

"You didn't forget my purse?"

"No, never fear."

"Good."

And Porthos and Mousqueton, each leading another horse, rode to their position.

D'Artagnan, left alone, took out flint and steel, and set fire to a tiny bit of tinder. Then he climbed on his horse, rode out into the street, and stopped in the midst of the soldiers in the yard. And there, while stroking the animal with one hand, with the other he pushed the burning tinder into its ear.

It was a thing only a master horseman like d'Artagnan could risk, for as soon as the animal felt the touch of the burning ember it uttered a shriek of pain, reared back, and began leaping around as if mad.

The soldiers, threatened by the flailing hooves, fell about and scattered.

"Help me! Help!" cried d'Artagnan. "Stop my horse! It's gone crazy!" And indeed, it had blood in its eyes and foam on its lips. "Help me!" d'Artagnan cried, but the soldiers didn't dare approach. "Help! Are you going to let him kill me? *The Lord Our Savior!*"

D'Artagnan had scarcely uttered this cry before the door burst open and out rushed Athos and Aramis, swords in hand. But thanks to d'Artagnan's ruse, the way was clear.

"The prisoners are escaping!" cried the sergeant. "The prisoners are escaping!"

"Wait! Stop!" shouted d'Artagnan, releasing the reins of his furious horse, which leapt forward, knocking over two or three men.

"Stop! Halt!" cried the soldiers, running to their weapons.

But the prisoners were already in the saddle, and once in the saddle they lost no time galloping toward the nearest city gate. Halfway up the street they met Grimaud and Blaisois, who were looking for their masters. At a sign from Athos Grimaud understood everything and fell in behind the little troop as it passed like a hurricane, while d'Artagnan, still shouting in feigned dismay, followed farther back. They passed through the gate in a blur, before the guards could even think about halting them, and found themselves in open country.

Meanwhile, the soldiers at the house continued shouting, "Halt! Stop!," while the sergeant, who realized he'd been fooled, tore at his hair. Just then a rider came galloping up, a sheet of paper in his hand. It was Mordaunt, returning with the order. "Where are the prisoners?" he cried, leaping down from his horse.

The sergeant couldn't find the strength to answer him, just pointed toward the gaping door and the empty room. Mordaunt rushed to the doorstep, understood everything, gave a cry that seemed to come from the very depths of his being, and fell fainting to the flagstones.

XVII

In Which It Is Shown that Even in the Most Difficult Situations, Great Hearts Never Lose Their Courage, and Strong Stomachs Never Lose Their Appetites

The little troop, without looking back or exchanging a word, rode on at the gallop, crossing a narrow river of which no one knew the name and passing a town on their left that Athos thought must be Durham.

At length they came upon a little wood, and the horses were turned toward it and given a final touch of the spur. As soon as they'd disappeared behind a curtain of leaves thick enough to hide them from the eyes of pursuers, they stopped to hold a council. The horses were given to two of the lackeys so they could breathe without being unsaddled or unbridled, while Grimaud was placed as a sentinel.

"First, come let me embrace you, my friend," said Athos to d'Artagnan, "you who are our savior, you who are the true hero among us!"

"Athos is right, and I admire you," said Aramis, taking d'Artagnan into his arms. "Think what you could do for an intelligent master, with that infallible eye, that arm of steel, and that conquering spirit!"

"That's all very well," said the Gascon, "and I accept these thanks and embraces on behalf of myself and Porthos, but we have no time to spare for that now."

The two friends, reminded by d'Artagnan of what they also owed to Porthos, took turns shaking his hand. "Now," said Athos, "it's a matter of not riding off at random like fools, and instead coming up with a plan. What are we going to do?"

"What are we going to do? *Mordioux,* that's not hard to say!"

"Then say it, d'Artagnan."

"We make our way to the nearest seaport, gather what resources we have, outfit a boat and cross over to France. As to me, I'll put up everything I've got down to my last sou. Our chief treasure is our lives, and right now, it must be said, they're hanging by a thread."

"What do you say, du Vallon?" asked Athos.

"Me, I agree completely with d'Artagnan's advice," said Porthos. "It's an ugly country, this England."

"You're determined to leave her, then?" Athos asked d'Artagnan.

"God's blood!" said d'Artagnan. "I can't see what there is to hold me."

Athos exchanged a look with Aramis. "Then go on, my friends," he said with a sigh.

"Go on! What?" said d'Artagnan. "You mean, 'Let's *all* go,' don't you?"

"No, my friend," said Athos. "We must part."

"We must part!" said d'Artagnan, flabbergasted.

"Bah!" said Porthos. "Why should we part, when we're finally together?"

"Because your mission is done, and you can and ought to return to France—but ours is not."

"Your mission isn't finished?" said d'Artagnan, looking at Athos in surprise.

"No, my friend," replied Athos, in that voice so gentle, yet so firm. "We came here to defend King Charles, we defended him poorly, and now we must save him."

"Save the king!" said d'Artagnan, looking at Aramis as he had at Athos. Aramis just nodded.

D'Artagnan's face took on an expression of deep compassion; he was beginning to think he was dealing with the mentally afflicted. "You can't seriously mean that, Athos," he said. "The king is surrounded by an army that's taking him to London. That army is commanded by a butcher, or the son of a butcher, named Colonel Harrison.* His Majesty's trial will take place as soon as they arrive in London,[25] I can assure you—I've heard enough right from the mouth of Oliver Cromwell to know what to expect."

Athos and Aramis exchanged a second glance.

"And with his trial complete, his sentence will soon be executed," continued d'Artagnan. "Oh, these Puritans don't waste any time once they go to work!"

"And to what judgment do you think the king will be sentenced?" asked Athos.

"I'm afraid it can be nothing but death. Too much blood has been spilled for forgiveness; they have to kill him. Do you know what Cromwell said when he came to Paris and was shown the Dungeon of Vincennes, where Monsieur de Vendôme had been held?"

"What did he say?" asked Porthos.

"'You must strike princes only at the head.'"

"I knew it," said Athos.

"And do you think he won't put this maxim into execution, now that he has the king?"

"I'm quite sure he will—which is all the more reason not to abandon that august head."

"Athos, you've gone mad."

"No, my friend," Athos replied mildly. "You see, when de Winter came to find us in France, he took us to see Madame Henriette, and Her Majesty did us the honor, Monsieur d'Herblay and me, to ask our assistance for her husband. We gave her our word, and our word holds. We committed our minds, our bodies, our very lives to him. Isn't that how you see it, d'Herblay?"

"Yes," said Aramis. "We gave our word."

"Then," continued Athos, "we have another reason, and here it is, so listen carefully: all France is in a shambles at the moment. We have a ten-year-old king who doesn't know what he wants yet; we have a queen blinded by a late romantic passion; we have a minister who treats France as a vast farm to be harvested, caring for nothing but how much gold he can gather through intrigue and Italian tricks; and we have the princes whose opposition to Mazarin is entirely personal and egotistical, and will end up winning nothing but a few scraps of power and sundry bars of gold. I have served them, but not out of respect—God knows I see them for who they are, and they don't rank high in my esteem—but rather on principle. Here, today, is something else: here, I find before me a terrible misfortune, a royal misfortune, a misfortune for all Europe, and I must act upon it. If we succeed in saving the king, it will be a fine thing—and if we die for him, it will be glorious!"

"So, you know in advance that it means your death," said d'Artagnan.

"We fear that it may, but our only sorrow is to die apart from you."

"What can you do in a land where you're a stranger, an enemy?"

"When I was young I traveled in England, and speak English like a native, and Aramis also has some knowledge of the language. Ah, if only we had you two, my friends! With you, d'Artagnan, and you, Porthos, the four of us reunited for the first time in twenty years, we could stand up not just to England, but to Scotland and Ireland into the bargain!"

"And did you promise this queen," replied d'Artagnan sarcastically, "to break into the Tower of London, kill a hundred thousand soldiers, to contest the will of an entire nation as well as the ambition of a man, when that man is named Cromwell? You haven't met that man, Athos—nor have you, Aramis. Hear me! He's a man of genius, who reminded me strongly of our old cardinal—the other, the great one, whom you knew so well. Don't exaggerate the extent of your obligations. In the name of heaven, Athos, you don't have a duty to throw away your life. When I look at you, I seem to see before me a reasonable person—but when I hear you talk, you sound like a madman. Porthos, back me up here: what do you think of this matter?"

"Nothing good," replied Porthos.

"Come," said d'Artagnan, impatient because Athos, instead of listening to him, seemed to hear only a voice within himself, "believe me, Athos, your mission is completed, and completed nobly. Come back to France with us."

"Friend," said Athos, "our resolution is unshakeable."

"Do you have some other motive for this that we don't know about?"

Athos just smiled.

D'Artagnan punched his thigh angrily, then resumed the battle, calmly stating all the most convincing reasons he could think of. But to all these reasons Athos merely responded with a serene and patient smile, and Aramis just shook his head.

"All right!" cried d'Artagnan, losing his temper at last. "Fine! If that's what you want, let's all leave our bones in this bastard of a country, where it's always cold, where good weather is mist, where mist is rain, and where rain is a deluge; where the sun looks like the moon, and the moon looks like cream cheese. Die here, die there, since we all must die, what does it matter?"

"The way to think about it, dear friend," said Athos, "is that we just die a little sooner."

"Bah! A little sooner, a little later, it's scarcely worth fussing about."

"If I'm astonished by anything," said Porthos sententiously, "it's that it hasn't happened already."

"Oh, it's on its way, Porthos, never fear," said d'Artagnan. "So, we're agreed, assuming Porthos doesn't oppose it . . ."

"Me?" said Porthos. "I'll go where you go. Besides, I think the speech the Comte de La Fère just made for us was very pretty."

"But what about your future, d'Artagnan? And your ambitions, Porthos?"

"Our future! Our ambitions!" said d'Artagnan airily. "Why should we worry about that, since we're saving a king? We just need to rescue the king, rally his friends, defeat the Puritans, reconquer England, return him to London and place him on his throne . . ."

"And then he'll make us dukes and peers," said Porthos, his eyes alight, as if already living the happy ending to this fable.

"Or he'll just forget us," said d'Artagnan.

"But no!" said Porthos.

"*Dame!* We've seen that already, friend Porthos. It seems to me we performed a service for Queen Anne of Austria that wasn't much less than what we propose to do for Charles I. That didn't stop Queen Anne from forgetting us for over twenty years."

"Even so, d'Artagnan," said Athos, "are you sorry you did her that favor?"

"No, *ma foi,*" said d'Artagnan, "and I even admit that in hard times I've found some consolation in the memory of it."

"And you know, d'Artagnan, that though princes may be ungrateful, God will remember."

"You know, Athos," said d'Artagnan, "I think if you met the Devil on earth, you could talk him into following you into heaven."

"And so?" said Athos, offering his hand to d'Artagnan.

"And so, we're agreed," said d'Artagnan. "I find England a charming country, and I'll stay—on one condition."

"What's that?"

"That no one tries to teach me English."

"Well!" said Athos triumphantly. "Now, my friend, I swear to you, by God who hears all, and by my name which I believe to be above reproach, that there is a power who watches over us, and that gives me hope that we shall all once more return safely to France."

"May it be so," said d'Artagnan, "though I confess I can't believe it."

"Our dear d'Artagnan!" said Aramis. "He represents among us a parliament's loyal opposition that always says *no,* but always does *yes.*"

"And who in doing so, somehow always save the country," said Athos.

"Well, now that that's settled," said Porthos, rubbing his hands, "let's turn our thoughts to dinner! For it seems to me that, no matter what perils we've faced, we've always found time to eat."

"Ah, yes!" said d'Artagnan. "Let's speak of dinner in a land where they eat boiled mutton at every meal, and drink nothing but beer. What were you thinking when you came to such a country, Athos? Ah, but pardon me," he added, smiling, "I forgot that you're no longer Athos. Never mind—let's hear your plan for dinner, Porthos."

"My plan!"

"Yes, don't you have a plan?"

"No, all I have is an appetite."

"*Pardieu!* Now that you mention it, so do I. We're going to have to find some food, or else take up eating grass like our horses . . ."

"Ah! When we were at the Heretic, do you remember what fine oysters we had?" said Aramis, who was not as detached from earthly pleasures as Athos.

"And the lamb cutlets they make in those salt marshes," said Porthos, licking his lips.

"But Porthos, don't we still have our friend Mousqueton," said d'Artagnan, "who made life so easy for you at Chantilly?"

"Indeed, we do have Mousqueton," said Porthos, "but since he became my intendant he's grown . . . and grown less active. But no matter, I'll summon him." And he called out agreeably, "Hey! Mouston!"

Mousqueton appeared, wearing a most pitiful expression.

"My dear Monsieur Mouston, what's the matter?" asked d'Artagnan. "Are you ill?"

"Monsieur, I'm very hungry," replied Mousqueton.

"Well! That's the very reason we called for you, my dear Monsieur Mouston. Could you please hunt up some nice rabbits and a few succulent partridges, like those from which you made such fricassees and soups at the Hôtel de . . . my faith, what *was* the name of that inn?"

"The Hôtel de . . . *ma foi,* I can't remember it either."

"No matter! While you're at it, lasso up some more bottles of that Burgundy that had such curative properties when your master had his, er, sprain."

"*Hélas,* Monsieur!" said Mousqueton. "I'm afraid what you ask for is quite hard to find in this dreadful country, and we might do better to ask for hospitality from the master of that little house one can see from the edge of the woods."

"Oh? You say there's a house nearby?" asked d'Artagnan.

"Yes, Monsieur," Mousqueton replied.

"Well, then, as you say, let's go ask the master of this house for some dinner. Messieurs, are you in accord with this idea of Monsieur Mouston's?"

"But what if the householder is a Puritan?" said Aramis.

"*Mordioux,* all the better!" said d'Artagnan. "If he's a Puritan, we'll tell him of the king's capture, and in honor of such news, he'll slaughter the fatted calf."

"And if he's a royalist?" said Porthos.

"In that case we'll look mournful, and he'll slaughter the black sheep."

"Such good cheer!" said Athos, smiling despite everything at the indomitable Gascon. "I think you could laugh at anything."

"What would you have?" said d'Artagnan. "I was born in a place without a cloud in the sky."

"Not like here," said Porthos, extending a hand to make sure what he'd felt on his cheek was a drop of rain.

"Then let's go," said d'Artagnan. "All the more reason for us to move on. Hey, Grimaud!"

Grimaud appeared.

"Grimaud, my friend, have you seen anything?" asked d'Artagnan.

"Nothing," replied Grimaud.

"What blunderers," said Porthos. "They haven't even pursued us. Now, if we'd been handling it . . . !"

"And a shame it is, too," said d'Artagnan. "A private place like this would be perfect for what I have to say to Mordaunt. This is a lovely spot to lay a man out."

"Decidedly, Messieurs," said Aramis, "I don't think the son is in the same class as his mother."

"Eh, my friend," said Athos, "give him a chance. We've been gone less than two hours, and he has no idea which way we went or where we are. Don't decide he's less of a threat than his mother until we've once more set foot in France, with none of us run through or poisoned."

"Then let's have dinner while we wait," said Porthos.

"My faith, yes," said Athos, "for I'm hungry too."

"Black sheep, beware!" said Aramis.

And the four friends, led by Mousqueton, advanced toward the house, already restored to their usual confidence, now that, as Athos had said, they were all four reunited.

XVIII

A Toast to Fallen Majesty

As they approached the house, our fugitives saw that the ground around it was torn up, as if a considerable troop of horsemen had preceded them; the marks were most pronounced near the door and showed that the troop had halted there.

"*Pardieu!*" said d'Artagnan. "It's as clear as writing: the king and his captors have passed here."

"The devil!" said Porthos. "In that case, they'll have eaten all the food."

"They might have missed a hen," said d'Artagnan, and he jumped from his horse and knocked on the door. But no one answered.

He pushed open the door, which was unlocked, and saw that the front room was empty and deserted.

"Well?" asked Porthos.

"I don't see anyone," said d'Artagnan. "Ah, wait!"

"What is it?"

"Blood!"

At this word, his three friends leapt off their horses and entered the first room, but d'Artagnan was already opening the door into the second, and by the expression on his face it was clear he'd found something.

The three friends approached and saw a young man lying on the floor in a pool of blood. One could see that he'd tried to get to his bed, but his strength had run out and he'd collapsed just short of it.

Athos, who thought he'd seen a movement, was the first to approach the unfortunate young man. "Well?" asked d'Artagnan.

"Well!" said Athos. "If he's dead, it hasn't been for long, because he's still warm. But no, his heart still beats. Hey, there, friend."

The wounded man sighed. From a bowl, d'Artagnan poured some water into his cupped hand and splashed it on his face. The man opened his eyes, tried to raise his head and fell back.

Athos tried to lift the man to lean him on his knee but saw that the man's wound was to his head; his skull was split, and blood still flowed from the gash. Aramis dipped a towel in the water bowl and applied it to the wound, and the coolness brought the man around so that he opened his eyes again. He looked with surprise at these men who seemed to pity him, and who, as much as they could, were trying to help him.

"You are among friends," said Athos in English. "Have no fear. But if you have the strength, tell us what happened."

"The king," murmured the wounded man. "The king is a prisoner."

"You saw him?" asked Aramis in the same language.

The man didn't answer. "Don't worry," said Athos, "we're loyal servants of His Majesty."

"Are you speaking the truth?" asked the wounded man.

"On our honor as gentlemen."

"Then I can tell you?"

"Speak."

"I'm the brother of Parry, His Majesty's valet."

Athos and Aramis remembered that it was by that name that Winter had addressed the servant they'd met in the corridor of the royal pavilion. "We know him," said Athos. "He never left the king's side!"

"Yes, that's him!" said the wounded man. "When the king was taken, he went with him, and when they neared my house, he thought of me. He asked in the name of the king if they could stop here. The request was granted; the king, he said, was hungry. They brought him into this room so he could take his meal, and placed sentries at the doors and windows. Parry knew this room, because several times, while His Majesty was at Newcastle, he'd come to see me. He knew there was a trap door in the floor that led to the cellar, and that from the cellar one could reach the orchard. He made a sign to me about it, and I understood. But one of the king's guardians must have seen the gesture and become suspicious. I knew nothing about that, I just wanted to save His Majesty. So, I pretended I needed to go out and get some wood, thinking there was no time to lose.

"I came back in through the outside door that opened into the cellar. I went to the trap door and slowly raised it, just as Parry was quietly bolting the inner door, and I beckoned to the king to follow me. But alas! He didn't want to do it—it was as if he didn't really want to escape. Then Parry clasped his hands and begged him, and we implored him not to lose this opportunity. Finally he decided to follow me into the cellar. I went in front, with the king a few steps behind me, when suddenly, in the passage to the outer door, a great shadow rose up in front of me. I tried to cry out to warn the king but didn't have time—I felt a blow like the entire house falling on my head and fell unconscious."

"Faithful servant!" said Athos. "Good and loyal Englishman!"

"When I came to, I was lying where they'd left me. I dragged myself out and around to the front, but the king and his captors were gone. It took maybe an hour to crawl inside this far before my strength was gone, and I passed out for a second time."

"And now, how do you feel?"

"Very bad," said the brother of Parry.

"Can we do anything for you?" asked Athos.

"Help me up onto the bed; I think I'll feel better there."

"Is there anyone we can send to for help?"

"My wife went to Durham and should be back any time now. But you, is there anything you need, anything you want?"

"We came here intending to ask you for some food."

"Alas! They took everything; there's not a crust of bread left in the house."

"Do you hear, d'Artagnan?" said Athos. "We'll have to find our dinner elsewhere."

"That hardly matters now," said d'Artagnan. "I've lost my appetite."

"My faith, me too," said Porthos.

They carried the man to his bed, and sent for Grimaud, who dressed his wound. In the service of the four companions, Grimaud had had occasion to patch them up so many times that he had the skills of a field surgeon.

Meanwhile the fugitives had gathered in the front room for a council. "Now we know what took place here," said Aramis. "It was indeed the king and his captors who passed through. We should go in the opposite direction. Don't you agree, Athos?"

Athos said nothing; he was thinking.

"Yes," said Porthos, "let's go the other way. If we follow the king's escort, we'll find everything eaten up and we'll die of hunger. This England is a cursed country, but at least till now I'd always been able to find a dinner in it. Dinner is my favorite meal."

"What do you think, d'Artagnan?" said Athos. "Do you agree with Aramis?"

"Not at all," said d'Artagnan, "in fact I think quite the opposite."

"What? You want to follow the escort?" said Porthos, shocked.

"No, I want to join up with them."

Athos's eyes sparkled with joy.

"Join up with the escort!" cried Aramis.

"Hear d'Artagnan out," said Athos. "You know he always has good ideas."

"No doubt about it," said d'Artagnan, "we must go where they won't search for us. They won't even think of looking for us among the Puritans, so among the Puritans we must go."

"Fine, my friend—good advice!" said Athos. "I was about to say the same thing myself."

"So, you agree with him?" asked Aramis.

"Yes. They'll think we want to leave England, so they'll be searching the ports. Meanwhile, we'll go to London with the king. Once in London, we're safe—it's easy to hide among a million people. Not to mention," said Athos, with a glance at Aramis, "the possible opportunities of such a journey."

"Yes," said Aramis, "I understand."

"Me, I don't understand at all," said Porthos. "but no matter. If d'Artagnan and Athos agree on a thing, it must be the right idea."

"But won't Colonel Harrison be suspicious of us?" asked Aramis.

"Him? *Mordioux!*" said d'Artagnan. "He's the one I'm counting on. Colonel Harrison will welcome us; he's seen us twice with General Cromwell, and knows we were sent from France by Mazarin. He'll treat us like brothers. Besides, isn't he the son of a butcher? He is, isn't he? Well, Porthos will show him how he can knock out an ox with a punch and overturn a bull by taking it by the horns. He'll love us."

Athos smiled. "You're the best comrade a man could have, d'Artagnan," he said, taking the Gascon's hand, "and I'm very glad we're together again, my son." That is, as we know, what Athos called d'Artagnan when deeply moved.

At that moment Grimaud called them in. The wounded man had been bandaged and was feeling better. The four friends bid him adieu and asked if there was any message they could convey to his brother. The brave man said, "Tell him he should let the king know they didn't quite kill me; no matter how unimportant I am, I'm sure His Majesty regrets my death and blames himself for it."

"Don't worry," said d'Artagnan, "he'll know it before nightfall."

The little troop resumed their march. There was no mistaking their path; the trail they had to follow was clearly visible across the fields.

After about two hours of silent march, d'Artagnan, who was in the lead, stopped at a turn in the road. "Ah ha!" he said. "Here are our men."

In fact, a considerable troop of riders could be seen about a half-league ahead.

"My dear friends," said d'Artagnan to Athos and Aramis, "give your swords to Monsieur Mouston, who will hold them for you, and don't forget for a moment that you're our prisoners."

Then they put their horses, which were beginning to tire, into a final trot, and soon caught up to the escort.

The king, at the head of the troop, surrounded by Colonel Harrison's soldiers, rode impassively, dignified and resigned. On seeing Athos and Aramis, to whom he'd not even had time to say farewell, he read in the glances of the two gentlemen that he still had two friends at hand, though he thought they were prisoners. A flush of pleasure colored the king's cheeks.

D'Artagnan reached the head of the column, where, leaving his friends guarded by Porthos, he rode straight to Harrison. The colonel recognized him from having seen him with Cromwell, and welcomed him as politely as a man of his character and background could manage. As d'Artagnan had foreseen, Harrison suspected nothing.

The troop stopped at an inn; it was at this halt that the king was to dine—only this time precautions were put into place to make sure he didn't escape. In the inn's common room a small table was placed for the king, and a large table for the officers. "Will you dine with me?" Harrison asked d'Artagnan.

"Would I?" said d'Artagnan. "That would give me great pleasure—but I have my comrade, Monsieur du Vallon, and our two prisoners whom we can't leave, and that would overcrowd your table. Maybe it would be better to set up another table in the corner, and send over to us whatever you can spare, because believe me, we're famished. Then we'll all be at dinner together, or at least in the same room."

"We'll do it," said Harrison. The matter was arranged as d'Artagnan had proposed, and when he returned to the colonel's dinner with his friends, he found the king already seated at his table being served by Parry. Harrison and his officers were gathered in the center of the room, and a side table awaited the friends in a corner.

The table at which the Puritan officers were seated was round, and by chance or deliberate choice, Harrison was sitting with his back to the king. The king watched the four gentlemen enter but seemed to pay them no special attention.

The four comrades went to the table set aside for them and seated themselves with their backs to the wall, facing the officers' table and that of the king.

Harrison, to do honor to his guests, sent them the best dishes from his table, though unfortunately for the four friends, there was no wine. This didn't matter to Athos, but d'Artagnan, Porthos, and Aramis grimaced every time they had to swallow beer, the drink of Puritans. "Faith, Colonel," said d'Artagnan, "we're very grateful for your gracious invitation, for, without you, we ran the risk of missing our dinner, and we'd already missed breakfast. My friend Monsieur du Vallon here shares my gratitude, as he was famished."

"I'm still hungry," said Porthos, saluting Colonel Harrison.

"And how did the grave calamity of your missing breakfast come about?" asked the colonel with a laugh.

"The reason is simple enough, Colonel," said d'Artagnan. "I was eager to catch up to you, and in my haste, I followed the same route you'd taken, a mistake an old forager like me should never have made, as I should have known that where experienced troops like yours pass, they leave nothing behind. You can understand our disappointment when, upon arriving at a pretty little house at the edge of a wood, a handsome dwelling with a red roof and green shutters, instead of finding chickens to roast and ham steaks to grill, we discovered a poor devil bathed in blood. . . . *Mordioux*, Colonel, my compliments to whichever of your officers delivered that blow, for it was so mighty it earned the admiration of my friend Monsieur du Vallon, who's no amateur when it comes to blows."

"Yes," said Harrison, laughing and catching the eye of an officer at his table, "when Groslow takes on such a task, no follow up is needed."

"Ah, so it was monsieur, here," said d'Artagnan, saluting the officer. "I regret that monsieur doesn't speak French, or I'd pay him my compliments directly."

"I'm ready to receive them and pay you back in kind, Monsieur," said the officer in reasonably good French. "I lived in Paris for three years."

"Well, Monsieur," continued d'Artagnan, "I'm pleased to tell you that your blow was so well struck that you nearly killed the man."

"I thought I'd killed him outright," said Groslow.

"No. It was a near thing, it's true, but he's not quite dead."

As he said this, d'Artagnan glanced at Parry, who stood behind the king looking pale as death, which showed that the remark had found its intended audience. As to the king, he had listened to the whole conversation with a heart bursting with anguish, for at first, he didn't understand the intentions of the French officer who spoke with such callous cruelty about the assault and was revolted. At d'Artagnan's last words, he finally breathed freely.

"Devil take it!" said Groslow. "I thought I'd done a more thorough job. If it wasn't so far back to that dog's house, I'd return and finish it."

"And you'd be right to do so, if you're afraid he'll come after you," said d'Artagnan, "for you know that when such a head wound doesn't kill instantly, it heals within a week." And d'Artagnan cast a second glance at Parry, on whose face joy was spreading, as Charles pressed his hand and smiled. Parry bowed to his master's hand and kissed it with respect.

"Truly, d'Artagnan," said Athos quietly, "you are both a man of your word and a man of wits. But what do you think of the king?"

"I like the look of him," said d'Artagnan. "He seems both noble and good."

"Yes, but he let himself be taken," said Porthos. "That was a mistake."

"I have a strong desire to drink the king's health," said Athos.

"Then let me propose a toast," said d'Artagnan.

"Please do," said Aramis.

Porthos looked at d'Artagnan in surprise, ever amazed by the endless ideas his Gascon spirit supplied his comrade.

D'Artagnan took up his tin goblet, filled it, and rose to his feet. "Messieurs," he said to his companions, "let's raise a glass to he who presides over our feast. Let's drink to our colonel, to let him know that we're at his service to London and beyond."

As he said these words, d'Artagnan looked at Harrison, who thought the toast was for him. He rose and saluted the four friends, who, their eyes fixed on King Charles, drank all together, while Harrison, on his side, drained his glass without suspicion.

Charles, in his turn, held out his glass to Parry, who poured in a few drops of beer—for the king had the same fare as the rest. He then raised it to his lips, and while looking at the four gentlemen, he drank with a smile full of nobility and gratitude.

"Come, Gentlemen," said Harrison, resting his glass without so much as a glance at his illustrious prisoner, "let's be on our way!"

"Where do we sleep tonight, Colonel?"

"At Thirsk," replied Harrison.

"Parry," said the king, rising and turning to his valet, "my horse. I wish to go to Thirsk."

"Faith," said d'Artagnan to Athos, "your king has completely captivated me, and I'm entirely at his service."

"If you really mean that," Athos replied, "I think we can see to it that he never arrives in London."

"How so?"

"Because before then we'll have spirited him away."

"This time, Athos," said d'Artagnan, "word of honor, you really are mad."

"Do you mean to say you're out of ideas?" asked Aramis.

"Come now!" said Porthos. "It's not impossible. All we need is a good plan."

"I don't have any ideas," said Athos, "but I'll leave coming up with a plan to d'Artagnan."

D'Artagnan just shrugged his shoulders, and they left.

XIX

D'Artagnan Comes Up with a Plan

Athos knew d'Artagnan better than d'Artagnan knew himself. He knew that dropping a thought into a fertile mind like the Gascon's was like planting a seed in a rich and well-watered field. So, he let his friend shrug his shoulders and ride along, while chatting to him about Raoul, a conversation which he'd avoided under another circumstance, it may be recalled.

As night fell they arrived at Thirsk. The four friends appeared completely uninterested in and indifferent to the security precautions for the king's custody. They retired to a private house, where they took precautions for their own security, gathering in a single room that had a reliable escape route in case of attack. Each lackey was given a sentry post; Grimaud slept across the doorway on a pallet of straw.

D'Artagnan was pensive and seemed for once to have no interest in talking. He didn't say a word, just paced back and forth from window to bed, whistling tunelessly. Porthos, who never saw anything beyond the obvious, spoke to him as usual, but d'Artagnan replied only in monosyllables. Athos and Aramis looked at each other and smiled.

The day had been tiring, and yet, with the exception of Porthos, for whom slumber was as dependable as hunger, the friends slept badly.

The next morning d'Artagnan was the first one on his feet. He had already gone down to the stables, checked on the horses, and given all the orders necessary for the day by the time Athos and Aramis got up. Porthos was still snoring.

At eight in the morning the entire troop set out, marching in the same order as the day before—though d'Artagnan left his group of friends and went to expand on the acquaintance with Mister Groslow begun the day before. The officer, who was still glowing from d'Artagnan's earlier praise, received him with a gracious smile. "In truth, Monsieur," d'Artagnan said to him, "I'm happy to find someone with whom I can speak my poor language. My friend Monsieur du Vallon is so melancholy a character he speaks scarcely four words in a day—while as for our prisoners, you understand that we don't engage them in conversation."

"They're royalist fanatics," said Groslow.

"All the more reason for them to sulk since we've taken the Stuart. I hope he'll be given a fine and fiery trial."

"Faith! That's what we're taking him to London for," said Groslow.

"And you don't mean to let him out of your sight, I imagine?"

"Plague! I should think not! As you see," the officer added, laughing, "we're giving him a truly royal escort."

"Yes, by day, there's no chance he might escape. But by night . . ."

"At night, our precautions are doubled."

"They must be pretty thorough."

"There are always eight men in his room."

"The devil!" said d'Artagnan "You do guard him well. But, besides these eight men inside, you must have a guard outside, right? You can't be too careful guarding a prisoner like this one."

"True! But on the other hand, what could two unarmed men do against eight armed guards?"

"What do you mean, two men?"

"The king and his valet."

"They gave the king permission to keep his valet?"

"Yes, the Stuart asked for that favor, and Colonel Harrison agreed. The excuse is that he's a king, so he can't dress or undress himself."

"Truly, Captain," said d'Artagnan, pushing his flattery campaign to see how far it would take him, "the more I listen to you, the more I admire the easy and elegant way you speak French. I realize you lived in Paris for three years, but I'm sure I could live in London for the rest of my life and never learn English that well. What were you doing in Paris?"

"My father, who's a merchant, had placed me in the office of his continental partner, who had sent his own son to work with my father. Such exchanges are customary between trading partners."

"And did you like Paris, Monsieur?"

"Yes, but you ought to have a revolution like ours. Not against your king, he's just a child, but against that thieving Italian who's your queen's lover."

"Ha! I quite agree with you, Monsieur, and we could do it, too, if we had only a dozen officers like you, sharp, vigilant, and determined! We'd soon see the end of that Mazarin, and give him a little trial like the one you're going to stage for your king."

"But I thought you were in Mazarin's service," said the officer. "Wasn't it he who sent you to General Cromwell?"

"Say rather that I'm in the service of the king. Knowing that Mazarin needed to send someone to England, I asked for the mission, for the express purpose of meeting the man of genius who now commands your three kingdoms. Then, when he invited me and Monsieur du Vallon to draw our swords for the honor of old England, you saw how we took up his offer."

"Yes, I know you led the charge with Mister Mordaunt."

"On his left side and his right, Monsieur. *Peste*, he's another brave and determined young officer. Did you see how he settled his score with his traitorous uncle?"

"Do you know him, then?" asked the officer.

"Very well indeed; I can even say we have a strong connection. Monsieur du Vallon and I came over from France with him."

"It sounded like you made him wait quite a while at Boulogne."

"What would you have?" said d'Artagnan. "I was like you, I had a king to guard."

"Oh?" said Groslow. "Which king is that?"

"Ours, *pardieu!* Our little king, Louis XIV." And d'Artagnan removed his hat.

The Englishman did the same out of politeness. "How long did you guard him?"

"Three nights, and, by my faith, I'll always remember those nights fondly."

"Is the young king easy to get along with?"

"The king? He was fast asleep."

"Then what are you talking about?"

"What I'm talking about is that my friends, the officers of the guards and the musketeers, came to keep me company, and we spent those nights drinking and gambling."

"Ah, yes," sighed the Englishman. "It's true, you Frenchmen make merry companions."

"You mean you don't play dice and cards while you stand guard?"

"Never," said the Englishman.

"How terribly boring! I must say, I feel sorry for you," said d'Artagnan.

"The fact is," the officer replied, "I dread my turn at guard duty. It's a long, long night with nothing to do."

"Yes, when one watches alone or with dull mates. But when we share duty with a jolly friend, and scatter gold and dice on the table, the night passes like a dream. So you don't care for dice or cards?"

"On the contrary!"

"You'd enjoy a few hands of lansquenet,[26] then?"

"I'm crazy about it—played it almost every night in France."

"And since you've been back in England?"

"I've touched neither cards nor dice-box."

"You poor fellow," said d'Artagnan, with an air of deep compassion.

"Listen," said the Englishman, "do something for me."

"What's that?"

"Tomorrow night I'm on guard."

"Around the Stuart?"

"Yes. Come spend the watch with me."

"Impossible."

"Impossible?"

"Completely."

"But why?"

"I play cards every night with Monsieur du Vallon. Sometimes we don't go to bed at all. . . . This morning, for example, we were still playing at dawn."

"Well?"

"Well, he'll be bored to death if we don't play."

"Is he a devoted player?"

"I've seen him lose two thousand pistoles on a hand and laugh it off."

"Bring him, then."

"How could I do that? What about our prisoners?"

"Ah, the devil! I forgot," said the officer. "Just tell your lackeys to guard them."

"I might as well just let them escape," said d'Artagnan. "Those lads are no kind of guards."

"Are your prisoners men of high rank, then?"

"*Peste!* I'll say! One is a rich seigneur of Touraine, and the other is a Knight of Malta[27] of an ancient house. We've set the ransom for both of them: two thousand livres in silver when we arrive in France. Believe me, we're not about to leave those men for a moment, especially with lackeys who know the prisoners are rich. We gave them a once-over, a pre-ransom search, and I confess it's their gold we're playing with every night, Monsieur du Vallon and I. But they might have a few more gemstones hidden away in their sleeves, even a diamond of price, so we guard them like misers guard their strongboxes. One or the other of us watches over them at all times."

"Ah! Hmm," said Groslow.

"So now you understand why I must refuse your noble offer—and with sorrow, because as I'm sure you know, nothing is more tiresome than to play the same games over and over, night after night, with the same partner. Luck goes back and forth equally between you, and at the end of a month you find you're both back where you started."

"No, there's one thing even more tiresome than that," said Groslow with a sigh, "and that's not playing at all."

"I imagine you're right," said d'Artagnan.

"But see here," said the Englishman, "your prisoners, are they dangerous men?"

"How do you mean?"

"Could they make a break for it?"

D'Artagnan laughed aloud. "Lord above!" he chuckled. "The seigneur is weak and trembling with fever, thanks to the climate of your charming country, while the Knight of Malta is as timid as a young girl. Though to be safe, we took away their pen knives and pocket scissors."

"All right, then," said Groslow, "just bring them along."

"Really? We could do that?"

"Why not? I have eight men."

"So?"

"So four can watch your prisoners, and four can guard the king."

"You know," said d'Artagnan slowly, "I think that could work—though we're putting you to a lot of trouble."

"Bah! Come anyway; we'll figure it out."

"Oh, I'm not worried about that," said d'Artagnan. "One can trust a man like you to handle anything."

At this final flattery, the officer gave one of those little chuckles of satisfied vanity that cement a new friendship between one who is pleased and one who pleases.

"Now that I think of it," said d'Artagnan, "why shouldn't we start tonight?"

"What?"

"Our game."

"No reason in the world," said Groslow.

"Why don't you come play lansquenet with us tonight, and we'll return the favor with you tomorrow night. That way, if there's anything about our 'fanatical royalists' that alarms you, well! We'll just play the one night and cancel the next."

"Perfect! Tonight at your place, tomorrow night at the Stuart's, and the night after that at mine."

"And then every night in London. Hey, *mordioux!*" said d'Artagnan. "You see, one can lead a merry life anywhere."

"Yes, when one falls in with Frenchmen, and they're Frenchmen like you," said Groslow.

"Especially ones like Monsieur du Vallon—what a merry soul he is! He's a furious Frondeur, and terrifies Mazarin, who employs him out of fear of opposing him."

"Yes, he's an imposing figure of a man," said Groslow, "but he has a pleasant face, and I like him without even knowing him yet."

"You'll like him even more when you get to know him better. But hey! They're calling me. My apologies, but unlike you, he's not clever, and can't do without me. You'll excuse me?"

"Of course!"

"Until tonight."

"At your place?"

"At our place."

The two men exchanged salutes, and d'Artagnan returned to his companions. "What the devil were you talking about with that bulldog?" said Porthos.

"My dear Porthos, don't speak that way about Monsieur Groslow, who is my new best friend."

"Your new best friend," said Porthos, "that murderer of peasants?"

"Hush, my dear Porthos! All right, yes, Monsieur Groslow may be a brute, but I've discovered that he has two excellent qualities: he's proud, and he's stupid."

Porthos, bewildered, stared wide-eyed, but Athos and Aramis looked at each other and smiled; they knew that d'Artagnan did nothing without a purpose.

"Soon enough, you'll come to appreciate him yourself," said d'Artagnan.

"How's that?"

"I'll introduce him to you tonight, when he comes to play cards with us."

"Oh ho!" said Porthos, his eyes lighting up. "Is he rich?"

"He's the son of one of London's leading merchants."

"And he likes lansquenet?"

"He loves it."

"And basset?"

"Crazy about it."

"He plays biribi?"[28]

"Like an expert."

"Good," said Porthos, "we'll have a pleasant evening."

"All the more pleasant as it promises us a better night tomorrow."

"What do you mean?"

"Yes, we host him at gaming tonight, and he hosts us tomorrow night."

"Where will that be?"

"I'll tell you later. Tonight, we must pay attention to just one thing: making sure we're worthy hosts to Monsieur Groslow. We're spending the night at Derby; send Mousqueton on ahead, and if there's a bottle of wine to be had in the city, have him buy it. It wouldn't hurt for him to find something tasty and prepare us a savory supper—though the prisoners won't join us because you, Athos, are trembling with a fever, and you, Aramis, are an effete Knight of Malta who doesn't like the harsh conversation of soldiers—it makes you blush. Do you hear me?"

"I hear you," said Porthos, "but devil take me if I understand you."

"Porthos, my friend, you know that I'm descended from the prophets on my father's side and the sibyls on my mother's, and that I speak only in parables and riddles; let those who have ears listen, and those who have eyes look! I can say no more at this time."

"No need, my friend," said Athos. "I'm sure that whatever you're doing will be done well."

"And you, Aramis, do you agree with Athos?"

"Completely, *mon cher* d'Artagnan."

"Behold," said d'Artagnan, "for here are true believers, and it's a pleasure to perform miracles for them. Not like the faithless Porthos, who only believes in what he can see and touch."

"I am, in fact," said Porthos with a shrewd look, "very incredulous."

D'Artagnan clapped him on the shoulder, and then, as the troop had arrived at their midday halt, the conversation was over.

At about five in the evening, as agreed, Mousqueton was sent on ahead. Mousqueton spoke no English, but since they'd been in England he'd been studying the methods of Grimaud, who never spoke a word, and nonetheless made himself understood by gestures. He'd asked Grimaud for some lessons, and thanks to studying with a master, he'd learned more than a little. Blaisois went with him.

That evening the four friends, riding down Derby's principal street, saw Blaisois waiting at the gate of a fine house; this was to be their lodging for the night.

All day they'd avoided the king for fear of arousing suspicion, and instead of joining Colonel Harrison's table for supper, they took that meal by themselves.

Groslow arrived at the appointed hour. D'Artagnan received him as if he were a friend of twenty years' standing. Porthos looked him up and down from head to toe and smiled, for he realized that despite the remarkable blow he'd given to Parry's brother, Groslow wasn't as mighty as he. Athos and Aramis did what they could to conceal their disgust at Groslow's crude and brutal nature.

In short, Groslow was pleased with his reception. Athos and Aramis played their parts. At midnight they retired to their room, the door of which was left open, on the pretext of keeping an eye on them. As they left, d'Artagnan went with them, leaving Porthos for a moment with Groslow.

When he returned, they played; Porthos won fifty pistoles from Groslow, and found, by the time he retired for the night, that the man's company was less disagreeable than he'd expected. As for Groslow, he promised d'Artagnan he'd get his revenge on Porthos next time, and took his leave of the Gascon, reminding him of their rendezvous that evening. We say that evening, because by the time the players finally broke up, it was four in the morning.

The day passed in the usual way; d'Artagnan went from Captain Groslow to Colonel Harrison, and from Colonel Harrison back to his friends. For one who didn't know d'Artagnan, he seemed to be in his usual cheerful mood—but to his friends, or Athos and Aramis anyway, he seemed to be in a fever of gaiety.

"What's he up to?" said Aramis.

"Just wait," said Athos.

Porthos said nothing, only counted, one after another, with a visible air of satisfaction, the fifty pistoles he'd won from Groslow.

Arriving that evening at Ryston, d'Artagnan assembled his friends. His face wore the expression of cheerful nonchalance it had shown all day; Athos gave Aramis a nudge and said, "The time approaches."

"Yes," said d'Artagnan, who'd heard him. "Yes, the time approaches. Tonight, Messieurs, we rescue the king."

Athos trembled, his eyes alight. "D'Artagnan," he said, doubt momentarily displacing hope, "this isn't a joke, is it? Such a joke would be the death of me!"

"It's unlike you, Athos, to doubt me this way," said d'Artagnan. "When have you seen me jest about a friend's heart or a king's life? I told you, and I repeat, that tonight we rescue Charles I. You asked me to find a plan, and the plan is found."

Porthos gave d'Artagnan a look of deep admiration. Aramis smiled like a man who's found hope.

But Athos was pale as death and trembled in every limb. "Tell us," he said.

Porthos opened his eyes wide, while Aramis hung on d'Artagnan's every word. "Did you hear that we've been invited to spend the evening with Monsieur Groslow?"

"Yes," responded Porthos. "He made us promise to give him his revenge."

"Good. And do you know where he's going to take this revenge?"

"No."

"In the king's quarters."

"In the king's quarters!" cried Athos.

"Yes, Messieurs, the king's quarters. Monsieur Groslow is on guard duty with His Majesty tonight, and, for his amusement, has invited us to keep him company."

"All four of us?" asked Athos.

"*Pardieu!* Certainly, all four of us—do you suppose we'd let our prisoners out of our sight?"

"Oh ho!" said Aramis.

"Go on," said Athos, excited.

"We'll go to join Groslow, we with our swords, you with your poniards; the four of us will overwhelm those eight imbeciles and their stupid commander. What do you say to that, Monsieur Porthos?"

"I say it'll be easy," said Porthos.

"We'll put Groslow's clothes on the king; Mousqueton, Grimaud, and Blaisois will be waiting around the first corner with horses; we'll jump into the saddle, and by dawn we'll be twenty leagues from here. Will this plot do, Athos?"

Athos placed his hands on d'Artagnan's shoulders and looked at him with his calm and gentle smile. "I declare, friend," he said, "there isn't another creature under the sun to equal you for nobility and courage. While we thought you indifferent to our troubles, you alone have found the answer we sought for in vain. I repeat once more, d'Artagnan, you are the best of us, and I bless you and love you, my dear son."

"And to think that I didn't think of it myself!" said Porthos, slapping his forehead. "It's all so simple."

"But as I see it," said Aramis, "we have to kill them all, don't we?"

Athos shuddered and turned pale.

"*Mordioux!*" said d'Artagnan. "You're right, and we must. I've thought it through every way I can, and I don't see how to avoid it."

"Come," said Aramis, "there's no point in fretting about it. How do we proceed?"

"I have a two-part plan," d'Artagnan replied.

"Let's hear the first part," said Aramis.

"You hold yourselves ready and await my signal, and when I give the word, each of us plunges a dagger into the heart of the soldier nearest to us. That puts four down right away, and evens the odds, as it leaves us four against five. These five surrender, and are bound and gagged, or they resist and are killed. If by any chance our host changes his mind and admits only Porthos and myself to the party, then, *dame!* We two will just have to do double the work. It will take longer and be louder, but you'll be nearby with swords and will rush in when you hear the commotion."

"But what if they overwhelm you?" said Athos.

"Ha!" said d'Artagnan. "These beer-drinkers are too heavy and awkward. Besides, Porthos will punch them in the throat, and they'll be killed before they can make a sound."

"Sounds good!" said Porthos. "We'll have a jolly little massacre."

"Dreadful!" said Athos. "Dreadful!"

"Bah! Monsieur the sensitive," said d'Artagnan, "you'd kill that many or more without hesitation in a battle. Besides, friend," he continued, "if you think the king's life isn't worth that price, just say so, and I'll send to Groslow to say I'm too sick to come."

"No," said Athos. "No, I'm wrong, my friend, and you're right. Forgive me."

At that moment the door opened, and a soldier appeared on the threshold. "Monsieur le Capitaine Groslow," he said in terrible French, "sends to advise Monsieur d'Artagnan and Monsieur du Vallon that he awaits them."

"Where?" asked d'Artagnan.

"In the quarters of the English Nebuchadnezzar," replied the soldier, a confirmed Puritan.

"Very good," Athos replied in excellent English, though a flush had risen on his face at this insult to royal majesty. "Tell Captain Groslow we're on our way."

The Puritan departed. The lackeys had been ordered to saddle eight horses, to stay mounted, and to keep together, in the street around the corner about twenty paces from the king's lodging.

XX

The Lansquenet Party

By that time, it was nine in the evening; the previous guards had been relieved at eight, and Captain Groslow's squad had been on duty for an hour.

D'Artagnan and Porthos, armed with their swords, and Athos and Aramis, each with a poniard hidden in his doublet, made their way toward the house that served as the prison of Charles Stuart. The latter two, humble and apparently disarmed, followed their conquerors like captives.

"Faith," Groslow said when he saw them, "I'd almost given up on you."

D'Artagnan approached him and said in a low voice, "In fact, Monsieur du Vallon and I were hesitant to come."

"But why?" asked Groslow.

D'Artagnan nodded toward Athos and Aramis.

"Ah!" said Groslow. "Because of their royalist sympathies? No matter. On the contrary," he said, laughing, "since they love the Stuart, let them see him."

"Will we spend the evening in the king's chamber?" asked d'Artagnan.

"Not there, but in the next room—and as the connecting door will remain open, it'll be exactly as if we were in his chamber. Did you bring enough money? Because I declare I intend to gamble like the devil tonight."

"Hear this?" said d'Artagnan, jingling the gold in his pockets.

"Ah, very good!" said Groslow, opening the door into the room. "I only precede you to show you the way, Gentlemen," he said, going in first.

D'Artagnan glanced at his friends. Porthos was as nonchalant as if this were an ordinary card party; Athos was pale but resolute; Aramis mopped his brow with a handkerchief.

The eight guards were at their posts: four were in the king's chamber, two at the connecting door, and two at the door through which the four friends entered. At the sight of their naked swords, Athos smiled, for that would make it a mêlée, not a massacre. From that moment his good humor returned.

Charles, whom they could see through the open door, was lying on his bed fully dressed, under a simple wool throw blanket. At his bedside, Parry sat reading a chapter from a Catholic Bible in a voice that was quiet, but loud enough for the king to hear. A coarse tallow candle, placed nearby on a black table, illuminated the king's resigned face, and the far more troubled face of his loyal servant. From time to time Parry paused, thinking that the king might have fallen asleep, but each time the king opened his eyes, smiled, and said, "Continue, my good Parry, I'm listening."

Groslow advanced to the threshold of the king's chamber, putting back on the hat he'd removed to receive his guests, looking for a moment with contempt at the simple and touching tableau of the old servant reading the Bible to his captive king. He made sure every man was at his assigned post, and, turning back to d'Artagnan, looked triumphantly at the Frenchman as if inviting a compliment on his tactics.

"Well done," said the Gascon. "*Cap de Diou!* You'd make a distinguished general."

"And do you think," asked Groslow, "that while I'm guarding him there's any chance the Stuart could be rescued?"

"Absolutely not," replied d'Artagnan, "unless an army of his friends rained down from heaven."

Groslow beamed with pleasure.

As Charles Stuart's eyes were closed throughout this exchange, it was impossible to tell if he was aware of the Puritan captain's insolence. But when he heard d'Artagnan's distinctive accent, he opened his eyes in spite of himself. Parry, meanwhile, trembled and stopped reading. "Why have you stopped, Parry?" said the king. "Continue—unless you're too tired, of course."

"No, Sire," said the valet, and he resumed his reading.

A table was prepared in the outer room, with a tablecloth, two lit candles, cards, dice, and a pair of dice boxes. "Gentlemen," said Groslow to Athos and Aramis, "seat yourselves facing the Stuart, as I do, because I love to watch him in captivity. Sit there, Monsieur d'Artagnan, across from me."

Athos flushed with anger, but d'Artagnan frowned and gave him a look. "Fine," he said. "You, Monsieur le Comte de La Fère, sit to the right of Mister Groslow; you, Monsieur le Chevalier d'Herblay, to his left; you, du Vallon, next to me. You'll back me, and those gentlemen will back Mister Groslow."

So it was arranged: with Porthos to his left, d'Artagnan could signal him with his knee, and since Athos and Aramis were facing him, he could communicate to them with a look.

At the names of the Comte de La Fère and the Chevalier d'Herblay, Charles had opened his eyes and raised his head, taking in at a glance all the actors of the scene.

Just then Parry turned a few pages in his Bible and read aloud this verse from Jeremiah: "God said: 'Hearken to the words of my servants the prophets, whom I sent unto you, both rising up early and sending them, but ye have not hearkened.'"

The four friends exchanged glances. Parry's words indicated that he and the king recognized they were there and understood why they'd come. D'Artagnan's eyes sparkled.

"You asked me just now if I'd brought enough money?" said d'Artagnan, placing twenty pistoles on the table.

"Yes," said Groslow.

"Well," d'Artagnan replied, "it's my turn to ask you that. Haul out your cash, my dear Mister Groslow, for I tell you now I'm not leaving here until I've won it all from you."

"I'm not going down without a fight," said Groslow.

"All the better," said d'Artagnan. "To battle, my dear Captain, to battle! Whether you know it or not, that's what we've come for."

"I'm sure of that!" said Groslow with his coarse laugh. "I know it doesn't feel like a real game for you Frenchmen without a few bumps and bruises."

In fact, Charles had heard it all, and understood everything. A light flush rose to his cheeks. The soldiers who guarded him saw him gradually stretch his weary limbs, and on the pretense of excessive heat from a stove glowing nearly white, slowly put off the Scottish blanket under which he lay fully clothed.

Athos and Aramis trembled with suppressed joy on seeing that the king was lying dressed and ready.

The party began. That night fortune had changed in favor of Groslow, and he won every pot. A hundred pistoles passed from their side of the table to his. Groslow was almost giddy.

Porthos, who had lost the fifty pistoles he'd won the night before, plus thirty pistoles of his own, was sullen, and kept nudging d'Artagnan with his knee, as if asking if it wasn't time to play a different game. Athos and Aramis also watched d'Artagnan closely, but he remained impassive.

The clock struck ten. From outside came the sound of the sentries passing. "How many times do they make the rounds?" asked d'Artagnan, drawing two more pistoles from his pocket.

"Five," said Groslow, "once every two hours."

"Good," said d'Artagnan. "Very prudent." And he gave Athos and Aramis a meaningful look, while responding for the first time to Porthos's prodding with a nudge from his own knee.

Meanwhile, attracted by the flitting cards and the sight of gold, so magnetic to all men, the soldiers who were on duty in the king's chamber had one by one approached the door, where they stood, rising on tiptoe to watch over d'Artagnan's and Porthos's shoulders. The pair at the outer door also approached, which suited the purposes of the four friends, who much preferred having them close at hand to having to chase them to the four corners of the room. The two door sentries held naked swords, but they leaned on their points as they watched the players.

Athos seemed to grow calm as the moment approached, his white and aristocratic hands playing with a *louis d'or*, which he bent and straightened as easily as if the gold were tin. Less master of himself, Aramis kept fumbling at his doublet, while Porthos, who always hated losing, kept plying his knee.

D'Artagnan stretched and glanced behind him, seeing between two soldiers where Parry stood while Charles leaned on one elbow, his hands clasped and appearing to address God in fervent prayer. D'Artagnan realized the moment had come, that everyone was at their post and awaiting only the words, "At last!," which were to be the signal. He cast a preparatory glance at Athos and Aramis, who pushed their chairs back slightly to have greater freedom of movement. He gave a second nudge with his knee to Porthos, who stood as if to stretch his legs, meanwhile ensuring that his sword was loose in its scabbard.

"*Sacrebleu!*" said d'Artagnan. "Another twenty pistoles gone! Truly, Captain Groslow, your luck has been in, but it can't last." He drew twenty more pistoles from his pocket. "A final turn, Captain. These twenty pistoles on a single last turn of the cards."

"In, then, for twenty pistoles," said Groslow. And he turned two cards: a king for d'Artagnan, and an ace for himself.

"A king," said d'Artagnan. "It's a good omen. Master Groslow," he added, "beware of the king." And there was something strange in d'Artagnan's voice that sent a chill through his opponent.

Groslow began to go through the deck, turning cards; if he turned an ace, he won; but if a king came up first, he lost.

He turned a king.

"At last!" said d'Artagnan.

At these words Athos and Aramis rose, while Porthos took a step back.

Poniards and swords were about to shine out when suddenly the outer door opened and Colonel Harrison appeared on the threshold, accompanied by a man wrapped in a cloak. Behind the man, light glittered on the muskets of five or six soldiers.

Groslow rose hastily, ashamed of being caught with wine, cards, and dice. But Harrison paid no attention to him, marching into the king's chamber and saying, "Charles Stuart, an order has come that you are to be escorted to London without delay, riding day and night. Prepare to leave immediately."

"And in whose name is this order given?" asked the king. "That of General Oliver Cromwell?"

"Yes," said Harrison, "and here is Mister Mordaunt who has just brought it, and who is charged with its execution."

"Mordaunt!" murmured the four friends, exchanging looks.

D'Artagnan stooped over the table and swept all the money he and Porthos had lost into his deepest pocket, while Athos and Aramis moved around behind him. At this movement Mordaunt turned, recognized them, and uttered a cry of savage joy.

"How happy he is to see us," d'Artagnan said to his friends. "We might be caught."

"Not yet," said Porthos.

"Colonel! Colonel!" said Mordaunt. "Surround the house, you've been betrayed. These four Frenchmen escaped from Newcastle and must intend to rescue the king. Arrest them!"

"You'll find, young man," said d'Artagnan, drawing his sword, "that's an order easier to give than to execute." Then, whirling his blade, he cried, "At them, my friends!"

Then he rushed toward the door, knocking over the pair of soldiers who guarded it before they had time to raise their muskets. Athos and Aramis followed, with Porthos as rear guard, and before the soldiers, officers, and colonel had time to take a breath, all four were in the street.

"Fire!" cried Mordaunt. "Shoot them!"

Two or three muskets went off but had no more effect than to show by their flashes the four fugitives as they disappeared safely around the street corner.

The horses were at the appointed place; the lackeys had only to throw the bridles to their masters, who leapt into the saddles like the consummate horsemen they were. "Ride!" said d'Artagnan. "Spur on!"

They took off after d'Artagnan, returning along the route they'd come during the day, that is, back toward Scotland. The town had neither gates nor walls, so they no difficulty in leaving it.

Fifty paces beyond the last house, d'Artagnan stopped. "Halt!" he said.

"What do you mean, 'Halt'?" cried Porthos. "Don't you mean, 'Ride like the wind'?"

"Not at all," d'Artagnan replied. "This time we'll be closely pursued; let's watch them ride out of town and chase us up the road to Scotland. After they've passed, we'll go in the opposite direction."

A few yards away ran a stream, with a bridge across it; d'Artagnan led his horse down under the arch, and his friends followed. They'd been there less than a minute before they heard the rapid gallop of an approaching troop of horsemen. Moments later, this troop passed over their heads, never suspecting that they were separated from those they sought by no more than the thickness of the bridge's arch.

XXI

London

When the noise of the horses was lost in the distance, d'Artagnan climbed up the bank of the stream, mounted, and began to ride across the fields, turning as much as possible toward London. His three friends silently followed, until they had ridden in a wide semicircle and left the town behind them.

"This time," said d'Artagnan, when he thought they were far enough from where they'd hidden to drop from a gallop to a trot, "this time I really think everything is lost, and the best thing we can do is to try to reach France. What do you think of that idea, Athos? Does that sound reasonable to you?"

"Reasonable, yes," Athos replied, "but I remind you that the other day you said something that sounded more admirable than reasonable, something noble and generous, when you said, 'Let us die here!'"

"Oh, death is nothing!" said Porthos. "Death shouldn't bother us, since we don't really know what it is. What tortures me is the idea of being beaten. The way things are going, we'd have to fight London, then the provinces, then all of England, and really we can't fail to lose in the end."

"We must follow this great tragedy to its conclusion, whatever it may be," said Athos. "We can't leave England until this is over. Do you think like I do, Aramis?"

"In every respect, my dear Count. And I must confess I look forward to the chance of once more meeting up with Mordaunt; it seems to me we have an account to settle with him, and it's not our practice to leave a matter without paying that sort of debt."

"Ah! Now that's something else," said d'Artagnan, "and there's a reason I can approve. I confess that if it meant meeting Mordaunt again, I'd be willing to wait in London for a year. Only let's find lodging with someone we can trust and where we can avoid suspicion, for at the moment Monsieur Cromwell is out for our blood, and from what I've seen, he doesn't joke around, this Cromwell. Athos, do you know of an inn in the city where we can find clean sheets, beef that isn't overcooked, and wine that isn't made with hops or juniper?"

"I think I can manage it," said Athos. "De Winter took us to a house run by a former Spaniard who is now a naturalized Englishman, thanks to the flow of guineas spent in his place by his new compatriots. What do you say, Aramis?"

"I say the idea of lodging at the house of Señor Perez sounds quite reasonable to me, and I endorse it. We'll invoke the memory of poor de Winter, whom Perez seemed to hold in high esteem. We'll tell him we're here as sightseers and observers, we'll each of us pay him a guinea a day, and with those precautions, I think we needn't worry."

"You did forget one precaution, Aramis," said d'Artagnan, "maybe the most important of all."

"What's that?"

"We must change the way we dress."

"Bah!" said Porthos. "Why should we change our clothes? I'm very comfortable in these!"

"So as not to be recognized," said d'Artagnan. "Our clothes are of a cut and color that says 'Frenchman' at first glance. Now, I'm not so attached to the cut of my doublet or the color of my breeches to risk, for love of them, being hanged at Tyburn or shipped off to the Indies. I'm going to buy myself a dark brown suit. I've noticed that these Puritan imbeciles dote on that color."

"But Athos, can you find your way back to the Spaniard's house?" said Aramis.

"Oh, absolutely! He lives in Green Hall Street, in Bedford's Tavern; I could find my way there with my eyes closed."

"I wish we were there already," said d'Artagnan. "My advice is that we get to London before dawn, even if it cripples our horses."

"Come, then," said Athos, "for unless my calculations are off, we can't be more than eight or ten leagues from there."

The friends rode their horses hard, and in fact arrived by five in the morning. At the city gate they were stopped by a sentry, but Athos told him in excellent English that they had been sent ahead by Colonel Harrison to notify his colleague Colonel Pride[29] of the imminent arrival of the king. This response elicited some questions about the taking of the king, but Athos gave such precise and positive details that if the guardians of the gate had any suspicions, they were quelled. The four friends were passed through amid all sorts of puritanical congratulations.

Athos had spoken truly—he led them right to Bedford's Tavern, where he reintroduced himself to the host. Perez was delighted to see him return with so many prosperous-looking guests, and gave orders to have his best rooms made ready.

Though it was barely daylight, our four travelers, upon arriving in London, had found the entire city in an uproar. The rumor that the king, escorted by Colonel Harrison, was approaching the capital, had spread since the day before, and many citizens had stayed up all night in hopes of catching a glimpse of the Stuart, as they called him, making his entrance.

The precaution of changing their clothing had been adopted unanimously, after some opposition from Porthos, and they put the plan into immediate execution. The host sent out for a variety of clothes on approval, as if he wanted to stock up his wardrobe. Athos donned a black suit that gave him the look of an honest bourgeois; Aramis, who didn't want to give up his sword, chose a dark outfit in a military cut; Porthos couldn't resist a red doublet and green breeches; while d'Artagnan, who'd already settled on his color, found just the dark brown suit he had in mind, which made him look like a retired sugar merchant.

As for Grimaud and Mousqueton, since they didn't wear livery, they were already in disguise; Grimaud looked like the calm, dry, and cautious kind of Englishman, while Mousqueton resembled the portly and complacent sort.

"Now for the important part," said d'Artagnan. "To avoid the insults of the populace, we must cut our hair. As we are no longer gentlemen of the sword, we must be Puritans of the hairstyle. It is, as you know, the key distinction between Covenanter and Cavalier."

But on this point, key distinction or not, Aramis stubbornly refused. He was determined to keep his hair, which was very handsome and of which he took the greatest care. It took Athos, who didn't care about such things, to set the example. Porthos submitted without difficulty to the ministrations of Mousqueton, who took some shears to his master's coarse and heavy mane. D'Artagnan gave himself a fanciful cut that made him look like a head on a medal from the times of François I or Charles IX.

"We look frightful," said Athos.

"So awful even a Puritan would shudder," said Aramis.

"I feel a chill on my scalp," said Porthos.

"And me, I feel like singing a psalm," said d'Artagnan.

"Now that we can't even recognize ourselves," said Athos, "and therefore have no fear of being recognized by others, let's go watch the entrance of the king. If they pushed on through the night, they can't be far from London."

They joined the waiting crowds, and after less than two hours loud shouts and commotion announced the arrival of Charles I. A carriage had been sent to meet him, and while it was still somewhat distant the gigantic Porthos, who was a head taller than the crowd around him, declared he could see the royal carriage approaching. D'Artagnan stood on tiptoe, trying to see, while Athos and Aramis listened to the those around them to hear their opinions. As the carriage passed, d'Artagnan recognized Harrison riding at one door and Mordaunt at the other. As for the people, Athos and Aramis heard nothing but insults and imprecations toward Charles.

Athos returned to the tavern in despair. D'Artagnan shook his head. "To persist seems pointless, and in fact I told you the situation was bad. As for me, I intend to stick with it, mostly for your sake, but also because I have a certain artistic interest in politics *à la mousquetaire*. It would be very satisfying to snatch their prey away from these louts and laugh at them. I'll give the idea some thought."

The next day, from the window that gave out onto the most populous parts of the city, Athos heard cried the Bill of Parliament that arraigned the ex-King Charles I, accusing him of treason and abuse of power. D'Artagnan stood by his side, while behind them Aramis consulted a map. Porthos was absorbed in finishing the final bites of a delicious breakfast.

"Parliament!" cried Athos. "Parliament couldn't possibly have passed such a bill!"

"Listen," said d'Artagnan, "I understand very little English, but as English is nothing but French very badly pronounced, when I hear, '*Parliament's bill*,' that must mean a bill of Parliament, or '*God damn me*,' as they say here."

Just then the host came in; Athos beckoned him to approach. "Has Parliament really passed this bill?" Athos asked in English.

"Yes, Milord—the Purified Parliament."

"The *Purified* Parliament! Are there two parliaments, then?"

"Friend host," interrupted d'Artagnan, "as I don't understand English, but we all understand Spanish, do us the pleasure to converse in that language. It's your native tongue, so you must enjoy speaking it when you get a chance."

"By all means," said Aramis.

As for Porthos, as we said, his attention was concentrated on a lamb chop he was occupied in picking clean.

"You were asking?" said the host in Spanish.

"We're asking," Athos replied in the same language, "about these two parliaments, the pure and the impure."

"Why, how bizarre!" said Porthos, slowly raising his head and looking at his friends in astonishment. "Suddenly I can understand English! I could follow every word you said."

"That's because we're speaking Spanish, old friend," said Athos with his usual sangfroid.

"Ah! The devil!" said Porthos. "What a shame—I thought I'd added a new language."

"When I say the Pure Parliament, Señor," replied the host, "I mean the one that Colonel Pride has purified."

"Ah ha!" said d'Artagnan. "Really, these people are quite ingenious; when we return to France I must recommend this means to Monsieur de Mazarin and Monsieur le Coadjuteur. The one will purify in the name of the Court, the other in the name of the People, and soon there will be no parliament at all."

"Who is this Colonel Pride," asked Aramis, "and how did he go about purifying the Parliament?"

"Colonel Pride," said the Spaniard, "is an old carter, a very clever man who had noticed something when driving his cart: when there was a stone blocking the way, it was easier to remove the stone than to try to drive the wheel over it. Of the two hundred fifty-one Members of Parliament, one hundred and ninety-one embarrassed him by blocking the wheel of his political cart. He picked them up as if they were stones and threw them out of the House."

"Bravo!" said d'Artagnan, who esteemed cleverness wherever he encountered it.

"And all those expelled were Stuartists?" asked Athos.

"Indeed, Señor, because you understand, they would have tried to save the king."

"*Pardieu!*" said Porthos, waving his fingers. "By my count, they made a majority."

"And you think," said Aramis, "that Charles will consent to appear before such a tribunal?"

"He'll have no choice," said the Spaniard. "If he tries to refuse, the people will force him."

"Thank you, Master Perez," said Athos. "That's what I needed to know."

"Do you begin to believe at last this is a lost cause, Athos?" said d'Artagnan. "Against such as these Harrisons, Joyces, Prides, and Cromwells, how could we defeat them?"

"It seems clear the king will be delivered to the tribunal," said Athos. "This 'purification' has silenced his partisans."

D'Artagnan shrugged his shoulders.

"But surely," said Aramis, "if they condemn the king, it will be to exile or prison, no more."

D'Artagnan gave a skeptical little whistle.

"We shall see," said Athos, "because we'll attend the hearings, I presume."

"You won't have long to wait," said the host. "They begin tomorrow."

"*Ah çà!*" said Athos. "Were the proceedings arranged before the king was even taken?"

"Must have been, starting from the day he was bought," said d'Artagnan.

"And you know," said Aramis, "that it was our friend Mordaunt who, if he didn't finalize the deal, at least made the first overtures in that little affair."

"Monsieur Mordaunt again," said d'Artagnan. "The first time he falls under my hand, I think I'll kill him."

"Bah!" said Athos. "That miserable wretch?"

"It's precisely because he is such a wretch that I'll kill him," said d'Artagnan. "Ah, my friend! I've done your will often enough you should indulge me in mine. So this time, whether you like it or not, that wretch Mordaunt is a dead man. I swear it."

"As do I," said Porthos.

"As do I," said Aramis.

"So voted, so approved!" cried d'Artagnan. "And quite suited to our roles as citizens and bourgeois. Now how about a walk around town? Not even Mordaunt would recognize us from four paces away in the kind of fog they have here. Let's go take in some fog."

"Yes," said Porthos, "it'll be a nice change from beer."

And the four friends went out to, as they say, take in the local air.

XXII

The Trial

The next day Charles I was conducted by a large detail of guards to the court where he would be judged.

The crowd thronged the streets and houses surrounding Westminster Hall;[30] reaching the area, the four friends were blocked by the nearly impassable obstacle of this living wall. Some swaggering rowdies in this crowd insulted Aramis so rudely that Porthos raised his formidable fist and brought it down on the floury face of a baker, instantly changing it from white to red as his features burst like crushed grapes. This caused a great commotion; three men attacked Porthos, but Athos knocked aside the first, d'Artagnan the second, and Porthos threw the third over his head. Many of the English, who are connoisseurs of boxing, admired these maneuvers and clapped enthusiastically. Instead of being overwhelmed by the mob, as they'd feared, they suddenly found the crowd prepared to hoist Porthos and his friends to their shoulders in triumph—but the four travelers, fearing to draw attention to themselves, managed to decline the honor. Yet they gained one thing by their Herculean exploit, in that the crowd opened before them, and they succeeded in doing that which moments before had seemed impossible, that is, to get close to the hall.

All London was pushing through the gates to the galleries, so that when the four friends finally got inside, they found the first three rows of benches already full. That was small loss to people who didn't want to be recognized, so they took places toward the rear and were happy with them—with the exception of Porthos, who'd wanted to show off his red doublet and green breeches and was sorry they weren't in the front row.

The benches were arranged as in an amphitheater, and from their location the four friends looked down on the entire assembly. By chance they had entered the central gallery, and found themselves facing the defendant's chair prepared for Charles I.

At about eleven in the morning the king appeared from a rear doorway. He entered surrounded by guards, but with an air of quiet dignity. As he looked around the hall he seemed confident and self-possessed, as if he were presiding over an assembly of submissive subjects, rather than answering the accusations of a rebel court.

The judges, proud of having a king to humiliate, were eager to begin abusing the rights they'd usurped. They sent an usher to inform Charles I that it was customary for the accused to remove his hat when before his judges.

Charles said not a word, just sat his broad-brimmed hat more firmly on his head, then turned and looked aside. When the usher had withdrawn, the king sat down on the defendant's chair facing the president, tapping at his boot with a riding crop he held in one hand. Parry, who'd entered with him, stood behind the chair.

D'Artagnan, instead of watching these ceremonies, was looking at Athos, whose face reflected all the emotions which the king, who had to control himself, managed to suppress. Athos was usually so cool and calm that this agitation worried him. He leaned toward Athos's ear and said, "I hope you're going to follow the example of His Majesty and not get yourself killed in this death trap."

"Don't worry," said Athos.

"Look around," continued d'Artagnan, "they're certainly afraid of something: the guards have been doubled, and the additional troops are armed, not with halberds, but muskets. That way they're ready for anything—the halberds are to keep back the crowd, but the muskets are for us."

"Thirty, forty, fifty . . . seventy men," said Porthos, counting the newcomers.

"Ho!" said Aramis. "Don't forget to count their commander, Porthos, as it seems to me he's one you don't want to miss."

"By God!" said d'Artagnan. And he turned pale with anger, for he'd recognized Mordaunt, who stood with naked sword commanding the musketeers behind the king, that is, facing the galleries. "Has he recognized us?" he continued. "If so, we should beat a quick retreat. I don't mind dying, but not in this trap—I'll choose my own death, not be shot like a fish in a barrel."

"No, he hasn't seen us," said Aramis. "He sees no one but the king. *Mordieu!* How he glares, the insolent dog. Does he hate His Majesty as much as he hates us?"

"*Pardieu!*" said Athos. "We took only his mother from him; the king robbed him of his name and fortune."

"That's right," said Aramis. "But hush! The president is rising to speak to the king."

President Bradshaw addressed the august defendant. "Stuart," he said, "listen as your parliamentary judges are named to you, and then address your observations to the tribunal."

The king, as if these words were spoken to someone else, turned his head and looked away.

The president waited, and as no answer came, he was silent for a moment. Out of one hundred and sixty-three Members of Parliament, only seventy-three were present, as the others, frightened by the idea of complicity in such an act, had stayed away. "Proceed with the trial," said Bradshaw, disregarding the absence of three-fifths of the assembly. And he began to name the members, present or absent. Those present responded in a voice strong or weak, depending on the courage of their convictions. The name of each absent member was followed by a short silence before the name was repeated.

The name of Colonel Fairfax[31] was spoken in its turn, and followed by the short, somber silence that denounced those absent members who didn't want to take part in this trial. "Colonel Fairfax?" Bradshaw repeated.

"Fairfax?" replied a mocking voice, which by its silvery tone was that of a woman. "He has the good sense to be elsewhere."

A huge burst of laughter greeted these words spoken with the audacity that women use to exploit their own weakness, that weakness that exempts them from retaliation.

"That's a woman's voice," said Aramis. "By my faith! I'd wager she's both young and pretty." He climbed a few steps higher to get a better view of the gallery the voice had come from. "Upon my soul," he said, "she is charming! See, d'Artagnan, how everyone is looking at her, and despite Bradshaw's glare, her chin is still high."

"That's Lady Fairfax herself," said d'Artagnan. "Remember her, Porthos? We saw her with her husband at General Cromwell's."

After a moment, the calm interrupted by this wry episode was restored, and the roll call resumed. "Once these clowns see that they lack the numbers for a quorum, they'll be forced to adjourn," said the Comte de La Fère.

"You still don't know them, Athos. Look at how Mordaunt smiles as he stares at the king. Does he look like a man who's worried that his victim will escape? No, that's the smile of hatred satisfied, of vengeance sure and certain. Ah, you evil basilisk! It'll be a happy day when I'm able to cross you with something more than just a look!"

"The king makes a handsome showing," said Porthos. "See how well turned out he is, despite being a prisoner. Why, the plume on his hat is worth at least fifty pistoles—look at it, Aramis."

With the roll call complete, the president gave the order to proceed to the reading of the indictment. Athos paled; he'd deluded himself once more. Even without sufficient members to sit as judges, the trial was to proceed—which could only mean the king had been condemned in advance.

"I warned you, Athos," said d'Artagnan, shrugging his shoulders. "But you're always so skeptical. Now I beg you, summon all your courage and listen without exploding when you hear all the petty horrors that man in black, with full license and privilege, is about to ascribe to the king."

In fact, never had more brutal accusations, never had such base insults, never had such a bloody indictment been brought against royal majesty. Previous generations had been content to simply assassinate their kings, saving all these insults for their corpses.

Charles I listened to the prosecutor's speech attentively, ignoring the abuse, overlooking the insults, disregarding the grievances, and when the litany of hatred reached its height, the prosecutor threatening almost to assume the role of executioner in advance, the king's only response was a contemptuous smile. It was, nonetheless, a terrible litany, in which the unhappy king heard all his indiscretions called conspiracies, and his mistakes denounced as crimes.

D'Artagnan, who let this torrent of insult go by with the disdain it deserved, nonetheless took note of some of the prosecutor's accusations. "The fact is," he said, "that if one punished kings for imprudence and folly, this poor king has earned some punishment; but it seems to me that what he's suffering here is quite cruel enough."

"In any case," replied Aramis, "the punishment shouldn't fall on the king, but on his ministers, since the first law of the English constitution is, *the king can do no wrong.*"

As for me, thought Porthos, looking at Mordaunt and thinking of nothing but him, *if it wouldn't disrupt the solemnity of this occasion, I'd jump from the gallery to the floor, be on Mordaunt in three bounds, and wring his neck. Then I'd swing him by the feet and knock down all those phony musketeers, those mockeries of the Musketeers of France. In the meantime d'Artagnan, who's smart and quick, would have found a way to rescue the king. Maybe I should speak to him about it.*

Meanwhile Athos, with his face flushed, fists clenched, and lips bitten bloody, was squirming on the bench, enraged by this protracted parliamentary insult and royal torment; the man of iron arm and mighty heart was reduced to a trembling frame with shaking hands.

Finally, the prosecutor finished his indictment, saying, "These charges are brought in the name of the English people."

There were murmurs from the galleries, and another voice, not female this time, but male and furious, thundered from behind d'Artagnan: "You lie! And nine-tenths of the English people hear your words in horror!"

It was the voice of Athos, who was beside himself, standing with arm outstretched, pointing in accusation at the accuser.

At this disruption king, judges, spectators, all turned their eyes to the gallery containing the four friends. Mordaunt turned like the others and recognized the gentleman around whom the other Frenchmen had risen, pale and menacing. His eyes flashed with grim joy as he realized he'd found those to whose death his life was devoted. With a furious gesture he called his twenty musketeers to arms, pointed to the benches where his enemies stood, and said, "Fire into that gallery!"

But then, quick as thought, d'Artagnan lifted Athos bodily, Porthos grabbed up Aramis, and they jumped down the steps, rushed out the corridor, hustled down the stairs, and lost themselves in the crowd outside. Meanwhile within, lowered muskets threatened three thousand spectators, whose loud cries for mercy defused the incident before it escalated into mayhem.

Charles had also recognized the four Frenchmen; he put one hand to his heart to control its beating, and the other to his eyes so as not to see his faithful friends slaughtered.

Mordaunt, pale and trembling with rage, naked sword in hand, dashed out of the hall at the head of ten halberdiers, searching the crowd, interrogating everyone, but finally returning empty-handed.

The uproar was hard to suppress, and it was half an hour before anybody could be heard once again. The judges thought the galleries were going to erupt. The spectators in the galleries saw the muskets pointed their way, and, caught between fear and anger, continued to be loud and agitated.

Finally, calm was restored. "And what have you to say in your defense?" asked Bradshaw of the king.

Then, in the tone of one judging rather than being judged, his head still covered, and rising, not in humility, but in majesty, Charles said, "Before questioning me, answer me this: I was free at Newcastle, where by negotiation I had concluded a treaty with these Houses. Instead of fulfilling your part of this treaty, as I fulfilled mine, you bought me from the Scots—and cheaply, I know, which speaks well for your government's thrift. But having bought me like a slave, do you really hope that means I am no longer your king? It does not. To answer you would be to forget that. I will not answer until you have established your right to question me. To answer you would be to acknowledge you as my rightful judges, and I see in you only my executioners."

And in the midst of a deathly silence, Charles, calm, proud, his head still covered, sat back down in his chair.

"Where are they, my Frenchmen?" murmured Charles, turning his eyes toward the gallery where he'd seen them for a moment. "I would like them to see that their friend, living, is worth defending—and dead, is worth weeping for." But in vain he scanned the crowd, asking God where to find those noble and consoling countenances—but he saw only stunned and fearful faces, and felt he was trapped between horror and hatred.

"Well, then," said the president, seeing that Charles was determined to remain unmoved, "we will judge you despite your silence. You are accused of treason, abuse of power, and assassination. The witnesses will swear to it. Therefore go, but at the next session we will address what you refuse to acknowledge this time."

Charles rose and turned toward Parry, whom he found pale and sweating. "But, my dear Parry," he said, "what's wrong? What agitates you so?"

"Oh, Sire!" said Parry, in a trembling voice, and with tears in his eyes. "Sire, while leaving the hall, please don't look to your left."

"Why is that, Parry?"

"Never mind, just do as I beg, my King!"

"But what is it?" said Charles, trying to see through the hedge of guards that surrounded him.

"It's just—you won't look, Sire, will you?—it's just that they've placed, on a table there, the axe they use to execute criminals. I beg you, Sire, don't look. It's hideous!"

"The fools!" said Charles. "Do they think I'm as cowardly as they are? Still, it was good of you to warn me; thank you, Parry." And then, the time having come to withdraw, the king went out amidst his guards.

To the left of the door, in fact, placed on a red carpet on a long table, shone the great white headsman's axe with its long haft well polished by the hands of the executioner. Arriving in front of it, Charles stopped, turned toward it with a laugh, and said, "Ah ha! The axe! Trying to play Scare-Me-Crow might seem a good idea to those who don't understand gentlemen—but you can't frighten me with an executioner's axe," he sneered, whipping it with his riding crop. "Thus, I strike you, and will now wait patiently like a Christian for you to return the blow."

And shrugging his shoulders he continued on his way, leaving stupefied those who'd crowded around the table to see what the king's face would look like when he saw the axe that was to separate his head from his body.

"Really, Parry," continued the king, "God forgive me! But these people seem to take me for a cotton merchant from the Indies rather that a gentleman accustomed to the shine of steel; do they think I have less nerve than a butcher?"

As he said these words, he arrived at the door to the street. A long line of people pressed forward, folk who, unable to gain admittance to the galleries, still wished to see the end of the spectacle even if they'd missed the most interesting part. The sight of this numberless multitude, studded with menacing faces, drew a sigh from the king. *So many people*, he thought, *and not a single faithful friend!*

But just as he thought these words of doubt and discouragement, a voice rang out from nearby, "Long live his fallen Majesty!"

The king turned eagerly, heart leaping and tears springing to his eyes. Before him was an old soldier of his guards who hadn't wanted to see his captive king pass by without paying him this final tribute.

But the next moment the unlucky man was struck down by the pommel of a sword wielded by a man the king recognized as Captain Groslow. "Alas!" said Charles. "Such a severe punishment for a minor fault."

Then, with a heavy heart, he went on his way, but he hadn't gone a hundred paces more before a furious fanatic, bursting between two soldiers in his hatred, spat in the king's face, as once an infamous Jew had spat in the face of Jesus of Nazareth.

Bursts of laughter and bitter insults sounded out together; the crowd surged back, then forward, heaving like a stormy sea, and for a moment it seemed to the king that in the middle of this living wave he saw the sparkling eyes of Athos. Charles wiped his face and said with a sad smile, "The poor churl! For a half-crown he'd have done the same to his own father."

He hadn't been mistaken; he really had seen Athos who, with his friends, were mingling with the mob to escort the royal martyr for a final time.

When the old soldier had saluted Charles, Athos's heart had swelled with joy, and when the beaten man came to, he found ten guineas in his pocket that had been placed there by the French gentleman. However, when the insolent churl spat in the prisoner's face, Athos had put his hand on his dagger.

But d'Artagnan clapped his hand over Athos's and said in a hoarse voice, "Wait!"

Never before had d'Artagnan given a direct command to the Comte de La Fère. Athos stopped himself. D'Artagnan gripped Athos by the arm, gestured to Porthos and Aramis to stay close, and took a position behind the angry lout, who was still laughing about his crude jest and being congratulated by some other fanatics.

The man began making his way toward the City of London. D'Artagnan followed, still gripping Athos's arm, beckoning Porthos and Aramis to follow as well.

The churl, who looked like a butcher's apprentice, went with a couple of companions down a lonely and narrow street that ran toward the river. D'Artagnan released Athos's arm and marched up behind the man who'd spat on the king. Arriving at the river bank, the three men realized they were being followed, stopped, and looked insolently at the Frenchmen, exchanging some mocking jests with each other. "I don't speak English, Athos," said d'Artagnan, "but you do, so you must act as interpreter."

As he spoke, they rushed past the three men, then immediately turned, and d'Artagnan marched up to the butcher's apprentice. He prodded the man's chest with his index finger and said, "Tell him this, Athos. 'You've behaved like a coward; you've insulted a defenseless man; you've defiled the face of your king; and you're going to die.'"

Athos, pale as a specter, translated this speech to the man, who, seeing d'Artagnan's preparations and the look in his eye, assumed an attitude of defense. At this movement, Aramis put his hand to his sword. "No, no steel!" said d'Artagnan. "Steel is for gentlemen." And seizing the butcher by the throat, he said, "Porthos, punish this wretch with a single blow."

Porthos raised his mighty arm, it whistled through the air like a stone from a catapult, and the heavy mass fell with a dull thud on coward's skull, crushing it. The man fell like an ox under a sledgehammer.

The man's comrades wanted to cry out, to flee, but their voices failed them, and their trembling legs folded beneath them. "Tell them this, Athos," continued d'Artagnan. "Say, 'Thus die all those who forget that the life of a prisoner is sacred, and that a captive king is therefore twice the representative of the Lord.'"

Athos repeated d'Artagnan's words. The two men, mute, their hair standing on end, stared at the corpse of their comrade, who was swimming in a pool of his own black blood. Then, coming out of their paralysis, they clasped their hands in supplication, turned and ran.

"Justice is done!" said Porthos, wiping his forehead.

"And now," said d'Artagnan to Athos, "doubt me no more, and trust me on this: I hereby assume responsibility for our efforts on behalf of the king."

XXIII

Whitehall

The Parliament condemned Charles Stuart to death, as was all too predictable. Political trials are always mere formalities, for the same passions that drive the accusations result in condemnations. Such is the terrible logic of revolutions.

Though our friends expected this condemnation, it filled them with grief. D'Artagnan, whose wits were never so resourceful as in these extreme situations, swore anew that he would try every possible means to avoid a bloody outcome to this tragedy. But how? So far, he had only vague ideas. Everything depended on the nature of the circumstances. The judges had decided the execution was to take place the next day, so to gain time it was essential to prevent that execution until a proper plan could be made. The only recourse seemed to be to abduct the official London executioner. With the executioner gone, the sentence couldn't be carried out. No doubt they would send for one from the nearest city, but at least it would gain them a day, and a day gained in such a case might be salvation! D'Artagnan charged himself with this difficult task.

It was just as essential to warn Charles Stuart of the attempt to save him, so that he might assist his rescuers as much as possible, or at least do nothing to thwart their efforts. Aramis took on this dangerous task. Charles Stuart had asked that Bishop Juxon be permitted to visit him in his prison at Whitehall. Mordaunt had gone to the bishop that very evening to acquaint him with the king's religious wishes, and to inform him of Cromwell's assent. Aramis resolved to obtain from the bishop, by persuasion or intimidation, whatever he might need in sacerdotal clothing or regalia that would enable him to penetrate the palace of Whitehall.[32]

For his part, Athos undertook to arrange a means for them to leave England in a hurry, whether they succeeded or failed.

As night fell, they arranged to meet back at the inn at eleven o'clock, and then each went on his way to execute his hazardous mission.

Whitehall Palace was guarded by three regiments of cavalry, as well as the constant attention of Cromwell, who used it as his headquarters and was continually marching from one chamber to another, meeting his agents or generals.

The condemned monarch, alone in the inner of his two rooms, lit only by a pair of candles, mused sorrowfully upon his former grandeur, as one in his last hour recalls scenes from his life at their most vivid and sweet.

Parry, in the next room, never left his master, and since his condemnation had been weeping constantly.

Charles Stuart sat, leaning on a table, looking at a locket containing pictures of his wife and daughter. He was waiting, first for Bishop Juxon, and after Juxon, for martyrdom. Sometimes his thoughts strayed to those brave French gentlemen who already seemed a hundred leagues away, fabulous, chimerical, like those figures from dreams that fade once we awake. In fact sometimes Charles wondered if everything that had happened to him wasn't just a dream, or perhaps a delirium from fever. At this thought he got up, and to break out of his trance took a few steps toward the window; but beneath the window he saw the gleam of his guards' muskets and was forced to admit that he was awake and his bloody dream was real.

Charles returned silently to his chair, leaned once more on the table, let his head fall on his hand, and thought. "Alas!" he said to himself. "If I had at least as a confessor one of those lights of the Church whose soul has plumbed all the mysteries of life, from great to small, perhaps his words could silence the dark voice that laments in my soul. But they'll send me a priest of mean spirit, someone whose career and fortune I unwittingly thwarted. He'll speak to me of God and death as if I were any other dying man, without caring or understanding that this doomed king is leaving a throne to a usurper, while his children don't even have bread to eat." Then, lifting the locket to his lips, he whispered, one by one, the names of his children.

It was a night of fog and gloom. The hour slowly tolled from the belfry of a neighboring church. The pale flames of the two candles were reflected in the corners of the tall chamber as flickering glints that shivered like ghosts. These phantoms were the painted ancestors of King Charles, whom the flickers seemed to draw out from their gold-framed portraits. Their reflections joined the last bluish flickers of the hearth's dying coal fire.

A great sadness took hold of Charles. He buried his face in his hands, thinking of the world and how beautiful it seems when we're about to leave it, of the caresses of his children so soft and so sweet, whom he'd never see again, and of his wife, that noble and courageous creature who'd supported him to the very end. He drew from his bosom the diamond cross and the Star of the Garter that she'd sent him by those generous Frenchmen, and kissed them; then, thinking she would see these objects again only once he was lying cold and mutilated in his tomb, he felt pass through him one of those icy shudders that death sends when he begins to wrap us in his mantle.

Then, in that royal chamber which recalled to him so many memories, in which so many courtiers had uttered so many flatteries, alone but for a broken servant too frail to help him, the king despaired and allowed his courage to succumb to weakness, darkness, and the winter cold; and then, sad to say, this king who'd resolved to die grandly, with a smile of noble resignation on his lips, wept in the shadows tears that fell on the table and dropped to the gold embroidered carpet below.

Suddenly there were footsteps from the corridor, the door opened, torches filled the room with smoky light, and an ecclesiastic, garbed in episcopal robes, entered, followed by two guards to whom Charles made an imperious gesture. The guards withdrew, and the chamber returned to its former gloom. "Juxon!" cried Charles. "Juxon! Thank you, my final friend—you arrive just in time."

The bishop cast an anxious sidelong glance at the man who sobbed in the corner of the foyer. "Come, Parry," said the king, "cry no more, for the consolation of God has come to us."

"If that's just Parry," said the bishop, "then I won't worry—but, Sire, permit me to salute Your Majesty and tell him who I am, and why I've come."

At that sight, and that voice, Charles was about to exclaim, but Aramis put a finger to his lips, and bowed deeply to the King of England. "The chevalier," murmured Charles.

"Yes, Sire," interrupted Aramis, and then raising his voice, said, "yes, it's Bishop Juxon, loyal chevalier of Christ, who comes at Your Majesty's request."

Charles clasped his hands; he'd recognized d'Herblay, and was stunned by these men who, though foreigners, with no motive other than the duty imposed by their own conscience, struggled almost alone against the will of a people and the destiny of a king. "You!" he said. "How did you come here? My God, if they recognize you, you're lost."

Parry was on his feet, his entire person expressing his feeling of simple and profound admiration.

"Don't worry about me, Sire," said Aramis, gesturing to the king for quiet. "Just worry about yourself. Your friends are watching out for you. What we'll do, I don't know yet—but four determined men can do much. In the meantime, don't close your eyes tonight, be surprised by nothing, and expect almost anything."

Charles shook his head. "Friend," he said, "don't you know there's no time to lose, and that if you wish to act, it must be now? Don't you know that at ten tomorrow morning I must die?"

"Sire, something will happen between now and then that will make the execution impossible."

The king looked at Aramis in astonishment.

Just then there was a strange noise beneath the king's window, like a cartload of wood being dumped.

"Do you hear that?" said the king.

The sound was followed by a cry of pain.

"I hear it," said Aramis, "but I don't understand the noise, and especially the cry."

"I don't know who made that cry," said the king, "but I can account for the noise. Do you know that they plan to perform the execution right outside this window?" And Charles gestured toward the somber and empty courtyard, peopled solely by soldiers and sentries.

"Yes, Sire," said Aramis. "I know it."

"Well, that pile of lumber is made up of beams and planks to construct my scaffold. Some worker must have been hurt unloading it."

Aramis shuddered in spite of himself.

"So, you see," said Charles, "there's no point in being so stubborn; I am condemned, let me submit to my fate."

"Sire," said Aramis, recovering his composure, "though they may erect a scaffold, they won't find an executioner."

"What do you mean?" asked the king.

"I mean that as we speak, Sire, the executioner is being bribed or abducted. Tomorrow the scaffold will be ready, but the executioner will be missing, and they'll postpone it another day."

"And then?" said the king.

"And then," said Aramis, "tomorrow night we will carry you off."

"But how?" cried the king, whose face lit with joy in spite of himself.

"Oh, Monsieur!" murmured Parry, clasping his hands. "Be blessed, you and yours."

"But how?" repeated the king. "I must understand, so I can assist you, if necessary."

"I don't know, Sire," said Aramis, "but the most skillful, brave, and devoted of us said to me as I left, 'Chevalier, tell the king that by ten o'clock tomorrow night he'll be free.' If he said it, it will happen."

"Tell me the name of this devoted friend," said the king, "that I may think of him with gratitude, whether he succeeds or not."

"D'Artagnan, Sire, the same man who nearly saved you before Colonel Harrison made his untimely entrance."

"You are indeed wonderful men," said the king. "If I'd been told such things were possible, I wouldn't have believed them."

"Now, Sire," Aramis replied, "listen to me. Don't forget for a single instant that we're preparing to save you. Take note of every gesture, every whistled song, every tiny sign that we're near you; see all, hear all, and be ready."

"Oh, Chevalier!" said the king. "What can I say to you? No words, even from the depths of my heart, can express my gratitude. If you succeed, your success won't be that you saved a king—for royalty is not so very great a thing. It will be that you saved a husband for his wife, a father for his children. Take my hand, Chevalier—this is the hand of a friend who will love you till his last breath."

Aramis wished to kiss the king's hand, but the king seized the chevalier's hand and pressed it to his heart. Just then a man entered without even bothering to knock; Aramis tried to pull his hand away, but the king held onto it.

He who entered was one of those Puritans, half-preacher and half-soldier, who clustered around Cromwell. "What do you wish, Sir?" the king said to him.

"I want to know if the confession of Charles Stuart is finished," said the newcomer.

"What does that matter to you?" said the king. "We're not of the same religion."

"All men are brethren," said the Puritan. "One of my brethren is going to die, and I come to prepare him for death."

"Enough," said Parry. "The king doesn't need your preparations."

"Be careful, Sire," Aramis said in a low voice, "he's probably a spy."

"After the reverend bishop leaves," said the king, "I shall hear you with pleasure, Sir."

The man narrowed his eyes and withdrew, but not before taking a good look at the supposed Juxon, a look that hadn't escaped the king. When the door was closed, he said, "Chevalier, I think you were right, and that man entered with evil intentions. Take care, and watch yourself on your way out."

"I thank Your Majesty," said Aramis, "but don't worry: under this robe I wear a coat of mail and a dagger."

"Go then, Monsieur, and may God keep you in safety, as I used to say when I was king."

Aramis went out; Charles escorted him to his door. Aramis pronounced his holy blessing, at which the guards bowed, passed majestically through the antechambers filled with soldiers, entered his carriage, followed by his two guards, who rode with him back to the bishopric, where they left him. Juxon was waiting there anxiously. "Well?" he said upon seeing Aramis.

"Well!" said the latter. "Everything went as planned; spies, guards, sentries, all took me for you, and the king blesses you while waiting for you to bless him."

"God protects you, my son, and your example has given me both hope and courage."

Aramis returned Juxon his robes and mantle and went out, after warning the bishop that they might have to rely upon him again.

He'd gone no more than ten steps up the street before he noticed he was being followed by a man wrapped in a large cloak. He stopped and put his hand on his dagger. But the man came straight up to him—and it was Porthos. "My dear friend!" said Aramis, taking his hand.

"You see, friend" said Porthos, "each of us has his mission; mine was to guard you, so you've been guarded. Have you seen the king?"

"Yes, and all is well. Now, where are the others?"

"We're to rendezvous at eleven o'clock at the inn."

"Then we have no time to lose," said Aramis.

In fact, half past ten was tolling from the bells of Saint Paul. The two friends hurried, and so arrived first. Athos came in right behind them. "All is well," he said, before they had a chance to ask him.

"What have you been doing?" said Aramis.

"I've hired a little sloop, slim as a felucca and light as a swallow. It awaits us at Greenwich, across from the Isle of Dogs; it has a captain and four crew, who, for fifty pounds sterling, will be at our disposal for the next three nights. Once we board with the king, we'll sail with the tide, slip down the Thames, and be on the open sea within two hours. Then like true pirates we'll hug the coast, or if the sea is clear we'll make for Boulogne. In case I'm killed, the name of the captain is Rogers, and the sloop is the *Lightning*. A handkerchief with its four corners knotted is the recognition sign."

A moment later d'Artagnan came in. "Reach into your pockets," he said, "because we need a hundred pounds sterling—and as for mine . . ." He turned his empty pockets inside out.

Within seconds, the sum was collected. D'Artagnan took it, went back out, and returned again a moment later. "There!" he said. "That's done. Whew! This is no easy task."

"The executioner has left London?" asked Athos.

"Well, no! That was too uncertain a solution—he might go out one door and come back in another."

"So, where is he?" asked Athos.

"In the cellar."

"In what cellar?"

"In the cellar of our inn! Mousqueton is posted in front of the door, and here's the key."

"Bravo!" said Aramis. "But how did you persuade the man to disappear?"

"The way you persuade everyone in this world, with money. It cost me dearly, but he agreed."

"And how much did it cost you, friend?" said Athos. "Because you know, now that we're once again like poor musketeers without house or home, all our expenses should be shared."

"It cost me twelve thousand livres," said d'Artagnan.

"Where ever did you find that?" asked Athos. "You had that much money?"

"No, but I had the queen's famous diamond!" d'Artagnan said with a sigh.

"Ah, that's true!" said Aramis. "I'd recognized it on your finger."

"You bought it back from Monsieur des Essarts?" asked Porthos.

"In a way," said d'Artagnan. "But it's written on high that it's fated not to stay with me. What would you have? Diamonds, as I understand it, have their sympathies and antipathies just like people—and it seems this one just doesn't like me."

"Well, maybe it will like the executioner," said Athos. "So much for him—but mightn't he have an apprentice or an assistant?"

"Yes, he had one, but we got lucky there."

"How's that?"

"Just when I thought I was going to have to strike yet another bargain, the young buck returned home with a broken leg. In an excess of zeal, he'd gone all the way to the courtyard under the king's window with the lumber cart carrying the planks and beams for the scaffold, and one of those beams had fallen on his leg and broken it."

"Ah!" said Aramis. "That explains the cry I heard from the king's chambers."

"Probably," said d'Artagnan. "Anyway, when leaving, he promised the carpenters he'd send some hard-working friends to take his place and help them get the scaffold done in time. And so, upon returning to his master's house, wounded though he was, he wrote to his friend Tom Low, who has a crew of woodworkers, asking them to go to Whitehall to fulfill his promise. Here's the letter he sent by a courier—he paid the messenger ten pence, but I bought the message for a guinea."

"And what the devil do you want with this letter?" asked Athos.

"Don't you get it?" said d'Artagnan, his eyes shining with intelligence.

"No, upon my soul!"

"Well, my dear Athos, since you speak English like John Bull himself— *you* are Master Tom Low, and we are your three woodworkers. Do you get it now?"

Athos uttered a cry of joy and admiration, ran to a wardrobe, and began drawing out an assortment of work clothes and throwing them to his friends. As soon as they were properly dressed they left the inn, Athos carrying a saw, Porthos a vise, Aramis an axe, and d'Artagnan a hammer and nails.

At Whitehall, the letter from the executioner's apprentice proved to the master carpenter that these were the men he'd been expecting.

XXIV

The Workmen

Toward the middle of the night, Charles heard a commotion beneath his window, a great racket of hammering, chopping, and sawing. As he had thrown himself fully dressed on his bed, and was just falling asleep, the noise woke him with a start. And, as in addition to its physical repercussions the sounds struck a blow to his soul, the awful thoughts of the day just ended returned to assail him again. Alone in the face of darkness and isolation, he didn't have the strength to endure this new torment, which wasn't supposed to be part of his punishment, so he sent Parry to tell the sentry to please ask the laborers to work more quietly, and have pity on the final sleep of he who used to be their king.

The sentry didn't want to leave his post, but he allowed Parry to pass. After going out and around the palace to approach the window, Parry saw built to the level of the balcony, from which the railing had been removed, a large unfinished wooden scaffold, around which the workers were beginning to hang black serge drapery. This scaffold, raised to the height of the window, that is, about twenty feet, had two lower levels beneath it. Parry, though repelled by this sight, looked over the eight or ten workmen who were building this somber structure, the noise of which was disturbing the king, and on the second level he saw two men using a crowbar to remove the last metal anchors of the railing from the balcony; one of them, a veritable colossus, was like a human battering-ram, shattering stone at every stroke. The other, who stood just below him, cleared the debris as it fell. It was apparently these two who were making the noise of which the king complained.

Parry climbed a ladder and approached them. "My friends," he said, "could you work a little more gently, I pray you? The king is trying to get some sleep, which he desperately needs."

The man pounding with the crowbar stopped and half turned, but as the man was standing above him in shadow, Parry couldn't make out his face in the darkness under the scaffold. The man below him also turned, and as he was nearer and his face was lit by the lantern, Parry could see him. The man looked him in the eye and raised a finger to his lips. Parry recoiled, stupefied. "Sure, right," said the workman in excellent English. "Return and tell the king that if he sleeps poorly tonight, he'll sleep better tomorrow night."

These harsh words, which, if taken literally, had a terrible meaning, were greeted by the other workmen on the scaffold with a burst of mocking laughter. Parry withdrew, walking like a man in a dream.

Charles was waiting for him impatiently. As Parry reentered, the sentry at the door peeked in curiously through the opening to see what the king was doing. Charles was in bed, sitting up and leaning on one elbow.

Parry shut the door and went to the king, the valet's face radiant with joy. "Sire," he said in a low voice, "do you know who those workmen are who are making so much noise?"

"No," said Charles, shaking his head sadly. "How could I know that? Do I know those men?"

"Sire," said Charles, his voice even lower as he leaned on the bed toward his master, "it's the Comte de La Fère and his comrades."

"They're building my scaffold?" the king said, astonished.

"Yes, and while doing so, they're making a hole in the wall."

"Hush!" said the king, looking around him in terror. "Did you see them?"

"I talked to them."

The king clasped his hands and raised his eyes to heaven; then, after a short but fervent prayer, he jumped out of bed, went to the window, and drew aside the curtain. The sentries on the balcony were still there, but beyond the balcony extended a dark platform upon which human shadows moved. Charles couldn't make out any details, but beneath his feet he felt the thump of the blows struck by his friends. And each of these blows was now repeated by his heart.

Parry hadn't been mistaken, he had in fact recognized Athos. It was he who, aided by Porthos, was carving a hole that was supposed to anchor the end of one of the transverse framing beams. This hole opened into a sort of crawlspace just beneath the floor of the royal bedchamber. Once in this narrow crawlspace, one could, with a crowbar and a good set of shoulders, which Athos had, loosen one of the floorboards; the king could then slip through this opening, emerge under the scaffold which was surrounded by black drapes, dress in the worker's outfit they'd brought for him, and then simply walk out with his four companions. The unsuspecting sentries, seeing only workmen coming from the scaffold, would let them pass. And then, as we said, the sloop was ready and waiting.

The plan was bold, easy, and simple, like all the best plans born of desperate resolution. Enacting it, Athos lacerated his beautiful, aristocratic hands in clearing the stone shards ripped out by Porthos. Already he could fit his head through the gap beneath the carvings that edged the balcony. In two more hours, it would be big enough to admit his entire body. Before dawn, the opening would be finished, hidden behind the folds of an interior curtain d'Artagnan would hang. D'Artagnan had passed himself off as a French tapestry hanger and was nailing up the black cloth with the care of the most skillful draper. Aramis was cutting off the excess where it hung to the ground, concealing the framework of the scaffold.

Daylight crept over the roofs of the houses. A bonfire of coal and peat had helped the workmen pass that cold night of the 29th and 30th of January 1649; at any given moment several of the laborers were taking a break from the work and gathering near it to warm themselves. Only Athos and Porthos never interrupted their labors. And so, at morning's first gleam, the opening was finished. Athos crawled inside, carrying with him the clothes intended for the king, wrapped in a bolt of black cloth. Porthos passed him the crowbar, and d'Artagnan hung over the hole a large but essential luxury, the curtain that concealed the opening.

Athos now had no more than two hours' work ahead of him before reaching the king—but thanks to the precautions taken by the four friends, they thought they had the whole day ahead of them, since, with the executioner missing, another would have to be summoned from Bristol.

Their work done, d'Artagnan resumed his brown suit, and Porthos his red doublet; as to Aramis, he went to visit Juxon, to go in with him, if possible, to visit the king. The three agreed to rendezvous at noon outside Whitehall to see what was going on.

Before leaving the scaffold, Aramis had approached the opening behind which Athos was hidden, to tell him he was going to try to visit Charles. "Goodbye then, and take heart," said Athos. "Tell the king what's happening and ask him to rap on the floor when he's alone, so I can continue my work in safety. If Parry could assist me by removing or loosening the hearthstone at the base of the chimney, which is probably a marble slab, that would be a big help. You, Aramis, should try to stay near the king. Speak loudly, very loudly, because they'll be listening beyond the door. When the time comes, if there's a single sentry inside the suite, kill him out of hand. If there are two, have Parry kill one while you kill the other; if there are three, die yourself if you must, but save the king."

"Never fear," said Aramis. "I'll bring two poniards so I can give one to Parry. Is that all?"

"Yes, go. But advise the king not to succumb to false generosity. If there's a struggle, while you're fighting, he must flee. With the hearthstone replaced over his head, and you dead or alive on top of it, it will take them at least ten minutes to find the hole by which he escaped. In ten minutes we can go far, and the king will be saved."

"It will be done as you say, Athos. Give me your hand, for we may never see each other again."

Athos threw his arms around Aramis's neck and hugged him tightly. "That's for you," he said. "Now, if I die, tell d'Artagnan that I love him like a son, and embrace him for me. Embrace also our good and brave Porthos. Adieu."

"Adieu," said Aramis. "I'm as sure now that the king will be saved as I'm sure that I've just shaken the most loyal hand in the world."

Aramis left Athos, went down from the scaffold in his turn, and returned to the inn whistling a popular pro-Cromwell tune. He found the other two seated near a good fire, drinking a bottle of port and eating cold chicken. Porthos ate while muttering insults about the infamous parliamentarians; d'Artagnan ate in silence, while reviewing the situation and considering contingency plans.

Aramis told them what he and Athos had agreed; d'Artagnan nodded in approval, and Porthos said, "Bravo! Besides, we'll be nearby when he makes his escape; there's plenty of room to hide under the scaffold. Between d'Artagnan, me, Grimaud, and Mousqueton, we can kill eight of his pursuers while you get away with the king; I don't count Blaisois, as he's only good for holding the horses. At a minute a man, that's eight minutes—though Mousqueton will kill only one, so that's seven. Still, in seven minutes you'll be able to ride a quarter of a league."

Aramis quickly ate a few bites, downed some wine, and went to change his clothing. "I'm off to the bishop's. Take charge of readying the weapons, Porthos; d'Artagnan, keep an eye on that executioner."

"Don't worry, Grimaud has relieved Mousqueton, and he's got it in hand."

"Nonetheless, redouble your watch, and don't be idle for a moment."

"Idle! My dear Aramis, ask Porthos: I don't stop for a moment, and I'm on my feet so much, I might as well be a dancer. *Mordioux!* How I love France at this moment, and how good it is to have a country of one's own, when one finds life so hard elsewhere."

Aramis left them as he'd left Athos, by embracing them. Then he went to see Bishop Juxon, to whom he made his request. Juxon quickly consented to bringing Aramis with him, as he'd foreseen the need to bring a deacon in the event the king wished to receive communion, and perhaps even hear mass said.

Dressed as Aramis had been the day before, the bishop got into his carriage. Aramis, disguised more by his pallor and sadness than by his deacon's robes, got in with him. The carriage halted at the gates of Whitehall at about nine o'clock in the morning. Nothing seemed changed; the antechambers and corridors, like the day before, were filled with guards. Two sentries were watching at the king's door, two others marched back and forth outside on the balcony and platform of the scaffold, on which the headsman's block had already been placed.

The king was filled with hope; on seeing Aramis again, this hope became joy. He embraced Juxon and shook Aramis's hand. The bishop spoke loudly enough for all to hear of their interview the day before. The king replied that the discussion they'd had the day before had borne fruit, and he desired to continue it. Juxon turned to his assistants and asked them to leave him and the deacon alone with the king. Everyone withdrew.

Once the door was firmly shut, Aramis said rapidly, "Sire, you are saved! The executioner of London has disappeared, and his apprentice broke his leg under Your Majesty's window—it was his cry we heard yesterday. Doubtless they've already noticed the absence of the executioner, but there's no replacement closer than Bristol, and it will take time to bring him, so we have until tomorrow at least."

"But the Comte de La Fère?" asked the king.

"He's two feet below you, Sire. Take the poker from the fireplace and rap the floor three times, and you'll hear him reply."

The king, with trembling hand, took the tool and knocked three times at equal intervals. Immediately, responding to the signal, three raps rang out from below. "So," said the king, "he who answers me there . . ."

"Is the Comte de La Fère, Sire," said Aramis. "He's preparing the way for Your Majesty's escape. Parry, for his part, will raise this marble hearthstone, and the passage will be open."

"But I don't have a prybar," said Parry.

"Take this stout dagger," said Aramis, "only take care not to dull the edge; you may need to cut something other than stone."

"Oh, Juxon!" said Charles, turning to the bishop and grasping his hands. "Juxon, hear the prayer of one who was once your king . . ."

"Who still is and who will always be," said Juxon, kissing the prince's hand.

"Pray all your life for this gentleman you see here, for another we hear beneath our feet, and for two others who, no matter where they are, work for my salvation, I am certain."

"Sire," replied Juxon, "you will be obeyed. Every day, so long as I live, I'll pray to God for these loyal friends of Your Majesty."

The miner continued his work for a time, sounding ever nearer. Suddenly a noise was heard from out in the antechamber. Aramis seized the poker and sounded the signal to stop working.

The noise approached, a march of equal and regular steps. The four men stood frozen, their eyes fixed on the door, which opened slowly and with a sort of solemnity.

Guards entered and formed two lines in the king's outer room. A commissioner of Parliament, dressed in black and with a gravity that augured ill, entered, saluted the king, and unrolling a parchment, read to him his sentence, as is customary when the condemned is about to be marched to the scaffold.

"What does this mean?" asked Aramis of Juxon.

Juxon just shrugged to show he was as ignorant as Aramis.

"So, it's for today?" asked the king, with an emotion perceptible solely to Juxon and Aramis.

"Weren't you warned, Sire, that it would be this morning?" replied the man dressed in black.

"And," said the king, "I must die like a common criminal by the hand of the London executioner?"

"The London executioner has disappeared, Sire," said the Commissioner of Parliament, "but a man has offered to take his place. The execution, therefore, will be delayed only so long as it takes you to put your affairs in order, temporal and spiritual."

A light sweat that beaded the roots of Charles's hair was the only trace of emotion he showed at this news.

But Aramis went livid. His heart ceased to beat; he closed his eyes and leaned hard on a table. Seeing this deep sorrow, Charles seemed to forget his own. He went to him, lifted his hands and embraced him. "Come, friend," he said, with a sad and gentle smile. "Courage."

Then, turning to the commissioner, he said, "Sir, I am ready. I desire only two things that won't delay you long, I think: first, to take communion, and second, to embrace my children and to tell them goodbye for the final time. Will that be permitted me?"

"Yes, Sire," replied the Commissioner of Parliament. And he went out.

Aramis, gripping the top of a chair, got hold of himself, and groaned from deep in his chest. "Oh, Monseigneur!" he cried, seizing Juxon's hands. "Where is God? Where is God?"

"My son," said the bishop firmly, "you do not see him because earthly passions hide him from you."

"My child," said the king to Aramis, "do not despair so. You ask where is God? God beholds thy devotion and my martyrdom, and, believe me, both will have their reward. Blame men, therefore, for what happens, and not God. It is men who put me to death, and men who make you weep."

"Yes, Sire," said Aramis, "yes, you're right; it's men whom I shall blame for this, and who shall be held to account."

"Now sit, Juxon," said the king, falling to his knees, "for it remains for you to hear me, and it remains to me to confess. Stay, Monsieur," he said to Aramis, who'd started to withdraw. "And you, Parry, stay. I have nothing to say, even in the privacy of penitence, that cannot be said before all. Stay—and I have but one regret, that the whole world cannot hear me as you hear me."

Juxon sat, and the king, kneeling before him like the humblest of the faithful, began his confession.

XXV

"Remember"

When the royal confession was finished, Charles received communion, and then asked to see his children. Ten o'clock was tolling; as the king had said, he hadn't delayed events by much.

However, the people crowding the streets surrounding the palace were already eager and ready; they knew that ten o'clock was the time fixed for the execution, and the king began to recognize that sound made by both a crowd and the sea, the one when agitated by its passions, the other by its storms.

The king's children arrived, first Princess Elizabeth, then the Duke of Gloucester—that is, a pretty blond girl with her eyes moistened with tears, and a young boy of eight or nine whose dry eye and disdainful look bespoke his proud birth. The boy had been crying all night, but before the world's eyes he would cry no more.

Charles felt his heart melt at the sight of these two children, whom he hadn't seen for two years and now met again only at the moment of his death. A tear rose in his eye and he turned to wipe it away, for he wanted to be strong before these two to whom he bequeathed such an inheritance of suffering and misfortune.

Beckoning to the young girl, he spoke first to her, recommending piety, resignation, and filial love. Then he took the young Duke of Gloucester and sat him on his knee, so that at the same time he could kiss his face and press him to his heart. "My son," he said, "you have seen in the streets and halls many people coming here; they come to take your father's head, and you must never forget it. Because you are among them and under their control, they may someday propose to make you king, advancing you ahead of the Prince of Wales or the Duke of York, your older brothers who are away, the one in France, the other I know not where. But you are not the king, my son, and cannot be while they live. Swear to me, then, that you will never place the crown on your head unless you have a legitimate right to that crown; for hear me, my son, if you did that, then a day would come when they would take away both head and crown, and you wouldn't be able to die at peace, as I do. Swear it, my son."

The child put his small hand on that of his father and said, "Sire, I swear it to Your Majesty."

Charles interrupted: "Henry," he said, "call me your father."

"Father," the child replied, "I swear to you they will have to kill me before I'll be made king."

"Good, my son," said Charles. "Now kiss me—you too, Elizabeth—and do not forget me."

"Never! No, never!" cried the two children, throwing their arms around the king's neck.

"Adieu," said Charles, "adieu, my children. Take them away, Juxon; their tears would steal from me the courage to die."

Juxon pried the poor children from their father's arms and returned them to those who'd brought them. Once the children were outside the doors were opened, and everyone in the antechamber was allowed in. The king, finding himself alone in the crowd of guards and the curious who were beginning to invade the chamber, remembered that the Comte de La Fère was nearby, under the room's parquet floor, unable to see and perhaps still hopeful. He was afraid that any noise might be taken by Athos as a signal to resume his task, thus betraying himself, so the king stood immobile, hoping that by his example the others around him would do the same.

The king was right, Athos really was just below his feet. He listened carefully, and, despairing at not hearing the signal to resume, he nearly began, in his impatience, to once more pry at the stone, but stopped at once, fearing to be heard. This horrible inaction lasted for two hours, during which a silence like death reigned in the royal chamber above.

Then Athos made up his mind to determine the cause of that somber silence that was troubled only by the surging sound of the crowd. He opened the hanging that hid the hole in the outer wall and climbed down to the first stage of the scaffold. Only four inches above his head were the planks of the platform that was the top of the scaffold.

The roar of the crowd, deep and menacing, which he had only distantly heard till then, made him start with terror. He crept to the edge of the scaffold, opened the black curtain at eye level, and looked. There was the cavalry ranked around the terrible structure, beyond the cavalry the rank of halberdiers, and beyond the halberdiers, the musketeers—and beyond the musketeers, the first lines of the people, who, like a restless ocean, were seething and roaring.

"What's happened, then?" Athos asked himself, trembling like the curtain whose edge he held. "The people press forward, the soldiers are under arms, and there, among the spectators, all eyes fixed on the window, I see d'Artagnan! What's he waiting for? What does he see? Great God, have they allowed the executioner to escape?"

Suddenly the drums rolled, stark and funereal, across the square, and the sound of steps, heavy and deliberate, resounded from above his head. It seemed a procession was marching across the floor of Whitehall, out onto the balcony, and then making the scaffold creak as it emerged into the square. Athos cast a final glance out into the yard, and the attitude of the spectators told him what the last hope in his heart had kept him from guessing.

The murmurs in the square had altogether stopped. All eyes were fixed on the window of Whitehall, all mouths hanging half-open, breath suspended as all awaited the terrible spectacle.

The sound of footsteps echoed from the hole beneath the king's apartment, and then from the scaffold above Athos's head, as the planks bent under added weight almost to the top of that distraught gentleman's head. It seemed two lines of soldiers had marched into place.

And then a noble voice, one Athos knew, pronounced these words from just above his head: "Colonel, I wish to address the people."

Athos shuddered from head to foot—for it was the king who spoke from above him on the scaffold.

In fact, after taking a few sips of wine and breaking a loaf of bread, Charles, weary of waiting for Death, had decided to go to meet him, and had given the signal to march.

Then a second window on the balcony was opened, and from the depths of the chamber within, the people could see a masked man advancing silently, who from the axe in his hand they recognized as the executioner. This man approached the block and laid down his axe, with a sound that Athos heard clearly.

Then, from behind this man, visibly pale but calm and marching steadily, Charles Stuart came forward flanked by two priests, between the two lines of halberdiers ranked along both sides of the scaffold, followed by some superior officers charged with presiding over the execution.

The sight of the masked man had provoked the crowd to murmurs. All were curious to know the identity of this unknown executioner who'd come forward to enact the terrible spectacle promised to the people, when they'd thought the spectacle postponed to the following day. The crowd devoured him with their eyes, but all they could see was a man of medium height, garbed entirely in black, and apparently of a certain age, for the tip of a graying beard extended past the bottom of the mask that covered his face.

But at the sight of the king, so calm, so noble, and so dignified, silence fell once again, and everyone heard him express his desire to speak to the people.

To this request, the person to whom it was addressed apparently responded with an affirmative gesture, for in a firm and resonant voice, which struck Athos to the heart, the king began to speak. He explained his conduct to the people and gave them advice for the future good of England.

"Oh!" Athos said to himself. "Is it really possible I'm hearing what I hear and seeing what I see? Is it possible for God so to abandon his representative on Earth to such a miserable death? And I can't even see him! I can't even bid him farewell!"

A noise came that sounded like the instrument of death being moved on the block. The king interrupted: "Do not touch the axe," he said. And he resumed his speech where he'd left off.

When the speech ended, an icy silence seemed to chill the air around the count's head. He touched his hand to his brow, and it ran with streams of sweat, though the air seemed frozen.

This silence was the sign of the final preparations.

When his address was over, the king looked over the crowd with an expression full of mercy, and then removed the medallion he wore, which was none other than the diamond plaque the queen had sent to him, and which he handed to the priest who accompanied Juxon. Then he drew from his breast a small diamond-crusted cross which, like the plaque, had come from Madame Henriette.

"Sir," said the king, addressing the priest next to Juxon, "I will keep this cross in my hand until the final moment; you will take it from me once I am dead."

"Yes, Sire," said a voice which Athos recognized as that of Aramis.

Then Charles, who until then had kept his head covered, removed his hat and set it down near him. He undid the buttons of his doublet, removed it and placed it near his hat. Then, as it was cold, he asked for his dressing gown, which he donned.

All these preparations were made with a frightful calm. It was as if the king were preparing to lie in his bed, not his coffin.

Finally, lifting his hair from his neck with his hand, he said to the executioner, "Will this bother you, Sir? If so, it could be tied up with a cord." Charles accompanied these words with a look that seemed to penetrate the unknown's mask. This look, so noble, so calm and self-assured, forced the man to turn his eyes away. But beyond the penetrating eyes of the king he met the fiery gaze of Aramis.

The king, receiving no answer, repeated his question. "It will suffice," said the man in a hollow voice, "if you spread the hair on your neck."

The king spread his hair with his hands, and then looked at the block. "This block seems quite low," he said. "Is there none higher?"

"It's the usual block," replied the masked man.

"Do you think you can cut off my head with a single blow?" asked the king.

"So I hope," replied the executioner.

There was in this phrase, *So I hope,* such a strange intonation that everyone shivered, except the king.

"Very well," said the king. "And now, executioner, listen."

The masked man took a step toward the king and leaned on his axe.

"I don't want you to surprise me," Charles said to him. "I'm going to kneel to pray, so don't strike just yet."

"And when shall I strike?" asked the masked man.

"When I lay my neck on the block, stretch out my arms, and say, 'Remember,' strike, and strike boldly."

The masked man nodded.

"Now is the time to leave the world," said the king to those around him. "Gentlemen, I leave you in the midst of a tempest, and precede you into that country that knows no storms. Adieu." He looked at Aramis and gave him a significant nod.

"Now," he continued, "step away, and allow me a quiet prayer. You, too," he said to the masked man. "This will take just a moment, and then I shall be all yours. But remember to wait for my signal."

Then Charles kneeled, made the sign of the cross, and leaned his lips toward the planks as if he would kiss the platform. He put one hand on the planks and the other on the block, and then whispered in French, "Comte de La Fère, are you there, and can you hear me?"

This voice struck straight through Athos's heart and pierced it like a blade of ice. "Yes, Majesty," he said, shakily.

"Faithful friend and generous heart," said the king, "I couldn't be saved, and indeed, didn't deserve it. Now, though it be a sacrilege, I tell you: I have spoken to the people, and I have spoken to God, but I speak my final words to you. To support a cause I believed was sacred, I lost the throne of my fathers and the heritage of my children. But there remains a million in gold, which was buried in the cellars of the keep at Newcastle just before I left that city. You alone know that this money exists, for you to use when you think the time is right in the best interests of my eldest son. And now, Comte de La Fère, bid me adieu."

"Adieu, M-majesty, saint, and martyr," stammered Athos, frozen with terror.

There was a moment of silence, during which it seemed to Athos that the king rose and changed his position. Then, in a clear and resonant voice, so he could be heard not just on the scaffold, but across the square, the king said, "*Remember.*"

Charles had scarcely finished the word before a terrible blow shook the planks of the scaffold; dust billowed from the black curtain and blinded the wretched count. Then, quickly and mechanically, Athos turned up his eyes, just as a drop of hot liquid fell on his forehead. He drew back with a shudder of horror, as the drops turned into a black cascade from above.

Athos, fallen to his knees, remained for some moments stricken with weakness and dismay. Gradually, as the murmurs died away, he realized that the crowd was leaving the square, but he remained a while longer, stunned and mute. Then, turning about, he dipped the corner of his handkerchief in the blood of the martyred king, before he descended, parted the curtain, and slipped out between two horses to merge with the departing crowd, in clothing similar to theirs.

He was the first to arrive back at the inn. Going up to his room, he looked at himself in a mirror, and saw his forehead was marked by a large red blot. He raised his hand to his brow, drew it away stained with the king's blood, and swooned.

XXVI

The Masked Man

Though it was only four o'clock in the afternoon, it was dark as night, the snow falling thick and damp. Aramis made his way to the inn where he found Athos, though not unconscious, thoroughly dazed. But at his friend's first words, the count emerged from the stunned lethargy into which he'd fallen.

"Outdone!" said Aramis. "Vanquished by fate."

"Defeated!" said Athos. "That noble and unhappy king!"

"Are you wounded?" asked Aramis.

"No, the blood is his." The count wiped his forehead.

"Where were you?"

"Where you left me, under the scaffold."

"And you saw it all?"

"No, but I heard everything. God defend me from another hour like the one I've just passed. Has my hair turned white?"

"Then you were aware I never left him?"

"I heard your voice up until the final moment."

"Here is the plaque he gave me," said Aramis, "and here the cross I took from his hand. He asked that they be returned to the queen."

"And here is a handkerchief to wrap around them," said Athos. And he drew from his pocket the handkerchief he'd soaked in the king's blood. "Now," he asked, "what has become of his poor cadaver?"

"By Cromwell's order, it's to be rendered royal honors. We put the body in a leaden coffin; the doctors are busy embalming the remains, and when they're done, the body will be taken to a chapel to lie in state."

"A mockery!" Athos muttered darkly. "Paying royal honors to one they assassinated!"

"It proves that though the king may die, royalty lives on."

"Alas!" said Athos. "It may be that the last king of ancient chivalry has passed from the world."

"Come, don't despair, Count," said a loud voice from the stairway, above the heavy footsteps of Porthos. "We're all but mortal, my poor friends."

"You're late, my dear Porthos," said the Comte de La Fère.

"Yes," said Porthos, "there were some people along my way who delayed me. They were dancing, the wretches! I took one by the neck and choked him a bit. Just then the Watch arrived. Fortunately, the one I'd been toying with wasn't able to speak for several minutes, and I took advantage of that to dash up a back street. The back street led to an alley, and that to another, and soon I was lost. I don't know London, I don't speak English, and I thought I'd never see you again—but here I am."

"But d'Artagnan," said Aramis, "what of him? Have you seen him?"

"We got separated in the crush, and I lost track of him," said Porthos.

"Oh," said Athos bitterly, "I saw him! He was in the front row of the crowd, admirably situated so he'd miss nothing. And as the spectacle was curious, no doubt he stayed to see the end."

"What? Now, Monsieur de La Fère," said a voice, calm but breathing hard from exertion, "is it like you to slander the absent?"

This reproach struck Athos to the quick. But the sight of d'Artagnan at the front of the crowd had hit him hard, so he replied, "I don't slander you, my friend. We were just worried about where you were, and I said where I'd seen you. You didn't really know King Charles well enough to love him, he was almost a stranger to you." As he said these words he extended his hand to his friend, but d'Artagnan pretended not to see the gesture and kept his hand under his cloak. Athos allowed his hand to drop slowly away.

"Whew! I'm tired," d'Artagnan said, and sat down.

"Have a glass of port," said Aramis, taking a bottle from the table and filling a glass. "Drink, it'll restore you."

"Yes, let's drink," said Athos, who, aware of the Gascon's resentment, hoped to touch glasses with him and amend it. "Let's drink, and then get out of this abominable country. The sloop awaits us; let's leave tonight. We have no more business here."

"You're in a great hurry, Monsieur le Comte," said d'Artagnan.

"This bloody soil burns my feet," said Athos.

"The snow doesn't have that effect on me," said the Gascon quietly.

"But what would you have us do now that the king is dead?" said Athos.

"So, Monsieur le Comte," said d'Artagnan airily, "you don't find that you have anything left to do in England?"

"Not a thing," said Athos, "other than to doubt in divine grace and curse my own weakness."

"Indeed!" said d'Artagnan. "Well, I, rustic that I am, who stood thirty feet from the scaffold the better to watch the fall of the head of this king I hardly knew, to whom I was apparently quite indifferent—I see things otherwise than Monsieur le Comte. I intend to stay."

Athos turned pale; these reproaches from his friend went straight to his heart.

"Really! So, you're staying in London?" said Porthos to d'Artagnan.

"I am. And you?"

"*Dame!*" said Porthos, looking awkwardly at Athos and Aramis. "*Dame!* Since I came with you, if you're staying, then I'll stay with you. I wouldn't leave you alone in this abominable country."

"Thanks, my good friend. Then I have a little enterprise to propose to you, which we shall undertake together once the count has departed, an idea that came to me while watching that spectacle you heard mentioned."

"What's that?" said Porthos.

"It's to find out the identity of that masked man who so obligingly offered to cut off the king's head."

"A masked man!" cried Athos. "Then you didn't allow the executioner to escape?"

"The executioner?" said d'Artagnan. "He's still in the cellar, where I assume he's making free with our host's bottles. But now that you mention it . . ." He went to the door. "Mousqueton!" he called.

"Monsieur?" replied a voice that seemed to come from the depths of the earth.

"You can leave the prisoner," said d'Artagnan. "It's all over."

"But then," said Athos, "who was the wretch who presumed to lay hands on the king?"

"An amateur executioner," said Aramis, "but one who, nonetheless, manages an axe with ease, for as the king hoped, it took only one blow."

"Were you able to see his face?" asked Athos.

"He wore a full mask," said d'Artagnan.

"But weren't you near to him, Aramis?"

"I saw only a bit of gray beard that stuck out below the mask."

"So, he was a man of some maturity?" asked Athos.

"Oh, that doesn't mean anything," said d'Artagnan. "One who wears a mask can wear a beard as well."

"I'm sorry now that I didn't follow him," said Porthos.

"Fortunately, my dear Porthos," said d'Artagnan, "that idea occurred to me while watching."

Athos understood everything. He rose. "Pardon me, d'Artagnan," he said. "When I doubted God, I even doubted you. Forgive me, my friend."

"We can probably find the time for that, at some point," said d'Artagnan with a half-smile.

"Well?" said Aramis.

"Well!" replied d'Artagnan. "I was looking, not at the king, as Monsieur le Comte thought—for I know what it's like for a man who's about to die, and though you'd think I'd be used to that sort of thing, it still dismays me—but rather at the masked executioner, and the idea came to me, as I mentioned, that I'd like very much to know who he was. Now, as we're in the habit of relying on each other, one hand calling for the others to join in and help, I automatically looked around to see if I could spot Porthos; I'd already recognized you near the king, Aramis, and I knew you, Count, were under the scaffold. And this is the part where I forgive you," he added, holding out his hand to Athos, "for I know how you must have suffered.

Anyway, I looked around and saw standing to my right someone with a head that had been split open and then sewn back up, as well as it could be, anyway, with black silk thread. '*Parbleu*,' I said to myself, 'that work looks familiar—in fact I think Grimaud did that sewing job.' And indeed, it was that unlucky Scotsman, Parry's brother—you remember, the one on whom Groslow amused himself by trying his strength, and who had only half a head when we found him."

"Absolutely," said Porthos. "The man with the black chickens."

"Just as you say! He was gesturing to someone on my left; I turned and recognized our honest Grimaud, completely occupied like me in staring at the masked executioner. '*Ohé,*' I said to him, and as this is one of the abbreviations the count uses when speaking with him, Grimaud thought it was his master who'd called, and turned like a clockwork. Seeing me instead, he pointed toward the masked man and said, '*Hein?*', which meant, 'Do you see him?' '*Parbleu!*' I replied. We knew we were in perfect accord.

"I turned back to our Scotsman, whose look said he understood as well. In the event, it all ended sadly, as you know. The people filed away as, little by little, evening came on. I'd withdrawn to a corner of the square with Grimaud and the Scotsman, whom I'd signaled to join us, and from there we watched the executioner. We could see him retire into the king's chamber to change his outfit, which was doubtless bloodstained. Then he clapped a black hat on his head, wrapped himself in a cloak, and disappeared further within. I guessed he was going to go through and come out and I ran around to the front entrance. In fact, a few moments later he came out and went down the stairs."

"You followed him?" cried Athos.

"We did!" said d'Artagnan. "Though not without some difficulty, I'll tell you! Every few minutes he turned to look behind him, and we had to hide ourselves or pretend indifference. If I'd been here on my own account, I'd have just killed him, but I'm not that selfish, so I saved that pleasure for you, Aramis, and you, Athos, as a small consolation. Finally, after half an hour's twisting march through the smallest and most crooked streets in the City of

London, he arrived at a small, lonely house, which seemed entirely deserted. Grimaud reached into his belt and drew a pistol. '*Hein?*' he asked, pointing. 'No,' I said, and put a hand on his arm. As I said, I had my own ideas.

"The masked man stopped in front of a low door and pulled out a key, but before putting it in the lock, he turned suddenly to see if he'd been followed. I huddled behind a tree, Grimaud ducked behind a lamppost, and the Scotsman, who had nowhere to hide, threw himself facedown in the street. No doubt our prey thought himself quite alone, for I heard the turning of the key; the door opened, and he disappeared."

"The wretch!" said Aramis. "In the time since you've returned, he'll have fled, and we'll never find him again."

"Come, Aramis," said d'Artagnan, "who do you think you're dealing with?"

"However," said Athos, "in your absence . . ."

"Well, in my absence, don't I have Grimaud and the Scot in my place? Before the man had time to take ten steps inside I'd circled around the house. At one of its doors, the one by which he'd entered, I posted the Scotsman and ordered that if the man in the black mask came out, he was to follow him. Grimaud would follow in his turn, and when the man reached his destination, Grimaud would come back and wait for us at the deserted house. Then I stationed Grimaud at the house's second door, with the same orders, and here I am. The prey is in the trap; now, who's in for the death blow?"

Athos threw himself into the arms of d'Artagnan, who was catching his breath and wiping his forehead. "Friend," Athos said, "in truth I don't deserve your forgiveness—I was wrong, a hundred times wrong. I should have trusted you, but deep inside us there's a wicked will that leads us to doubt."

"Hmm!" said Porthos. "Might the executioner by any chance be Monsieur Cromwell, who, to be sure the work was done right, decided to do it himself?"

"Maybe—but no. Cromwell is short and stout, while the masked man is slender, and tall if anything."

"Some condemned soldier, perhaps, who was offered amnesty as payment," said Athos, "as was done with poor Chalais."[33]

"No, no," continued d'Artagnan. "He didn't march like an infantryman or step out like a man of the cavalry. He walked with dignity and stood with poise. Unless I'm badly mistaken, we're dealing with a gentleman."

"A gentleman!" cried Athos. "Impossible! It would be a disgrace to the entire aristocracy."

"A pretty prey!" said Porthos, with a laugh that made the windowpanes shake. "A pretty prey, *mordieu!*"

"Are you still leaving the country, Athos?" asked d'Artagnan.

"No, I'm staying," replied the gentleman, with a gesture so menacing it promised no good for the one he was staying for.

"Then, swords all!" said Aramis. "And let's lose not a moment."

The four comrades quickly resumed their gentlemen's clothing and buckled on their swords. They called up Mousqueton and Blaisois, ordered them to settle accounts with their host, and to prepare for immediate departure, as in all probability they'd be leaving London that very night.

Dark night had fully arrived, while the snow continued to fall, drawing a vast white shroud across the regicide city; it was about seven in the evening, and there were few passersby still in the streets, talking with friends and family in low voices about the terrible events of the day. The four comrades, enveloped in their cloaks, made their way through the squares and streets of the city, so busy during the day, so deserted at night. D'Artagnan led the way, pausing from time to time to take note of the crosses he'd scratched on the walls they passed, but the night was so dark it was often difficult to make out the shallow marks. However, d'Artagnan had so carefully memorized each post, sign, and fountain along the way that within half an hour he and his three companions came within sight of the lonely house.

D'Artagnan thought for a moment that Parry's brother had disappeared, but he was mistaken; the robust Scotsman, accustomed to winters in his mountains, had sat down with his back against a borne, and like a statue that had fallen from its pedestal, insensible to the weather, lay covered in snow; but at the approach of the four men he rose.

"Come," said Athos, "here's another true and loyal servant. God's truth! The good folk are less rare than we think. That's encouraging."

"Don't be in such a hurry to plait garlands for our Scotsman," said d'Artagnan. "I think the fellow is here on his own account. I've heard that the men who hail from the north side of the Tweed are a vengeful sort. Let Master Groslow beware! He'll have a bad quarter of an hour if this man catches up with him." He separated from his friends, approached the Scot and made himself known. Then he beckoned the others to join him.

"Well?" said Athos in English.

"No one has come out," replied Parry's brother.

"Good. Stay with this fellow, Porthos, and you too, Aramis. D'Artagnan is going to lead me to Grimaud."

Grimaud, no less wily than the Scotsman, had pushed himself into the hollow of a bare willow tree, which he'd converted to a sentry-box. Failing at first to see him, d'Artagnan worried for a moment that the masked man had moved on and Grimaud had followed him. Then a head emerged from the tree and he heard a light whistle.

"*Ohé!*" said Athos.

"*Hein,*" replied Grimaud.

They approached the willow.

"So," d'Artagnan asked, "has anyone gone out?"

"No—but someone has gone in," said Grimaud.

"A man or a woman?"

"A man."

"Ah ha!" said d'Artagnan. "Then they are two."

"I wish they were four," said Athos. "It would make it more equal."

"Maybe there are four," said d'Artagnan.

"How's that?"

"Couldn't other men have been in the house when these later two arrived?"

"You could look," said Grimaud, pointing to an upper window through whose shutters a few rays of light shone out.

"True enough," said d'Artagnan. "Let's call the others."

And they returned to the first door to beckon the others, who hastily rejoined them. "Have you seen anything?" they asked.

"No, but we're about to," replied d'Artagnan, indicating Grimaud, who, clinging to crevices in the wall, was already five or six feet off the ground. The four drew nearer as Grimaud continued his ascent with the dexterity of a cat. Finally, he got a hand around one of the hooks used to hold one of the shutters open against the outer wall, while his feet found purchase on a molding that gave him solid support, and he made a sign to say that he'd reached his goal. Then he leaned toward the gap in the shutter.

"Well?" asked d'Artagnan.

Grimaud raised a hand with two fingers extended.

"Speak," said Athos. "We can't see your signs. How many are there?"

With an effort, Grimaud forced himself to talk. "Two," he said. "One is facing me, but the other has his back turned."

"Good. Which one is facing you?"

"The man I saw enter second."

"Do you know him?"

"I thought I'd recognized him, and I wasn't wrong; he's short and stout."

"Who is he?" the four below hissed urgently.

"General Oliver Cromwell."

The four friends looked at each other. "And the other?" asked Athos.

"Slim and rather tall."

"It's the executioner," said d'Artagnan and Aramis at the same time.

"I see only his back," replied Grimaud. "But wait, he's turning, and if he's removed his mask, I'll see him . . . Ah!"

Grimaud, as if stabbed to the heart, let go of the iron hook and fell backward with a muffled groan. Porthos caught him. "You saw him?" asked the four friends.

"Yes," said Grimaud, hair standing on end and sweat bursting from his brow.

"The tall, slender man?" said d'Artagnan.

"Yes."

"Was it the executioner?" asked Aramis.

"Yes."

"Well, who is he?" said Porthos.

"Him! Him!" stammered Grimaud, pale as death, grasping for his master's hands with his own trembling fingers.

"Him? Who?" demanded Athos.

"Mordaunt . . . !" whispered Grimaud.

D'Artagnan, Porthos, and Aramis gasped with joy and gratification.

But Athos recoiled, passed his hand across his brow, and murmured, "It is fate."

XXVII

Cromwell's Safe House

It was indeed Mordaunt that d'Artagnan had followed without recognizing him. After entering the house, he had removed his mask and false beard, climbed the stairs, opened a door, and, in a chamber lit by a single lamp hung with dark-colored curtains, found himself facing a man who was sitting at a desk and writing.

This man was Oliver Cromwell.

As we now know, Cromwell kept two or three of these retreats in London, safe houses known only to his most loyal aides. Mordaunt, it will be recalled, could be counted among the latter. When he entered, Cromwell raised his head. "It's you, Mordaunt," he said. "You come late."

"General," replied Mordaunt, "I wanted to see the ceremony through to the end, and that delayed me."

"Oh?" said Cromwell. "I didn't think you such a curious man."

"I'm always curious to see the fall of one of Your Honor's enemies, and this one was not the least of them. But you, General—weren't you at Whitehall?"

"No," Cromwell said.

There was a moment of silence. "Have you heard the details?" asked Mordaunt.

"No. I've been here since the morning. I know only that there was a conspiracy to save the king."

"Ah! How do you know that?" asked Mordaunt.

"No matter. Four men disguised as workers were to spirit the king away from prison and escort him to Greenwich, where a ship awaited them."

"And knowing that, Your Honor chose to remain here, far from White-hall, quiet and passive!"

"Quiet, yes," replied Cromwell, "but what do you mean, passive?"

"But what if the plot had succeeded?"

"That would have been fine with me."

"I thought Your Honor regarded the death of Charles as a surgery, an operation necessary for the good of England."

"Well!" said Cromwell. "That's still my opinion. But so long as he died, that was all that mattered. It might have been better, perhaps, if he'd died somewhere other than on a scaffold."

"Why's that, Your Honor?"

Cromwell merely smiled.

"Your pardon," said Mordaunt, "but as you know, General, I'm just a novice to politics, and wish to learn from all the lessons my master provides."

"Because it would have been said that I'd had him condemned out of justice but had let him escape out of mercy."

"But what if he'd actually gotten away?"

"Impossible."

"Impossible?"

"Yes, my precautions were in place."

"And does Your Honor know these four men who plotted to save the king?"

"It was those four Frenchmen, two of whom were sent by Madame Henriette to her husband, and two by Mazarin to me."

"And do you think, Sir, that Mazarin ordered them to do what they've done?"

"It's possible, but he'll just disavow them."

"You believe so?"

"I'm sure of it."

"Why is that?"

"Because they failed."

"Your Honor had given me two of these Frenchmen when they were merely guilty of having borne arms for Charles I. Now that they're guilty of a conspiracy against England, will Your Honor give me all four?"

"Take them," said Cromwell.

Mordaunt bowed with a smile both fierce and triumphant.

"Stop," said Cromwell, seeing that Mordaunt was about to begin thanking him. "Let's return, if you please, to the unlucky King Charles. Did the people shout and cry out much?"

"Very little, except to say, 'Long live Cromwell!'"

"Where were you located?"

Mordaunt studied the general for a moment to try to read whether he was asking a rhetorical question and actually knew the whole truth. But Mordaunt's burning gaze couldn't penetrate the dark depths of Cromwell's mind. "I was located where I could see and hear everything," replied Mordaunt.

It was Cromwell's turn to start fixedly at Mordaunt and Mordaunt's turn to be inscrutable. After a few seconds' regard, he turned his eyes away indifferently. "It seems," said Cromwell, "that the amateur executioner did his job well. The blow, or so I'm told at least, was struck as if by the hand of a master."

Mordaunt recalled that Cromwell had said he knew no details, and was now convinced that the general had attended the execution in secret, watching from behind some curtain or tapestry. "In fact," Mordaunt said, voice calm, face impassive, "one blow was enough."

"Perhaps it was a man who knew the trade," said Cromwell.

"You think so, Sir?"

"Why not?"

"The man didn't carry himself like an executioner."

"And who but an executioner," asked Cromwell, "would take on such a dreadful task?"

"Perhaps," said Mordaunt, "some personal enemy of King Charles, who had taken a vow of vengeance and has now accomplished his vow; perhaps some gentleman who had grave reasons to hate the late king, and who, knowing he was about to flee and escape, undertook the task of wearing the mask and wielding the axe less as an executioner than as an instrument of fate."

"That's possible," said Cromwell.

"And if it were so," said Mordaunt, "would Your Honor condemn such an act?"

"It's not for me to judge," said Cromwell. "That would be a matter between him and God."

"What if Your Honor knew this gentleman?"

"I do not know him, Sir," replied Cromwell, "and I will not know him. What does it matter whether it was this man, that man, or some other? From the moment Charles was condemned, it wasn't a man who would take his head, it was the axe."

"And yet," said Mordaunt, "but for this man, the king would have been saved."

Cromwell smiled.

"But you said so yourself—they'd have carried him off."

"They'd have taken him to Greenwich, where the four saviors had a sloop awaiting. But the sloop was crewed by four men of mine, with five barrels of black powder in the hold. Once at sea, my four men would have left in the longboat—and you're not such a novice, Mordaunt, as to need me to explain the rest."

Mordaunt nodded. "The sea would have taken them all."

"Exactly. The explosion would have done what the axe had not. King Charles would have disappeared, annihilated. It would be said that, fleeing from human justice, he'd been overtaken by heavenly vengeance; we'd been his judges, but God had been his executioner. That's what your masked gentleman cost us, Mordaunt. You see, I'm right in not wanting to know him—for in truth, despite his excellent intentions, I can't be grateful to him for what he's done."

"Sir," said Mordaunt, "as always I humbly bow before you. You are a profound thinker, and the idea of the powder-packed sloop is sublime."

"Rather, it's absurd, since it's become useless. No idea in politics is sublime unless it bears fruit; an aborted or incomplete plan is just a folly." Cromwell rose. "You will go to Greenwich tonight, Mordaunt, and ask for the master of the sloop *Lightning*. You will show him a white handkerchief with a knot in each corner, which is the agreed-upon signal. Tell his men to go ashore and arrange to have the powder returned to the arsenal—unless . . ."

"Unless . . ." replied Mordaunt, whose face lit up with mad joy at Cromwell's words.

"Unless this sloop as prepared would be useful for your own purposes."

"Ah, Milord! Milord!" cried Mordaunt. "God, in choosing you to do his will, has given you his vision, which sees everything and misses nothing!"

"I think you just called me *milord*," Cromwell laughed. "That's fine, since we're amongst ourselves, but be careful not to let such a word slip out in front of our fools of Puritans."

"Won't Your Honor be called by that title soon?"

"I hope so," said Cromwell, "but that time has not yet come." Cromwell turned and took up his cloak.

"You're going now, Sir?" asked Mordaunt.

"Yes," said Cromwell. "I slept here last night and the night before that, and you know it's against my policy to sleep in the same bed three nights in a row."

"Then," said Mordaunt, "Your Honor gives me liberty for the rest of the night?"

"And even through tomorrow if need be," said Cromwell, smiling. "Today you've done enough in my service that, if you have personal affairs to settle, you should be granted the time to do it."

"Thank you, Sir. I hope to spend this time well."

Cromwell nodded to Mordaunt, turned away, and then turned back again. "Are you armed?" he asked.

"I have my sword," said Mordaunt.

"And who awaits you at the door?"

"No one."

"Then you should come with me, Mordaunt."

"Thank you, Sir, but your long route through the underground passage will cost me too much time, and from what you told me, I may not have any to spare. I'll use the outer door."

"Go, then," said Cromwell. He pressed a concealed lever that opened a door so hidden behind a tapestry not even the sharpest eye could spot it. He went past the open door, which then, moved by a steel spring, closed behind him. This was one of those secret exits that, as history tells us, Cromwell had installed in all of his safe houses. It led to an underground tunnel a hundred paces long that passed under the street and opened in the garden grotto of another house, one that faced away from the house the future Protector had just left.

It was during the latter part of this scene that, through the gap in the shutters, Grimaud had spied on the two men whom he eventually recognized as Cromwell and Mordaunt. We have seen the effect of his news on the four friends.

D'Artagnan was the first to come to his senses. "Mordaunt!" he said. "By heaven! It's God himself who sends him to us."

"Yes," said Porthos. "Let's break down the door and get at him."

"On the contrary," said d'Artagnan, "do nothing, and make no noise; if Mordaunt is, as Grimaud says, with his worthy master, there must be some hard men in iron armor not fifty paces from here. *Holà!* Grimaud, stop shaking and come here."

Grimaud approached. He was firm again, fury in him having replaced fear. "Good man," said d'Artagnan. "Now go back up to that window and tell us if Mordaunt still has company. If he does, or is about to go to bed, we'll just have to wait until he's alone. If he comes out, we'll take him as he leaves. If he turns in alone, we'll enter by the window—that's always quieter and less difficult than a door."

Grimaud began to climb quietly back up to the window. "Guard the other exit, Athos and Aramis," said d'Artagnan. "I'll stay here with Porthos." His two friends obeyed.

"Well, Grimaud?" hissed d'Artagnan.

"He's alone," said Grimaud.

"You're sure?"

"Yes."

"We didn't see his companion come out."

"Maybe he left by the other door."

"What's he doing?"

"He's donned his cloak and is putting on his gloves."

"He's ours!" murmured d'Artagnan.

Porthos put his hand to his poniard and began to draw it from its sheath. "Not so fast, friend Porthos," said d'Artagnan. "This is not a case of striking first. We've got him and must do things in the proper order. We have questions to ask, and explanations to make, because this is the final outcome of that business in Armentières. Let's hope Mordaunt doesn't have any offspring—but if he does, this time we exterminate the entire nest."

"Hush!" said Grimaud. "He's getting ready to leave. He approaches the lamp—blows it out—I can see nothing."

"Come down, then!"

Grimaud leapt down and landed on his feet, the snow absorbing the sound. D'Artagnan said, "Go and warn Athos and Aramis to stand one to each side of the door, as Porthos and I will do here. Let them clap their hands if they get him, and we'll do the same."

Grimaud disappeared.

"Porthos, Porthos," said d'Artagnan, "better hide those big shoulders of yours against the wall, friend—if he sees them, he won't come out."

"Oh, I do so hope he comes out this way!" Porthos flattened himself against the wall to one side of the door, and d'Artagnan did the same on the other.

Mordaunt's footsteps could be heard coming down the staircase. A door somewhere inside creaked on its hinges; within, Mordaunt looked out suspiciously, but thanks to the pair's precautions, he saw nothing. He turned the key in the lock, opened the outer door and stepped onto the threshold—where found himself face-to-face with d'Artagnan. He tried to pull the door shut, but Porthos grabbed the knob and jerked it open.

Porthos clapped three times. Athos and Aramis came running. Mordaunt was livid, but he didn't say a word or call out for help. D'Artagnan marched straight in on Mordaunt, thrusting him back bodily, to the foot of the staircase and up it. The light from a hanging lamp enabled the Gascon to keep an eye on Mordaunt's hands in case he went for a weapon, but Mordaunt knew that even if he killed d'Artagnan, he'd just have to face the other three, so he was careful not to make any threatening moves, or even to defend himself. Reaching the landing, Mordaunt, his back against the door, felt cornered, and no doubt thought it was all over with him, but he was wrong—d'Artagnan merely reached around him and opened the door. He and Mordaunt were then in the room where a few minutes earlier the young man had been speaking with Cromwell.

Porthos came in behind d'Artagnan; he had taken the hanging lamp on his way up and brought it in with him, and he used this first lamp to light a second. Athos and Aramis followed him through the door, which they locked behind them.

"Here, have a seat," said d'Artagnan, presenting a chair to the young man. The latter took the chair and sat down, pale but calm. Three paces in front of him, Aramis placed three chairs in a line for himself, d'Artagnan, and Porthos. Meanwhile, Athos, seeming overwhelmed, went and took a seat in the room's farthest corner, apparently determined to remain a spectator to events.

Porthos sat to the left of d'Artagnan, Aramis to his right. Porthos rubbed his hands together with nervous impatience. Aramis was smiling, but biting his lips till they bled. Only d'Artagnan seemed fully in command of himself. "Monsieur Mordaunt," he said, "after so many days apart from each other, chance seems to have brought us together again. Let's have a little talk."

XXVIII

A Little Talk

Mordaunt, surprised so completely and unexpectedly, and marched upstairs in fear for his life, found his thoughts in disarray. Ambushed, he was overcome by terror, a man who found himself in the hands of mortal enemies he'd been certain were safely elsewhere.

But once he was seated, and saw that he was granted a reprieve, for whatever reason, he concentrated his thoughts and summoned his strength. D'Artagnan's fiery gaze, burning with menace, electrified rather than intimidated him, for the look was open in its anger and hatred. That set Mordaunt to prepare to seize, by force or by cunning, any opportunity for recovery that offered itself, and he gathered himself together—much as a bear, pursued into its den and seemingly cornered, eyed every movement of the hunter who'd trapped him there. He only glanced down for a moment at the long sword that hung at his hip, and as he sat on the chair d'Artagnan had indicated, he brought the hilt forward with his left hand until it was near to his right.

D'Artagnan was quiet, waiting for his prey to burst into one of those threatening tirades with which he'd mocked them in the past.

Aramis said to himself, "Now we'll hear some double-talk."

Porthos gnawed at his mustache, muttering, "God's death! There's more than one way to crush this little serpent!"

Athos withdrew further into his corner, motionless and pale as a marble statue, albeit a statue whose brow was beaded with sweat.

Mordaunt said nothing. Once he'd assured himself that his sword's hilt was at hand, he nonchalantly crossed his legs and sat, silent.

This silence couldn't last long before it became ridiculous. D'Artagnan understood the ploy, and since he was the one who'd invited Mordaunt to sit and talk, he felt it behooved him to start the conversation. "It seems to me, Monsieur," he said with brittle courtesy, "that you change your costume nearly as often as those Italian commedia mimes that Cardinal Mazarin brought over from Bergamo, and which he doubtless took you to see during your visit to France."

Mordaunt said nothing.

"A few minutes ago," d'Artagnan continued, "you were disguised—I mean *dressed*—in an assassin's garb, and now . . ."

"And now, on the contrary, I wear the garb of one who is to be assassinated?" replied Mordaunt in a voice calm and curt.

"Why, Monsieur!" said d'Artagnan. "How can you say such a thing when in the company of gentlemen, and with such a long sword still at your side?"

"There is no sword long enough, Monsieur, to counter four swords and four daggers, not to mention the swords and daggers of your men-at-arms outside."

"Pardon me, Monsieur, if I correct you," said d'Artagnan, "but the men outside aren't soldiers, just our lackeys. I'd like to keep our talk on a truthful basis."

Mordaunt answered only by tightening his lips in an ironic smile.

"But that's beside the point, and so I return to my question," d'Artagnan said. "I had the honor to ask you, Monsieur, why you'd changed your appearance. The mask seemed to cause you no inconvenience, and I thought the gray beard rather suited you. And as to that axe which you wielded so famously, it seems to me it might come in handy right about now. Why did you give it up?"

"Because, knowing of the event at Armentières, I assumed I'd find myself between four executioners and be outnumbered four axes to one."

"Monsieur," replied d'Artagnan, supremely cool, though the twitch of an eyebrow revealed that he was beginning to heat up, "Monsieur, though you are thoroughly vicious and corrupt, you're also very young, so I'll overlook your frivolous remarks. Yes, frivolous—for the scene at Armentières in no way compares to your present situation. We couldn't very well offer your mother a sword and challenge her to fence with us. But you, Monsieur, a young cavalier who handles the dagger and pistol as we've seen you do so well, and who wears a sword as long as that one, are certainly a person of whom one has the right to ask the favor of a meeting."

"Oh ho!" said Mordaunt. "So, it's a duel you want?" And he rose, eyes flashing, as if he were ready to take up the challenge at once. Porthos, always ready for a fight, got up as well.

"Patience, patience," said d'Artagnan, still cool. "There's no rush, and we all want to make sure this thing is done according to the rules. Sit down, friend Porthos—and you, Monsieur Mordaunt, calm yourself. We're going to settle this matter properly. Will you admit, Monsieur Mordaunt, to a desire to kill one or another of us?"

"One and all of you," replied Mordaunt.

D'Artagnan turned to Aramis and said, "It's fortunate, I'm sure you agree, Aramis, that Monsieur Mordaunt is so well acquainted with the nuances of the French language that it will enable us to arrange the affair without the least misunderstanding." Turning back to Mordaunt, he continued, "Dear Monsieur Mordaunt: I hereby inform you that these gentlemen all return your fine sentiments and would be delighted to kill you as well. Moreover, I can assure you that they *would* kill you, honorable gentlemen that they are, except for what I'm about to tell you, which is this." And with these words d'Artagnan threw his hat on the floor, pushed his chair out of the way, and gestured to his friends to do the same. Then he saluted Mordaunt and said with perfect French grace, "At your command, if you please, Monsieur— for unless you object I claim the honor of challenging you. My sword is shorter than yours, but never mind—hopefully my arm will make up for it."

"Stop right there!" said Porthos, stepping forward. "I'm going first, and without any more talk."

"No, Porthos, allow me," said Aramis.

Athos stayed motionless, like a statue—even his breathing seemed to have stopped.

"Messieurs, Messieurs," said d'Artagnan, "rest assured, you'll each have your turn. Observe this gentleman's eyes and see the passionate hatred we inspire in him. Notice how nimbly he draws his sword; admire with what care he inspects the ground for objects that might trip him. Well, then! Doesn't all this indicate that Monsieur Mordaunt is a worthy opponent, and will survive long enough to face you—provided I let him? Be patient, like Athos, whose calm I can't recommend enough, and allow me this initiative I've taken. Besides," he continued, drawing his sword with terrible resolve, "I have particular business with monsieur, and I *will* be first. I want it, and will have it."

It was the first time d'Artagnan had ever spoken so imperatively to his friends—until then, he'd been content to merely think that way. In response, Porthos stepped back, and Aramis tucked his sword under his arm. Athos remained motionless in his dark corner, not calm, as d'Artagnan had said, but suffocated and barely breathing.

D'Artagnan said to Aramis, "Return your sword to its sheath, Chevalier, or monsieur might think you harbor intentions you do not." Then, turning to Mordaunt, he said, "Monsieur, I await you."

"And I, Messieurs, listen and wonder. You discuss who will be first to fight me, but you don't consult me on the matter, a business which concerns me, I think, more than a little. It's true, I do hate all four of you—but not to the same degree. And though I hope to kill all four of you, I have more chance of killing the first than the second, the second than the third, and the third than the fourth. Therefore, I claim the right to choose my first adversary. If you deny me this right, just kill me outright—I'll refuse to fight you."

The four friends looked at each other. "That's fair," said Porthos and Aramis, both of whom hoped the choice would fall on them. Athos and d'Artagnan said nothing, but their silence was taken as assent.

"Well!" said Mordaunt into the midst of the profound and solemn silence that reigned in that mysterious house. "In that case, I choose for my first adversary the one who, believing himself no longer worthy of the name Comte de La Fère, calls himself . . . Athos!"

Athos rose from his corner as if a spring had thrust him—but to his friends' surprise, after a moment of silence, he shook his head and said, "Monsieur Mordaunt, a duel between the two of us is impossible. That honor must be offered to another." And he sat back down.

"Ah!" said Mordaunt. "There's one who fears me already."

"A thousand thunders!" cried d'Artagnan, advancing a step toward the younger man. "Who calls Athos afraid?"

"Let him say what he will, d'Artagnan," said Athos, with a smile mixing sadness and contempt.

"Is your decision final, Athos?" replied the Gascon.

"Irrevocable."

"All right, we'll say no more about it." Then, turning to Mordaunt, he said, "You've heard, Monsieur, that the Comte de La Fère will not do you the honor to duel with you. Choose someone else to replace him."

"If I don't fight him first, I don't care whom I fight," said Mordaunt. "Put your names in a hat, and I'll draw one by chance."

"There's an idea," said d'Artagnan.

"Indeed, that solves it," said Aramis.

"It never occurred to me," said Porthos, "and yet, it's so simple."

"Come, Aramis," said d'Artagnan, "write our names in that pretty little hand with which you wrote to Marie Michon to warn that monsieur's mother wanted to assassinate Milord Buckingham."

Mordaunt reacted to this new gibe without so much as blinking; he stood, arms crossed, appearing about as calm as a man can be in such a circumstance. If it wasn't courage, it was at least pride, which strongly resembles it.

Aramis went to Cromwell's desk, tore off three slips of paper of equal size, wrote his name on one and his comrades' on the other two, and showed them to Mordaunt, who, without reading them, nodded to indicate they were fine with him. Aramis rolled them up, put them in a hat, and presented it to the young man. Mordaunt plunged his hand into the hat and drew out one of the three slips, which he disdainfully dropped on the desk without reading it.

"Ah, you young serpent!" murmured d'Artagnan. "I'd give up my chances of promotion to Captain of the Musketeers to ensure that slip bore my name!"

Aramis unrolled the slip, and no matter how calm and cool he hoped to be, his hands trembled with hatred and longing. "D'Artagnan!" he said loudly.

D'Artagnan uttered a cry of joy. "Ha!" he said. "There *is* justice in heaven!" Then, turning to Mordaunt, he added, "I hope, Monsieur, you have no objection to make?"

"None, Monsieur," said Mordaunt, flourishing his blade and trying its point on his boot.

As soon as d'Artagnan was sure his wish was granted, and this man wouldn't escape him, a calm, even tranquility settled upon him, and he began the ritual of preparations for that grave affair known as a duel. He turned back his cuffs and scraped the sole of his right boot on the floor, none of which stopped him from noticing, for the second time, the care with which Mordaunt looked around the room, assessing locations and distances. "Are you ready, Monsieur?" he said at last.

"It's I who await you, Monsieur," replied Mordaunt, raising his head and giving d'Artagnan a strange look impossible to describe.

"Then take care, Monsieur," said the Gascon, "for I have some skill with the sword."

"As do I," said Mordaunt.

"All the better—it sets my conscience to rest. *En garde!*"

"One moment," said the young man. "Give me your word, Messieurs, that you will engage me only one at a time."

"Is it for the pleasure of insulting us that you ask this, little serpent?" said Porthos.

"No, it's as monsieur here said, to set my conscience to rest."

"It must be for another reason than that," murmured d'Artagnan, shaking his head and looking around anxiously.

"Faith of a gentleman!" said Aramis and Porthos together.

"In that case, *Gentlemen,*" said Mordaunt, "put yourselves in a corner, like Monsieur le Comte de La Fère, who, while he may not wish to fight, seems at least to know the rules of combat. Give us space; we will need it."

"So be it," said Aramis.

"So many complications!" said Porthos.

"Do as he asks, Messieurs," said d'Artagnan. "We mustn't leave monsieur the slightest pretext for misconduct, although it seems to me that's what he's looking for."

This new jape had no more effect on Mordaunt than the last. Porthos and Aramis went into the corner opposite to that of Athos, so that the two adversaries found themselves in command of the center of the chamber, lit like a stage from the side by the two lamps standing on Cromwell's desk. Needless to say, the parts of the room farthest from the lamps were the least well lit.

"Come," said d'Artagnan, "are you ready at last, Monsieur?"

"I am," said Mordaunt.

Each took a step forward at the same time, and their blades crossed.

D'Artagnan was too accomplished a fencer to amuse himself, as they say in the academy of arms, by feeling out his adversary. He went right into a brilliant and rapid feint, which was parried by Mordaunt. "Oh ho!" he said, with a satisfied smile. And, without wasting any time, thinking he saw an opening, he made a straight lunge, quick as lightning.

Mordaunt parried in *quarte* so tightly that the point of his sword traced a circle no larger than a girl's finger ring.

"I begin to think we're going to amuse ourselves," said d'Artagnan.

"Yes," murmured Aramis. "Amuse yourself, but be alert."

"*Sangdieu*, my friend! Take care," said Porthos.

Mordaunt smiled in his turn.

"You have a nasty smile, Monsieur," said d'Artagnan. "Was it Satan who taught you to smile like that?"

Mordaunt's only reply was an attempt to bind d'Artagnan's sword with a strength the Gascon hadn't expected from an opponent so slight in the body—but, thanks to a parry no less skillful than his adversary's, he diverted Mordaunt's steel, which slid past rather than into his chest.

Mordaunt took a quick step backward. "Ah! You break?" said d'Artagnan. "You turn? As you please, for I gain by not having to look at your horrid smile. Now we move into the shadows—all the better! You have no idea how terrible you look, Monsieur, especially when you're afraid. Turn and look me in the eyes and you'll see an honest face, something your mirror will never show you."

To these words, which were perhaps a bit rude, but which served d'Artagnan in his practice of trying to distract his adversary, Mordaunt said nothing at all, meanwhile continuing to dance back and around, until he and d'Artagnan had completely changed places. His feral smile grew ever broader, which made the Gascon suspicious. "Come, come, time to end this," murmured d'Artagnan. "This scoundrel has limbs of iron, and he hits hard!"

And he pressed even harder on Mordaunt, who continued to back away, evidently as a deliberate tactic, keeping his blade firmly in line, and without making any mistakes of which d'Artagnan could take advantage. However, as the duel was taking place in a room with limited space, Mordaunt's heel soon touched the wall behind him, and he leaned back on the wall with his left hand.

"Ha!" said d'Artagnan. "You'll retreat no further, my pretty friend! Messieurs," he continued, narrowing his eyes and frowning, "have you ever seen a scorpion nailed to a wall? No? Well, watch this . . ."

And in a single second, d'Artagnan made three terrific lunges at Mordaunt, who parried desperately. All three struck but delivered only light wounds. D'Artagnan was astounded; his three friends gasped, mouths gaping.

D'Artagnan was now too close to thrust again and took a half step back to commence a fourth lunge, all these moves blending into each other seamlessly. But just as, after a light and rapid feint, he began a lightning thrust, the wall before him seemed to split open, and Mordaunt disappeared into the gap. D'Artagnan's point probed after him, but the wall shut as quickly as it had opened, and his blade was caught and broken off.

D'Artagnan took a step back. The wall was closed and solid.

Mordaunt had maneuvered, while defending himself, until he was in front of the secret door by which he'd seen Cromwell leave. Reaching it, he'd found the hidden lever with his left hand and pushed it—and then he'd disappeared, like an evil genie who has the power to pass through walls.

The Gascon uttered a furious oath, which was echoed, from beyond the iron panel, by wild laughter, a laugh so devilish that even the skeptical Aramis shivered at the sound. "To me, Messieurs!" shouted d'Artagnan. "We'll break this door down."

"He's the Devil himself!" said Aramis, running to help his friend.

"He got away! God's blood, he got away!" howled Porthos, hurling himself shoulder-first against the panel, which, held fast by its mechanism, didn't even budge.

"No. It's for the best," murmured Athos.

"I suspected something, *mordioux!*" said d'Artagnan, exhausting himself in useless blows against the wall. "I suspected something when the wretch kept turning around the room, I *knew* he was up to something with his damned dancing, but who could have expected this?"

"It's the Devil looking out for his own," cried Aramis.

"No, it's a benevolent God protecting us from sin!" said Athos.

"Really, Athos," said d'Artagnan, shrugging his shoulders and turning his back on the door, which stubbornly refused to open. "You're losing it. How can you say such things to people like us? *Mordioux!* Don't you understand the situation?"

"Situation? What situation?" asked Porthos.

"In this game, it's either kill or be killed," d'Artagnan replied. "Is it essential to your program of expiation, Athos, that Monsieur Mordaunt should be allowed to sacrifice us on the altar of his filial piety? If so, please tell us now."

"Oh, d'Artagnan! My friend!"

"Come on, now, this is just too pathetic. That wretch is about to call down on us a hundred of Cromwell's Ironsides, who will grind us into powder. Let's go! Move it! Five more minutes here, and we're done for."

"Yes, you're right!" said Athos.

"Let's go!" said Aramis.

"But where are we going *to*?" asked Porthos.

"To our inn, old friend, to grab our gear and our horses, and from there, if God allows it, back to France, where the houses have honest walls. Our sloop awaits us—my faith, let's use it."

And d'Artagnan, matching the deed to the word, sheathed his sword, picked up his hat, opened the door and ran down the staircase, followed closely by his three companions. Outside the door the fugitives asked their lackeys for news of Mordaunt, but they'd seen no one else come out.

XXIX

The Sloop *Lightning*

D'Artagnan had guessed right: Mordaunt knew he hadn't much time and didn't waste a moment of it. He knew how decisive and quick his enemies were and resolved to act accordingly. This time the musketeers faced an adversary worthy of them.

After carefully making sure the door was solidly shut behind him, Mordaunt slipped down into the underground passage, sheathed his now-useless sword and then, emerging in the garden of the neighboring house, paused to catch his breath. "Good!" he said. "These wounds are nothing, or nearly nothing: two scratches on the arm, and another on the chest. I deliver better wounds than these—just ask the Executioner of Béthune, Uncle Winter, and King Charles! Now there's not a second to lose, for even a second might save them, and they must all die together, destroyed by the thunder of men, since we can't rely on God. They shall disappear, annihilated, disintegrated. Now I must run till my legs can no longer carry me, until my heart bursts in my chest, so long as I arrive before them."

And Mordaunt began to sprint toward the nearest cavalry barracks, which was about a quarter of a league away. He covered that quarter of a league in five minutes.

Arriving at the barracks, he made himself known, demanded the stable's best horse, jumped into the saddle, and took to the road. A quarter of an hour later he was in Greenwich. "Here's the port," he said to himself. "That dark blot over there is the Isle of Dogs. Good! I must be half an hour ahead of them, maybe even an hour. Fool that I was—in my haste I damned near gave myself a heart attack. Now," he added, standing in his stirrups the better to see through the masts and cordage of the ships lining the docks, "the *Lightning*, where is the *Lightning*?"

As he said this to himself, as if to answer his thoughts a sailor sitting on a coil of ropes rose and took a few steps toward Mordaunt, who drew a handkerchief from his pocket and waved it for a moment in the air. The man seemed attentive but remained where he was. Mordaunt quickly tied a knot in each corner of his handkerchief, showed it again, and the man came up to him. (This was, it will be recalled, the agreed-upon signal.) The sailor was wrapped in a large hooded cloak that hid his figure and his face. "Sir," the sailor said, "have you by chance come from London for a jaunt on the sea?"

"Yes, most particularly to the Isle of Dogs," replied Mordaunt.

"There it is. And would the gentleman have a particular preference? One vessel over another? A steady ship, perhaps, or a ship that's fast . . . ?"

"As lightning," Mordaunt replied.

"Well, then, it's my ship the gentleman is looking for, and I'm the skipper."

"I begin to believe it," said Mordaunt, "especially if you haven't forgotten the recognition sign."

"Here it is, Sir," said the sailor, drawing from inside his cloak a handkerchief with a knot at each corner.

"Good!" cried Mordaunt, leaping down from his horse. "Now, there's no time to lose. Have my horse led to the nearest stable and take me to your vessel."

"But your companions?" asked the sailor. "I was told to expect four, plus some lackeys."

"Listen," said Mordaunt, stepping up to the sailor, "I'm not the one you're waiting for, just as you're not the one they expect to find. You took the place of Captain Rogers, didn't you? You're here by order of General Cromwell, and I come from him."

"I know," said the skipper, "because I recognize you—you're Captain Mordaunt."

Mordaunt started. "There's nothing to fear," said the skipper, lowering his hood. "I'm a friend."

"Captain Groslow!" cried Mordaunt.

"In person. The general remembered that I'd formerly been a naval officer and charged me with this mission. Has something changed?"

"No, nothing. On the contrary, everything is going according to plan."

"I thought that the death of the king . . ."

"The king's death has only hurried their flight—in a quarter of an hour, maybe only ten minutes, they'll be here."

"Then what are you going to do?"

"Embark along with you."

"Oh? Does the general doubt my zeal?"

"No—but I want to attend to my own vengeance. Is there anyone who can take care of my horse?"

Groslow whistled, and another sailor appeared. "Patrick," said Groslow, "take this horse to the stable of the nearest inn. If you're asked to whom it belongs, tell them it's to an Irish lord."

The sailor led the horse away without saying anything.

"Now you," said Mordaunt, "aren't you afraid that they'll recognize you?"

"No fear of that in this outfit, wrapped in both this cloak and the dark night. Even you didn't recognize me, so there's little chance they will."

"True enough," said Mordaunt. "Besides, they'd hardly be expecting to encounter you. Is everything ready?"

"Yes."

"Is the . . . *cargo* loaded?"

"Yes."

"Five barrels full?"

"And fifty empty."

"That's right."

"We claim we're shipping a cargo of port to Antwerp."

"Perfect. Now get me aboard and then return to your post, for they'll be arriving soon."

"I'm ready."

"Oh—it's important that none of your people see me board."

"There's only one man aboard at the moment, and I'm as sure of him as I am of myself. Besides, he doesn't know you. The crew, though ready to follow orders, has been told nothing."

"Good. Let's go." They went down to the bank of the Thames. A long-boat was moored to the shore by a chain tied to a bollard. Groslow assured Mordaunt that everything was fine, loosed the boat from its chain, and jumped in, quickly proving by his rowing prowess that he hadn't forgotten his trade as a sailor. Within five minutes they were clear of the sprawl of buildings that, even at that time, already encumbered the approaches to London, and Mordaunt could see, as a shadow ahead, the small sloop sway-ing at anchor within four or five cable-lengths of the Isle of Dogs.

As they approached the *Lightning*, Groslow gave a peculiar whistle, and a man's head appeared above the rail. "Is that you, Captain?" the man asked.

"Yes, throw down the ladder." And Groslow, swarming up the rope ladder like a squirrel, soon joined him at the rail. "Come on up," Groslow said.

Mordaunt said nothing, just grabbed the ropes and climbed up the side of the ship with extraordinary grace and agility; driven by his desire for vengeance, he seemed capable of anything.

As Groslow had foretold, the *Lightning*'s duty sailor didn't seem to notice that his captain had returned with a companion.

Mordaunt and Groslow went forward toward the captain's cabin, a sort of shed on the foredeck pieced together out of planks. "And where will *they* stay?" asked Mordaunt.

"At the other end of the vessel," Groslow replied. "Captain Rogers had given up the main cabin to his honorable passengers."

"And they'll have no reason to come to this end?"

"Absolutely none."

"Perfect! I'll hide in your cabin. Return to Greenwich and get them. Your ship has a longboat?"

"The one that brought us."

"She seemed light and nimble."

"As a canoe."

"Tie her to the stern by a hempen line so it follows in our wake, and put the oars in it so it's ready to depart at a cut of the rope. Pack it with rum and biscuits; if by chance the sea is bad, your men won't be sorry to find supplies at hand to comfort themselves."

"It'll be done as you say. Do you want to see the powder kegs?"

"No, not till you return. Then I want to trim the fuse myself, to make sure it's not too long. Take care to hide your face so they don't recognize you."

"Don't worry."

"Get going, I hear ten o'clock sounding from Greenwich."

In fact, the tolling of a bell, repeated ten times, was sounding sadly across the water, while dark clouds began to roll across the night sky like silent waves.

Groslow went out the door, which Mordaunt closed tightly behind him. Then, having ordered the sailor on duty to keep watch with utmost alertness, he went down into his boat and rowed away rapidly with foam at either oar.

The wind was cold and the jetty deserted when Groslow landed at Greenwich; several barks had just departed with the tide. As Groslow stepped ashore, he heard horses galloping on the gravel of the high road. "Oh ho!" he said to himself. "Mordaunt said there was no time to lose, and here they are."

In fact, it was the musketeers, or at least their vanguard, which consisted of d'Artagnan and Athos. As they arrived in front of Groslow they pulled up, as if guessing that he was the one they were to deal with. Athos dismounted, unwrapped a handkerchief with a knot at each corner, and waved it in the wind, while d'Artagnan, ever cautious, leaned forward on his saddle, one hand near his holsters.

Groslow, unsure if these cavaliers were the ones he awaited, had stepped back behind one of the bollards used to anchor ships' cables, but upon seeing the agreed-upon signal, he approached the gentlemen. His face was so deep in the hood of his cloak it was impossible to see his features, though the night was so dark that hardly mattered. However, Athos's piercing eye divined, despite the gloom, that this wasn't Rogers who stood before him. "What do you want?" he said to Groslow, taking a step back.

"I wish to inform you, Milord," replied Groslow, affecting an Irish accent, "that if you're looking for Captain Rogers, you won't find him."

"How's that?" asked Athos.

"Because this morning he fell from a high mast and broke his leg. But I'm his cousin; he told me about the whole business, and asked me to take over for him, escorting wherever they wished the gentlemen who'd have a hand-kerchief knotted at all four corners, like this one I have in my pocket." And Groslow pulled out the same handkerchief he'd already shown Mordaunt.

"Is that all?" asked Athos.

"No, Milord—there were also seventy-five livres promised if I brought you safe and sound to Boulogne or any other point in France you designated."

"What do you think, d'Artagnan?" asked Athos in French.

"Tell me first what he said," the latter replied.

"Oh, that's right, I forgot you don't understand English," said Athos. And he recounted to d'Artagnan the conversation he'd just had with the skipper.

"That sounds reasonable enough," said the Gascon.

"And to me as well," replied Athos.

"Besides," said d'Artagnan, "if this man is lying to us, we can always blow his brains out."

"And then who would pilot us home?"

"You would, Athos—you know so many things, I've no doubt you know how to navigate a ship as well."

"*Ma foi,*" said Athos with a smile, "my friend, you've found me out—my father intended me to serve in the navy, and I still have some vague notions of navigation."

"You see?" said d'Artagnan.

"Go and fetch our friends, d'Artagnan, and hurry back; it's already nearly eleven, and we've no time to lose."

D'Artagnan rode back toward two riders who, pistols in hand, were posted *en vedette* by a sort of long shed before the first houses of the town, watching the road in both directions; three other horsemen could be seen waiting beyond. The vedettes were Porthos and Aramis, while the three riders were Mousqueton, Blaisois, and Grimaud—though the last, on closer inspection, was double, as he carried on his crupper Parry's brother, who was to return with their horses to London and sell them to settle their accounts. Counting on this means to cover their expenses, the four friends had retained their cash, which gave them a sum that, though not large, should be enough to deal with delays and contingencies.

D'Artagnan beckoned to Porthos and Aramis to follow him, and the latter made signs to their lackeys to dismount and bring their baggage. Parry's brother parted, not without regret, from his new friends; they'd proposed to bring him to France, but he'd obstinately refused. "The reason is obvious: he has plans for Groslow," said Mousqueton, who recalled that it was Groslow who'd split open his head.

The little troop rejoined Athos. By then d'Artagnan had resumed his usual wariness; he found the quay too deserted, the night too dark, and the ship captain over-plausible. He'd told Aramis of the substitution for Rogers, and Aramis, no less wary than he, had echoed his suspicions.

A slight clicking of his tongue against his teeth conveyed the Gascon's anxieties to Athos. "We have no time for suspicions," said Athos. "The sloop awaits us—let's go."

"Besides," said Aramis, "we can go and still be careful about it. Just keep an eye on that skipper."

"And if he plays us false, I'll smash him flat," said Porthos.

"Well said," replied d'Artagnan. "Let's go, then. Get in, Mousqueton." D'Artagnan raised a hand to signal his friends to wait, letting the lackeys make the first trip across the plank from the jetty to the longboat. The three servants got aboard without any trouble. Athos followed them, then Porthos, then Aramis. D'Artagnan came last, while continuing to shake his head.

"What the devil are you worried about, friend?" said Porthos. "Upon my word, you'd put fear into a Caesar."

"This is a port," replied d'Artagnan, "but I don't see a guard, or an inspector, or a customs agent."

"And that's a problem? Who wants them?" said Porthos. "Everything is going smooth as silk."

"Too smoothly, Porthos. But never mind, we'll trust in God's grace."

As soon as the plank was removed, the skipper sat down at the helm and motioned to a sailor who, armed with a gaff, kept the bow away from other vessels as they maneuvered their way out of the labyrinth of anchored ships. A second sailor stood on the port side, oar at the ready. When they were clear, his companion put down the gaff, the oars were deployed, and the boat began to pick up speed. "At last, we're leaving!" said Porthos.

"But alas for us!" said the Comte de La Fère. "For we're leaving alone."

"Yes, but at least we're all together, and leaving without a scratch—that's some consolation."

"We're not home yet," said d'Artagnan. "I fear further trouble."

"Dear friend," said Porthos, "you croak like a raven! Trouble? Who will bother us on a night as dark as this, when you can't see twenty paces?"

"Yes, but tomorrow morning?" said d'Artagnan.

"Tomorrow morning we'll be in Boulogne."

"I hope so with all my heart," said the Gascon, "and admit to my weakness. Here, Athos, you'll laugh—but as long as we were within range of the jetty or the ships moored there, I expected a volley of musketry to break out at any moment."

"But that's impossible," said Porthos sensibly, "because they'd also be firing on the skipper and his sailors."

"Bah! Do you think that would stop Monsieur Mordaunt for a second?"

"Well," said Porthos, "at least I lived long enough to hear d'Artagnan confess that he's afraid."

"I don't just confess it, I'm proud of it. I'm not a rhinoceros like you. *Ohé!* What's that there?"

"The *Lightning*," said the skipper.

"So, we've arrived?" asked Athos in English.

"We've arrived," the captain said.

In fact, three strokes of the oars later, they hove to the side of the small vessel. The duty sailor was waiting and unrolled the ladder; he'd recognized the boat.

Athos, with the agility of a mariner, mounted first; Aramis, with the skills gained by long experience with forbidden entrance by ropes and other means, went second; d'Artagnan, climbing like a Gascon mountaineer, was next; followed by Porthos, who hauled himself up with the brute force that, for him, took the place of skill.

The lackeys had a harder time of it. Not Grimaud, who was slim and wiry as a gutter cat, but for the portly Mousqueton and the awkward Blaisois, the sailors on the longboat had to lift them within range of the mighty arms of Porthos, who grabbed them by the collars and hoisted them onto the deck.

The captain escorted his passengers to the cabin prepared for them, a single room which they were to occupy together, and then tried to leave under the pretext of having to go give orders to set sail. "A moment," said d'Artagnan. "How many men do you have aboard, skipper?"

"I don't understand," the man replied in English.

"Ask him in his own language, Athos."

Athos repeated d'Artagnan's question. "Three," Groslow replied, "not counting me, of course."

D'Artagnan understood, as in responding the skipper had held up three fingers.

"Ah!" said d'Artagnan. "Only three. That makes me feel better. Nonetheless, Athos, while you're settling in, I'll take a look around the ship."

"And I," said Porthos, "will see about getting us some supper."

"A noble project and an act of charity, Porthos—I salute you! Athos, lend me Grimaud, because, having spent time with his friend Parry, he's picked up a little English; he can serve as my interpreter."

"Go, Grimaud," said Athos.

A glowing lantern hung from the bridge; d'Artagnan took it in one hand, put a pistol in the other, and said to the skipper, "*Come.*" That, along with *Goddamn,* was the only word he knew in English.

D'Artagnan opened the main hatch and descended into the tween-decks. The steerage was divided into three compartments: the one he entered stretched aft from the mizzenmast to the end of the poop deck, extending beneath the floor of the cabin where Athos, Porthos, and Aramis were preparing to spend the night; the second compartment, in the middle of the sloop, was offered to house the lackeys; while the third, toward the prow, extended under the improvised captain's cabin wherein Mordaunt was hidden. "Ho!" said d'Artagnan, descending the ladder from the hatch while holding out the lantern, extending it forward. "So many barrels! It looks like Ali Baba's cavern."

(The *Thousand and One Nights* had just been translated[34] and was very fashionable at the time.)

"What'd you say?" asked the captain in English.

D'Artagnan understood him from his tone of voice. "I want to know what's in these barrels," d'Artagnan asked, resting the lantern on one of the kegs.

The skipper made a movement toward the ladder but restrained himself. "P-port," he replied.

"Ah! Port wine?" said d'Artagnan. "Then at least we won't die of thirst." He turned back to Groslow, who was mopping his brow. "And are they all full?" he asked him.

Grimaud translated the question. "These here are full, the rest are empty," Groslow replied in a voice that, despite himself, betrayed his anxiety.

D'Artagnan tapped on the barrels, finding that five were full, while the rest sounded hollow. Then, to the abject terror of the Englishman, to see farther aft he passed the lantern right between two of the filled kegs—but seeing nothing, he said, "Let's move on," and turned toward the door to the second compartment.

"Wait," said the Englishman, pausing to catch his breath. "I have the key." And, slipping past d'Artagnan and Grimaud, with a trembling hand he inserted the key into the door and unlocked the second compartment, where Mousqueton and Blaisois were already preparing their supper. They saw nothing of interest or concern, peering into every corner of the cabin by the light of the lamp that had been lit by their worthy companions.

They passed quickly through the waist and went forward to visit the third compartment. This was the home of the sailors; three or four hammocks were hanging from the ceiling, as was a table hung upside-down by its legs, beside which two worm-eaten and shaky benches formed the whole of the furnishings. D'Artagnan looked behind two or three sails hanging from the walls, but seeing nothing suspicious, went up a ladder and emerged onto the vessel's bow. "And this small cabin?" he asked.

Grimaud translated the musketeer's words into English. "That's my cabin," said the skipper. "Do you want to see it?"

"Open the door," said d'Artagnan.

The Englishman obeyed. D'Artagnan extended his arm, holding the lamp, through the doorway, stuck his head in, and seeing the little room really was in use as a cabin, he said, "Good. If there's an army aboard, it isn't hiding here. Let's go see what Porthos has found for our supper."

He thanked the skipper with a nod and returned aft to the cabin of honor to rejoin his friends. Porthos hadn't found anything edible, it seemed, or if he had, fatigue had prevailed over hunger, for he was deeply asleep when d'Artagnan entered. Athos and Aramis, lulled by the first rollers of the sea, had begun to close their eyes, but they reopened them when they heard their comrade enter. "Well?" said Aramis.

"All is well," said d'Artagnan, "and we can sleep in peace."

At this assurance, Aramis allowed his head to drop back; Athos gave an affectionate nod; and d'Artagnan, who, like Porthos, had more need for sleep than food, dismissed Grimaud, drew his sword, wrapped himself in a cloak, and lay down in front of the door in such a way that it was impossible to enter without the panel hitting him.

XXX

The Port Wine

Within ten minutes the masters were asleep, but not so the servants, who were quite hungry, and even worse, thirsty. Blaisois and Mousqueton were beginning to make their bed, which consisted of a plank and a travel trunk, while nearby on a hanging table, swaying as the ship rolled, were balanced a jug of beer and three glasses.

"This cursed rolling!" said Blaisois. "I feel like it'll make me as sick as I was on the way over."

"And we have nothing to stave off seasickness but some barley bread and this brew of hops!" said Mousqueton. *"Pouah!"*

"But what about your wicker-wrapped flask, Monsieur Mouston?" asked Blaisois, who'd finished making the bed, and stumbled over to the table where Mousqueton had just seated himself. Blaisois managed to get onto a chair, and said, "Your wicker-wrapped flask—did you lose it?"

"No, Parry's brother held onto it," said Mousqueton. "These devils of Scots are always thirsty. What about you, Grimaud?" asked Mousqueton of his companion, who'd just returned from escorting d'Artagnan on his tour. "Are you thirsty?"

"As a Scotsman," replied the laconic Grimaud. And he sat down near Blaisois and Mousqueton, drew a notebook from his pocket and began to balance the accounts of their little society, of which he was the purser.

"Oh! *Là!*" said Blaisois. "My insides are turning over."

"For this symptom," said Mousqueton in a doctor's tone, "I prescribe some food."

"You call this food?" said Blaisois, with a pitiful look, pointing at the bread and beer.

"Blaisois," said Mousqueton, "remember that bread is the true food of the French people—and not even the French can always get it. Ask Grimaud."

"Yes, but beer?" replied Blaisois, with a rapidity that did honor to the French spirit of debate. "Beer, now—is that any kind of a true drink?"

"As to that," said Mousqueton, caught and somewhat embarrassed for an answer, "I must admit that beer is as abhorrent to the French as wine is to the English."

"Really, Monsieur Mouston?" said Blaisois, doubting, for once, the worldly wisdom of Mousqueton, for which he usually had the deepest admiration. "Really? The English don't like wine?"

"They hate it."

"But I've seen them drink it, though."

"Only as a penance. And the proof," continued Mousqueton, rising to his theme, "is that an English prince was drowned in a barrel of malmsey wine! I heard all about it from Monsieur l'Abbé d'Herblay."

"Drowned? The fool," said Blaisois. "I'd love to suffer such a fate."

"You could," said Grimaud, totaling his figures.

"What do you mean, *you could*?" said Blaisois.

"What I said," continued Grimaud, carrying the four and adding it to the top of the next column.

"I could? Explain yourself, Monsieur Grimaud."

Mousqueton remained silent during Blaisois's interrogation, but it was clear that it had gotten his attention.

Grimaud carried his calculation to the end, and then said, "Port wine," extending his hand toward the first compartment he'd visited with d'Artagnan and the skipper.

"What? In those barrels I saw when the door was opened?"

"Port wine," repeated Grimaud, starting a new computation.

"I've heard of this port," said Blaisois to Mousqueton. "It's an excellent wine from Spain."

"Excellent?" said Mousqueton, running his tongue over his lips. "I'll say it is! Monsieur le Baron de Bracieux has some in his cellars."

"If we asked these Englishmen, do you suppose they'd sell us a bottle?" inquired the honest Blaisois.

"Sell!" said Mousqueton, succumbing to his old instincts for banditry. "It's easy to see, young man, that you've not yet had much experience of life. Why should one buy when one can take?"

"Take!" said Blaisois. "To covet our neighbor's goods? That's written down as forbidden, it seems to me."

"Oh? Where?" asked Mousqueton.

"In the Commandments of God or the Church somewhere, I'm sure of it. It's written, *Covet not thy neighbor's goods, nor his wife.*"

"That's a child's reasoning, Monsieur Blaisois," said Mousqueton in his most patronizing tone. "A child's! Where does it say in these scriptures you quote that an Englishman is your neighbor?"

"Nowhere, that's true," said Blaisois. "Or at least, I can't remember it."

"A child's reasoning, I repeat," said Mousqueton. "My dear Blaisois, if you'd spent ten years on campaign like Grimaud and me, you'd know how to distinguish between the goods of your neighbors and the goods of your enemies. Now, an Englishman is our enemy, I think, and this port wine belongs to the English. Therefore, since we're French, we're entitled to take it. Don't you know the proverb that what's taken by you is denied to the enemy?"

This pronouncement, spoken with all the authority of Mousqueton's long experience, overwhelmed Blaisois. He bowed his head as if to submit, but suddenly raised it again like a man armed with an irresistible argument. "And our masters—will they share your opinion, Monsieur Mouston?" he said.

Mousqueton smiled with disdain. "Oh, maybe I should just go wake our illustrious lords from their well-deserved sleep and ask them! 'Messieurs, your servant Mouston is thirsty, can he have a drink?' Do you suppose it matters to Monsieur de Bracieux if I'm a little thirsty?"

"It's just so very expensive a wine," said Blaisois, shaking his head.

"If it were gold in liquid form, Monsieur Blaisois, our masters would still take it if they wanted it," said Mousqueton. "Why, Monsieur le Baron de Bracieux alone is rich enough to drink a cellar-full of port, even at a pistole per swallow. I can't see why," continued Mousqueton, magnificent in his pride, "if our noble masters would partake of it, that we, their loyal servants, should be deprived of it."

And Mousqueton, rising, took the jug of beer, emptied it out a port-hole to the last drop, and advanced majestically toward the door of the aft compartment. "But no! Locked!" he cried. "These English devils, how suspicious they are!"

"Locked!" said Blaisois, no less disappointed than Mousqueton. "Plague take it! What rotten luck! And now I feel my insides heaving more and more."

"Locked!" repeated Mousqueton, with a face whose expression showed Blaisois he fully shared the younger man's disappointment.

"But didn't I hear you say, Monsieur Mouston," ventured Blaisois, "that once in your youth, at Chantilly I think it was, you fed both your master and yourself by taking partridges by snare, carp by fishing line, and bottles by lasso?"

"Yes, indeed," Mousqueton replied. "It's the honest truth, as Grimaud here can tell you. But that wine cellar had an air-vent, and the wine was in bottles. I can't throw a lasso through a solid bulkhead or use it to lift a keg that weighs twice what you do."

"No, but you can pry two or three planks out of the wall," said Blaisois, "and make a hole with a hand-drill into a barrel."

Mousqueton stared wide-eyed at Blaisois, amazed to discover in the man unexpected qualities. "That's true," he said, "but I'd need a chisel to pry the planks, and a gimlet to drill the hole."

"Tool case," said Grimaud, drawing a line under his final balance.

"Oh, right! Our tool case," said Mousqueton. "I forgot about that."

Grimaud, in fact, was not just the purser of the troop, but also its handyman, equipped with a tool bag as well as a ledger. Now, as Grimaud was a man of both foresight and caution, this canvas case, which was rolled up in his baggage, contained an assortment of tools of the finest quality. In it Mousqueton quickly found a gimlet of suitable size, which he appropriated. For a chisel, he drew from his belt his dagger, which was stout and sharp. Mousqueton picked a section of the bulkhead where the planks were loose and went right to work.

Blaisois watched him working with an admiration tinged by impatience, making recommendations from time to time about how to pull a nail or pry a plank, advice notable for its intelligence and clarity.

After five minutes, Mousqueton had removed three boards. "There," said Blaisois. But Mousqueton was the opposite of the frog in the fable who thought himself larger than he was. Unfortunately, though he'd managed to decrease his name by a third, the same wasn't true of his body. He tried to pass through the opening, but was dismayed to find that to do so he'd have to remove three or four additional boards. He sighed and picked up his tools to go back to work.

But Grimaud, who'd finished his computations, had joined them, showing a great interest in the operations underway, and had noted Mousqueton's thwarted attempt to reach the Promised Land. "Let me," said Grimaud.

These two words were worth more from Grimaud than a whole sonnet from anyone else, so Mousqueton paused and turned around. "What, you?" he asked.

"I can get through."

"So you could," said Mousqueton, looking over his friend's long, slender body. "You could get through, and easily."

"That's right, and he knows which barrels are the full ones," said Blaisois, "since he was in the cellar already with Monsieur le Chevalier d'Artagnan. Let Monsieur Grimaud pass, Monsieur Mouston."

"I could do it just as well as Grimaud," said Mousqueton, a little piqued.

"Yes, but it'll take longer, and I'm thirsty. My inwards are getting worse and worse."

"Go ahead, Grimaud," said Mousqueton, giving the jug and the gimlet to the man assuming his place on the mission.

"Rinse out the glasses," said Grimaud. Then he gave a little bow to Mousqueton, as if asking his pardon for finishing the expedition he'd so brilliantly begun, and then, lithe as a snake, he slipped through the opening and disappeared.

Blaisois was thoroughly delighted. Of all the exploits accomplished in England by the extraordinary members of their little troop, this one seemed to him the most miraculous. "Now, Blaisois," said Mousqueton, with a look of superiority he didn't even try to conceal, "now you'll see how old soldiers can find drink when they're thirsty."

"The cloak," said Grimaud, from within the cellar.

"Ah, right," said Mousqueton.

"What does he want?" asked Blaisois.

"To have the opening concealed with a cloak."

"Why do that?" asked Blaisois.

"Oh, innocent one!" said Mousqueton. "What if someone comes in?"

"Ah! That *is* right," said Blaisois, in even greater admiration. "But he won't be able to see in there."

"Grimaud will be fine," replied Mousqueton. "He has eyes like a cat."

"Lucky for him," said Blaisois. "If I don't have a candle, I can't take two steps without barking my shins."

"You were never in the service," said Mousqueton, "or you'd have learned how to find a needle in a dark closet. But hush! I think I hear someone coming."

Mousqueton gave out a low whistle of alarm, familiar to all the lackeys from their younger days, sat back down at the table and gestured to Blaisois to do the same. Blaisois obeyed.

The door opened. Two men came in, both wrapped in cloaks. "Oh ho!" said one of them. "A quarter past eleven, and not yet asleep? That's against the rules. Make sure that in another quarter of an hour everyone's in bed and snoring."

The two men crossed to the doorway to the compartment Grimaud had gone into, opened the door, entered, and closed it behind them.

"Woe!" whispered Blaisois, trembling. "Grimaud is doomed!"

"He's a canny fox, that Grimaud," murmured Mousqueton.

And they waited, holding their breath with heads cocked to listen.

Ten minutes passed, during which no noise was heard that indicated Grimaud was discovered. Then Mousqueton and Blaisois saw the door open again, the two cloaked men came out, locked the door with the same care they'd taken to unlock it, and went out, renewing the order to go to bed and put out the lights.

"Should we obey?" asked Blaisois. "There's something strange about all this."

"They said in a quarter of an hour, so we still have five minutes," replied Mousqueton.

"Should we warn our masters?"

"Let's wait for Grimaud."

"What if they killed him?"

"Grimaud would have cried out."

"You know he's practically a mute."

"We'd have heard the blow."

"What if he doesn't come back?"

"Here he comes now."

In fact, at that moment Grimaud drew back the cloak that concealed the opening and his face appeared, pale, his eyes wide with fright, their pupils like pinpoints in dishes of white milk. He crawled in, carefully holding the beer jug in one hand. It was filled with some substance, which he brought near the smoky lamp to see better. Then he murmured a single syllable— "*Oh!*"—with an expression of such profound terror that Mousqueton recoiled in fear, and Blaisois nearly fainted.

Nevertheless, they both glanced curiously into the beer jug.

It was full of black powder.

Now convinced that the vessel's cargo was gunpowder rather than wine, Grimaud leapt up and out the hatch and rushed to the cabin wherein slept the four friends. He gently pushed open the door, which immediately awakened d'Artagnan, who was sleeping against it. Seeing Grimaud's dismayed expression he began to cry out, but Grimaud quickly raised a finger to his lips, and then, with a puff of breath one wouldn't have thought could issue from such a slim body, from a distance of three feet he blew out the night-lamp.

D'Artagnan raised himself on one elbow, Grimaud knelt next to him, and then, quivering, Grimaud whispered into d'Artagnan's ear a story so dramatic it needed neither gesture nor expression to emphasize it.

During this account, Athos, Porthos, and Aramis continued sleeping like men who hadn't slept for a week, while in the tween-decks, Mousqueton did up his doublet as a precaution, as Blaisois, gripped by terror, the hair standing up on his head, tried to do the same.

Here is what had happened: scarcely had Grimaud disappeared through the opening into the aft compartment before, searching, he encountered a barrel. He knocked, and it echoed, empty. He tried another, also empty, but the third, which he thumped twice to make sure he wasn't mistaken, gave back a sound so dull that Grimaud recognized it had to be full. Feeling the keg for a good place to set the gimlet, his hand struck a spigot. "Good!" said Grimaud. "That saves me the trouble." He positioned his beer jug, opened the tap on the keg, and felt the contents flow from one to the other.

Having first closed the spigot as a precaution, Grimaud was lifting the jug to his lips, so as not to bring his companions a brew he couldn't answer for, when he heard Mousqueton's low alarm whistle. He expected some watchman on a night round, so he slipped between two barrels and hid himself behind a crate.

A moment later the door opened, then closed again after admitting the two cloaked men we saw passing Blaisois and Mousqueton and giving the order for lights out. One of them had a dark-lantern, its glass sides carefully closed, and tall enough that the flame burned well below its top. In addition, the glass was wrapped in thick paper that absorbed most of the light.

This man was Groslow.

The other, his face shaded by a broad-brimmed hat, had in his hand something long, flexible, and coiled like a whitish rope. Grimaud, thinking they'd come to the cellar following the same urge as he, to sample the port wine, nestled further back behind his crate, while thinking that if he was discovered, his crime was no worse than theirs.

Arriving at the barrel in front of Grimaud's crate, the two men stopped. "Do you have the fuse?" asked the one carrying the lamp, speaking English.

"Right here," said the other.

At the voice of the latter, Grimaud felt a cold shiver shake him to the marrow of his bones. He slowly raised his head above the edge of the crate until he could see, under the broad brim of the hat, the pale features of Mordaunt.

"How long will it take to burn down?" asked Mordaunt.

"Five minutes, more or less," said the skipper.

This was another voice that was no stranger to Grimaud. He glanced from one to the other and recognized Mordaunt's companion as Groslow.

"All right, then," said Mordaunt. "Warn your men to be ready to go, without telling them why. The longboat is trailing the sloop?"

"Like a dog on the end of a leash."

"Then, when the clock shows a quarter past midnight, gather your men and go quietly down into the longboat . . ."

"After first having lit the fuse?"

"I'll handle that. I want to be certain of my vengeance. The oars are in the boat?"

"Everything is ready."

"Good."

"That's it, then."

Mordaunt knelt down and inserted one end of the fuse into the spigot, so he'd only have to light the other end. Then he drew out his watch. "You understand? At a quarter past midnight, in other words . . ." He rose and looked at his watch. "In twenty minutes."

"Yes, Sir," replied Groslow. "Only, I must point out that the part of this mission you've reserved for yourself is dangerous, and it would be safer to have one of the men set off the fireworks."

"My dear Groslow," said Mordaunt, "you know the French proverb: *If you want something done right, do it yourself.* I intend to put that into practice."

Grimaud had heard everything, and understood most of it, while what he saw made the situation quite clear: for there was Mordaunt, laying the fuse, and uttering that proverb, which for fidelity he'd spoken in French. In final confirmation, Grimaud carefully reached into the jug that Mousqueton and Blaisois were waiting so impatiently for, rubbed its contents between his fingers, and felt the grains of a coarse powder.

Mordaunt and the skipper moved away. At the door they paused, listening. Mordaunt said, "Listen to how soundly they sleep!"

Through the ceiling could be heard the snores of Porthos. Groslow said, "They've been placed in our hands like a gift from God."

"And this time," said Mordaunt, "not even the Devil could save them!"

Smiling, the pair went out.

Grimaud waited until he'd heard the key turn in the lock, and when he was sure he was alone, he slowly rose against the wall. "Oh!" he said, wiping huge beads of sweat from his forehead with his sleeve. "How lucky it was that Mousqueton was thirsty!"

He scurried back through the opening in the bulkhead, hoping it had just been a dream—but when he saw the black powder in the jug, he knew it was no dream, but instead a deadly nightmare.

D'Artagnan, as one might imagine, listened to this story with increasing attention, and without even waiting for Grimaud to finish, he got swiftly up, put his mouth near the ear of Aramis, who slept on his left, put a hand on his shoulder to prevent sudden movement, and whispered, "Get up, Chevalier, but quietly."

Aramis awoke. D'Artagnan repeated his warning and lifted his hand. Aramis got up. "You have Athos to your left," d'Artagnan said. "Warn him as I warned you."

Aramis easily awoke Athos, who was a light sleeper, as is usually the case with those of a refined nature. They had a more difficult time awakening

Porthos, who was inclined to resist being drawn from sleep and ready to protest aloud, until d'Artagnan placed a firm hand over his mouth.

When all were up, our Gascon extended his arms around them and drew their heads close together, nearly touching. "Comrades," he said, "we must get off this vessel immediately, or we're all dead."

"Bah!" said Athos. "Now what?"

"Do you know who's the skipper of this ship?"

"No."

"Captain Groslow."

The shudder that ran through the three musketeers told d'Artagnan he was beginning to get their attention. "Groslow!" said Aramis. "The devil!"

"Who is this Groslow?" asked Porthos. "I don't remember him."

"The one who broke open Parry's head and is about to take our own."

"Oh ho!"

"And his lieutenant, can you guess who *he* is?"

"His lieutenant? He has none," said Athos. "There's no lieutenant on a sloop with a crew of four."

"Yes, but our Monsieur Groslow is no ordinary captain. He has a lieutenant, and his lieutenant is Monsieur Mordaunt."

This time it was more than a shudder that passed through the musketeers, it was a spasm. These invincible men were nonetheless subject to a single mysterious and fatal influence, a terror which only that name could produce in them.

"What do we do?" said Athos.

"Take over the sloop," said Aramis.

"And kill him," said Porthos.

"The sloop is mined," said d'Artagnan. "Those barrels I took for barrels of port are kegs of powder. When Mordaunt is confronted, he'll blow everything up, friends and enemies together, and by my faith as a gentleman, he's such bad company that I have no desire to go anywhere with him, especially to heaven or hell."

"Do you have a plan?" asked Athos.

"Yes."

"What is it?"

"Do you have confidence in me?"

"Command us," said the three musketeers together.

"Then, let's go!" D'Artagnan went to the stern window, which was low but broad enough to allow passage, and opened it gently on its hinges. "This is our road," he said.

"*Diable!*" said Aramis. "That's a cold road, *cher ami.*"

"Stay here if you like—it will be hot soon enough!"

"But we can't swim to land."

"The longboat trails in our wake on a rope—see it there? When we're all in the boat, we'll cut the rope. That's the whole plan. Let's go, Messieurs."

"One moment," said Athos. "The lackeys?"

"Here we are," said Mousqueton and Blaisois, whom Grimaud, to concentrate all their forces in the cabin, had brought up quietly through the hatch.

Meanwhile the three friends stood motionless, contemplating the grim spectacle d'Artagnan had revealed by opening the window. It was a daunting scene indeed, and anyone who's seen it knows there's nothing more striking than a stormy night sea, dark waves rolling and crashing under the flickering light of a midwinter moon. "*Cordieu!*" said d'Artagnan. "Are we hesitating? If we're afraid to go, how will the lackeys manage it?"

"I won't hesitate," said Grimaud.

"Monsieur," said Blaisois, "I must warn you, I can swim only in rivers."

"And I, I don't swim at all," said Mousqueton.

Meanwhile d'Artagnan was slipping over the sill. "You're decided, then, friend?" said Athos.

"Yes," replied the Gascon. "Come, Athos, you who are the superior man, put your mind over matter. You, Aramis, command the lackeys. You, Porthos, kill anyone who tries to stop us."

And d'Artagnan, after shaking hands with Athos, chose a moment when the sloop's bow pitched up so its stern sank down, and slipped into the water, which was already up to his waist.

Athos followed immediately before the sloop could pitch down again; when the stern came up, the tow-rope rose out of the water, and they could see where it led to the longboat. D'Artagnan swam toward the rope and grabbed it. He clung to the rope by one hand, just his head out of the water, until a second later Athos joined him.

Two more bodies plunged into the water behind the sloop. They saw the heads of Aramis and Grimaud. "Blaisois worries me," said Athos. "Did you hear what he said, d'Artagnan, about swimming only in rivers?"

"If you can swim at all, you can swim anywhere," said d'Artagnan. "To the boat! To the boat!"

"But Porthos? I don't see him yet."

"Oh, Porthos will come, don't worry—he swims like Leviathan himself."

In fact, Porthos was delayed, as a scene, half drama, half comedy, played out between him, Mousqueton, and Blaisois. The latter two, frightened by the roaring wind, alarmed by the sound of the waves, and terrified of the roiling black water, were backing away rather than advancing. "Come on! Come on!" said Porthos. "Into the water!"

"But, Monsieur, I can't swim," said Mousqueton. "Leave me here."

"And me too, Monsieur," said Blaisois.

"I'd just be an embarrassment, taking up room in the boat," said Mousqueton.

"And I'd just drown before I even got to it," said Blaisois.

"Why, I'll strangle you both if you don't get going," said Porthos, grabbing them by their throats. "Forward, Blaisois!"

Blaisois's only answer was a groan stifled by Porthos's mighty hand, as the giant, taking him by the neck and the ankles, slid him like a plank out the window and into the sea face-first.

"Now, Mouston," said Porthos, "I hope you won't abandon your master."

"Ah, Monsieur!" said Mousqueton, with tears in his eyes. "Why did you have to return to the service? We were doing so well at the Château de Pierrefonds!" And without further reproach, having turned philosophical and obedient, thanks to the example of Blaisois's fate, Mousqueton jumped headlong into the sea—an act of supreme loyalty, as he considered himself already drowned.

But Porthos wasn't a man to abandon a faithful companion. The master followed his servant so closely that their double impact made a single great splash—and when Mousqueton returned to the surface, blind and blinking, he found himself borne up by Porthos's great hand, effortlessly advancing toward the rope with the majesty of a sea god. At the same time Porthos felt something thrashing near his other arm and seized it by the hair: it was Blaisois, for whom Athos was already coming. "Don't bother, Count," said Porthos. "I don't need you."

And indeed, with a vigorous kick of his mighty legs, Porthos rose like the giant Adamastor[35] above the waves, and three seconds later found himself among his companions.

D'Artagnan, Aramis, and Grimaud helped Mousqueton and Blaisois to climb into the boat. Then it was the turn of Porthos, who, throwing himself across the bow, managed to avoid causing the craft to capsize. "And Athos?" asked d'Artagnan.

"Here I am!" said Athos, who, like a general commanding the rear guard, had waited until everyone else was aboard the longboat. "Are we all together?"

"All," said d'Artagnan. "And you, Athos, do you have your poniard?"

"Yes."

"Then sever the rope and get in."

Athos drew his poniard from his belt and cut the tow-rope, and the sloop sailed onward, while the longboat stayed where it was, with no motion but that given it by the waves.

"Come aboard, Athos!" said d'Artagnan. And he offered his hand to the Comte de La Fère, who found a place on a thwart in the middle. "Just in time," said the Gascon, "as I think we're about to see something interesting."

XXXI

Destiny

In fact, d'Artagnan had scarcely spoken when a low whistle was heard from the sloop, which was beginning to disappear into the mist and gloom. "That must mean something," said the Gascon.

Just then a lantern appeared on deck, making shadows dance at the stern. Suddenly a terrible cry, a cry of despair, echoed over the water—and as if this cry had chased away the clouds, the veil that had wreathed the moon slid away, and in the pale, silver moonlight the sloop was silhouetted against the horizon.

On the ship shadows ran back and forth, crying out seemingly at random. From the midst of this chaos Mordaunt appeared on the after deck with a torch in his hand. The shadows flitting to and fro across the ship were Groslow and his men, who'd gathered at the time appointed by Mordaunt, who, after listening at the cabin door to make sure the musketeers were asleep, had been reassured by the silence. Indeed, how could he have suspected what had happened? Mordaunt had then opened the aft hatch and hurried down, where, burning with vengeance and blinded by God, he'd set fire to the fuse.

Meanwhile, Groslow and his sailors had gathered at the stern. "Grab the rope," Groslow ordered, "and pull in the longboat."

One of the sailors put a leg over the rail, seized the rope and pulled—and it came right up without resistance. "The tow-rope is cut!" the sailor cried. "The boat's gone!"

"What! The boat's gone!" said Groslow, rushing to the rail. "That's impossible!"

"Maybe so," said the sailor, "but see for yourself—there's nothing in our wake, and here's the end of the rope."

It was then that Groslow uttered that cry of despair heard by the musketeers. "What is it?" demanded Mordaunt, coming up from the hatch, torch in hand, and darting toward the stern.

"Our enemies have escaped—they've cut the rope and fled in the longboat!"

Mordaunt leapt to the cabin door and kicked it open. "Empty!" he cried. "Oh, the demons!"

"We'll go after them," said Groslow. "They can't have gotten far, and we can ram and sink them."

"But no, the fire!" said Mordaunt. "I set the fire!"

"To what?"

"To the fuse!"

"A hundred hells!" Groslow shouted, racing toward the hatch. "Maybe there's still time!"

Mordaunt's only reply was a horrific laugh. Then, his face twisted by hatred more than by terror, raising his eyes to the sky to howl a final blasphemy, he threw the torch into the sea and followed it, hurling himself into the waves.

Just as Groslow set foot on the ladder into the hold, the ship erupted like the mouth of a volcano. A jet of fire exploded into the sky like a hundred cannon firing at once; the air was alight with flaming debris, and then the sloop *Lightning* was gone, blown to burning splinters that flew and fell and went out as they touched the sea. Except for a fading hiss, it was as if nothing had been there at all. The sloop had disappeared beneath the surface, and Groslow and his men were annihilated.

The four friends had seen every detail of the drama. For an instant the sea had been lit up for at least a league, and they could have been glimpsed each frozen in a different attitude, showing the terror they couldn't help but feel, despite their hearts of bronze. Next the rain of fire fell all around them, but the volcano was quickly extinguished, and darkness rushed back to swallow them, a small boat tossing on a stormy sea.

For a moment they remained stunned and silent. Porthos and d'Artagnan, each of whom had taken an oar, held them out mechanically over the water, leaning heavily on them, hands clenched. *"Ma foi,"* said Aramis, the first to break the deathly silence, "this time I think it's finally over."

"Help me, Milords! Help! Save me!" came a lamenting voice, that seemed to the four friends to rise from the waves like some spirit of the seas.

They looked at each other. Athos trembled. "It's him!" he said. "It's his voice!"

They all remained silent, for they all, like Athos, had recognized that voice. They only stared, eyes wide, toward where the sloop had disappeared, trying to peer through the darkness.

After a moment they could distinguish a man swimming vigorously toward them. Athos extended his arm, pointing him out to his companions. "Yes, yes," said d'Artagnan, "we see him all right."

"Him again!" said Porthos, breathing like a bellows. "What! Is he made of iron?"

"My God!" murmured Athos.

Aramis and d'Artagnan were whispering to each other.

Mordaunt made a few more strokes, and then, raising a hand from the water in distress, he called, "Have pity, Messieurs, in the name of heaven! I feel my strength ebbing away—I'm going to die!"

That voice pleading for help was so vibrant, so penetrating, that it awakened compassion in Athos's heart. "How pitiful," he murmured.

"Great!" said d'Artagnan. "And you're falling for it! Look, he's swimming toward us again. Does he think we're going to take him aboard? Row, Porthos, row!"

And setting the example, d'Artagnan plunged his oar into the water. Two long strokes sent the boat another twenty paces.

"Oh! You can't abandon me like that! You can't leave me to drown! You can't be so cruel!" Mordaunt wailed.

"Oh?" said Porthos to Mordaunt. "I think we've got you at last, my lad, and there's no way out for you but through the gates of hell!"

"Oh, Porthos," murmured the Comte de La Fère.

"Leave me alone, Athos—you're becoming ridiculous with your misplaced charity! If he gets within ten feet of the boat, I swear I'll break his head open with this oar."

"Have mercy! Oh, don't leave me, Messieurs—have mercy, have pity on me!" cried the young man, panting and blowing out water whenever a wave passed over his head.

D'Artagnan, who, without taking his eye off Mordaunt for a second, had completed his colloquy with Aramis, rose and said, "Mordaunt, begone, if you please. Your repentance is too recent for us to have any confidence in it. Allow me to point out that the ship in which you intended to fry us all still steams just below the surface, and your current situation is a bed of roses compared to what you had in mind for us, and actually brought upon Groslow and his men."

"Messieurs!" pleaded Mordaunt, even more despairingly. "I swear to you my repentance is real. Messieurs, I'm so young, I'm barely twenty-three! I was carried away by a natural resentment, I just wanted to avenge my mother! You, oh, surely you would have done no differently."

"*Pfah!*" said d'Artagnan, seeing that Athos was weakening. "That's as may be."

Mordaunt was only three or four strokes from the boat, and the approach of death seemed to grant him supernatural strength. "Alas!" he cried. "I'm doomed to die! You'll murder the son as you murdered the mother! But think, by all laws human and divine, a son *must* avenge his mother. Besides," he added, joining his hands in prayer, "if it was a crime, since I repent of it, since I ask to be pardoned, I must be forgiven." Then, as if his strength was failing, he sank until a wave passed over his head, silencing his pleas.

"Oh! It tears me apart!" said Athos.

Mordaunt reappeared, blinking and blowing.

"And I say that now we finish this," replied d'Artagnan. "Monsieur the assassin of your uncle; Monsieur the executioner of King Charles; Monsieur the incendiary saboteur, I urge you to allow yourself to sink quietly—because if you come a single stroke closer, I'll break your head with my oar."

Mordaunt, as if in despair, swam a stroke nearer. D'Artagnan took his oar in both hands, and Athos rose. "D'Artagnan! D'Artagnan!" he cried. "My son, I beg of you. This unhappy man is about to die, and it's abominable to let a man die when you can extend your hand, and by doing so save him. Oh, my heart revolts against such cruelty, I can't resist it—he must live!"

"*Mordieu!*" swore d'Artagnan. "Why not just turn yourself over to this wretch with your hands and feet already tied? It would at least be quicker. Ah, Comte de La Fère, do you want to die by his hand? Well! I, *your son,* as you call me, I *don't* want it."

It was the first time d'Artagnan had ever resisted a plea when Athos had called him his son.

Aramis coldly drew his sword and gripped it between his teeth. "If the regicide puts his hand on the gunwale," he gritted, "I'll cut it off."

"And I," said Porthos, "listen . . ."

"What are you going to do?" asked Aramis.

"I'm going to jump in the water and strangle him."

"Oh, Messieurs!" cried Athos feelingly. "Be men, be Christians!"

D'Artagnan uttered a sigh that ended in a groan, Aramis laid down his sword, and Porthos sat down.

"Look," continue Athos, "see how death is painted on his face. His strength is at its end, and in a minute more, he'll sink to the bottom of the abyss. Ah, do not inflict this terrible remorse upon me, don't force me to die of shame in my turn. My friends, grant me the life of this unhappy man, and I'll bless you, I'll . . ."

"I'm dying," gasped Mordaunt. "Help me! Help . . ."

"Hold on a minute," said Aramis, addressing d'Artagnan. Then, turning to Porthos, "One more pull at the oars," he said.

D'Artagnan didn't reply by word or gesture—he was beginning to feel overwhelmed, half by the appeals of Athos, half by the scene playing out before him. So Porthos plied his oar alone, and since it had no counterweight, the boat pivoted in place, a motion that brought Athos closer to the dying man. "Comte de La Fère!" wheezed Mordaunt. "Monsieur le Comte! It's you I implore, you I beg, have pity on me. . . . Are you there, Monsieur? Everything grows dark. . . . I'm dying! Oh, help me!"

"Here I am, Monsieur," said Athos, leaning forward and extending his arms toward Mordaunt with his innate air of nobility and dignity. "Here I am. Take my hand and enter our vessel."

"I can't watch this," said d'Artagnan. "I'm nauseated." He turned toward his two friends, who were leaning away from his side of the boat, as if they feared the man to whom Athos extended his hand.

Mordaunt made a supreme effort, lifted himself, seized the hand stretched out to him and clung to it as if it was his last hope. "Good!" said Athos. "Put your other hand here." And he offered his shoulder as another point of support, so that his head nearly touched that of Mordaunt, and the two mortal enemies embraced like two brothers.

Mordaunt grabbed Athos by the collar. "Easy, Monsieur," said the count. "You're saved now, rest easy."

"*See, Mother!*" shrieked Mordaunt, with flaring eyes and an accent of hatred impossible to convey. "I can offer you only one victim, but at least it's the one you would have chosen!"

And as d'Artagnan shouted, Porthos raised his oar, and Aramis sought an opening for a thrust, the boat tipped alarmingly and dumped Athos into the water. Then Mordaunt, with a cry of triumph, wrapped his arms around his victim's neck and his legs around his arms, paralyzing him like a serpent constricting its prey. Struggling for a moment, without crying out or calling for aid, Athos tried to stay on the surface, but jerk by jerk he disappeared, until all they could see was his long floating hair. And then there was only a bubbling whirlpool to show where the sea had swallowed them both.

Mute with horror, frozen, paralyzed by outrage and fear, the three friends gaped helplessly, eyes dilated, arms outstretched. They were like statues, yet despite their immobility, the pounding of their hearts was audible, almost visible. Porthos was the first to come to himself, and tearing his hair out with his hands, he cried with a sob, "Oh, Athos! Athos! Noble heart! Woe! Woe to us who let you die!"

"Ah! Woe!" repeated d'Artagnan.

"Woe," murmured Aramis.

At that moment, in the middle of a vast circle of sea lit by the light of the moon, four or five strokes from the longboat, a whirlpool like that which had formed at the sinking appeared and enlarged, and they saw reappear first a swirl of hair, then a pale face with staring but dead eyes, then a body which, having risen chest-high from the sea, settled on its back and tossed limply at the whim of the waves.

A poniard was embedded in the cadaver's chest, its pommel glinting with gold.

"Mordaunt! Mordaunt!" cried the three friends. "It's Mordaunt!"

"But Athos?" said d'Artagnan.

All at once the boat leaned to port under a new and unexpected weight, and Grimaud gave a cry of joy. All turned to where Athos, pale, eyes dull and hand trembling, clung to the gunwale. Eight eager arms immediately drew him up and into the boat, where Athos was warmed, reanimated, and reborn beneath the attentions and embraces of his friends, drunk with joy.

"You're not hurt, I hope?" asked d'Artagnan.

"No," said Athos. "What about . . . him?"

"Oh! This time, thank God, he's dead. Look!" And d'Artagnan, forcing Athos to gaze in the direction he pointed, showed him the corpse of Mordaunt tossing on the waves, a body that, sometimes floating, sometimes submerged, still seemed to pursue the four friends with a look of fury and mortal hatred.

Finally, the body rolled over and sank. Athos followed it with a gaze filled with pity and melancholy.

"Well done, Athos. Bravo!" said Aramis, with an effusion that was rare for him.

"A mighty blow!" said Porthos.

"I have a son," said Athos. "I wanted to live."

"At last," said d'Artagnan, "God has spoken!"

"It wasn't I who killed him," murmured Athos. "It was destiny."

XXXII

In Which Mousqueton, Having Avoided
Being Roasted, Escapes Being Eaten

A deep and lengthy silence reigned in the longboat after the terrible scene just recounted. The moon, which had revealed itself for a moment as if God willed that no detail of this event should escape the sight of the viewers, disappeared again behind the clouds. Everything returned to that darkness which is so frightful in desert areas, especially so on that liquid desert called the ocean, and nothing could be heard but the whistle of the west wind as it crested the waves.

Porthos was the first to break the silence. "I've seen many things," he said, "but nothing has disturbed me as much as what I just saw. And yet, though I'm troubled, I must confess I'm also very, very happy. I feel like a hundred pounds has been removed from my chest, and I can breathe again at last." And Porthos breathed in and out with a sound that did honor to the power of his mighty lungs.

"As for me," said Aramis, "I can't yet join you in that feeling, Porthos—I'm still appalled. It's as if I can't believe my own eyes, I must doubt what I've seen, and I keep looking around the boat, expecting every minute to see that wretch rising up, the poniard in his hand that he's drawn from his heart."

"Oh, no fear of that!" replied Porthos. "The blade went in just under the sixth rib and was buried to the hilt. That's not a reproach, Athos, there's no shame in that blow. That was a proper stab, and no mistake. And so, I'm alive, and I'm breathing, and I'm happy."

"Not so quick to the victory parade, Porthos!" said d'Artagnan. "We've never been in more danger than we are now—for while a man can kill another man, he can't fight the elements. Now we're lost at sea, at night, without a pilot, in a frail boat; if we're capsized by wind or wave, we're done for."

Mousqueton sighed sadly.

"You, d'Artagnan, are ungrateful," said Athos. "Yes, ungrateful to doubt Providence at the very moment when it's saved us all so miraculously. Do you think we would be guided by His hand through so many perils only to be abandoned? Not so. We were sailing on a west wind, and that wind still blows." Athos looked up and found the North Star. "There's the Plough,[36] and therefore east, and France, are to starboard. We'll sail before the wind, and if it doesn't change it will bring us near either Calais or Boulogne. If the boat capsizes, we're strong enough and good enough swimmers, five of us anyway, to right it again, or at least to hang on to it if that's beyond our strength. Plus, we are in the shipping lane of all the vessels that sail from Dover to Calais and from Portsmouth to Boulogne; if the water retained ruts like the land, we'd be in a valley carved by their keels. It's impossible for us not to be picked up by some fishing boat."

"But what if we aren't picked up, and the wind turns to blow from the north?"

"Ah. In that case," said Athos, "we wouldn't reach land until we'd crossed the Atlantic."

"Before that happened, we'd die of hunger," said Aramis.

"Yes, that's very probable," said the Comte de La Fère.

Mousqueton uttered a second sigh more doleful than the first.

"*Ah çà*, Mouston," said Porthos, "why must you sigh like that? I'm getting tired of it."

"I'm just cold, Monsieur," said Mousqueton.

"That's impossible," said Porthos.

"Impossible?" said Mousqueton, astonished.

"Certainly. You're coated with so many layers of fat it's impossible for the air to penetrate it. It's something else—speak up, tell me."

"Well, yes, it is, Monsieur. It's these very layers of fat that you admire that frighten me so."

"And why's that, Mouston? Speak freely, these gentlemen will permit it."

"Because, Monsieur, I remember that in the library at the Château de Bracieux there are a number of travel books, including the accounts of Jean Mocquet,[37] the famous explorer for King Henri IV."

"Well?"

"Well, Monsieur," said Mousqueton, "in those books are many stories of nautical misadventures much like the one that threatens us now!"

"Go on, Mouston," said Porthos, "you interest me."

"Well, Monsieur, in such cases, Jean Mocquet says that the starving travelers have the frightful habit of eating each other, starting with . . ."

"With the fattest!" cried d'Artagnan, unable to contain his laughter, despite the gravity of the situation.

"Yes, Monsieur," replied Mousqueton, somewhat abashed by this hilarity, "and allow me to say I don't see what's so funny about it."

"Here you see devotion personified by my brave Mouston!" replied Porthos. "In your imagination, did you already see yourself dismembered and eaten by your master?"

"Yes, though my joy at the thought of thus saving Monsieur is not unmixed with some sadness. But I wouldn't regret my death too much, Monsieur, so long as I could be sure it would be useful to you."

"Mouston," said Porthos, touched, "if we ever again see my estate of Pierrefonds, you shall have, for yourself and all your descendants, the vineyard on top of the hill."

"And you will name it the Vineyard of Devotion, Mouston," said Aramis, "to pass down through the years the memory of your near-sacrifice."

"Chevalier," said d'Artagnan, still laughing, "you'd join in partaking of Mouston, wouldn't you, after fasting for two or three days?"

"My faith, no," replied Aramis. "I'd much rather eat Blaisois; we haven't known him nearly as long as Mouston."

It must be assumed that this exchange of pleasantries, though mainly aimed at lifting Athos's spirit after what had just happened, made the lackeys more than a little uncomfortable, with the exception of Grimaud, who knew that in the event of famine he'd be the last chicken plucked. So

Grimaud, silent as usual, was taking no part in the conversation, and was rowing as best he could, an oar in each hand.

"Are you rowing, then?" said Athos.

Grimaud nodded.

"Why are you rowing?"

"To keep warm."

In fact, though the other castaways shivered with cold, the silent Grimaud was sweating from exertion.

Suddenly Mousqueton uttered a cry of joy and raised a bottle over his head. "Oh!" he said, passing the bottle to Porthos. "Oh, Monsieur, we're saved! The boat is stocked with provisions." And rummaging under the bench from which he'd already drawn that precious specimen, he brought out a dozen such bottles, followed by bread loaves and salted beef. Needless to say, this discovery cheered everyone, except for Athos.

"*Mordieu!*" said Porthos, who, it will be remembered, had been already hungry when he boarded the sloop. "It's amazing how hungry one gets after such an emotional episode!" And he emptied a bottle without pausing and then ate a third of the bread and beef himself.

"Now sleep, Messieurs" said Athos, "or at least try. I'll take the first watch."

To men other than our hardy adventurers such a proposal would have been absurd. They were wet to the bone, there was an icy wind, and the emotional storm they'd passed through should have been more than enough to deprive them of rest—but for these swashbucklers, with iron nerves and exhausted bodies, sleep was easily found despite the circumstances, coming almost as soon as it was called. Each of them, confident in their pilot, found what comfort he could and tried to profit from the advice of Athos, who, sitting at the tiller with his eyes fixed on the stars, sought not only the path toward France, but perhaps also the face of God. Through the night he sat and watched alone, as he'd promised, thoughtful and alert, steering the small boat on its proper route home.

After some hours of sleep, the travelers were awakened by Athos. The first glimmers of dawn were lightening the blue sea, and about ten musket-shots off the bow they could see a black mass on the waves beneath a tall triangular sail, long and slim like a swallow's tail.

"A ship!" said the four friends in one voice, followed by those of their lackeys. In fact, it was a Dunkirk flute sailing toward Boulogne. The four musketeers, Blaisois, and Mousqueton all raised their voices in a single cry that rang out across the heaving waves, while Grimaud, without saying a word, put his hat on the end of an oar and waved it to attract the attention of anyone who might not have heard the shouts.

A quarter of an hour later, the flute's boat took them in tow, and shortly after that they set foot on the ship's deck. On the behalf of his master, Grimaud offered twenty guineas to the skipper for passage, and with a favorable wind, by nine o'clock that morning our Frenchmen set foot on the soil of their native land.

"*Mordieu!* How strong one is on his own ground!" said Porthos, pushing his large feet deep into the sand. "Let them come at me now, whoever they may be, and they'll see who they're dealing with! *Morbleu!* I could defy a whole kingdom!"

"And I say, Porthos," said d'Artagnan, "be careful what you ask for. It seems to me we're attracting attention here."

"Of course!" said Porthos. "They admire us!"

"That doesn't comfort me, Porthos," replied d'Artagnan. "I see men in outfits of official black, and I must confess that in our situation the sight of officials worries me."

"They're the port's customs agents," said Aramis.

"Under the old cardinal, the great one," said Athos, "they'd have paid more attention to us than to cargo and merchandise. But under the current regime, rest assured, friends, they're more interested in duties and tariffs than in passengers."

"I don't trust them," said d'Artagnan. "I'm heading into the dunes."

"Why not the town?" said Porthos. "I'd rather rest in a comfortable inn than in these godforsaken sandy wastes that are no use to anyone but rabbits. Besides, I'm hungry."

"Suit yourself, Porthos!" said d'Artagnan. "But as for me, I think people in our situation are safest in the open country." And d'Artagnan, certain he'd be followed by the others, plunged into the dunes without waiting for a response from Porthos.

The little troop followed him and soon slipped behind the dunes without attracting any further attention. "And now," said Aramis, after they'd gone about a quarter of a league, "let's talk."

"No," said d'Artagnan, "let's flee. We've escaped from Cromwell, from Mordaunt, and from the sea, three abysses that nearly swallowed us—but there's no escaping from Monsieur Mazarin."

"You're right, d'Artagnan," said Aramis, "and my advice is that, for safety, we should split up."

"Indeed, Aramis, we must separate," said d'Artagnan.

Porthos wanted to speak in opposition to this idea, but d'Artagnan persuaded him by a hand gesture to remain silent. Porthos was usually obedient to these signals from his comrade, whom he good-naturedly recognized as his intellectual superior. So he swallowed his words before speaking them.

"But why should we separate?" said Athos.

"Because Porthos and I were sent to by Monsieur de Mazarin to serve Cromwell," said d'Artagnan, "and instead of serving Cromwell we served King Charles I, which is not at all the same thing. If we return as companions of Messieurs de La Fère and d'Herblay, our guilt is proven—whereas if we return by ourselves, our guilt remains in doubt, and doubt is something we can work with. I hope to lead Mazarin up the garden path."

"He's right, so he is!" said Porthos.

"You forget that we're your prisoners," said Athos. "We've given you our parole, and as prisoners we could go with you to Paris. . . ."

"Really, Athos," interrupted d'Artagnan, "it's shameful for a man of sense like you to reason like a third-grade schoolboy. Chevalier," he continued, addressing Aramis, who, hand proudly on his sword, seemed to have been won over to Athos's opinion at his first words, "Chevalier, please understand that in this situation, my wary nature is fully aroused. By ourselves, Porthos and I risk nothing at the end of the day—but if they tried to stop the four of us to arrest you two, well! Seven swords would come out, and this business, already bad enough, would be made infinitely worse for all of us. Look, if one pair of us gets into trouble, isn't it better to have the other pair at liberty to get them out of it, by bribery, ruse, or force? Besides, we might be able to obtain separately—you from the queen, we from Mazarin—the pardon we'd be refused as a group. Come, Athos and Aramis, you take the road to the right, and Porthos and I will take the road to the left. You gentlemen can make your way through Normandy, while we take the direct route to Paris."

"But if one pair gets taken along the way, how can they warn the other of the disaster?" asked Aramis.

"That's easy enough," d'Artagnan replied. "Let's agree on itineraries from which we won't deviate. You go by Saint-Valery, then Dieppe, then follow the direct route from Dieppe to Paris; we'll go by way of Abbeville, Amiens, Péronne, Compiègne, and Senlis, and at each inn or tavern where we stop, we'll write on the wall with a dagger point, or scratch on a window with a diamond, directions that will guide any comrade who comes looking for us."

"Ah, my friend," said Athos, "how I would admire the resources of your head if I weren't so occupied with adoring your heart." And he offered his hand to d'Artagnan.

"Does the fox have genius, Athos?" said the Gascon, shrugging. "No, he just knows a few tricks, like how to steal chickens, evade hunters, and find his way by day or night, that's all. So, is the matter settled?"

"It's settled."

"Then let's divide the money," said d'Artagnan. "We must have around two hundred pistoles left. What's the tally, Grimaud?"

"One hundred and eighty half-louis, Monsieur."

"That'll do. Ah, *vivat!* Here comes the sun! Welcome, friend sun! Though you're not as bright as you are in Gascony, at least here I can recognize you. Bonjour! You make me blink."

"Come, come, d'Artagnan," said Athos, "don't pretend to be such an iron man, we see those tears in your eyes. Be honest with us, as we all are— it's one of our greatest strengths."

"I guess," said d'Artagnan, "that it just isn't possible, Athos, to take leave of such friends as you and Aramis without feeling it when you're riding into danger."

"Of course not," said Athos, "so come into my arms, my son!"

"*Mordieu!*" said Porthos, sobbing. "I think I'm weeping. How foolish!"

And the four friends wrapped themselves in a circle of their arms. At that moment these four men, united in a fraternal embrace, had but a single soul.

Blaisois and Grimaud were to follow Athos and Aramis; Mousqueton would suffice for both Porthos and d'Artagnan. They divided the money equally, as they always had; then, after each had clasped hands with all the others, the four gentlemen separated and set off on the agreed-upon routes, though not without turning back to call out final farewells that echoed across the dunes.

At length they lost sight of each other. "*Sacrebleu*, d'Artagnan!" said Porthos. "I must get this off my chest right now, because I can't stay angry with you in my heart—I have to say I think, for once, you've made a mistake!"

"How so?" asked d'Artagnan, with his sly smile.

"Because if, as you say, Athos and Aramis are in real danger, this is no time to abandon them. I confess I was about ready to go with them, and may yet despite all the Mazarins in the world."

"And you'd be right to do so, Porthos, if that were the case," said d'Artagnan. "But consider this small fact which is nonetheless large enough to change everything: it's not our friends who are in the greatest danger, it's us—and it's not to abandon them that we separate, but to protect them."

"Really?" said Porthos, eyes wide in astonishment.

"No doubt about it. If they're taken, they just spend some time in the Bastille—whereas if we fail to make our case and are imprisoned, we lose our heads on the Place de Grève."[38]

"Oh!" said Porthos. "That's not exactly the barony you promised me, d'Artagnan!"

"Bah! That may not be as out of reach as you think, Porthos. Remember the proverb: all roads lead to Rome."

"But why are we in greater danger than Athos and Aramis?" asked Porthos.

"Because all they did was try to carry out the rescue mission given them by Queen Henriette, while we betrayed the assignment Mazarin gave us. Sent as envoys to serve Cromwell, instead we served King Charles; instead of helping to bring down that crowned head, condemned as he was by all those villains, Mazarin, Cromwell, Joyce, Pride, Fairfax, and so forth, we nearly saved him."

"Faith, that's true," said Porthos. "But do you really think, my friend, that in the midst of all these great events that Cromwell has had time to think of notifying . . ."

"Cromwell thinks of everything; Cromwell has time for everything; and believe me, dear friend, we'd better lose no time ourselves, for every minute is precious. We won't be safe until we've had a chance to talk to Mazarin, and even then . . ."

"The devil!" said Porthos. "What *are* we going to tell Mazarin?"

"Let me handle it—I have a plan. He who laughs last laughs best, after all. Monsieur Cromwell is powerful, and Monsieur Mazarin is cunning, but I'd rather bandy words with those two than juggle fire with the late Monsieur Mordaunt."

"Ah!" said Porthos. "How pleasant it is to say *the late Monsieur Mordaunt.*"

And the two, without wasting a moment, set off on the road to Paris, followed by Mousqueton, who, after having been too cold all night long, was too hot inside a quarter of an hour.

XXXIII

The Return

Athos and Aramis followed the route outlined for them by d'Artagnan, traveling as rapidly as they could. It seemed to them that if they might be arrested, they'd be better off if it happened near Paris. Every evening, afraid of being taken during the night, they traced the agreed recognition sign on a wall or a window—but every morning they awoke still free, to their continuing surprise.

As they approached Paris, the great events they'd witnessed in England, culminating in the execution of her king, began to fade like last night's dreams, while the events that had taken place in Paris and the provinces in their absence began to seem real and urgent. During their six weeks' absence, so many little things had happened that together they almost constituted a single great event. The Parisians, when they awoke to find themselves without queen regent or king, had been dismayed by their departure, and the absence of Mazarin, so long desired, didn't make up for the loss of the royal fugitives. The first emotion the Parisians felt when they learned of the flight to Saint-Germain, an escape we allowed our readers to witness, was like the terror felt by a child when he awakens in the night to find himself alone. Even the Parliament was moved, and it decided to send a deputation to the queen to ask her not to deprive Paris of her royal presence.

But the queen was still under the double influence of the triumph at Lens and the pride of having so well executed their escape. The deputation was not only denied the honor of seeing her, they were kept waiting in the street, where the chancellor—that same Chancellor Séguier whom we saw in the first book in this series stubbornly pursuing a letter right into the queen's corset—presented the deputies with the Court's ultimatum, which stated that if parliament didn't humble itself by repealing all the resolutions to which the throne objected, then on the following day Paris would find itself besieged. At that very moment, in preparation for this siege, Gaston, the Duc d'Orléans, had occupied the bridge to Saint-Cloud, while Monsieur le Prince, emboldened by his victory at Lens, garrisoned Charenton and Saint-Denis.

Unfortunately for the Court, which could have won considerable support with a moderate response, this threatening reply produced an effect opposite to what was intended. It wounded parliament in their pride, and, feeling themselves supported by the citizenry after the release of Broussel had shown their strength, they replied to this ultimatum with a statement that since Cardinal Mazarin was the notorious source of all these conflicts, he was therefore declared an Enemy of the State, and commanded to leave the Court that very day and all of France within a week—after which, if he didn't obey, he was fair game for attack by every subject of the crown.

This aggressive response, which the Court never expected, put both the Parisians and Mazarin beyond what could be resolved by the law. It only remained to be seen which side would prevail by force, the Parliament or the Court.

The Court began preparations for attack, and Paris for defense. The citizens had begun undertaking the work that's always theirs in times of unrest, that is, erecting barricades and tearing up the streets, when they saw aid arrive in the persons of the Prince de Conti, brother of the Prince de Condé, and of the Duc de Longueville, Condé's brother-in-law, both escorted by the coadjutor. The citizens were encouraged by both the leadership of two Princes of the Blood and by the strength of their numbers. By this time, it was January 10, 1649. After a heated debate among the rebel princes, the Prince de Conti was named generalissimo of the King's Armies of Paris, with the Ducs d'Elbeuf and de Bouillon[39] and Maréchal de La Mothe as his lieutenant generals. The Duc de Longueville, without office or title, had to content himself with assisting his brother-in-law the Prince de Conti.

As for Monsieur de Beaufort, he arrived from the Vendômois, bringing his haughty demeanor, his long, shining hair, and that popularity with the common Parisians that earned him the title of King of the Markets.

The Parisian army quickly organized itself with that speed the bourgeois could show when some strong feeling prompted them to adopt the guise of soldiers. On the 19th, this improvised army had attempted a sortie beyond the walls, more to announce their existence rather than for any serious purpose. They marched beneath a flag bearing this singular motto: We Seek our King.[40]

The last few days of January were occupied in petty raids outside the city that had no result but the theft of some livestock and the burning of a few houses. It was on February 1 that our four companions disembarked at Boulogne and began their journey toward Paris in two pairs, each taking its own route. Athos and Aramis, toward the end of the fourth day, found themselves skirting Nanterre to avoid encountering anyone from the queen's faction. Athos was impatient with such ignoble precautions, but Aramis had tactfully pointed out to him that they had no right to be reckless given the mission they were charged with by King Charles on his scaffold, a mission supreme and sacred that could only be discharged at the feet of Queen Henriette. Athos conceded the point.

The travelers found the capital's outer *faubourgs* guarded and under arms. At the city gate the sentry refused to let the two gentlemen proceed further and called for his sergeant. The sergeant came out right away, puffed up with the officious pride of the citizen playing soldier. "Who might you be, Messieurs?" he demanded.

"Two gentlemen," Athos replied.

"Where do you come from?"

"From London," said Aramis.

"What are you doing coming to Paris?"

"Completing a mission for Her Majesty the Queen of England."

"*Ah çà!* Today everyone is the Queen of England's friend!" replied the sergeant. "I've got three other gentlemen inside with passes to enter to visit Her Majesty. Where are your passes?"

"We don't have any."

"What? You don't have any!"

"No, we've just arrived from England, as we told you. We know nothing of the current state of political affairs, having left Paris before the king's departure."

"Ha!" said the sergeant, with a knowing look. "You're Mazarinists who want to sneak in to spy on us."

"My good man," said Athos, who till now had been letting Aramis do the talking, "if we were Mazarinists, we'd have every pass possible, all stamped and correct. In your situation, believe me, it's those whose papers are perfectly in order of whom you should be most suspicious."

"Go into the guardhouse," said the sergeant. "You can tell your story to the post commander."

He gestured to the sentry, who stepped aside; the sergeant entered first, and the two gentlemen followed him into the guardhouse.

The guardhouse was packed with bourgeois and laborers; some played cards, others drank and danced. In one corner, almost out of sight, were the three gentlemen the sergeant had said had already entered, and who were waiting while the commander reviewed their passes. That officer occupied the next room, his high rank and importance earning him a chamber to himself.

The first activity upon the entry of the newcomers was, from opposite sides of the guardroom, a quick and inquiring look at each other from both groups of gentlemen. Those first to enter were wrapped in long cloaks and hidden by collars and cowls; one of them, the shortest of the three, kept himself behind the other two.

At the sergeant's announcement that the men he escorted in were probably Mazarinists, the three earlier gentlemen turned their heads and paid closer attention. The shortest of the three took a step backward further into the shadows.

Hearing the declaration that the newcomers had no passes, the unanimous opinion of the guards on hand seemed to be that they should be denied entry. "On the contrary," said Athos, "since I can see we're dealing with reasonable people, I think it quite likely we will be allowed to enter.

It will be easy enough to send our names in to Her Majesty the Queen of England, and if she deigns to recognize us, it won't inconvenience you in the least to let us pass."

At that these words the short gentleman in the shadows started with surprise. He pulled his collar up even higher, but this knocked off his hat; he bent down, grabbed it, and quickly replaced it on his head.

"Good God!" said Aramis, nudging Athos with his elbow. "Did you see that?"

"What?" asked Athos.

"The face of the shortest of those three gentlemen?"

"No."

"It looked to me like—but that's impossible . . . !"

At that moment the sergeant, who had gone into the officer's chamber to consult with his commander, came out, beckoned to the three gentlemen, and gave them some papers. "These passes are in order," he said, "and you may enter, Messieurs."

The trio nodded, and hastened to take advantage of the opening that, upon the order of the sergeant, appeared before them. Aramis followed them with his eyes, and when the shortest of them went by, he gripped Athos's hand. "What is it, old friend?" the latter asked.

"I . . . I could almost swear . . ." Then, addressing the sergeant, he said, "Tell me, Monsieur, do you know the three gentlemen who just passed through?"

"Only by the names on their passes, of Messieurs de Flamarens,[41] de Châtillon,[42] and de Bruy, three gentleman Frondeurs on their way to rejoin the Duc de Longueville."

"How strange," said Aramis, speaking mainly to himself. "I thought I recognized the short one as Mazarin himself."

The sergeant burst out laughing. "Him, to come in here at the risk of being hanged? Not likely!"

"Ah!" said Aramis. "I may have been mistaken; I don't have the infallible eye of d'Artagnan."

"Who speaks the name of d'Artagnan?" demanded the commanding officer, who just then appeared on the threshold of his chamber.

"Oh!" blurted Grimaud, his eyes widening.

"What?" asked Aramis and Athos at the same time.

"Planchet!" replied Grimaud. "Planchet in an officer's collar!"

"Messieurs de La Fère and d'Herblay, returned to Paris!" cried the officer. "What joy! No doubt you've come to join the party of the princes!"

"As you see, my dear Planchet," said Aramis, while Athos smiled to see how high the old comrade of Mousqueton, Bazin, and Grimaud had risen in the ranks of the citizen army.

"And Monsieur d'Artagnan, whom I just heard you mention, Monsieur d'Herblay, dare I ask if you have news of him?"

"We parted from him four days ago, *mon cher ami,* and were under the impression he would precede us to Paris."

"No, Monsieur, I'm sure he hasn't returned to the capital. Perhaps he went instead to Saint-Germain."

"I don't think so, as we're supposed to meet him at the Hôtel de La Chevrette."

"I just passed by there today."

"And the lovely Madeleine had no news of him?" asked Aramis with a smile.

"No, Monsieur, and I don't mind telling you she seemed anxious about it."

"In fact, we moved quickly, and didn't lose any time getting here," said Aramis. "So, if you'll permit me, Athos, I'll forego further questions about our friend, and pay my compliments to Officer Planchet."

"Oh, Monsieur le Chevalier!" said Planchet, bowing.

"Lieutenant?" said Aramis.

"Lieutenant, and with the promise to be a captain."

"And very handsome you look," said Aramis. "How did all these honors come about?"

"Well, Gentlemen, do you recall that it was me who rescued Monsieur de Rochefort?"

"Yes, *pardieu!* He told us himself."

"Thanks to that deed I was nearly hanged by Mazarin, which naturally made me very popular with the people."

"And thanks to that popularity, you've become . . ."

"No, thanks to something even better. You know, Messieurs, that I served in the Piedmont Regiment, where I rose to the rank of sergeant."

"Yes."

"Well, one day, when no one could get the ranks of citizen militia to line up, some putting their left foot forward and the others their right, I succeeded in getting them to all march together. They made me a drill officer on the spot."

"That explains it," said Aramis.

"So," said Athos, "you have a crowd of nobles on your side now?"

"Indeed! To lead us, as you've no doubt heard, we have Monsieur le Prince de Conti, the Duc de Longueville, Monsieur le Duc de Beaufort, the Duc d'Elbeuf, and the Duc de Bouillon, plus the Duc de Chevreuse, Monsieur de Brissac, the Maréchal de La Mothe, Monsieur de Luynes, the Marquis de Vitry, the Prince de Marcillac, Marquis de Noirmoutiers, Comte de Fiesque, Marquis de Laigues, Comte de Montrésor, Marquis de Sévigné, and others, I think."

"And Monsieur Raoul de Bragelonne?" asked Athos, voice full of emotion. "D'Artagnan told me he'd commended him to your care upon parting, my good Planchet."

"He did, Monsieur le Comte, as if Raoul was his own son, so I haven't lost sight of him for a moment."

"Then," Athos said in a voice edged with joy, "he is well? No accident has befallen him?"

"None, Monsieur."

"And he's residing . . . ?"

"At the Grand Charlemagne, as always."

"How does he pass the time?"

"Sometimes with the Queen of England, sometimes with Madame de Chevreuse. He and the Comte de Guiche never leave one another's sides."

"Thank you, Planchet, thank you!" said Athos, offering him his hand.

"Oh, Monsieur le Comte!" said Planchet, taking his hand and shaking it.

"Really, Count! Familiarity with an old lackey?" said Aramis in a low voice. "What are you thinking?"

"But, friend," said Athos, "he gives me news of Raoul."

"And now, Messieurs," asked Planchet, who'd missed the exchange, "what are your intentions?"

"To reenter Paris, if you give us your permission, my dear Monsieur Planchet," said Athos.

"I? Grant permission to you! You're mocking me, Monsieur le Comte, for I'm entirely at your service." And he bowed.

Then, turning to his men, "Let these gentlemen pass," he said. "I know them—they're friends of Monsieur de Beaufort."

"Long live Monsieur de Beaufort!" cried every voice in the post, and a way was opened for Athos and Aramis.

The sergeant approached Planchet and whispered, "What! Without a passport?"

"Even without a passport," said Planchet.

"Take care, Captain," continued the sergeant, addressing Planchet by the promised title, "take care—one of the three men who passed through just now warned me in a low voice to be wary of these gentlemen."

"But I," said Planchet majestically, "I know them personally, and will answer for them."

Having said this, he then shook hands with Grimaud, who seemed honored by the attention.

"Au revoir, Capitaine," said Aramis in his bantering tone. "If we run into trouble, we'll just drop your name to get us out of it."

"Monsieur," said Planchet, "in this as in all things, I am your servant."

"That fellow has wit, and plenty of it," said Aramis as he mounted his horse.

"And how could he not?" said Athos, mounting his own steed. "After years of brushing d'Artagnan's hat, some brains were bound to rub off on him."

XXXIV

The Ambassadors

The two friends immediately left the guardhouse, following the slope of the street down into Paris, but upon arriving at the foot of the hill, they saw with astonishment that the streets had become rivers, and the squares were lakes. Following the endless rains of the month of January, the Seine had overflowed, and the river had invaded half of the capital.[43]

Athos and Aramis bravely entered the flood on their horses, but soon the poor animals were in water up to their breasts, and the two gentlemen decided they'd be better off taking a boat. They hired one and ordered the lackeys to take the horses and wait for them in the markets of Les Halles.

It was thus by boat that they made their way to the Louvre. By that time, it was full night, and with the light of a few pale lanterns flickering across the water from patrol boats and glittering from the steel of their crews' weapons, their challenges and replies echoing between them, Paris appeared in a new aspect that enthralled Aramis, who was always susceptible to the martial appeal of warlike scenes.

They arrived at the queen's suite, but were compelled to wait in the ante-chamber, as just then Her Majesty was giving an audience to some gentlemen who had news from England.

"As do we," Athos said to the servant who'd made this announcement. "We not only have news from England, we've just come from there."

"What are your names, Messieurs?" asked the servant.

"Monsieur le Comte de La Fère and Monsieur le Chevalier d'Herblay," said Aramis.

"Ah! In that case, Messieurs," said the servant, hearing the names that the queen had so often hopefully uttered, "it's another matter entirely, and I think Her Majesty would be displeased if I delayed you even a moment.

Follow me, if you will." And he went on ahead, followed by Athos and Aramis.

Arriving at the queen's chamber, he gestured to them to wait, and then opened the door. "Madame," he said, "I hope Your Majesty will pardon me for disobeying her orders when she hears I enter to announce Monsieur le Comte de La Fère and the Chevalier d'Herblay."

At these names the queen let out a cry of joy, which the two gentlemen could hear from where they waited. "Poor queen!" murmured Athos.

"Oh! Have them enter! Have them enter!" shouted the young princess as she dashed to the door. The poor child never left her mother the queen, trying by her filial attentions to help her forget the absence of her sister and two brothers. "Come in, come in, Messieurs," she said, opening the door herself.

Athos and Aramis presented themselves. The queen was seated in an armchair, and before her stood two of the three gentlemen they'd encountered in the guard house. These were Monsieur de Flamarens and Gaspard de Coligny, Duc de Châtillon, brother of that Coligny who'd been killed seven or eight years earlier in a duel in the Place Royale—a duel over Madame de Longueville. At the announcement of the newcomers, they stepped back and anxiously exchanged a few words in low voices.

"Well met, Messieurs!" called the Queen of England, seeing that it really was Athos and Aramis. "Here you are, our faithful friends, but state couriers travel even faster than you. The Court was informed of affairs in London before you reached the gates of Paris, and here are Messieurs de Flamarens and de Châtillon come from Her Majesty Queen Anne of Austria to bring us the latest news."

Aramis and Athos looked at each other; the serenity and joy that shone from the queen's eyes filled them with surprise and dismay. "Please continue," she said, addressing Flamarens and Châtillon. "You said that His Majesty Charles I, my august husband, was condemned to death despite the wishes of the majority of his English subjects?"

"Y-yes, Madame," stammered Châtillon.

Athos and Aramis looked at each other in even greater astonishment.

"And that, led to the scaffold," continued the queen, "at the very scaffold, my lord and king was saved by his outraged people?"

"Yes, Madame," replied Châtillon, in a voice so low the two gentlemen, though listening closely, could scarcely hear him.

The queen joined her hands in pious thanks, while her daughter wrapped her arms around her mother's neck and embraced her, eyes overflowing with tears of joy.

"Now, it only remains for us to present Your Majesty our humble respects, and withdraw," said Châtillon, who seemed abashed, and flushed when he met Athos's fixed and piercing gaze.

"Not just yet, Messieurs," said the queen, detaining them with a gesture. "A moment, please! For here are Messieurs de La Fère and d'Herblay, who, as you may have heard, have just come from London, and who might, as eyewitnesses, know details you haven't yet heard. You could share these new details with my royal sister the queen. Speak, Messieurs, speak—I'm listening. Don't hide anything from me or spare me a single detail. So long as His Majesty still lives, and his royal honor is safe, nothing else can bother me."

Athos turned pale and clutched at his heart. "What is it?" said the queen, who saw this movement and his pallor. "Tell me, Monsieur, I beg you."

"Pardon me, Madame," said Athos, "but I don't wish to add anything to these gentlemen's account before giving them the chance to acknowledge that perhaps they were mistaken."

"Mistaken!" gasped the queen, nearly choking. "Mistaken! What's happened? Oh, my God!"

"Monsieur," said Flamarens to Athos, "if we are mistaken, the error comes from Queen Anne of Austria, and you wouldn't presume, I suppose, to contradict her. You wouldn't be so bold as to give Her Majesty the lie."

"From the queen, Monsieur?" replied Athos in his calm and sonorous voice.

"Yes," murmured Flamarens, dropping his gaze.

Athos sighed sadly.

"Would it not come instead from the man who accompanied you, and whom we saw with you at the guardhouse of the Barrière du Roule?" said Aramis, with his mocking politeness. "For, unless we're mistaken, the Comte de La Fère and I, there were three of you when you entered Paris."

Châtillon and Flamarens winced.

"Oh, explain yourself, Count!" cried the queen, her anguish growing from moment to moment. "On your forehead I read despair, your hands tremble, your mouth hesitates to announce some terrible news. . . . Oh, *mon Dieu, mon Dieu!* What's happened?"

"Dear Lord, have pity on us!" said the young princess, falling on her knees beside her mother.

"Monsieur," said Châtillon, "if you bear deathly news, no true man would have the cruelty to announce such news to the queen."

Aramis approached Châtillon almost near enough to touch him. "Monsieur," he said, lips tight and eyes glinting, "I'm sure you wouldn't presume to try to tell Monsieur le Comte de La Fère and myself what we can and cannot say here. Or would you?"

During this brief altercation, Athos, still with his head bowed and his hand on his heart, approached the queen and said, in a voice choked with emotion, "Madame, those of royal blood, who by their nature are superior to other men, have been granted hearts able to bear greater misfortunes than those of common people, for their hearts partake of their superiority. Therefore, it seems to me we must not act toward a great queen like Your Majesty as we would toward a woman of our own lesser state. O Queen, fated to join the martyrs of the earth, these tokens are the result of the mission with which you honored us."

And Athos, kneeling before the trembling, paralyzed queen, drew from within his doublet, in its original case, the Order set in diamonds the queen had given to Lord Winter upon his departure, and the wedding ring which, before his death, Charles had entrusted to Aramis; since Athos had received them, these objects had never left his side. He opened the case and handed it to the queen with a mute and profound sorrow.

The queen reached out her hand, took up the ring, brought it convulsively to her lips, and then, without even a sigh or a sob, she turned pale, half rose, and fell unconscious into the arms of her daughter and her ladies.

Athos kissed the hem of the dress of the unlucky widow, and then stood tall with a majesty that impressed all who saw him. "I, the Comte de La Fère," he said, "a gentleman who has never lied, swear before God first, and this poor queen second, that all that it was possible to do to save the king we did, on the soil of England. Now, Chevalier," he added, turning to Aramis, "let us go—our duty here is finished."

"Not just yet," said Aramis. "We have a message to give these two gentlemen." And turning back to Châtillon, he said, "Monsieur, would you care to step out, if only for a moment, to receive the message I can't convey in front of the queen?"

Châtillon bowed without a word as a sign of assent. Athos and Aramis went out first, followed by Châtillon and Flamarens; they crossed the antechamber silently, but beyond, in the gallery, Aramis led them all to a window embrasure at the far end. Before the window he stopped, turned to the Duc de Châtillon, and said, "Monsieur, you have permitted yourself, it seems to me, to treat us with some disrespect. This was not at all proper, especially in men who came to deliver to the queen the message of a liar."

"Monsieur!" cried Châtillon.

"What *have* you done with Monsieur de Bruy?" asked Aramis mockingly. "Has he gone to change his face, which too closely resembled that of Monsieur de Mazarin? We know there are a selection of Italian comedy masks in the wardrobes of the Palais Royal, from Harlequin to Pantaloon."

"I think you're deliberately provoking us!" said Flamarens.

"Do you? Well, you're smarter than your reputation, then."

"Chevalier! Chevalier!" said Athos.

"Let me do this," said Aramis, peeved. "You know very well I don't like leaving unfinished business behind me."

"Be it so, then, Monsieur," said Châtillon, no less haughty than Aramis.

Aramis bowed. "Messieurs," he said, "another man than I or Monsieur le Comte de La Fère would have you arrested, for we have some friends here in Paris—but we offer you a way out that avoids such concerns. Come out into the garden with us for five minutes."

"Willingly," said Châtillon.

"Hold on, Messieurs," said Flamarens. "Your offer is tempting, but at the moment it's impossible for us to accept it."

"And why is that?" said Aramis, sarcastically. "Has spending time with Mazarin made you too cautious?"

"Oh! Listen to him, Flamarens," said Châtillon. "Not to reply would be a stain on my honor and my name."

"On that we agree," said Aramis.

"But you won't reply, nonetheless," said Flamarens, "and I think these gentlemen will support me on this."

Aramis shook his head in a gesture of incredible insolence.

Châtillon's eyes widened and he put his hand to his sword.

"Duke," said Flamarens, "you forget that tomorrow you're commanding an expedition of the highest importance, one appointed by Monsieur le Prince and approved by the queen. Until tomorrow evening you belong to them."

"Very well—on the morning of the day after tomorrow," said Aramis.

"The day after tomorrow," said Châtillon. "That's a long way off, Messieurs."

"I'm not the one asking for a delay," said Aramis, "though it seems to me it might not be as long you think, if we happen to meet you on this 'expedition.'"

"Indeed, Monsieur, we might meet then, and with great pleasure," said Châtillon, "if you will take the trouble to look for us at the gates of Charenton."

"So near, Monsieur? To have the honor of meeting you I'd go, not just a league or two, but to the end of the world."

"Very well! Until tomorrow, Monsieur."

"I count upon it. Go, then, and rejoin your cardinal. But first swear on your honor that you won't inform him of our return."

"You make conditions?"

"Why not?"

"Because that's the right of the victors, and you've not yet won, Messieurs."

"Then let's draw and finish this now. It doesn't matter to us who does or doesn't command this expedition tomorrow."

Châtillon and Flamarens looked at each other; there was so much mockery in Aramis's words and attitude that Châtillon could barely maintain control, but after a word from Flamarens he restrained himself. "All right, so be it," he said. "Our companion, whoever he was, will be told nothing of these events. But you promise you'll find me at Charenton tomorrow, won't you, Monsieur?"

"Count on it," said Aramis.

The four gentlemen then bowed, and this time it was Châtillon and Flamarens who led the way out of the Louvre, followed by Athos and Aramis.

"Who's all this anger for, Aramis?" asked Athos.

"By God! For those who've earned it."

"What did they do to you?"

"What did they . . . you mean you didn't see it?"

"No."

"They sneered when you swore we'd done our duty in England. Sneered! Now, either they believed it, or they didn't; if they believed it, then they did it to insult us; and if they didn't believe it, that's an even worse insult, so it's important to show them that we're good at something. Anyway, I'm not sorry they've postponed our meeting until tomorrow, as I think we have an even tastier task for tonight than drawing swords."

"What would that be?"

"What, by God? We have to detain Mazarin."

Athos curled his lip in disdain. "Aramis, you know that sort of thing doesn't suit me."

"Why not?"

"It's too much like a surprise attack or ambush."

"Really, Athos, you'd make a pretty strange army commander; you'd insist on fighting only in broad daylight, you'd warn your adversary of the hour when you planned to attack him, and you'd be careful not to let any combat occur at night, lest you be accused of taking advantage of the darkness."

Athos smiled. "Everyone must be true to his nature," he said. "Besides, you don't know the current situation, and whether arresting Mazarin would be good or bad, a travesty or a triumph."

"Just say right out, Athos, that you disapprove of my proposal."

"No, on the contrary it sounds like good strategy, however . . ."

"However, what?"

"I think you shouldn't have made those gentlemen swear to say nothing about us to Mazarin, because by doing so, you essentially commit us to doing nothing against him."

"I've committed nothing to anyone, I swear. I regard myself as completely free to act. Come on, Athos, let's go!"

"Where?"

"To find Monsieur de Beaufort or Monsieur de Bouillon; we'll inform them of the matter."

"All right, but on one condition: that we start with the coadjutor. He's a priest, an expert in matters of conscience, so we can share our secret with him."

"Him?" said Aramis. "He'll spoil everything, do it himself and take all the credit. Let's go to him last."

Athos smiled. There seemed to be something behind his smile that he was thinking but didn't say. "Well, so be it!" he said. "Who shall we start with, then?"

"With Monsieur de Bouillon, if you please; he's the closest."

"Very well, but may we make another visit first?"

"What?"

"I'd like to stop by the Hôtel du Grand Charlemagne to embrace Raoul."

"Of course! I'll go in with you and we'll embrace him together."

They returned to their hired boat and were rowed back to Les Halles. There they found Grimaud and Blaisois, who'd held their horses for them, and all four made their way to Rue Guénégaud. But Raoul wasn't at his hôtel—during the day he'd received a message from Monsieur le Prince and had departed with Olivain shortly thereafter.

XXXV

The Generalissimo's Three Lieutenants

As they'd agreed, upon leaving the Grand Charlemagne, Athos and Aramis made their way toward the hôtel of Monsieur le Duc de Bouillon. The sky was dark, and though it was approaching the usually quiet hours of the depths of the night, the town buzzed with the myriad sounds of a city under siege. There were barricades every few yards, chains stretched from borne to borne, and a bivouac in every square; patrols met and exchanged passwords, couriers rode between the headquarters of the different commanders, while the more peaceful citizens, at their windows, had animated and anxious conversations with their more militant neighbors in the streets, who loitered with halberds on their shoulders or arquebuses on their arms.

Athos and Aramis hadn't gone a hundred paces before they were stopped by the sentries at a barricade, who demanded the evening's password, but they replied that they were on their way to Monsieur de Bouillon's to bring him important news, and the militia were contented with giving them a guide who, under the pretext of accompanying them and opening the way, could keep an eye on them. This guide went before them, singing,

> *The brave Monsieur de Bouillon*
> *Is afflicted by the gout*

This was one of the latest triolets, or satirical street songs, popular doggerel with innumerable verses that mocked everyone of importance on all sides.

As they neared the Hôtel de Bouillon, they passed a little troop of three horsemen who must have known all the passwords, since they rode without guide or escort. Upon reaching the next barricade they just whispered a few words that enabled them to pass, with the deference due to their apparent rank. When Athos and Aramis noticed the trio, they pulled up short. "Oh ho!" said Aramis. "Do you see that, Count?"

"Yes," said Athos.

"What do you think of those riders?"

"What do you think, Aramis?"

"I think those are our three shadows."

"Yes, I definitely recognize Monsieur de Flamarens."

"And I, Monsieur de Châtillon."

"Which makes the cavalier in the brown cloak . . ."

"None other than the cardinal."

"In person."

"But how the devil do we happen to encounter them in the neighborhood of the Hôtel de Bouillon?" asked Aramis.

Athos smiled, but said nothing.

Five minutes later they were knocking on the duke's gate. The door was guarded by a sentry, as was appropriate for a superior of high rank, and a courier was posted in the courtyard, waiting to carry any orders that might be issued by the lieutenant general of Monsieur le Prince de Conti. As the triolet had said, the Duc de Bouillon was a martyr to the gout, and was laid up in bed, but despite this grave condition, which had kept him out of the saddle for a month—in other words, since Paris had been under siege—he nonetheless sent word he was ready to receive Messieurs le Comte de La Fère and Chevalier d'Herblay.

The two friends were admitted into the chambers of the Duc de Bouillon. The invalid was in bed in his room, surrounded by an array of the most martial décor imaginable. All around, hanging on the walls, were swords, pistols, cuirasses, and arquebuses, and one might easily think that, once he was no longer crippled by gout, Monsieur de Bouillon would be eager to take the battle to the enemies of parliament. Meanwhile, to his great regret, he said, he was forced to keep to his bed.

"Ah, Messieurs!" he exclaimed, upon seeing his two visitors, and making an effort to half-rise from his bed, which caused him to wince in pain. "You are fortunate men! You can go forth, ride, and fight for the cause of the people. But I, as you see, am nailed to my bed. Ah, the devil take this gout!" he said, grimacing anew. "Devil take it!"

"Monseigneur, we've just arrived from England," said Athos, "and our first concern upon reaching Paris was to come and get news of your health."

"Many thanks, Messieurs, many thanks!" replied the duke. "It's bad, my health, as you can see . . . devil take this gout! But you say you've come from England? And King Charles is well, from what I've just heard?"

"He is dead, Monseigneur," said Aramis.

"What?" said the duke, astonished.

"He died on the scaffold, condemned by the Parliament."

"Impossible!"

"We were present at his execution."

"Then what of this story from Monsieur de Flamarens?"

"Monsieur de Flamarens?" said Aramis.

"Yes, he was just here."

Athos smiled. "With two companions?" said he.

"Yes, with two companions," the duke replied. Then, with some anxiety, he asked, "Did you encounter them?"

"Yes, I think we passed them in the street," said Athos. And he smiled at Aramis, who looked back in some surprise.

"Devil take this gout!" hissed Monsieur de Bouillon, apparently rather ill at ease.

"Monseigneur," said Athos, "it must call on all your devotion to the Parisian cause for you to continue, suffering as you are, at the head of their armies, and we greatly admire your perseverance, Monsieur d'Herblay and I."

"What would you have, Messieurs? One does what one must, as you show by your own examples, so brave and devoted. It's thanks to you that my dear colleague the Duc de Beaufort has his liberty and perhaps his life, but one must sacrifice oneself to public affairs. And so, as you see,

I do sacrifice myself—but I swear, I'm nearly at the end of my strength. My heart and my head are fine, but this devilish gout is killing me, and I confess that if the Court complied with my demands—which are quite justified, since I'm only asking for an indemnity promised me by the old cardinal himself when he confiscated my principality of Sedan—yes, if I were compensated by domains of equal value, along with a back payment for the non-enjoyment of my property during the period since it was taken from me, that is, for eight years—and if the title of prince was accorded to my house, and if my brother Turenne was reinstated to his command, why, I'd retire immediately to my estates and leave the Court and the Parliament to settle things between them however they may."

"And you would be quite right, Monseigneur," said Athos.

"Is that your true opinion, Monsieur le Comte de La Fère?"

"Absolutely."

"And you as well, Monsieur le Chevalier d'Herblay?"

"Indeed."

"Well! I assure you then, Messieurs, that in all probability that's the course I'll adopt," replied the duke. "Right now, the Court is making overtures to me, and I must decide whether to accept them. Heretofore I've rejected them, but if men like you tell me I've been wrong, and moreover since this devilish gout makes it impossible for me to render any service to the Parisian cause, then by my faith, I believe I'll follow your advice and accept the proposition made to me by Monsieur de Châtillon."

"Accept, Prince, accept," said Aramis.

"*Ma foi,* yes. I'm even sorry I didn't take it tonight . . . but there's a conference tomorrow, so we'll see."

The two friends saluted the duke. "Go, Messieurs," said the latter, "you must be very tired from your journey. Poor King Charles! But in the end, it was partly his own fault, and at least we can console ourselves that France has nothing to reproach itself for in this, and that we did everything we could to save him."

"We can bear witness to that," said Aramis, "as I'm sure Monsieur de Mazarin will be happy to hear."

"Well, there it is! I'm glad you can provide him such a testimony. He has a good heart, the cardinal, and if he weren't a foreigner, well! The people would do him justice. *Aiee!* Devil take this gout!"

Athos and Aramis went out, followed down the corridors by Monsieur de Bouillon's cries; it was evident the poor duke was suffering like the damned.

Arriving at the door, Aramis asked Athos, "Well! What do you think?"

"About what?"

"About Monsieur de Bouillon, *pardieu!*"

"My friend, I think I agree with that triolet sung by our guide:

> *The brave Monsieur de Bouillon*
> *Is afflicted by the gout.*

"Quite so," said Aramis. "And that's why I didn't say a word to him about the object of our visit."

"Very prudent—it just would have given him a fresh attack. Let's go see Monsieur de Beaufort."

And the two friends set out for the Hôtel de Vendôme. Ten o'clock was sounding as they arrived. The Hôtel de Vendôme was guarded as well as that of de Bouillon and presented just as warlike an appearance. There were sentries, couriers posted in the courtyard, stands of weapons, and horses saddled and holstered. Two riders were coming out of the gate as Athos and Aramis entered, obliging them to step their horses back to let them pass.

"Oh ho, Messieurs," said Aramis, "what a night this is for meetings. I confess that, having met so much tonight, I'll be truly dismayed if we fail to meet tomorrow."

"Oh, as to that, Monsieur," replied Châtillon, for it was indeed he and Flamarens who were coming out of the Duc de Beaufort's gate, "I think you can rest easy on that score—for if we meet so often when we're not looking for each other, I'm sure we'll find each other when we are."

"I hope so, Monsieur," said Aramis.

"Me, I don't hope, I'm sure of it," said the duke.

Flamarens and Châtillon continued on their way, while Athos and Aramis entered and dismounted. They had scarcely handed their bridles to their lackeys and removed their cloaks when a man approached, peered at them by the flickering light of the lantern hung above the middle of the courtyard, gave a cry of surprise, and leaped into their arms. "Comte de La Fère!" said the man. "Chevalier d'Herblay! How do you happen to be in Paris?"

"Rochefort!" said the two friends together.

"The same! As you probably know, we just arrived from the Vendômois four or five days ago and are preparing some trouble for Mazarin. You're still with us, I presume?"

"More than ever. And the duke?"

"He's furious with the cardinal. You know our dear duke! And he's riding high—he's practically the King of Paris and can't go anywhere without being mobbed."

"Ah, good for him!" said Aramis. "But tell me, wasn't that Messieurs de Flamarens and de Châtillon who left just now?"

"Yes, they came for an audience with the duke, coming from Mazarin, no doubt, but I'm sure they found out exactly who they're dealing with here."

"I'm sure they did!" said Athos. "Could one have the honor of calling on His Highness?"

"This very moment! You know that for you he'll always be in. Follow me—I claim the honor of presenting you."

Rochefort marched ahead, and all doors were opened for him and the two friends. They found Monsieur de Beaufort about to sit down to the table; the thousand interruptions of the evening had delayed his supper until just then, but despite the gravity of that circumstance, the moment the prince heard the names Rochefort announced, he slid back his chair, rose, and eagerly advanced toward the pair. "Ah, *pardieu!*" he said. "You're always welcome, Messieurs. You'll join me for supper, won't you? Boisjoli, notify Noirmont that I have two guests. You know Noirmont, don't you Messieurs? He's my maître d'hôtel, the successor to Father Marteau, who baked those excellent pies you remember. Boisjoli, have him send one in, though not like the one he made for La Ramée. Thank God, we've no use tonight for rope ladders, daggers, or choke-pears!"

"Monseigneur," said Athos, "though we're well aware of his talents, don't bother your illustrious maître d'hôtel on our account. Tonight, with the permission of Your Highness, we just desire the honor of asking news of his health and seeing if he has orders for us."

"Oh, as to my health, it's as you see, Messieurs, excellent. A constitution that can resist five years in Vincennes under the hospitality of Monsieur de Chavigny can withstand anything. As for giving you orders, my faith, I swear I don't know what orders I'd give you, since there are so many others giving orders in their own names that, soon enough, I doubt I'll be giving any at all."

"Really?" said Athos. "I thought the Parliament was counting on the unity between the people's commanders."

"Ah, yes, our unity—there's a thing of beauty. There's no conflict with the Duc de Bouillon, since he has the gout and can't get out of bed, which is one way of getting along, but with Monsieur d'Elbeuf and his ox-like sons . . . Have you heard the triolet about the Duc d'Elbeuf, Messieurs?"

"No, Monseigneur."

"Really!" The duke began to sing:

Monsieur d'Elbeuf and his beefy sons
Are awfully fierce in the Place Royale
They stomp their feet and shake their fists
Monsieur d'Elbeuf and his beefy sons
But comes the call to the battlefield
Their warlike bluster disappears

Monsieur d'Elbeuf and his beefy sons
Are awfully fierce in the Place Royale

"But that's not the case with the coadjutor, I hope," said Athos.

"It's the opposite with the coadjutor, which is even worse. Lord protect us from pugnacious prelates who wear armor under their vestments! Instead of biding in his archbishopric chanting *Te Deums* for victories we haven't won yet, or praying for us in our defeats, do you know what he's done?"

"No."

"He's raised a regiment he's named the Corinthian after his arch-bishopric,[44] and he's appointing lieutenants and captains like a Marshal of France, and colonels like a king."

"Yes," said Aramis, "but when it comes to fighting, surely he stays in his episcopal palace?"

"Not in the least, my dear d'Herblay! When it's time for battle, he fights. Now, since the death of his uncle has given him a seat in parliament, he's everywhere at once: in parliament, in council, in battle. Of course, the Prince de Conti is the general in appearance, but what an appearance that is—a hunchbacked general! Everything's going wrong, Messieurs, every-thing's going wrong."

"And therefore, Monseigneur, Your Highness is discontented?" said Athos, exchanging a look with Aramis.

"Discontented, Count? Say instead that My Highness is furious. We've reached the point, I don't mind telling you, though I wouldn't say it to others, the point where if the queen acknowledged the wrongs she's done me, revoked my mother's exile, and restored me to the Admiralty, which belonged to my father and was promised me upon his death, well! I'd be just about ready to train some dogs to say that in France there are some thieves even greater than Monsieur de Mazarin."

This time it was more than a glance Athos and Aramis exchanged, it was a significant look and a smile. Now even if they hadn't met them outside, they'd have known that Messieurs de Châtillon and de Flamarens had been there—so they didn't breathe a word about Mazarin's presence in Paris. "Monseigneur, we are satisfied," said Athos. "We came to visit Your Highness at this late hour with no other object than to prove our devotion, and to tell him we are at his disposal as his most loyal servants."

"And you have proven to be my most faithful friends, Messieurs! If I'm ever reconciled with the Court, I'll show you, I hope, that I'll still be a friend to you and to those gentlemen, what the devil are they called—d'Artagnan and Porthos?"

"Yes, d'Artagnan and Porthos."

"Yes, that's it! But most of all, you understand, to you, Comte de La Fère and Chevalier d'Herblay."

Athos and Aramis bowed and withdrew. "My dear Athos," said Aramis, "I do believe you consented to accompany me, God be thanked, just to teach me a lesson."

"We're not done, though," said Athos. "The evening isn't complete until we've seen the coadjutor."

"Then let's go see our archbishop," said Aramis. And they turned toward the Île de la Cité.

As they once more approached the center of Paris, Athos and Aramis were again blocked by the flood and had to hire a boat. It was now after eleven o'clock, but everyone knew there was no wrong time to visit the coadjutor; his inexhaustible energy turned night into day and day into night.

The episcopal palace rose before them out of the water, and one would have said, from the number of boats swarming around the mansion, that this wasn't Paris, but Venice. The skiffs came and went in every direction, poling into the labyrinth of the streets of the Cité, or pulling away toward the Arsenal or over to Quai Saint-Victor, as if skimming across a lake. Some of these boats were mute and mysterious, but others were noisy and gleaming with lanterns. The two friends glided through this aquatic traffic and joined those approaching their destination.

The ground floor of the episcopal palace was inundated, but ladders had been placed against the walls, so that the chief result of the flood was that, instead of entering by the doors, they went in through the windows. In this way Athos and Aramis ended up in the prelate's antechamber, a hall crowded with lords and lackeys, for a dozen seigneurs were on hand awaiting their turn.

"*Mon Dieu*, Athos!" said Aramis. "Are we going to give this fop of a coadjutor the pleasure of making us wait in his antechamber?"

Athos smiled. "My friend," he said, "we must be patient with the inconveniences of dealing with the important. Since the coadjutor is one of the seven or eight kings reigning in Paris, naturally he has a court."

"Maybe so," said Aramis, "but we're no mere courtiers."

"Then we'll send in our names, and if he won't receive us, well! We'll leave him to his affairs and the affairs of France. It's just a matter of finding the right lackey and slipping a half-pistole into his hand."

"You're right," said Aramis, "but if I'm not mistaken . . . yes, it's him. Bazin! Over here, you clown!"

Bazin, who, resplendent in his church vestments, was just then majestically crossing the antechamber, stopped and turned, frowning, to see who was so insolent as to address him in such a manner. But as soon as he recognized Aramis the tiger became a lamb, and approaching the two gentlemen, he said, "What! It's you, Monsieur le Chevalier! You arrive just when we were most anxious about you! Oh, I'm so happy to see you again!"

"Fine, fine, Master Bazin, but a truce to compliments," said Aramis. "We've come to see Monsieur le Coadjuteur, and as we're pressed for time, we need to see him at once."

"Of course!" said Bazin. "Right away—the waiting room is no place for seigneurs of your standing. Only he's locked in a secret conference right now with a Monsieur de Bruy."

"De Bruy!" said Athos and Aramis together.

"Yes! I'm the one who announced him, so I remember the name perfectly. Do you know him, Monsieur?" added Bazin, turning to Aramis.

"I believe so."

"That's more than I could say," said Bazin. "He was so wrapped up in his cloak and hat that I couldn't see his face no matter how I tried. But I'll go in to announce you, and maybe this time I'll get a glimpse."

"Never mind that," said Aramis. "We'll give up on seeing Monsieur le Coadjuteur tonight—isn't that so, Athos?"

"As you like," said the count.

"Yes, his business with Monsieur de Bruy is far too important for us to interrupt."

"Shall I inform the archbishop that Messieurs had stopped by?"

"No, it isn't worth the trouble," said Aramis. "Let's go, Athos." And the two friends marched out through the crowd of lackeys, followed by Bazin, who emphasized their importance with the effusiveness of his farewells.

"Well, then?" asked Athos when he and Aramis were once more in their boat. "Do you begin to see that we would have been doing our good friends no favor by calling out the guards to arrest Monsieur de Mazarin?"

"You are wisdom incarnate, Athos," replied Aramis.

Discussing the matter, what particularly struck the two friends was of how little importance to the Court of France were those terrible events in England that seemed to occupy the attention of the rest of Europe. In fact, in all of Paris, except for a poor widow and a royal orphan who wept in a dark corner of the Louvre, no one seemed aware that a king called Charles I had ever existed, and that this king had just died on the scaffold.

The two friends arranged to meet again at ten the next morning, for, though the night was well along, when they arrived at the door of their lodgings Aramis announced that he still had several important visits to make, and left Athos to enter alone.

As ten was sounding the next morning they were reunited. For his part, Athos had been out and about since six. "Any news?" he asked.

"None—no one has seen d'Artagnan anywhere, and Porthos has yet to show himself. You?"

"Nothing."

"The devil!" said Aramis.

"This delay isn't natural," said Athos. "They took the most direct route, and should have arrived before us."

"Plus, we both know how quickly d'Artagnan travels," added Aramis. "He's not the man to lose any time, knowing we're waiting for him. . . ."

"He was figuring, you remember, on being here by the fifth."

"And here it is the ninth. The agreed-upon waiting period expires tonight."

"What do you intend to do," asked Athos, "if we have no news by tonight?"

"*Pardieu!* We should head out looking for them."

"Very well," said Athos.

"What about Raoul?" asked Aramis.

A cloud passed over the count's expression. "I admit I'm anxious about Raoul," he said. "He had a message yesterday from the Prince de Condé, went to rejoin him at Saint-Cloud, and hasn't been back."

"Have you seen Madame de Chevreuse?"

"She wasn't at home. And you, Aramis—I imagine you must have gone by Madame de Longueville's?"

"I did indeed."

"Well?"

"She wasn't at home either, but at least she left the address of her new lodgings."

"Where is that?"

"You'd never guess in a thousand tries."

"How can I guess where she'd be at midnight? For I presume you went straight there after you left me last night. How am I supposed to guess the nighttime abode of the most lovely and energetic of all the lady Frondeurs?"

"At the Hôtel de Ville,[45] *mon cher!*"

"The Hotel de Ville? Has she been appointed the new Merchants' Provost?"

"No, she's appointed herself the Acting Queen of Paris—and since she didn't dare establish her court in the Palais Royal or the Tuileries, she's installed herself in the Hôtel de Ville, where at any moment she's due to present an heir to our dear Duc de Longueville."

"You didn't inform me she was in that condition, Aramis," said Athos.

"Oh, really? It must have slipped my mind—I beg your pardon."

"Now what are we going to do until tonight?" asked Athos. "It sounds like we have some time on our hands."

"Not at all, *mon ami,* we have our work cut out for us."

"Really? Where?"

"Just outside Charenton, *morbleu!* I hope, as promised, to meet there a certain Monsieur de Châtillon whom I've long detested."

"Why is that?"

"Because he's the brother of a certain Monsieur de Coligny."

"Ah, right, I forgot—that Coligny who presumed to be your rival. He was cruelly punished for his audacity,[46] you know, and you ought to be satisfied with that."

"Yes, but what would you have? It's not enough for me. I'm hot-blooded by nature; it's the only thing that's holding me back from advancement in the Church. Of course, you know, Athos, that you don't have to go with me."

"Come, now," said Athos, "you're joking!"

"In that case, *mon cher,* if you're going with me, we've no time to lose. The drums are beating, the cannons are rolling, and I saw the militia lining up for battle in front of the Hôtel de Ville. There's certainly going to be a battle beyond Charenton, as the Duc de Châtillon told us yesterday."

"I would have thought," said Athos, "that last night's conferences would have changed those warlike plans."

"It will change what follows, but they have to fight regardless, if only to cover for the conferences."

"Those poor people!" said Athos. "Going out to get themselves killed so Sedan can be returned to Monsieur de Bouillon, Monsieur de Beaufort can enjoy the Admiralty, and the coadjutor can be made a cardinal!"

"Come, now, *mon cher*," said Aramis. "Admit you wouldn't be so concerned about this battle if it didn't look like Raoul will be mixed up in it."

"You may be right, Aramis."

"Well, then, let's go to where the fighting is—it's the best way to find d'Artagnan, Porthos, and maybe even Raoul."

"Alas!" said Athos.

"My good friend," said Aramis, "now that we're in Paris, you really must lose this habit of sighing ruefully. When it's wartime, Athos, *morbleu*, go to war! Are you a man of the sword, or are you turning priest? Here, look how gloriously the militia marches by. It stirs the blood! And their captain, look there—what could be more warlike?"

"They're coming out of the Rue du Mouton—sadly appropriate for such sheep."

"But with a drummer leading the way, just like real soldiers! Look at that officer, the way he struts and swaggers!"

"Hey!" said Grimaud.

"What?" asked Athos.

"Planchet, Monsieur."

"Ha! Lieutenant yesterday, captain today, and doubtless a colonel tomorrow," said Aramis. "Within a week the fellow will be a Marshal of France."

"Let's ask him what's going on," said Athos.

And the two friends approached Planchet, who, prouder than ever of his new rank, deigned to explain to the gentlemen that he was ordered to take up position in the Place Royale with two hundred men, there to act as a reserve and rear guard for the Parisian army until ordered to advance on Charenton.

Since Athos and Aramis were on his side, they escorted Planchet to his position. Planchet maneuvered his men on the Place Royale very skillfully, arranging them in echelon behind a long column of militia that stretched to the Rue Saint-Antoine, awaiting the signal for battle. "This day will be a hot one," said Planchet in an aggressive tone.

"Yes, no doubt," said Aramis, "but you're a long way from the enemy."

"Oh, you'll see, Monsieur—we'll decrease that distance," replied a citizen soldier.

Aramis bowed, then turned toward Athos. "I don't care to park myself all day in the Place Royale with these people," he said. "What do you say to going to the front? We'll get a better view from there."

"And Monsieur de Châtillon isn't going to come looking for you in the Place Royale, is he? Let's go forward, my friend."

"And don't you also have a couple of words to say to Monsieur de Flamarens?"

"Friend," said Athos, "I've resolved not to draw my sword again unless it's absolutely necessary."

"And since when have you decided that?"

"Since I last drew my poniard."

"Oh, fine! Another souvenir of Monsieur Mordaunt. *Mon cher*, the last thing you need is to feel remorse for having killed that devil."

"Hush!" said Athos, putting a finger to his mouth with that sad smile that was unique to him. "Let us speak no more of Mordaunt—it will bring only misfortune."

And Athos spurred his horse toward Charenton, skirting the Faubourg Saint-Antoine, then the valley of Fécamp, which teemed with armed bourgeois. It goes without saying that Aramis was less than an arm's-length behind.

XXXVI

The Battle of Charenton

As Athos and Aramis rode forward, passing various units formed in columns on the road, they saw men in shining cuirasses bearing rusty weapons, and bright new muskets next to ancient halberds. "I think we've found the actual battlefield," said Aramis. "Do you see that cavalry unit standing there at the foot of the bridge, pistols at the ready? . . . Ah, take care—horse artillery coming toward us!"

"*Ah çà!*" said Athos. "Where have you taken us? It looks to me like we're now in the middle of the royal army. Isn't that Monsieur de Châtillon himself riding forward with his staff?" And Athos put his hand on his sword, while Aramis, thinking that perhaps they had ridden beyond the Parisian lines, reached for his pistols.

"Bonjour, Messieurs," said the duke, pulling up. "I can see you don't know the current situation, so allow me to enlighten you. We're under truce during negotiations; Monsieur le Prince is talking things over with the coadjutor, Monsieur de Beaufort, and Monsieur de Bouillon. Now, either affairs will be settled, and we'll meet another day, Chevalier, or they won't be settled, and we'll meet on the battlefield."

"Monsieur, you get right to the point," said Aramis. "Permit me to ask you one question."

"Do so, Monsieur."

"Where is this diplomacy taking place?"

"In Charenton itself, in the second house on the right, as you go in toward Paris."

"And this conference comes as a surprise?"

"Not exactly, Messieurs. It seems to stem from the new proposals made to the Parisians by Monsieur de Mazarin last night."

Athos and Aramis looked at each other and laughed. They knew better than anyone what those proposals were, to whom they'd been made, and who had made them.

"And this house where the diplomats are meeting," asked Athos, "it belongs to . . . ?"

"To Monsieur de Clanleu, who commands your troops at Charenton.[47] I say your troops, because I presume you gentlemen are Frondeurs."

"More or less," said Aramis.

"What do you mean, more or less?"

"It's hard for anyone to say what they are nowadays, as you should know better than anyone, Monsieur."

"We are for the king and the princes," said Athos.

"That doesn't tell me much," said Châtillon. "I mean, the king is with us, and his generals are Prince Gaston and the Prince de Condé."

"Perhaps," said Athos, "but His Majesty's true place is with us and the Princes de Conti, de Beaufort, d'Elbeuf, and de Bouillon."

"That's as may be," said Châtillon. "It's no secret that I have little sympathy for Monsieur de Mazarin, and all my interests are in Paris; I'm in the middle of a litigation there that all my fortunes depend upon. I was just consulting with my lawyer. . . ."

"In Paris?"

"No, in Charenton, with Monsieur Viole. You may have heard his name, as he's an excellent lawyer—a bit stubborn perhaps, but he's not a Member of Parliament for nothing. I'd hoped to meet him last night, but our business prevented me from attending to my own affairs. But affairs must be attended to, so I took advantage of the truce, and that's how you come to see me here now."

"Monsieur Viole conducts his consultations in the open air?" asked Aramis, laughing.

"Indeed, Monsieur, and on horseback, as today he's commanding a hundred pistoleers for the Parliament. I paid him a visit, and to do him honor, I brought with me these two small cannon, at the head of which you seemed so astonished to see me. I must admit I didn't recognize him at first, wearing a long sword over his lawyer's robe and with two pistols thrust through his belt. It gives him a warlike air that would amuse you should you happen to meet him."

"If he's that curious a sight, we might take the time to go look for him," said Aramis.

"You'll have to hurry, Monsieur, for the conference can't go on much longer."

"And if it ends without agreement," said Athos, "are you going to try to take Charenton?"

"Those are my orders; I command the attacking troops and will do my best to succeed."

"Then, Monsieur," said Athos, "since you command the cavalry . . ."

"Pardon me! I'm the commander in chief."

"Better still! You must know all your officers, I mean all those who are of good extraction."

"I do, or nearly so."

"Be good enough to tell me whether you have under your command the Chevalier d'Artagnan, Lieutenant of the Musketeers."

"No, Monsieur, he's not among us. It's been six weeks since he departed Paris and is said to be on a mission to England."

"I knew that, but I thought he was back."

"No, Monsieur, and as far as I know no one has seen him return. I can speak with authority on this subject as the King's Musketeers are one of our units, commanded by Monsieur de Cambon in the absence of Monsieur d'Artagnan."

The two friends looked at each other. "As I feared," said Athos.

"It's strange," said Aramis.

"They must have run into trouble on the way."

"It's been eight days, and tonight the deadline expires. If no news comes tonight, then tomorrow we go looking for them."

Athos nodded, then turned back to the duke. "And Monsieur de Brage-lonne, a young man of fifteen attached to Monsieur le Prince?" asked Athos, almost embarrassed to expose his paternal feelings before the cynical Aramis. "Has he the honor to be known to you, Monsieur le Duc?"

"Yes, certainly," replied Châtillon. "He arrived this morning with Monsieur le Prince—a charming young man! Is he a friend of yours, Monsieur le Comte?"

"Yes, Monsieur," said Athos, warmly. "So much so, that I wonder if I might see him. Is that possible?"

"Entirely possible, Monsieur. Just follow me and I'll escort you to headquarters."

"*Holà!*" said Aramis, turning. "There's some new commotion behind us, I think."

"In fact, I see a large troop of riders approaching!" said Châtillon.

"I recognize Monsieur le Coadjuteur under his Frondeur's hat."

"And I, Monsieur de Beaufort with his white plumes."

"They're coming at the gallop. Monsieur le Prince is with them. Ah! Now he's separated from them."

"They're sounding the tattoo!" cried Châtillon. "Do you hear? We must find out what's happening."

Indeed, the soldiers were running to their arms, the cavalrymen were getting back into their saddles, the trumpets sounded, and the drums beat as Monsieur de Beaufort drew his sword.

On his side, Monsieur le Prince gave the signal for recall, and those officers of the royal army who'd been visiting the Parisian troops rode toward him.

"Messieurs," said Châtillon, "the truce is over, it seems. We're going to fight. Withdraw into Charenton, as I'll be attacking shortly. Look, there's the signal from Monsieur le Prince."

In fact, a cornet waved the standard of the prince back and forth three times. "Au revoir, Monsieur le Chevalier!" cried Châtillon. And he departed at a gallop to rejoin his escort.

Athos and Aramis turned toward their side and saluted the coadjutor and Monsieur de Beaufort as they approached. As for Monsieur de Bouillon, at the end of the conference he'd had a terrible attack of gout and had to be carried back into Paris on a litter. In exchange the Duc d'Elbeuf, accompanied by his four sons as a staff, was roaming the ranks of the Parisian army as a marshal-at-large.

Meanwhile, between Charenton and the royal army there opened a broad gap, a region emptied out as if to prepare it to receive an imminent carpet of corpses. "Truly, this Mazarin is the shame of France," said the coadjutor as he tightened the sword belt he wore, in the fashion of the old military prelates, atop his episcopal robes. "He's nothing but a farmer who wants to harvest all France like a crop. The realm has no hope for peace and happiness until he's gone from it."

"Apparently they couldn't agree on a new color for the coadjutor's hat,"[48] Aramis said behind his hand.

Monsieur de Beaufort approached, sword waving. "Messieurs," he said, "diplomacy has proven useless. We proposed exile for this coward of a Mazarini, but the queen was quite emblematic in her recusal. She absolutely stands by her minister, so we have but one reservoir, and that's to congruously defeat him!"

"Hear, hear!" said the coadjutor. "Monsieur de Beaufort speaks with all his usual eloquence."

"Fortunately," said Aramis, "he corrects the defects of his speech with the effects of his sword."

"*Pfah!*" said the coadjutor with contempt. "He's done precious little so far in this war, I swear." And he drew his own sword. "Gentlemen," he cried, "there's the enemy coming on hard—now let's show him he can't have our half of this road!"

And without seeming to care whether he was supported or not, he charged off to lead the advance. His regiment, which was named the Corinthian after his archbishopric, followed close behind him—and the battle was joined.

For his part, Monsieur de Beaufort sent the cavalry, under the command of Monsieur de Noirmoutiers, toward Étampes, where they were to meet and escort in a convoy of supplies desperately needed by the Parisians. Monsieur de Beaufort intended, as always, to support the citizens.

Monsieur de Clanleu, in command of Charenton, stood waiting with the best of his troops, prepared to resist any assault, and even, in the event the enemy was repulsed, to attempt a sortie.

Within half an hour the combat was raging on all sides. The coadjutor, envious of Beaufort's reputation for bravery, had hurled himself into the fray, and had performed marvels of courage. His true vocation, as we know, was for the sword, and he was happy whenever he could draw it from its sheath, whatever the reason. But on this occasion, if he performed well as a soldier, he did a terrible job as a commander. With seven or eight hundred men he'd launched an attack on three thousand, who maintained a disciplined formation and smashed the coadjutor's attacking soldiers, who fell back in disorder onto the town's ramparts. There a barrage from Clanleu's artillery checked the advance of the royal troops, shaking them, but they quickly regrouped behind a cluster of houses and a small stand of trees.

Clanleu thought to seize the moment and charged the royal army at the head of two regiments—but as we said, the royalists had regrouped, and countercharged, led by Monsieur de Châtillon himself. This charge was so fierce and well-disciplined that Clanleu and his men were thrown back and almost enveloped. Clanleu sounded the retreat, and his troops were regaining their order as they fell back, step by step, when suddenly Clanleu fell, mortally wounded.

Châtillon saw him fall and announced far and wide that he was killed, which heartened the royal army, while the two regiments who'd been led out by Clanleu were completely demoralized. As a result, Clanleu's soldiers thought only of saving themselves and regaining Charenton's ramparts, where the coadjutor was trying to reform his own broken regiment.

Suddenly a squadron of Parisian cavalry bore in on the flank of the victors, who were pursuing the fugitives right into the town's entrenchments. Athos and Aramis charged at their head, Aramis with sword and pistol in his hand, Athos with his sword in its scabbard and his pistol in its holster. Athos was as calm and cool as if on parade, though his handsome and noble face was saddened at the sight of so many men slaughtering each other, sacrificed on the one hand to royal obstinacy, and on the other to the resentment of the princes.

Aramis, on the other hand, was a killing machine, inflamed by fury. His eyes blazed, his lips, so finely drawn, curved in a grim smile, and his nostrils flared at the smell of blood. Every one of his sword thrusts went home, and every blow with his pistol's pommel hit hard, dropping a wounded man trying to rejoin the fight.

On the opposing side, in the ranks of the royal army, two cavaliers, one wearing a gilded cuirass, the other a simple buff coat over a blue velvet doublet, charged to the fore. The cavalier in the gilded cuirass collided with Aramis and aimed a sword-thrust at him, which Aramis parried with his usual skill. "Ah, it's you, Monsieur de Châtillon!" cried the chevalier. "Greetings, I was waiting for you!"

"I hope I didn't keep you waiting too long, Monsieur," said the duke. "In any case, here I am."

"Monsieur de Châtillon," said Aramis, drawing from his saddle holster a second pistol which he'd reserved for this contingency, "if you've already emptied your pistol, I think you might be a dead man."

"But I haven't, thank God!" said Châtillon.

And the duke, raising his pistol at Aramis, cocked it and fired. But Aramis tilted his head just as he saw the duke pull the trigger, and the ball passed over him. Aramis shook his head. "You missed me. But by God, I won't miss you."

"If I give you the chance!" roared Châtillon, spurring his horse into Aramis's and raising his sword high.

Aramis awaited his moment with the terrible smile that was peculiar to him at such times. Athos, seeing Châtillon closing with Aramis like lightning, opened his mouth to cry, "Shoot!" just as the pistol was fired.

Châtillon threw his arms wide and fell back on his horse's crupper. The ball had entered his chest just above the edge of his cuirass. "I'm dead!" murmured the duke. And he slid from his horse to the ground.

"Ah, Monsieur, I warned you, and now I'm sorry I kept my word so well!" said Aramis. "Is there anything I can do for you?"

Châtillon beckoned him with a gesture, and Aramis was preparing to dismount, when suddenly he was struck hard in the side. It was a sword thrust, but his own cuirass turned the blade. He swiftly turned and seized his attacker by the wrist, and then cried out, at the same time as Athos: "Raoul!"

The young man simultaneously recognized the face of the Chevalier d'Herblay and the voice of his father and dropped his sword. Several Parisian cavalrymen closed in on Raoul, but Aramis covered him with his rapier. "This man is my prisoner! Ride on!" he cried.

Athos, meanwhile, grabbed his son's horse by the bridle and drew it out of the mêlée. At the same time Monsieur le Prince, supporting Monsieur de Châtillon's advance, appeared in the fray, easily recognizable by his shining eagle's eye and shrewd and skillful attacks. Seeing him, the regiment of the Archbishop of Corinth, which despite his efforts he hadn't been able to regroup, turned and routed, fleeing through the Parisian cavalry into Charenton, which they ran through without stopping.

The coadjutor, carried on by the general retreat, passed near Athos, Aramis, and Raoul. "Alas!" said the jealous Aramis, who couldn't resist enjoying the embarrassment of the coadjutor. "But in your capacity as archbishop, Monseigneur, you must recognize the aptness of the Scriptures."

"And what the devil do the Scriptures have to do with what's happening here?" asked the coadjutor.

"Why, Monsieur le Prince is treating you today as Saint Paul did the first of the Corinthians."

"Say, now!" said Athos. "That's not a bad joke, but we have no time for such witticisms. Onward, onward—or rather backward, for it looks to me like the Frondeurs have lost the battle."

"It's all the same to me!" said Aramis. "I just came here to meet Monsieur de Châtillon. And meet him I did, so I'm content—a duel with a Châtillon, now, that's something!"

"Plus, you took a prisoner," said Athos, indicating Raoul. And the three cavaliers went on their way at a gallop.

The young man had been overcome by joy when he'd found his father. They rode as close as they could, the young man's left hand in Athos's right.

Once they were clear of the battlefield, Athos asked the young man, "What were you doing in the midst of that mêlée? That wasn't where you belonged, it seems to me, and you weren't armed for it."

"I wasn't supposed to be in the fight today, Monsieur. I was sent as a courier to the cardinal, and was heading toward Rueil, when I saw Monsieur de Châtillon ride to the charge, and was moved to charge along with him. On the way he told me that two cavaliers of the Parisian army were looking for me, and one was named the Comte de La Fère."

"What? You knew we were there, but still tried to kill your friend the chevalier?"

"I didn't recognize the chevalier all armored for war," said Raoul, coloring, "though I should have known him by his coolness and skill."

"Thanks for the compliment, my young friend," said Aramis, "and it's clear where you learned your manners. But you say you were going to Rueil?"

"Yes."

"To the cardinal?"

"Yes, Monsieur. I have a dispatch from Monsieur le Prince for His Eminence."

"Then you must take it to him," said Athos.

"Not so fast with the chivalry, Count. What the devil! Our fate, and more importantly the fate of our friends, may be in this dispatch."

"But this young man must not fail in his duty," said Athos.

"First of all, Count, this young man is a prisoner, don't forget. This is all in accord with the rules of war. The loser doesn't get to dictate terms to the victor. Give me this dispatch, Raoul."

Raoul hesitated, looking toward Athos for guidance. "Give him the dispatch, Raoul," said Athos. "You are the prisoner of the Chevalier d'Herblay."

Raoul gave up the dispatch with some reluctance. Aramis, less scrupulous than the Comte de La Fère, took the dispatch and opened it, looked it over, and handed it to Athos, saying, "You're a believer, Athos—read this letter, and you'll see in it something that Providence thought we should know."

Athos frowned, but the idea that the letter might have something to say about d'Artagnan persuaded him to overcome his distaste and read it. What he read was as follows:

> *Monseigneur, in order to reinforce Monsieur de Comminges's guards, I send to you this evening the ten men you requested. They are picked men, soldiers quite capable of restraining that dangerous duo now in Your Eminence's custody.*

"Oh ho!" said Athos.

"Well?" said Aramis. "And what dangerous duo might this be, that needs ten men added to those of Comminges to restrain them? Who could that be but d'Artagnan and Porthos?"

"We'll spend the rest of the day searching Paris for them," said Athos, "but if we have no news by nightfall we take the road to Picardy, and I'll answer for it that, given d'Artagnan's quick mind, we'll soon know if we're on the right track."

"Search Paris we shall then, starting with Planchet, who ought to know if his old master is in town."

"Ah, poor Planchet! You speak of him so lightly, Aramis, when he was probably massacred in today's fiasco. All these belligerent bourgeois were probably cut down like wheat."

As this was all too likely, the two friends were anxious as they reentered Paris through the Porte du Temple and made their way to the Place Royale to learn the fate of that poor militia. But to their surprise they found the whole unit, soldiers and captain, still drinking and dicing in the Place Royale, while their families, who'd heard the sound of cannon toward Charenton, probably despaired of their lives.

Athos and Aramis inquired once again with Planchet, but he'd heard nothing of d'Artagnan, and told them he couldn't leave his post without orders from his superiors. At five o'clock they were released to go home, where they told everyone they were returning from the battle, though they'd never been out of sight of the bronze equestrian statue of Louis XIII in the Place Royale.

"A thousand thunders!" said Planchet, returning to his shop in the Rue des Lombards. "We got our arses kicked today! I'll never get over it."

XXXVII

The Road to Picardy

Athos and Aramis were safe in Paris, and knew very well that as soon as they set foot outside the city walls they were in great danger—but what was danger to such men as these? Instinctively, they felt that the climax of this second Odyssey was drawing near, and this was no time to hang back and give less than their all.

Besides, Paris was by no means a tranquil refuge. Provisions were beginning to run short, riots were breaking out, and when one of the Prince de Conti's generals felt the need to assert himself, putting down a small riot gave him the opportunity. Monsieur de Beaufort had taken advantage of one of these riots to plunder the personal library of Monsieur de Mazarin—for money, he said, to buy food for the suffering people.

Athos and Aramis left Paris during this disturbance, which took place on the evening of the same day the Parisians were beaten at Charenton. They left behind a Paris in misery, stalked by famine, plagued by fear, and divided into rival factions. As Parisians and Frondeurs, they expected to find the same misery, fears, and intrigues in the enemy camp. But on their way to Saint-Denis, they were surprised to hear that in Saint-Germain the Court was laughing, singing, and carrying on happily.

The two gentlemen took the back roads, at first to avoid the Cardinalists while they were in the Île-de-France, and later to avoid the provincial Frondeurs once they passed into Normandy, where they would have been brought before Monsieur de Longueville, who would then decide whether they should be treated as friends or enemies.[49] Once they'd avoided these two perils, they rejoined the main road from Boulogne to Abbeville, following it step by step, trace by trace.

For a while they were empty-handed; several innkeepers had been interrogated without yielding so much as a clue, when in Montreuil Athos's sensitive fingers detected something rough on a tavern table. Lifting the tablecloth, he found beneath it the following letters deeply incised with the edge of a blade: *Port . . . d'Art . . . 2 February.*

"Good news," said Athos, showing the inscription to Aramis. "We'd planned to stay here tonight, but now that we have some evidence, let's continue."

They remounted their horses and rode to Abbeville. There they were stymied by the city's large number of inns. They could hardly visit them all—how could they guess in which one their friends had stayed?

"Believe me, Athos," said Aramis, "we're not going to find anything at Abbeville. If we're stumped by which inn to choose, our friends would have been the same. If it was only Porthos we were after, well, Porthos would have picked the most magnificent hôtel, and we'd be sure to find traces of his passage. But d'Artagnan has no such weakness, and though Porthos would plead that he was dying of hunger, d'Artagnan would press on, inexorable as fate. We'll have to seek for him elsewhere."

They continued on their way but found nothing more. This was the most distressing and tedious task ever undertaken by Athos and Aramis, and without the triple motivation of honor, friendship, and gratitude to drive them, our two travelers would soon have given up looking for tracks, questioning passersby, searching for signs, and examining every face.

Their search brought them to Péronne. Athos was beginning to despair; his noble and sensitive nature blamed himself for the dilemma in which he and Aramis found themselves. He must have missed something obvious— no doubt they hadn't pressed their questions persistently enough, or pursued their investigations cleverly enough. They were ready to leave the town and turn back the way they had come, when, just inside the city gates, on a white wall at a street corner near the ramparts, Athos spotted something. It was a drawing in black as if made with a clinker, a childish sketch depicting two cavaliers galloping in a frenzy, one of whom held up a sign on which was written in Spanish, "They're after us."

"Ah ha!" said Athos. "That's as clear as day. Pursued though he was, d'Artagnan paused here for five minutes and put his time to good use. This shows that their pursuers couldn't have been too close behind them; maybe they got away."

Aramis shook his head. "If they'd escaped, we would have caught up with them by now, or at least heard of them."

"You're right, Aramis. Onward!"

The anxiety and impatience of the two gentlemen was now beyond description. The anxiety was in the tender and generous heart of Athos, the impatience in the nervous spirit of Aramis, so easily distraught. They galloped for three or four hours with the frenzy of the two cavaliers on the mural. Suddenly, in a narrow gorge between two steep cliffs, they found the road half blocked by an enormous boulder. Its point of origin could be seen halfway up the slope, where a fresh hole in the cliff face showed where it had been pried out. The size and mass of the thing proved that it would have taken the arm of a giant like Enceladus or Briareus[50] to move it.

Aramis stopped. "This is clear enough!" he said, looking at the boulder. "If Ajax of Telamon hasn't passed here, then it must have been Porthos. Count, let's examine this prodigious rock."

They dismounted and went to look. The boulder had clearly been placed to bar the road to horsemen, but there had evidently been enough riders in pursuit to shift it partway to the side. The two travelers examined every inch of the boulder they could see but found nothing of interest. They called Blaisois and Grimaud to help, and between the four of them, they were able to roll it enough to expose its underside. There they found inscribed, "We're pursued by eight light horse. If we reach Compiègne, we'll stop at the Peacock and Crown; the host is a friend."

"Positive news at last, and now we have a course to follow," said Athos. "On to the Peacock and Crown!"

"Yes," said Aramis, "but if we actually intend to arrive there, we'd better rest the horses first—they're nearly done in."

Aramis was right. They stopped at the next auberge; each horse was given a double ration of oats soaked in wine, allowed three hours to rest, and then they set out again. The men themselves were staggering with fatigue, but hope sustained them.

Six hours later, Athos and Aramis entered Compiègne and asked directions to the Peacock and Crown. They were shown to an inn with a sign representing the god Pan with a crown on his head. The two friends dismounted from the horses without pausing to puzzle out the meaning of the sign, which at any other time Aramis would have criticized. They found the inn's honest host, a man as broad and bald as a Chinese Buddha, and asked if recently he'd had two gentlemen lodgers who'd been pursued by light horse. The host, without saying a word, opened a chest and drew out a broken rapier. "Do you recognize this?" he said.

Athos knew it at a glance. "That's d'Artagnan's sword," he said.

"The larger man or the smaller?" asked the host.

"The smaller," Athos replied.

"I see you are friends of those gentlemen."

"Well! What happened to them?"

"They came into my courtyard on dying horses, but before they had time to shut the gate eight light horse cavalrymen came in after them."

"Eight!" said Aramis. "I'm astounded that men of the stature and ability of d'Artagnan and Porthos could be arrested by only eight men."

"No doubt, Monsieur, and these eight men would have failed if they hadn't been reinforced by twenty soldiers from the Royal Italian Regiment, which is garrisoned in this town. Your friends were literally overwhelmed by numbers."

"Arrested!" said Athos. "Do you know on what grounds?"

"No, Monsieur, they were taken away at once, and didn't have time to say anything. Only, once they were gone, I found this broken sword on the battlefield while helping to pick up the two dead and five or six wounded."

"And the two captives," asked Aramis, "were they injured at all?"

"No, Monsieur, I don't think so."

"Well, that's some consolation," Aramis said.

"And do you know where they were taken?" asked Athos.

"Toward Louvres."

"Let's leave Blaisois and Grimaud here," said Athos. "They can return tomorrow to Paris with the horses, which in any event have had it for today. We can continue by post-horse."

"Post-horse it is," said Aramis.

They sent for the hired horses. While they were waiting, the two friends took a quick meal; they hoped, if they learned anything at Louvres, to be able to follow it up immediately.

They arrived at Louvres, where there was only one inn, which served ratafia, that famous local liqueur[51] whose reputation survives even today. "Let's look around," said Athos. "D'Artagnan won't have missed the opportunity to ask to be allowed a glass of ratafia, and in the process leave us a clue."

They entered, stepped up to the counter, and asked for two glasses of the local liqueur, hoping that d'Artagnan and Porthos had done the same. The counter of the bar was covered with tinplate, one part of which was marred by scratches made by the prong of a buckle: "Rueil. D."

"They're at Rueil!" said Aramis, who was the first to spot the inscription.

"Then let's go to Rueil," said Athos.

"That's stepping into the jaws of the wolf," said Aramis. "Rueil is the cardinal's headquarters."

"If I were as much Jonah's friend as I am d'Artagnan's," said Athos, "I'd have followed him into the belly of the whale—and you would too, Aramis."

"Decidedly, my dear Count, I think you make me better than I am. If I were alone, I'm not at all sure I'd go to Rueil without first taking a number of precautions—but where you go, I go as well."

They got fresh horses and set out for Rueil.

Athos, without knowing it, had given Aramis the best advice they could follow. The deputies of parliament had just arrived at Rueil for those famous conferences that were to last for three weeks, resulting in the "Lame Peace"[52] that was later broken when Monsieur le Prince was arrested. So, the town of Rueil was crowded with Parisians: advocates, presidents, councilors, and parliamentarians of all sorts, jostling against, from the Court, any number of gentlemen, officers, and guards; it was easy, in all that confusion, to remain as anonymous as one liked. Besides, the conferences were occurring under truce, and arresting two gentlemen at that moment, even if they were prominent Frondeurs, would have violated the laws of diplomacy.

The two friends thought that everyone would be as concerned with their problems as they were, so they mingled with both sides, expecting to hear something about d'Artagnan and Porthos, but all they heard was talk about articles and amendments. Athos was in favor of going straight to the prime minister. "*Mon ami,*" said Aramis, "that's a fine idea, except for the fact that our safety lies in our obscurity. If we draw attention to ourselves, we'll immediately join our friends in the depths of some dark dungeon where not even the Devil could get us out. Let's find them, by all means, but on purpose, not by accident. They were arrested at Compiègne, and certainly brought to Rueil, as we confirmed at Louvres; once at Rueil, they would have been interrogated by the cardinal, who would then either hold them nearby under guard or send them on to Saint-Germain. They're not in the Bastille, because that's in the hands of the Frondeurs with Broussel's son as its governor. And they didn't execute them, as the death of d'Artagnan would make a big noise. As to Porthos, I think he's as immortal as God, though less patient. So let's not despair, be patient ourselves, and wait here at Rueil, for I'm convinced they're being held somewhere nearby. But what's wrong? You've turned pale!"

"I just remembered," said Athos, in a voice that almost trembled, "that when this château was the country headquarters of Monsieur de Richelieu he equipped it with some frightful oubliettes, some prison-pits . . ."

"Not to worry," said Aramis. "Monsieur de Richelieu was a nobleman, our equal in birth and our superior in position. He could, like the king, tap the head of even the greatest *grands,* and shake those heads on their shoulders. But Monsieur de Mazarin is a peasant who at best can have us taken by the collar like a policeman. Believe me, d'Artagnan and Porthos are here at Rueil somewhere, alive and well kept."

"In that case," said Athos, "we should go to the coadjutor and get official credentials for the conference, so we can enter the château itself."

"And mingle with all those frightful Men of the Robe? What are you thinking, *mon cher*? Do you believe we'd hear a single word about where d'Artagnan and Porthos are being held? No, I think we need to find some other means."

"Well!" said Athos. "In that case I return to my first thought, which is that the best means is to be open and direct. I'll go not to Mazarin, but to the queen, and I'll say, 'Madame, release to us your two good servants and our two good friends.'"

Aramis shook his head. "As a last resort that's always there, Athos, but believe me, don't try it unless you have to. It will still be available if needed. In the meantime, let's continue our investigations."

Thus, they continued their search, and learned many things under a thousand pretexts, each more ingenious than the last, and spoke to so many people, that at last they found a light horse cavalryman who admitted he was one of the troop who'd escorted d'Artagnan and Porthos from Compiègne to Rueil. With the testimony of this light horseman, they were finally certain that they were in the right town.

Athos kept coming back to his idea of an audience with the queen. "To see the queen," said Aramis, "you must first see the cardinal, and as soon as you see the cardinal, mark what I say to you, Athos, we *will* be reunited with our friends, but not in a way we'll enjoy. And I confess, that's a method of reunion I'd prefer to avoid. Let's keep our liberty so we have freedom to act."

"I'm determined to see the queen," said Athos.

"Very well, *mon ami*, but if you're set on this madness, warn me, I beg you, a day in advance."

"Why is that?"

"So, I can take advantage of the warning to make a trip to Paris."

"To see who?"

"*Dame!* How do I know? Probably Madame de Longueville; she's all-powerful there, and will help me. Just make sure you find a way to inform me that you've been arrested, and I'll do my best to return."

"Why not risk the arrest with me, Aramis?" said Athos.

"No, thank you."

"Once arrested the four of us will be reunited, and then I think we'll be fine. Within twenty-four hours all four of us will be free."

"*Mon cher,* since I killed Châtillon, who was the darling of the ladies of Saint-Germain, I'm too notorious to risk being put in prison. The queen would listen to Mazarin's advice about me, and Mazarin's advice would be to put me on trial."

"Do you really think, Aramis, that she loves this Italian as much as they say?"

"She once loved an Englishman a great deal."

"Ah, my friend, she truly is a woman!"

"Not at all, Athos, and don't fool yourself: she's a queen."

"Dear friend, I'm going to pay my respects and ask for an audience with Anne of Austria."

"Then adieu, Athos—I'm going to go raise an army."

"To do what?"

"To come back and besiege Rueil."

"Where shall we meet again?"

"At the foot of the cardinal's gallows."

And the two friends separated, Aramis to return to Paris, and Athos to take the first steps necessary to be granted an audience with the queen.

XXXVIII

The Gratitude of Anne of Austria

Athos found it easier than he expected to see Anne of Austria—at the first request he was granted an audience, for the following day after her morning *lever*, to which he was entitled to attend by right of birth.

The halls of the château at Saint-Germain were thronged with courtiers; never at the Louvre or the Palais Royal had Anne of Austria had more. But this crowd mainly consisted of the secondary nobility, as all the highest-ranking gentlemen of France were aligned with Monsieur de Conti, Monsieur de Beaufort, and the coadjutor.

Nonetheless, gaiety ruled the day at this Court. A peculiarity of this civil war was that more couplets were fired off than cannon. The Court wrote verses mocking the Parisians, who replied with triolets mocking the Court, and the wounds inflicted, though not mortal, were still deeply felt, for they were the burning wounds of ridicule.

But in the midst of this general hilarity and frivolous futility, one question preoccupied every mind: would Mazarin remain the minister and favorite, or would Mazarin, who seemed to have blown in from the south like a cloud, be blown away again now that the winds were against him? Everyone hoped for and wanted that—so much so that the minister came to feel that all the flattery and homage paid to him by the courtiers were mere lies covering hatred disguised by fear and self-interest. He was anxious, not knowing what to expect or whom he could rely upon.

Monsieur le Prince himself, who commanded for him, never missed a chance to mock or humiliate him. After two or three occasions when Mazarin had tried to exert his authority in the presence of the victor of Rocroi, and the prince had looked away coldly, that made it clear that, if he defended the minister, it was with neither conviction nor enthusiasm.

So, the cardinal fell back on his relationship with the queen, who was his only reliable support. But there had been several minor incidents that made him feel like even this support was wavering.

When the hour for his audience arrived, the Comte de La Fère was told that though it would take place, he would have to wait a few minutes, as the queen was consulting with her minister. This was true: Paris had just sent a new deputation which was intended at last to move negotiations forward, and the queen was consulting with Mazarin as to how she should receive these deputies. Matters of State were at a fever pitch among the high and mighty, and Athos could hardly have chosen a worse time to inquire after his friends, tiny atoms lost in the whirlwind of great affairs.

But Athos was unyielding once his mind was made up, especially when his decision derived from his conscience and was dictated by his duty. He insisted on being introduced, saying that, though he was no deputy of Monsieur de Conti, de Beaufort, de Bouillon, d'Elbeuf, or the coadjutor, nor of Madame de Longueville, Broussel, or parliament, and came on his own account, he nonetheless had matters of importance to speak of to Her Majesty.

Her consultation completed, the queen summoned Athos to her study. The audiencer introduced and named him. His was a name that had been too often heard in the ears of Her Majesty and too often felt in her heart for Anne of Austria not to recognize it; yet she remained impassive, regarding this gentleman with that direct and challenging gaze that is accepted only from those women who are queens, by beauty or by blood.

"Do you come to offer to render us a service, Count?" asked Anne of Austria after a moment of silence.

"Yes, Madame, a service yet again," said Athos, shocked that the queen appeared not to recognize him. Athos had a great and generous heart, and thus made a very poor courtier.

Anne furrowed her brow. Mazarin, seated at a side table and leafing through a stack of papers like a simple secretary, raised his head. "Speak," said the queen.

Mazarin resumed leafing through his papers.

"Madame," replied Athos, "two of our friends, two of the most intrepid servants of Your Majesty, Monsieur d'Artagnan and Monsieur du Vallon, who were sent to England by Monsieur le Cardinal, suddenly disappeared the moment they set foot back in France, and no one knows what has become of them."

"Well?" said the queen.

"Well!" said Athos. "I request Your Majesty in her benevolence to discover what has happened to these gentlemen—reserving the option, if need be, to appeal to her for justice."

"Monsieur," replied Anne of Austria, with that haughtiness that, toward the undeserving, became arrogance, "this is the matter with which you choose to disturb us in the midst of our consideration of great affairs? A matter for the police? Well, Monsieur, as you know, or should know, since we are no longer in Paris, we have no involvement with the police."

"I think that Your Majesty," said Athos, bowing with frosty respect, "would have no need to inquire of the police to discover what has become of Messieurs d'Artagnan and du Vallon; she has only to question the cardinal about these two gentlemen, as Monsieur le Cardinal could inform her without having to consult anything other than his recollections."

"Why, God be my witness!" said Anne of Austria, with that disdainful curl of the lips unique to her. "I believe you are *questioning* me."

"Yes, Madame, and I have nearly the right to do so, for it involves Monsieur d'Artagnan—Monsieur *d'Artagnan*, if you understand me, Madame," he said, hoping to reach the conscience of the woman behind the mask of the queen.

Mazarin saw that it was time to come to Anne of Austria's aid. "Monsieur le Comte," he said, "I will inform you of something Her Majesty is unaware of, which is what has become of those two gentlemen. They disobeyed orders and have been arrested."

"I implore Your Majesty," said Athos, firmly and without replying to Mazarin, "to rescind these judgments regarding Messieurs d'Artagnan and du Vallon."

"What you request is a matter of discipline and does not concern me, Monsieur," the queen said.

"Monsieur d'Artagnan never made such a reply when acting in the service of Your Majesty," said Athos, bowing with dignity.

He backed two steps toward the door, when Mazarin stopped him. "You have also come from England, Monsieur?" he said, while gesturing to calm the queen, who had visibly paled and was about to issue a stern order.

"Where I attended the final moments of King Charles I," said Athos. "Poor king! Guilty at most of weakness, for which his subjects punished him severely. But thrones are trembling at the moment, and it's a difficult time for those with devoted hearts who serve the interests of princes. That was the second time that Monsieur d'Artagnan had traveled to England; the first time was for the honor of a great queen, the second for the life of a great king."

"Monsieur," said Anne of Austria to Mazarin, in a tone that couldn't conceal her true feelings, "see if anything can be done for these gentlemen."

"Madame," said Mazarin, "I'll do what I can to please Your Majesty."

"Do as Monsieur le Comte de La Fère asks. Isn't that how you name yourself, Monsieur?"

"I have had another name, Madame, and am also known as Athos."

"Madame," said Mazarin, with a smile that indicated he understood her true desires, "you can rest assured that your wishes shall be fulfilled."

"Do you hear, Monsieur?" said the queen.

"Yes, Madame, and I expected nothing less from Your Majesty's justice. Then I'll soon see my friends again, isn't that so, Madame? That is what Your Majesty intends?"

"Yes, Monsieur, you shall see them again. These days, you're with the Fronde, aren't you?"

"Madame, I serve the king."

"Yes, but in your own way."

"My own way is that of all true gentlemen, and I know no other," said Athos haughtily.

"Go then, Monsieur," said the queen, dismissing Athos with a gesture. "You've obtained what you wanted, and we've learned all we needed to know."

Then, once the door had closed behind Athos, she said to Mazarin, "Cardinal, have this insolent gentleman arrested before he leaves the Court."

"That had already occurred to me," said Mazarin, "and I'm glad Your Majesty has given the order before I could even ask for it. These hard-heads who persist in our time with the high-handed practices of the previous reign are a nuisance, and since we already have two of them under lock and key, let's add the third."

Athos had not been entirely taken in by the queen. There was something in her tone that had seemed to threaten even while promising. But he was not a man to act upon mere suspicion, especially since he'd been told straight out that he would see his friends again. He waited, therefore, in the antechamber adjacent to the study, thinking that d'Artagnan and Porthos might be brought to him, or he might be escorted to where they were.

While waiting, he strolled to the window and gazed mechanically down into the courtyard. There he saw a deputation of Parisians entering, coming to set the final agenda of the conferences and to pay their respects to the queen. It was a crowd of councilors and presidents of parliament, advocates and attorneys, with a few Men of the Sword mixed in with the Men of the Robe. An imposing escort awaited them outside the gates.

Athos was looking more closely, as he thought he saw someone he recognized, when he felt a tap on his shoulder. He turned and said, "Ah, Monsieur de Comminges!"

"Yes, Monsieur le Comte, in person, and charged with a mission for which I hope you will accept my apologies."

"What's that, Monsieur?" asked Athos.

"To ask you to please give me your sword, Count."

Athos smiled, and opening the window, he shouted, "Aramis!"

A gentleman turned around—the man Athos thought he'd recognized was, in fact, Aramis. He made the count a friendly salute.

"Aramis," called Athos, "I'm arrested."

"Indeed," Aramis replied coolly.

Athos turned back to Comminges, politely presented him the hilt of his sword, and said, "Here is my sword; please keep it with care and return it to me when I'm released from prison. It was given to my grandfather by King François I. In his time, they armed gentlemen, rather than disarming them. Now, where are you taking me?"

"Well . . . to my room, first," said Comminges. "The queen will designate your destination later."

Athos followed Comminges out without saying another word.

XXXIX

The Royalty of Monsieur de Mazarin

The arrest had made no noise, caused no scandal, and gone virtually unnoticed. It had in no way hindered the course of events, and the deputation sent by the City of Paris was solemnly informed that they would be duly admitted to an audience with the queen.

The queen received them, silent and superb as always, and she heard the grievances and pleas of the deputies; however, when the speeches were finished, no one would have been able to say, based on Anne of Austria's impassive expression, whether she had listened to them.

On the other hand, Mazarin, who was also present at the audience, understood very well what the deputies wanted: it was, clearly and simply, his dismissal.

With the speeches completed, since the queen remained mute, Mazarin said, "Messieurs, I join you in imploring the queen to put an end to the troubles of her subjects. I've done all I can to help them, and yet you say the people believe that I'm responsible for their ills—I, a poor foreigner who has failed to please the French. Alas! I'm misunderstood by all, and the reason is clear: as prime minister I followed in the footsteps of the greatest man ever to support the scepter of the Kings of France. The memory of Monsieur de Richelieu overwhelms me. If I were ambitious, I'd fight the weight of that memory, but I'm not, and I'll prove it to you. I surrender. I'll do what the people ask. If the Parisians have done wrong— as who has not, Messieurs?—well, Paris has been punished. Enough blood has flowed, enough misery has stricken a capital deprived of both king and justice. It's not for me, a private citizen, to be so audacious as to come between a queen and her realm. Since you demand that I retire, well, then! I'll retire."

"In that case," Aramis said into the ear of his neighbor, "peace is declared and further conferences are needless. All we have to do is send Monsieur Mazarini under guard across the nearest foreign border, and make sure he doesn't return there or elsewhere."

"Not so fast, Monsieur, not so fast," said the Man of the Robe to whom Aramis had spoken. "*Peste!* Such haste! It's clear you're a Man of the Sword. First there's a whole list of compensations and indemnities to be settled."

"Monsieur Chancellor," said the queen, turning to our old acquaintance Séguier, "you will chair the conferences, to be held at Rueil. Monsieur le Cardinal has said things that have deeply moved me, which is why I will not address the deputation here. As to who is to stay and who is to go, I owe the cardinal too much to constrain him in any way. Monsieur le Cardinal shall do as he sees fit."

A fleeting pallor crossed the intelligent visage of the prime minister, and he looked at the queen anxiously. Her face was so impassive that, like the others, he couldn't read what was passing in her heart.

"But while awaiting Monsieur de Mazarin's decision," the queen added, "I ask you to think only of the interests of the king."

The deputies bowed and withdrew.

"What was that?" said the queen, when the last of them had left the hall. "Would you yield to these councilmen and lawyers?"

"For Your Majesty's happiness, Madame," said Mazarin, fixing the queen with his piercing gaze, "there is no sacrifice I wouldn't make."

Anne lowered her head and fell into one of those reveries increasingly common with her. The memory of Athos arose in her mind. His brave demeanor, his tone at once so firm and dignified, the ghosts he conjured with a word, reminded her of a past intoxicating and poetic: of youth, of beauty, of love at the age of twenty; of the brutal battles of those who'd fought for her, of the heroism of those obscure defenders who'd saved her from the double hatred of Richelieu and the king—and of the bloody death of Buckingham, the only man she'd ever truly loved.

Mazarin watched her, and now that she thought she was alone and no longer had a world of enemies spying upon her, he easily followed her thoughts as they passed across her face, as one sees in a clear lake the reflections of clouds passing in the heavens.

"Must we yield to the storm," murmured Anne of Austria, "bargain for peace, and wait patiently and religiously for better times?"

Mazarin smiled bitterly at these words, which indicated that she'd taken her minister's proposal seriously.

Anne's head was bowed, and she didn't see his smile, but hearing no answer, she looked up. "Well! You say nothing, Cardinal; what are you thinking?"

"I think, Madame, that this insolent gentleman we had Comminges arrest for us alluded to Monsieur de Buckingham, whom you allowed to be assassinated, to Madame de Chevreuse, whom you allowed to be exiled, and to Monsieur de Beaufort, whom you had imprisoned. But if he alluded to me, it was because he doesn't really know what I am to you."

Anne of Austria trembled as she did when struck in her pride; she blushed and, to suppress a reply, ground her sharp nails into her beautiful hands.

"He's a man of sound advice, of honor and of spirit, and a man of great resolve," Mazarin continued. "But you're aware of that, aren't you, Madame? Well, I wish to show him, as a personal favor, the extent to which he is mistaken about me. Because what his allies just proposed to me is close to an abdication, and an abdication requires careful consideration."

"An abdication!" said Anne. "I thought, Monsieur, that it was only kings who abdicated."

"And am I not almost a king, and King of France at that?" replied Mazarin. "Thrown over the foot of the royal bed at night, Madame, my minister's robe, I assure you, looks no different than a monarch's mantle."

This was one of the humiliations to which Mazarin most often subjected her, and before which she always bowed her head. Only Elizabeth and Catherine II were able to be both mistresses and queens for their lovers.

Anne of Austria looked with a touch of terror at the menacing presence of the cardinal, who at times like these could exert a domineering bravado.

"Monsieur," she said, "didn't I say, and didn't you hear me tell those people that you shall do as you please?"

"Ah! In that case," said Mazarin, "I think it shall please me to remain. It may be in my interest, but even more than that, I dare say it will be your salvation."

"Stay then, Monsieur, I desire nothing else—but preserve me from insults."

"You mean the pretensions of those rebels and the tone in which they express them? Patience! They've chosen to fight upon my own ground: the conference. We will defeat them with delay. Already they grow hungry; it will be worse a week from now."

"Oh, *mon Dieu*, yes, Monsieur, I know how that will turn out. But it's not them I refer to; they're not the ones who inflict the deepest injuries."

"Ah, now I understand you! You speak of the memories perpetually evoked by those three or four gentlemen. But now they're our prisoners, and they're just guilty enough that we can hold them as long as is convenient. Only one is still beyond our power and defies us. But what the devil! He'll join his companions soon enough. We've done harder things than that, it seems to me. I already have the most intractable pair locked up at Rueil, where I can keep an eye on them, and today they'll be joined by the third."

"So long as they remain prisoners, all will be well," said Anne of Austria, "but some day they must be free."

"Yes . . . if Your Majesty sets them free."

"Ah!" continued Queen Anne, half to herself. "This is where I regret Paris."

"Why's that?"

"Because the Bastille, Monsieur, is so strong and so discreet."

"Madame, with the conferences we'll have peace, with peace we'll have Paris, and with Paris we'll have the Bastille! And there our four myrmidons will rot."

Anne of Austria frowned lightly, while Mazarin kissed her hand to take his leave of her. With this act, half humble, half gallant, Mazarin departed. Anne followed him with her eyes, and as he walked away one might have seen a disdainful smile curl her lips. "In my time," she murmured, "I once rejected the love of a cardinal who never said, 'I will do,' but rather 'I have done.' That one knew retreats safer than Rueil, darker and more silent than the Bastille. Ah! Everything decays!"

XL

Precautions

After leaving Anne of Austria, the cardinal took the road to his estate at Rueil. Mazarin always traveled well accompanied in those times of trouble, often in disguise. The cardinal, as we've said, looked very well in the outfit of a Man of the Sword.

In the courtyard of the old château at Saint-Germain, he entered a carriage, which followed the road that crossed the Seine at Chatou. Monsieur le Prince has furnished him with an escort of fifty light horse, not so much to protect him as to show the deputies that Condé had troops to spare, and could deploy them however he thought best.

Athos, on horseback but unarmed and guarded by Comminges, followed the cardinal's carriage without saying a word. Grimaud, who'd been left at the gate of the château by his master, had realized he'd been arrested when Athos called out to Aramis, and at a gesture from the count he'd followed Aramis when he'd left, silently and as if nothing had happened. For a fact, Grimaud, who'd served his master for twenty-two years, had seen him survive so many adventures that nothing worried him anymore.

The deputies, immediately after their audience, had taken the road that returned to Paris, preceding the cardinal's party by about five hundred paces. Athos, therefore, could see ahead of him the back of Aramis, whose gilded baldric and proud demeanor drew his eye quite as much as the habits of long friendship and the hopes of deliverance he placed in him.

Aramis, for his part, didn't seem the least bit interested in whether he was being followed by Athos, and turned to look only when they arrived at Chatou. He thought Mazarin might leave his prisoner in the little fort that guarded the bridge, which an officer commanded for the queen. But no: Athos continued past Chatou in the cardinal's entourage.

Where the road forked toward Paris or Rueil, Aramis turned again. This time his expectations were fulfilled, as Mazarin turned toward Rueil, and Aramis could see his prisoner, following, as he disappeared into the wood. At just that moment Athos, as if moved by an identical thought, also turned to look back. The two friends exchanged a slight nod, and Aramis raised a finger to his head as if in salute. Athos understood that his friend was telling him that he had an idea.

Ten minutes later Mazarin entered the courtyard of the Château de Rueil, which had been bequeathed to him by the cardinal his predecessor. As he was stepping down from his carriage at the foot of the main staircase, Comminges approached him and asked, "Where would it please Your Eminence for the Comte de La Fère to be lodged?"

"In the pavilion of the orangery, facing the guards' post. I want the Comte de La Fère treated with honor while he's a prisoner of Her Majesty the queen."

"Monseigneur," ventured Comminges, "he requests the favor of being allowed to join Monsieur d'Artagnan, who occupies, as Your Eminence has ordered, the hunting pavilion across from the orangery."

Mazarin thought for a moment; Comminges could see that he was calculating. "It's a strong post," the officer said, "forty reliable men, veteran soldiers all, mostly German mercenaries who have no connections to the Frondeurs and no interest in the Fronde."

"If we put those three men together, Monsieur de Comminges," said Mazarin, "we'd have to double that guard, and we don't have enough men for such prodigalities."

Comminges smiled; Mazarin saw his expression and understood it. "You don't know them, Monsieur de Comminges—but I do know them, both directly and by tradition. I sent them to aid King Charles,[53] and by performing miracles they very nearly saved him; it's only due to an accident of fate that dear King Charles is not amongst us today."

"But if they served Your Eminence so well, why has Your Eminence had them imprisoned?"

"In prison?" said Mazarin. "Since when is Rueil a prison?"

"Since it holds prisoners," said Comminges.

"These gentlemen aren't my prisoners, Comminges, they're my guests," said Mazarin, smiling his sly smile. "Guests so precious I keep their windows barred and their doors locked for fear that they'll tire of keeping me company. But though they seem like prisoners, I esteem them nonetheless, and the proof is that I'd like to visit Monsieur de La Fère for a little private talk. To make sure our conversation will remain undisturbed, you will escort him, as I've already requested, to the pavilion of the orangery. You know that's along the route of my usual evening walk; well, on my walk, I'll stop in and have a talk with him. As much as he seems my enemy, I have a good deal of sympathy for him, and if he's disposed to be reasonable, we may get somewhere."

Comminges bowed and returned to where Athos was waiting, apparently calmly, but anxious underneath. "And so?" he asked the Lieutenant of the Guards.

"Monsieur," replied Comminges, "it seems it can't be done."

"Monsieur de Comminges," said Athos, "I've been a soldier all my life, so I know what it means to follow orders—but beyond your orders, there might still be a favor you could do me."

"With all my heart, Monsieur," replied Comminges, "since I know who you are, and what services you formerly rendered Her Majesty, and since I know how close you are to that young man who so bravely came to my rescue the day Broussel was arrested. I'm your man, so far as I can be within the limits of my orders."

"Thank you, Monsieur, I desire nothing more, and will ask for nothing of you that will compromise you in any way."

"If it's only a small compromise, Monsieur," said Comminges, smiling, "ask anyway. I don't much care for Monsieur Mazarini; I serve the queen, and it's only that that leads me to serve the cardinal. I serve the one with joy, but the other only reluctantly—so speak, and I'll listen."

"If it isn't inconvenient that I know Monsieur d'Artagnan is here," said Athos, "then can I presume it wouldn't be inconvenient to let him know that I'm here?"

"I have received no orders regarding that, Monsieur."

"*En bien!* In that case, do me the favor of giving him my regards, and informing him that I'm now his neighbor. You can tell him at the same time what I overheard just now, that Monsieur de Mazarin has placed me in the pavilion of the orangery so he can visit me, and that I intend to profit from this honor he grants me to seek to mitigate our captivity."

"It can't last long," said Comminges. "The cardinal himself told me this place is no prison."

"There are those notorious oubliettes," Athos said with a smile.

"Oh, that's out of the question!" said Comminges. "Yes, I've heard the stories, but a man of low birth, like the cardinal, an Italian who's come to find his fortune in France, wouldn't dare to commit such an outrage against men like you. Things were different in the time of the old cardinal, who was a great lord, but Monsieur Mazarin? Come, now! Such dungeons are only for enemies of the crown, and a coward like him wouldn't dare call you such. Your arrest is known, Monsieur, and that of your friends will soon be known, and all France would hold him accountable if he contrived for you to disappear. No, rest easy, for years the oubliettes of Rueil have been no more than a story to frighten children. Abide here without fear. For my part, I'll inform Monsieur d'Artagnan of your arrival. Why, a fortnight from now you might be doing a similar favor for me!"

"I, Monsieur?"

"No doubt about it! Couldn't I just as easily end up a prisoner of Monsieur le Coadjuteur?"

"Believe me, Monsieur, in that case I should do my best to oblige you," said Athos, bowing.

"Will you do me the honor of dining with me, Monsieur le Comte?" asked Comminges.

"Thank you, Monsieur, but I'm in a dark mood, and would be a sad guest this evening. But the invitation is appreciated."

Comminges then led the count to a chamber on the ground floor of the pavilion adjacent to the orangery, the approach to which was a grand court-yard crowded with soldiers and courtiers. This courtyard was surrounded by halls in the shape of a horseshoe; at its center were the apartments of Monsieur de Mazarin, one of its wings ended in the hunting pavilion, where d'Artagnan was held, and the other ended in the pavilion of the orangery, where Athos was lodged. Beyond these two wings stretched the park.

Athos, arriving in the room he was to occupy, saw through its single barred window other walls and a roof across the way. "What is that building?" he said.

"That's the back of the hunting pavilion where your friends are detained," said Comminges. "Unfortunately, its windows on this side were blocked up in the time of the old cardinal, as these buildings have been used to hold prisoners more than once, so Monsieur de Mazarin is really just restoring them to their old uses. If those windows weren't blocked up, you'd have the consolation of being able to communicate with your friends by gestures."

"Are you sure, Monsieur de Comminges," said Athos, "that the cardinal will do me the honor of visiting me?"

"At least that's what he said, Monsieur."

Athos sighed, looking at his barred window.

"In fact, it might as well be a prison," said Comminges. "It even has bars on the window. But really, what came over you, a flower of the nobility, to commit your courage and loyalty to those toadstools of the Fronde! If there was any gentleman I expected to see on the staff of the royal army, Count, it was you. But you, the Comte de La Fère, a Frondeur of the party of Broussel, of Blancmesnil, of Viole! *Fi donc!* You don't belong with those Men of the Robe. You, of all people!"

"*Ma foi,* Monsieur, one must be either a Frondeur or a Mazarinist," said Athos. "I considered both names and chose the former—it at least has a French ring to it. Besides, I'm not a Frondeur with Broussel, Blancmesnil, and

Viole, but with Monsieur de Beaufort, Monsieur de Bouillon, and Monsieur d'Elbeuf—with princes, not with presidents, councilors, and attorneys. And you, just look at that blank wall over there and see for yourself the pleasant result of serving the cardinal! That, Monsieur de Comminges, should tell you something about the gratitude of a Mazarin."

"Yes," replied Comminges with a smile, "especially if I repeat what Monsieur d'Artagnan has been saying about him for the last week."

"Poor d'Artagnan!" said Athos, with that charming melancholy that was one of the features of his character. "A man so brave, so good, and so terrible to anyone who threatens those he loves. You have two difficult prisoners there, Monsieur, and I pity you if you're responsible for holding those indomitable men."

"Indomitable!" said Comminges, still smiling. "Now, Monsieur, you're just trying to frighten me. It's true that on the first day of his incarceration, Monsieur d'Artagnan issued challenges to all the soldiers and lower officers, doubtless in hopes of getting a sword in his hand. He kept it up for another day, but then became as calm and as sweet as a lamb. Now he sings Gascon ditties that have us doubled over with laughter."

"And Monsieur du Vallon?" asked Athos.

"Ah! Now that's different. I admit I find him a fearsome gentleman. On the first day he forced open the door with a single thrust of his shoulder, and I half expected to see him break out of Rueil the way Samson came out of Gaza. But his mood changed along with Monsieur d'Artagnan's, and now he seems so accustomed to his captivity, he makes jokes about it."

"So much the better," said Athos.

"Were you expecting something else?" asked Comminges, suddenly recalling what Mazarin had said about these prisoners in light of what the Comte de La Fère had said and beginning to feel anxious.

For his part, Athos was thinking that this cooperative behavior on the part of his friends was certainly due to some plan of d'Artagnan's and thought it best not to continue calling them dangerous. "What, from them?" he said. "They're just a pair of hotheads—one's a Gascon, the other a Picard. They catch fire easily but burn out quickly. The proof is in the story you just told me."

That matched Comminges's own opinion, and he withdrew somewhat reassured, leaving Athos alone in that broad chamber where, according the cardinal's orders, he was to be treated with the consideration due to a gentleman. Athos expected to get a better idea of his real situation after the promised visit from Mazarin.

XLI

Brains and Brawn

Now let's pass from the orangery to the hunting pavilion. At the end of the courtyard, past a portico of Ionic columns that led to the dog kennels, an oblong building capped the end of the wing opposite the orangery, which ended the other wing of the half-circle. It was on the ground floor of this pavilion that Porthos and d'Artagnan were confined, sharing the long hours of a captivity abhorrent to both their temperaments.

D'Artagnan paced like a captive tiger, eyes narrowed, growling when he passed the bars of a window that looked out onto a back courtyard. Porthos lay quietly digesting an excellent dinner, the remains of which had just been taken away. The one seemed to have lost his mind, but was thinking; the other seemed to be thinking, but was asleep—though his sleep was a nightmare, if his broken and incoherent snores were any indication.

"See there?" said d'Artagnan. "The light is failing. It must be nearly four o'clock. We've been here for a hundred and eighty-three hours."

"Hum!" said Porthos, pretending to answer.

"Do you hear me, Enchanted Sleeper?" said d'Artagnan, annoyed that anyone could sleep in the daytime when he could barely sleep at night.

"What?" said Porthos.

"Did you hear me?"

"Did you say something?"

"I said," resumed d'Artagnan, "that we've been in here a hundred and eighty-three hours."

"It's your own fault," said Porthos.

"How is it my fault?"

"I offered to get us out."

"By bending the bars or smashing the door?"

"That's right."

"Porthos, people like us don't just purely and simply walk away."

"My faith," said Porthos, "*I'm* pure and simple enough to just walk away."

D'Artagnan shrugged. "There's more to the matter than just getting out of this pavilion."

"Dear friend," said Porthos, "since your mood seems a little better today, explain to me why there's more to the matter than getting out of this pavilion."

"Because we don't have weapons or the password, that's why, and won't get fifty paces across the courtyard before we're stopped by a sentry."

"*Eh bien!*" said Porthos. "We'll knock out the sentry, and then we'll have weapons."

"Yes, but they're tough nuts, these Germans, and before we knock him out he'll give a shout, and then the hounds will be after us. We'll be taken like foxes, we who are lions, and then we'll be thrown into the oubliettes, where we won't even have the consolation of seeing the frightful gray sky over Rueil, which no more resembles the sky of Tarbes[54] than the moon resembles the sun. *Mordioux!* If we had an ally outside, someone who could give us information on the moral and physical layout of the château, what Caesar called the *mores locaque,* or so I've been told, at least . . . bah! To think that I had time on my hands for twenty years, and yet never thought to study the defenses of the Château de Rueil."

"So what?" said Porthos. "Let's go anyway."

"Old friend," said d'Artagnan, "do you know why master pastry chefs never work with their own hands?"

"No," said Porthos, "but I'd be flattered to have you tell me."

"They're afraid that, in front of their students, they might make cakes that are over-baked or fallen soufflés."

"Because?"

"Because then they'd be laughed at, and no master pastry chef should be an object of mockery."

"And what do master pastry chefs have to do with us?"

"Because we, in our adventurous exploits, must never fail so badly that it's laughable. In England we failed, we were beaten, and that's enough of a blot on our reputation."

"By whom were we beaten?" asked Porthos.

"By Mordaunt."

"Oh, yes, by Monsieur Mordaunt. But then we drowned him."

"So we did, and that will restore us somewhat in the eyes of posterity, assuming posterity pays any attention to us. But listen to me, Porthos—though Monsieur Mordaunt was no one to take lightly, Monsieur Mazarin is of a very different order than Mordaunt and isn't someone we can just drown. Therefore, let's just keep our eyes open and await our chances, because," d'Artagnan added with a sigh, "while we two may be the equal of eight, we'd be better off if we were four. You know what I mean."

"Isn't that the truth," said Porthos, adding his sigh to that of d'Artagnan.

"Well, then, Porthos, do as I do, and march back and forth until our friends come to us or, failing that, we get a good idea. Just don't go on sleeping all the time—nothing addles the mind like too much sleep. As for what awaits us, I think it's not as bad as I feared at first. I don't think Monsieur de Mazarin is considering removing our heads, because our heads can't be removed without a trial, a trial would make a lot of noise, that noise would attract our friends, and they wouldn't let Monsieur de Mazarin do it."

"You sure can think a thing through," said Porthos, admiringly.

"Yes, I'm not bad," said d'Artagnan. "And then, you see, if we're not tried, and hold onto our heads, they have to either keep us here or transport us elsewhere."

"Yes, that's so," said Porthos.

"Well! Either way, it's impossible that neither Aramis, that shrewd schemer, nor Athos, that wise sage, will figure out where we are. And then, *ma foi,* it will be time!"

"True, and we're pretty well off here, all things considered—except for one."

"What's that?"

"Didn't you notice, d'Artagnan, that they've fed us braised mutton three days in a row?"

"I hadn't, but if they do it a fourth time, rest assured that I shall personally lodge a complaint!"

"And sometimes I miss my home; it's been a long time since I've seen my châteaux."

"Bah! No need to worry about those, you'll see them again. Do you think Monsieur de Mazarin is going to have them knocked down?"

"You don't suppose he's capable of such an outrage, do you?" asked Porthos anxiously.

"No, though it wouldn't have been beyond the old cardinal. This one's too small to take big risks."

"You reassure me, d'Artagnan."

"Then put the best face on things that you can: make jokes with the guards; befriend them since we can't bribe them; speak pleasantly to them when they go past our window. So far, you've only shown them your fist, and the more you show it, Porthos, the less they'll respect it. Ah, what I wouldn't give to have just five hundred louis."

"Me, too," said Porthos, determined not to be less generous than d'Artagnan. "Why, for that I'd give a hundred pistoles."

The two prisoners had just reached this point in their conversation when Comminges came in, preceded by a sergeant and two men who brought supper in a basket full of bowls and plates.

"Oh, great!" said Porthos. "Mutton again!"

"My dear Monsieur de Comminges," said d'Artagnan, "I warn you that my friend, Monsieur du Vallon, has been driven to extremity by the torment of Monsieur de Mazarin feeding him the same meal every day, and is capable of anything."

"I'll eat only half of this unless the rest is taken away immediately!" declared Porthos.

"Away with the mutton," said Comminges. "Bring something Monsieur du Vallon will find appetizing, especially since the good news I'm about to share is bound to give him an appetite."

"Has Monsieur de Mazarin died?" asked Porthos.

"No, I'm sorry to say he's in good health."

"Too bad," said Porthos.

"Then what's your news?" asked d'Artagnan. "It's a meal so rare in prison that I hope you'll excuse my impatience, Monsieur de Comminges. Especially since you say the news is good."

"Would you be pleased to hear that the Comte de La Fère is also in good health?" replied Comminges.

D'Artagnan's eyes widened. "I'd be delighted to hear that!" he said. "More than delighted."

"Well! I'm charged by him to give you his best compliments and report that he's in fine fettle."

D'Artagnan nearly jumped for joy. A quick glance at Porthos shared his thought: *If Athos knows where we are, and sends us word of it, he's about to act on it.*

Porthos wasn't usually very good at reading such glances, but he knew Athos, and was struck by the same idea as d'Artagnan, so this time he got it.

"But," asked the Gascon tentatively, "did the Comte de La Fère tell you personally to convey his compliments to myself and Monsieur du Vallon?"

"Yes, Monsieur."

"Then you saw him?"

"Certainly."

"Where was that? If it's not too much to ask."

"Right nearby," replied Comminges, smiling.

"Right nearby!" repeated d'Artagnan, eyes sparkling.

"So near that if the windows that face the orangery weren't bricked up, you could see where he is from here."

He's scouting out the environment of the château, thought d'Artagnan, then said aloud, "You met him in the park, perhaps, while hunting?"

"Oh, much closer than that—there, beyond that wall," said Comminges, knocking on the plaster.

"Beyond that wall? What's beyond that wall? They brought me here by night, so devil take me if I have any idea where I am."

"Then imagine this," said Comminges.

"I'll imagine whatever you like."

"Imagine there was a window in this wall."

"All right. And?"

"And then you could see the Comte de La Fère at his own window!"

"Monsieur de La Fère is staying at the château?"

"Yes."

"In what capacity?"

"In the same capacity as you."

"Athos is a prisoner?"

"You know very well," said Comminges, laughing, "that there are no prisoners at Rueil, since it isn't a prison."

"Enough wordplay, Monsieur: Athos was arrested?"

"Yesterday, at Saint-Germain, after leaving an audience with the queen."

D'Artagnan's arms dropped limp to his sides. He looked like he'd been struck by lightning. Pallor slowly drained his sun-browned complexion. "Prisoner!" he repeated.

"Prisoner!" Porthos repeated after him, crushed.

Suddenly d'Artagnan raised his head, but only Porthos saw the brief light in his eyes. Then he lowered it again in apparent dejection.

"Come, come," said Comminges, who had a real affection for d'Artagnan, after he'd rescued him from the Parisians on the day of Broussel's arrest. "Don't be upset, it's not sad news I bring you, I promise. These are just the chances of war. Be pleased at the chance that brings your friend closer to you and Monsieur du Vallon, and don't be cast down."

But this exhortation did nothing to cheer up d'Artagnan, who continued apparently stricken with gloom. "And how did he look?" asked Porthos, who, seeing that d'Artagnan was letting the conversation drop, put in a word of his own.

"He looked well," said Comminges. "At first, like you, he took it hard, but when he heard that the cardinal was planning to visit him this evening . . ."

"Oh?" said d'Artagnan. "Monsieur le Cardinal is going to pay a visit to the Comte de La Fère?"

"Yes, so he said, and the Comte de La Fère, hearing that, charged me to tell you that he would take advantage of this favor to plead your cause, and his."

"Ah, our dear count!" said d'Artagnan.

"Some cause," growled Porthos, "some favor! *Pardieu!* The Comte de La Fère, whose family ranks with the Montmorencys and the Rohans, is to plead with Monsieur de Mazarin."

"No matter," said d'Artagnan, in a soothing tone. "When you think about it, my dear du Vallon, it's quite an honor for the count. It's a hopeful sign, such an honor for a prisoner—so great, in fact, that Monsieur de Comminges must be mistaken about it."

"What? Me, mistaken?"

"Surely it isn't Monsieur de Mazarin who will visit the Comte de La Fère, but the Comte de La Fère who will visit Monsieur de Mazarin."

"No, not at all," said Comminges, who insisted on the accuracy of his statements. "I just repeat what the cardinal told me: it is he who will visit the Comte de La Fère."

D'Artagnan tried to catch Porthos's eye to convey to him the importance of this but failed. "Is it then the habit of the cardinal to take an evening walk through the orangery?" he asked.

"Every night," said Comminges. "It seems that's where he goes to meditate on affairs of state."

"Then I begin to believe that Monsieur de La Fère will receive a visit from His Eminence," said d'Artagnan. "He'll be accompanied, of course."

"Yes, by two soldiers."

"And he conducts business in front of soldiers?"

"The soldiers are Swiss from those cantons where they speak only German. Besides, they'll probably wait outside the door."

D'Artagnan ground his fingernails into the palms of his hands so his face would show only what he wanted it to show. "Monsieur de Mazarin should take care not to visit the Comte de La Fère alone," said d'Artagnan, "as the count is liable to be furious."

Comminges laughed. "*Ah çà!* What is it with you? Are you all cannibals? Monsieur de La Fère is a perfect gentleman—besides, he has no weapons. And at the first cry from His Eminence, the two soldiers would come running."

"Two soldiers," said d'Artagnan, seemingly consulting his memory. "Two soldiers—yes, that's why I hear two men called every evening, and why I see them pacing back and forth for a half an hour sometimes outside my window."

"That's when they're waiting on the cardinal, or rather Bernouin, who summons them when the cardinal comes out."

"They look like good men," said d'Artagnan.

"They're from a regiment that was at Lens, and which Monsieur le Prince has given to the cardinal to do him honor."

"Ah, Monsieur," said d'Artagnan, as if to sum up this whole conversation, "perhaps His Eminence will be lenient, and grant our liberty to Monsieur de La Fère."

"I desire it with all my heart," said Comminges.

"Then, if he forgot to make this visit, you wouldn't find it inconvenient to remind him of it?"

"Not at all."

"Ah! That makes me feel a bit better." Anyone who could have read the Gascon's soul would have seen how much of an understatement this was. "Now," he continued, "if I could ask a final favor, Monsieur de Comminges."

"I'm at your service, Monsieur."

"When will you see the Comte de La Fère again?"

"Tomorrow morning."

"Will you wish him good day for us, and ask him to request from the cardinal the same favor he's obtained?"

"You'd like the cardinal to visit you here?"

"No, I'm not so bold or so demanding as that. If His Eminence would just do me the honor to listen to me, that's all I ask."

"Oh!" murmured Porthos, shaking his head. "I would never have believed d'Artagnan could sink so low! How far we have fallen."

"I'll see to it," said Comminges.

"And also assure the count that you've seen I'm in good health, and that though sad, I'm resigned."

"It pleases me, Monsieur, to hear you say that."

"And say the same thing about Monsieur du Vallon."

"What, me? Not at all!" cried Porthos. "I'm not resigned at all."

"But you will be resigned, my friend."

"Never!"

"Oh, he will be resigned, Monsieur de Comminges," said d'Artagnan. "I know him better than he knows himself, and I know he has a thousand excellent qualities he doesn't even suspect—including resignation. Now shut up, my dear du Vallon, and resign yourself."

"Adieu, Messieurs," said Comminges, "and have a good night!"

"We'll try."

Comminges bowed and went out. D'Artagnan watched him with downcast eyes and a resigned expression—but as soon as the door was shut behind the guard officer, he leapt toward Porthos and hugged him with such joy that no one could doubt it. "Oh ho!" said Porthos. "What now? Are you losing your mind, my poor friend?"

"I am," said d'Artagnan, "because we're saved!"

"And how can you say that?" said Porthos. "On the contrary, it looks to me like we're all taken, except for Aramis, and that our chances of getting out are diminished by one-half now that Athos is in Mazarin's mousetrap."

"Not at all, Porthos, old friend. That mousetrap was strong enough for two, but it's too weak for three."

"I have no idea what you're talking about," said Porthos.

"No matter," said d'Artagnan. "Let's sit down to supper and fortify ourselves—we're going to need all our strength tonight."

"We are? What are we doing tonight?" said Porthos, intrigued in spite of himself.

"Traveling, most likely."

"But . . ."

"Let's sit down and eat, my friend—ideas come to me when I'm eating. After supper, when my ideas are complete, I'll share them with you."

However impatient Porthos was to hear d'Artagnan's plan, he knew his friend's methods, so he sat down to supper without another word, and ate with an appetite that showed the confidence he had in d'Artagnan's imagination.

XLII

Brawn and Brains

Their supper was silent, but by no means sad, for from time to time d'Artagnan's face was illuminated by one of those shrewd smiles that lit his expression when he was in good humor. Porthos didn't miss a single one of these smiles, and to each one he laughed or made some remark to show his friend that, while he had no idea what d'Artagnan was thinking, he could at least acknowledge the process.

At dessert d'Artagnan sat back in his chair with his legs crossed, with the look of a man well satisfied with himself. Porthos placed his elbows on the table, his chin on his hands, and looked at d'Artagnan with an admiring gaze that was the perfect expression of his unfailing good nature.

"Well?" said d'Artagnan, after a moment.

"Well?" repeated Porthos.

"You were saying, old friend?"

"Me! I didn't say anything."

"You did. You said you wanted to get out of here."

"Oh, that! Yes, I'd love to do that."

"And you added that it was only a matter of breaking down a door or a wall."

"It's true, I did say that, and I'd even say it again."

"And I answered you, Porthos, that it was a bad idea, and we wouldn't get a hundred paces before we were taken again, without clothes to disguise ourselves and weapons to defend ourselves."

"It's true, we'd need clothing and weapons."

"*Eh bien!*" said d'Artagnan, rising. "In that case we must get them, friend Porthos, and something else as well."

"Where?" said Porthos, looking around.

"Don't bother searching, it's too soon; everything will come to us at its proper time. When was it we saw those two Swiss guards last night?"

"An hour after sunset, I think."

"Then if they return when they did last night, we won't have more than another quarter of an hour to wait before we have the pleasure of seeing them."

"Yes, a quarter of an hour at the most."

"Your arm is in pretty good shape, isn't it, Porthos?"

Porthos unbuttoned his cuffs, rolled up his sleeves, and looked complacently at his brawny arms, as big around as most men's thighs. "But yes," he said, "pretty good."

"Strong enough to twist, without too much trouble, these fire tongs into a hoop and this ash shovel into a corkscrew?"

"Certainly," said Porthos.

"Show me," said d'Artagnan.

The giant took the two indicated objects and, with the greatest ease and without apparent effort, performed the feats his companion had requested. "You see?" he said.

"Magnificent!" said d'Artagnan. "You are truly gifted, Porthos."

"I once heard," said Porthos, "of a certain Milo of Croton[55] who did some extraordinary things, such as breaking a rope that was tightened around his brow by flexing his head muscles, killing an ox with his fist and carrying it home on his shoulders, stopping a horse by grabbing its hind feet, and so forth. When I was at Pierrefonds I made them read to me about all these feats, and I did everything he did, except for bursting a rope by swelling my temples."

"Your strength has never been in your head," said d'Artagnan.

"No, it's in my arms and shoulders," replied Porthos naïvely.

"Well, my friend! Let's see you go to the window and take out one of the bars. Wait a moment until I put out the lamp."

Porthos approached the window, took a central bar in both hands, gripped it tightly, pulled it toward him, and bent it in the middle like a bow, so that both ends came out of the stone sill where for thirty years they'd been sealed in cement.

"And there, my friend," said d'Artagnan, "is something even the old cardinal could never have done, man of genius though he was."

"Should I yank the others?" asked Porthos.

"No, I think that will do it; a man should be able to pass through that gap."

Porthos thrust his shoulders and chest through the opening. "Yes," he said.

"Indeed, a very pretty opening, just what we need. Now stick out your arms."

"Where?"

"Through the gap in the window."

"What for?"

"You'll see when the time comes. Try it."

Porthos obeyed, as obedient as a soldier, thrusting his arms out between the bars.

"Perfect!" said d'Artagnan.

"Our plan goes forward?"

"On wheels, old friend."

"Good. Now what do I do?"

"Nothing."

"Then we're done?"

"Not yet."

"I'd like to understand," said Porthos.

"All right, old friend, I'll catch you up. The door of the guardroom over there opens out, as you see."

"Yes, I see."

"They're going to send out into our courtyard, which Monsieur de Mazarin crosses to get to the orangery, the two guards who will accompany him."

"They're coming out now."

"Hopefully they'll close the door behind them . . . good, they did!"

"And now?"

"Hush! They might hear us."

"But how will I know what to do?"

"I'll tell you each step as the time comes."

"All right, but I'd rather . . ."

"What, and lose the pleasure of surprise?"

"Good point," said Porthos.

"Hush!"

Porthos stood mute and motionless.

In fact, the two soldiers were approaching the window, rubbing their hands, because it was February and cold. Just then the door to the guard-house reopened and one of the soldiers was called back. He left his companion and went back through the door.

"Is the plan still on?" whispered Porthos.

"Better than ever," replied d'Artagnan in the same tone. "Now, listen: I'll call this soldier over and chat with him, as I did last night with one of his comrades, remember?"

"Yes, though I didn't catch a word of what he said."

"He did have a pretty thick accent. But don't miss a word of what I'm about to tell you, Porthos: it's all in the execution."

"Good. Execution is my strong suit."

"Don't I know it; I'm counting on that."

"Tell me."

"So, I'll call the soldier over to chat with him."

"You already said that."

"I'll lean to the left, so as he steps up on that bench under the window to talk to me, he'll be on your right."

"What if he doesn't step up?"

"He will, don't worry. When he steps up on the bench, you reach your mighty arm through the gap and grab him by the neck. Then like Tobias grabbing the great fish by the gills, you'll drag him into our room, squeezing him tightly so he can't scream."

"Got it," said Porthos. "But what if I strangle him?"

"At worst, it'll mean one less Swiss, but I doubt you'll strangle him. Just lay him down gently on the floor so we can tie and gag him. Then we'll have one uniform and a sword."

"Wonderful!" said Porthos, regarding d'Artagnan with deep admiration.

"Eh!" shrugged the Gascon.

"Fine—but a single uniform and sword aren't enough."

"Well! Doesn't he have a comrade?"

"Good point," said Porthos.

"Now, when I cough, you reach out for him."

"All right!"

The two friends took their appointed positions, with Porthos out of sight around the edge of the window. "Good evening, comrade," said d'Artagnan in his friendliest voice, not too loudly.

"*Gut* evening, Mon-sieur," replied the soldier.

"It's not too warm for a walk," said d'Artagnan.

"*Brrr,*" said the soldier.

"Then I imagine a glass of wine would sound good to you?"

"A glass of vine vould be velcome."

"The fish bites!" d'Artagnan murmured to Porthos.

"I understand," said Porthos.

"How about a whole bottle?" said d'Artagnan.

"A pottle!"

"Yes."

"A whole pottle?"

"I have an extra, and it's all yours if you'll drink to my health."

"*Ja,*" said the soldier, drawing nearer.

"Here, come and get it, my friend," said the Gascon.

"Villingly! Ah, *gut*, here is a bench."

"Now, isn't that convenient?"

"I'll just step up . . . now, here I am, my friend."

And d'Artagnan coughed.

At the same moment Porthos reached out, fast as lightning. His fingers closed like steel pincers around the soldier's neck, and he dragged him suddenly through the opening, despite the risk of skinning him on the bars, and laid him down on the floor. There d'Artagnan, giving the Swiss just enough time to take a breath, gagged him with his own scarf, and immediately began to strip him of his clothes with the speed and dexterity of a man who'd learned his trade on the battlefield.

Then the soldier, bound and gagged, was stuffed into the fireplace, which our friends hadn't yet lit that evening. "And now we have a sword and a uniform," said Porthos.

"I'll take these," said d'Artagnan. "If we're going to get you a set, we'll have to do that again. Watch out! The other soldier is coming from the guardhouse."

"I don't think we should try the same thing again," said Porthos. "They always say lightning doesn't strike twice. If I missed my grab, all would be lost. I'll slip out, jump him when he goes by, and pass him in already bound and gagged."

"Even better," replied the Gascon.

"Get ready," said Porthos, sliding out through the opening.

It worked out just as Porthos had promised. The giant crouched behind a topiary, and when the soldier passed, he grabbed him by the neck, gagged him, shoved him like a mummy between the window bars, and then followed him inside.

The second prisoner was stripped as they had the first. He was laid down on the bed and bound to it with belts, and as the bed was solid oak, and the belts were doubled, he was as firmly restrained as the other.

"There," said d'Artagnan, "that's perfect. Now, try on his coat, Porthos, and see if it fits; if it doesn't, the baldric will be enough, along with this hat with its red feather."

By chance the second Swiss was a large fellow, so Porthos split only a few seams when he donned the man's coat, and everything else was fine. For several minutes nothing was heard but the rustling of cloth as Porthos and d'Artagnan hastily donned their disguises.

"Ready," both said at the same time. "As for you, comrades," added d'Artagnan, turning toward the two soldiers, "so long as you lie there gently, nothing will happen to you—but if you make a fuss, you're dead."

The soldiers didn't budge. They were still feeling the effects of Porthos's grip, and knew this was a serious matter, and no joke.

"Now," said d'Artagnan, "are you ready to understand the rest, Porthos?"

"Yes," said Porthos. "I am alert."

"Well, we go down into the courtyard."

"Yes."

"We take the place of these two fellows."

"Good."

"We patrol back and forth."

"That's fine, it will keep us warm."

"When the valet calls, like last night and the night before, we obey."

"What do we say?"

"We don't say anything, if possible."

"Fine. I like that better."

"We say nothing, we just pull our hats down and escort His Eminence."

"To where?"

"To his meeting with Athos. Do you think he'll be happy to see us?"

"Oh ho!" cried Porthos. "I get it now!"

"Be careful how loud you say so, Porthos, because we haven't done it yet," said the Gascon, cheerfully.

"What happens when we've done it?" said Porthos.

"Follow me," replied d'Artagnan. "Time will tell."

And passing through the opening in the bars, he slipped into the court-yard. Porthos followed him, though with more difficulty. The two bound soldiers in the room could be heard shivering in fear.

Scarcely had d'Artagnan and Porthos touched the ground before a door opened across the courtyard and the voice of the valet de chambre cried, "Attention!"

The next moment the door to the guardroom opened and a voice called, "La Bruyère and Barthois, on duty!"

"It seems my name is La Bruyère," said d'Artagnan.

"And mine is Barthois," said Porthos.

"Where are you?" called the valet, whose eyes hadn't yet adjusted to the darkness, so he couldn't make out our two heroes in the gloom.

"Here we are," said d'Artagnan. Then, turning to Porthos, he whispered, "How goes it, Monsieur du Vallon?"

"*Ma foi*, it goes well! I just hope it lasts."

The two soldier-impostors fell in gravely behind the valet. He led them into a vestibule, then into an antechamber that seemed to be a waiting room, and indicating two stools, he said, "Your orders are simple: let no one enter here but one—and that one you must obey in everything. Do you hear me? And stay here until I relieve you."

D'Artagnan was well known to this valet de chambre, who was none other than Bernouin, who, over six or eight months, had admitted him to the cardinal's presence a dozen times. Instead of replying, he looked down and muttered something that he hoped sounded German rather than Gascon.

As for Porthos, d'Artagnan had made him promise that under no conditions would he speak. If pushed to extremities, he was allowed to solemnly swear, "*Der Teufel.*"

Bernouin went out, shutting the door behind him. "Uh-oh," said Porthos, hearing a key turn in the lock. "It appears to be the fashion here to lock people up. It looks to me like we've just traded one prison for another, the orangery. I'm not sure we're any better off."

"Porthos, my friend," said d'Artagnan in a low voice, "trust in Providence, and let me think this through."

"Think all you want," said Porthos, soured by the way things were going.

"We came about eighty paces, and climbed six steps," murmured d'Artagnan. "And now, as the illustrious Monsieur du Vallon says, we must be in the pavilion of the orangery. The Comte de La Fère can't be far, but the doors are all closed."

"That's no problem!" said Porthos. "With a shove of my shoulder . . ."

"Good God, Porthos, settle down," said d'Artagnan. "Save your strength until we need it. Didn't you hear him say someone will be coming here?"

"I did."

"Well, that someone will open the doors *for* us."

"But listen," said Porthos, "if that someone recognizes us, and starts shouting, all is lost. Because I don't imagine you want me to strangle a man of the Church like I would a German or Englishman."

"God save us, no!" said d'Artagnan. "While the young king might be grateful, the queen would never forgive us, and we really should spare her feelings. Besides, to spill blood unnecessarily? Never! I have my plan—let's stick to it, and later we'll laugh."

"Fine by me," said Porthos. "I could use a laugh."

"*Chut!*" said d'Artagnan. "Here comes the 'someone.'"

The sound of a light step was heard from the vestibule. The hinges of the door squealed, and a man appeared dressed in a cavalier's outfit beneath a large brown cloak, with a wide felt hat over his eyes and a lantern in his hand.

Porthos backed against the wall, but he couldn't make himself so small the man in the cloak couldn't see him. He held out his lantern and said, "Light this from the ceiling lamp."

Then, addressing d'Artagnan, he said, "You have your orders."

"*Ja,*" replied the Gascon, determined to confine himself to that specimen of the German language.

"*Tedesco,*" said the cavalier, "*va bene.*"

And advancing to the door opposite to the one from which he'd entered, he opened it and passed through, closing it behind him.

"And now what do we do?" asked Porthos.

"Now, friend Porthos, if that inner door is locked, we're going to put your shoulder to use. But everything in its time, when all is prepared. First let's barricade the outer door before we follow the cavalier."

The two friends then went to work using all the room's furniture to blockade the outer door, which fortunately opened inward, making the effort worthwhile. "There," said d'Artagnan. "That will make sure we can't be surprised from behind. And now, forward!"

XLIII

Monsieur Mazarin's Oubliette

Upon trying the door through which Mazarin had disappeared, d'Artagnan found that it was locked. "Here's where we put your shoulder to work," said d'Artagnan. "Push, friend Porthos, but gently, quietly—don't break anything, just pry it open."

Porthos pressed his broad shoulder against the door panel, which bent enough that d'Artagnan could get the point of his sword between the bolt and the lock's faceplate. The bolt gave way, and the door opened.

"As I've always said, friend Porthos, doors, like women, yield best to sweet persuasion."

"You, Monsieur," said Porthos, "are a philosopher."

"In we go," said d'Artagnan.

In they went, to a small chamber. Beyond, through a glass door, glowed the cardinal's lantern, which rested on the ground outside. By its light they could see the potted orange trees of the Château de Rueil extending off in two double lines, with a wide path down the center and a small alley to each side.

"But no cardinal," said d'Artagnan, "only his lantern. Where the devil did he go?"

He went out to explore one side of the path, pointing Porthos toward the other, then suddenly saw that one of the tree-tubs on the left was out of line, and in its former place was a gaping hole. Ten men would have had difficulty lifting that great ceramic pot, but by some mechanism it had rotated away from the slab it stood upon.

D'Artagnan, as we've said, saw the cavity the tree had concealed, and in this hole the steps of a narrow spiral staircase. He called Porthos over with a gesture and showed him the pit and the stairs. The two looked at each other in astonishment. "If all we wanted was gold," said d'Artagnan, "we'd have just made our fortune, and would be rich for the rest of our lives."

"How's that?"

"Don't you understand, Porthos? In all probability at the foot of these stairs is the famous treasure trove of the old cardinal, which everyone talks about. All we'd have to do is go down, tie up the cardinal, fill a box, drag it up the stairs, and put the orange tree back in its place. No one in the world would know where our fortune had come from—and the cardinal would be in no position to tell."

"That would be quite a coup for a mercenary or rogue," said Porthos, "but unworthy, it seems to me, of two gentlemen."

"Agreed," said d'Artagnan. "That's why I said, 'if all we wanted was gold'—but we're after something else."

At that moment there was a noise from the pit. D'Artagnan started, and then leaned forward to listen, hearing a hard and metallic sound, like the clanking of a sack of gold. A door closed below, and the first glimmers of a light shone up the stairs.

Mazarin had left his lantern in the orangery to make it look like he'd gone for a walk, then had lit a wax taper to carry into his underground vault. "Say hey!" he said in Italian as he mounted the stairs, hefting a bulging sack of Spanish *reals*. "This is enough to buy off five Councilors of Parliament and two Parisian generals. I, too, am a great general, though I make war in my own way . . ."

D'Artagnan and Porthos crouched in the side aisles of the orangery, each behind a potted tree, and waited.

Mazarin emerged within three steps of d'Artagnan and pressed a lever hidden in the wall. The slab rotated, and the orange tree atop it returned to its original location.

Then the cardinal snuffed out his candle and replaced it in his pocket, picked up his lantern, and said to himself, "Now to go see Monsieur de La Fère."

Good, that's our destination as well, thought d'Artagnan. *We'll all go together.*

All three began to march, Monsieur de Mazarin down the middle aisle, and Porthos and d'Artagnan, quietly, along the side alleys. The two hung back just enough to avoid the bars of light that shone from the cardinal's lantern between the rows of trees.

Mazarin reached a second glass door without noticing he was followed, the soft sand of the paths deadening the footsteps of his unseen companions. He turned left, into a corridor Porthos and d'Artagnan hadn't noticed before, then stopped, thoughtfully, before a door. "Ah! *Diavolo!* I forgot Comminges's advice that I should bring the soldiers and place them outside the door in case of trouble with this devil. Back we go."

And, with an impatient gesture, he turned to retrace his steps. "Don't trouble yourself, Monseigneur," said d'Artagnan, smiling, with a courtly bow and his hat in his hand. "We followed Your Eminence each step of the way, and here we are now."

"Yes, here we are," said Porthos, with the same polite gestures.

Mazarin darted bewildered looks from one to the other, recognized them both, and dropped his lantern with a moan of terror. D'Artagnan picked it up; luckily it hadn't been extinguished by its fall. "Oh! Such imprudence, Monseigneur," he said. "We can't go about without a light! Your Eminence might bump into some crate or fall down a hole."

"Monsieur d'Artagnan!" murmured Mazarin, paralyzed with astonishment.

"Yes, Monseigneur, in person, and I also have the honor to present Monsieur du Vallon, my dear friend, whom Your Eminence has been so kind as to take such an interest in."

And d'Artagnan shone the lamp onto the delighted face of Porthos, who was beginning to understand everything, and was quite proud of it.

"You were on your way to see Monsieur de La Fère," said d'Artagnan. "Far be it from us to interfere with that, Monseigneur. Please lead on, and we'll follow."

Mazarin began to get hold of himself. "Have you been in the orangery for long, Messieurs?" he asked in a trembling voice, as he thought of the visit he'd just made to his treasure vault.

Porthos opened his mouth to reply, but d'Artagnan silenced him with a gesture, and Porthos's mouth slowly closed.

"We arrived just moments ago, Monseigneur," said d'Artagnan.

Mazarin sighed in relief: he no longer feared for his treasure, merely his own life. A kind of smile passed over his lips. "Come," he said, "I'm in the snare, Messieurs, and admit defeat. You want your freedom, no? I give it to you."

"Oh, Monseigneur!" said d'Artagnan. "You're very good to us—but as we already have our freedom, we prefer to ask for something else."

"You have your freedom?" said Mazarin, suddenly frightened.

"No doubt about it—while on the other hand, you, Monseigneur, have lost yours. That's the way of war, Monseigneur; now there's just the matter of your ransom."

Mazarin shuddered from head to toe. His piercing gaze tried in vain to read the mocking visage of the Gascon and the impassive features of Porthos, but both their faces were hidden in the shadows, and the Cumaean Sibyl herself couldn't have divined anything from them.

"Ransom my freedom! *Ransom,*" repeated Mazarin.

"Yes, Monseigneur."

"And how much will it cost me, Monsieur d'Artagnan?"

"*Dame,* Monseigneur, I don't know yet. We'll go ask the Comte de La Fère, if Your Eminence will permit. If Your Eminence would deign to open the door that leads to him, we'll have everything settled within ten minutes."

Mazarin trembled.

"Monseigneur," said d'Artagnan, "Your Eminence will recognize that so far we have shown all due respect and asked politely—but we're obliged to warn you that we have no time to lose. Open up, Monseigneur, if you please, and remember, above all, that at the first move you make to attempt to escape or cry out, we, who are in a very difficult situation, may be forced to go to extremes."

"Don't worry, Messieurs," said Mazarin, "I won't try anything. I give you my word of honor."

D'Artagnan made a sign to Porthos not to take his eye off Mazarin for a moment, and then said, "Now, Monseigneur, let's all go in together."

XLIV

Negotiations

Mazarin unlocked the bolts and opened the double door, where just inside Athos was waiting to receive the illustrious visitor Comminges had told him to expect. Seeing Mazarin on his threshold, he bowed and said, "Your Eminence could have come without the escort; the honor of your visit is too great for me to forget myself."

"But my dear Count," said d'Artagnan, "it wasn't His Eminence who wanted us along, it was du Vallon and I who insisted on it—perhaps somewhat improperly, but we had a great desire to see you."

At this voice, this mocking accent, and the familiar figure that went with that voice and accent, Athos started in surprise. "D'Artagnan! Porthos!" he cried.

"In person, dear friend."

"In person!" repeated Porthos.

"What does this mean?" asked the count.

"What it means," replied Mazarin, trying to recover some of his self-possession by forcing a smile, "is that the roles have reversed, and that instead of these gentlemen being my prisoners, I am now theirs, so that you see me obliged to submit to the situation rather than to command it. But, Messieurs, I warn you that unless you cut my throat, your triumph won't last long. My turn will come, and when it does . . ."

"Ah, Monseigneur, don't make threats—it's unbecoming," said d'Artagnan. "We intend to be nothing but sweet and gentle with Your Eminence! Let's set aside anger and ill-humor and try to keep it friendly, shall we?"

"I ask no better, Messieurs," said Mazarin. "But if we're negotiating my ransom, I don't want you to think your situation is better than it is. By taking me in the snare, you took yourselves with me. How will you get out of it? You can see the bars and the locked gates, see, or rather guess at, how many sentries guard these bars and gates, how many soldiers throng the courtyards, and take stock of your true position. As you can see, I'm being frank with you."

Good! thought d'Artagnan. *He's bargaining. Now hold on, for here comes the tricky part.*

"I offered you your freedom," continued the minister. "I offer it to you again. If you don't take it, within the hour you'll be discovered, attacked, and probably forced to kill me, which would be a horrible crime, unworthy of loyal gentlemen like yourselves."

He's right, thought Athos, and like every noble idea that passed through his elevated mind, his thought could be read in his eyes.

"And therefore," said d'Artagnan, to counter the hope that Athos's silent agreement had given Mazarin, "we recognize that we turn to violence only as an absolute last resort."

"On the other hand," continued Mazarin, "if you accept your freedom from me and let me go . . ."

"What?" interrupted d'Artagnan. "You want us to accept our freedom from you, even though, as you said yourself, you can take it back again five minutes later? And knowing you, Monseigneur," added d'Artagnan, "that's exactly what you'd do."

"No, really, faith of a cardinal! . . . You don't believe me?"

"Monseigneur, I don't believe cardinals who were never ordained as priests."

"All right, then—faith of a minister!"

"But you're not a minister now, Monseigneur, you're a prisoner."

"Then, faith of a Mazarin! I'm still that, I hope."

"Hmm!" said d'Artagnan. "I once heard of a Mazarin who didn't keep his promises, and I fear he might have been one of Your Eminence's ancestors."

"Monsieur d'Artagnan," said Mazarin, "you have no shortage of wits, and I regret ever quarreling with you."

"Then, Monseigneur, let's make up our differences. I ask nothing better."

"Well," said Mazarin, "what if I set you free with a guaranteed security, something visible and tangible . . . ?"

"Ah! That's another thing," said Porthos.

"Let's hear it," said Athos.

"Let's see it," said d'Artagnan.

"But first of all, do you accept?" asked the cardinal.

"Explain your proposal, Monseigneur, and then we'll see."

"Take note of the fact that you're locked up here."

"But you're well aware, Monseigneur," said d'Artagnan, "that we have, in extremity, a last resort."

"What's that?"

"We can all die together."

Mazarin shuddered. "There," he said, "at the end of that corridor, is a door to which I have the key. That door opens onto the park. Take this key and go; you're armed, alert, and quick. After a hundred paces, on your left you'll find the wall surrounding the park; go over it, and a few steps beyond it you'll be on the road and free. And as I have reason to know, if you're attacked, that won't be much of an obstacle to your escape."

"Ah! *Pardieu*, Monseigneur, that's tangible indeed!" said d'Artagnan. "Where is this key you'd like to offer us?"

"Here it is."

"Then, Monseigneur," said d'Artagnan, "please lead us to this door."

"Willingly," said the minister, "if that will make you feel better."

Mazarin, who had never hoped to get off so cheaply, led them cheerfully up the corridor and unlocked the door. It opened onto the park, and the three fugitives immediately felt the chill night wind, which swept down the corridor and blew snow in their faces.

"The devil!" said d'Artagnan. "It's a wretched dark night, Monseigneur, and we don't know the way. Since Your Eminence has come so far, perhaps Monseigneur would go a bit further and lead us to the wall."

"So be it," said the cardinal. And setting off without hesitation in a straight line, he led them quickly toward the wall, and in less than a minute all four were at its foot.

"Are you satisfied, Messieurs?" asked Mazarin.

"I should say so! *Peste*, we're not that hard to please! What an honor— three poor gentlemen escorted by a Prince of the Church! By the way, Monseigneur, you noted just now that we're quick, alert, and armed?"

"Yes . . ."

"That's not entirely true—only I and Monsieur du Vallon have weapons. The count has none, and if we meet a patrol, we'll need to defend ourselves."

"That's true, I suppose."

"Then do you suppose you could find us another sword?" asked Porthos.

"Monseigneur will lend the count his own," said d'Artagnan, "since it's of no use to him."

"Happily," said the cardinal. "I even invite Monsieur le Comte to keep it in memory of me."

"He's very gallant, isn't he, Count?" said d'Artagnan.

"Indeed," replied Athos, "and I promise Monseigneur to keep it near me always."

"What an exchange of compliments!" said d'Artagnan. "It's deeply moving. Doesn't it bring tears to your eyes, Porthos?"

"Yes," said Porthos, "that, or the wind. I think it might be the wind."

"Now up you go, Athos," said d'Artagnan, "and quickly."

Athos, aided by Porthos, who lifted him like a feather, clambered onto the top of the wall.

"Now jump, Athos."

Athos jumped and disappeared down the other side of the wall.

"Are you on the ground?" called d'Artagnan.

"Yes."

"Safely?"

"Perfectly so."

"Porthos, keep an eye on Monsieur le Cardinal while I go up—no, I can manage without help. Just watch the cardinal, that's all."

"I'm watching," said Porthos. ". . . Well?"

"You're right, it's higher than I thought; just lend me your back, but without letting go of the cardinal."

"I won't let go."

Porthos lent his back to d'Artagnan, who, thanks to his support, was on top of the wall in an instant. Mazarin looked aside, concealing a smile.

"Are you there?" asked Porthos.

"Yes, my friend, and now . . ."

"Now, what?"

"Now, pass Monsieur le Cardinal up to me—and if he starts to shout, muffle him."

Mazarin wanted to cry out, but Porthos enveloped him in both hands and lifted him up to d'Artagnan, who, in his turn, hoisted the cardinal by the collar and sat him down beside him atop the wall. "Monsieur," d'Artagnan said, "drop down at once, next to Monsieur de La Fère, or I'll kill you out of hand—faith of a gentleman!"

"Monsieur, Monsieur!" cried Mazarin. "You're breaking your promise!"

"Me? And just when did I promise you anything, Monseigneur?"

Mazarin groaned. "I gave you your freedom, Monsieur," he said. "Your liberty was my ransom."

"To be sure. But what of the ransom for that great treasure buried beneath the orangery, where one pushes a lever hidden in the wall, which pivots a stone slab, which reveals a certain staircase—what of that, Monseigneur?"

"*Jésous!*" said Mazarin, clasping his hands together. "*Jésous mon Diou!* I'm ruined . . . ruined."

Ignoring these laments, d'Artagnan gripped him under the arms and lowered him gently into the hands of Athos, who stood solid and impassive at the base of the wall. Then, turning to Porthos, d'Artagnan said, "Take my hand and come on up."

Porthos clambered up with an effort that made the whole wall shake, gaining the top. "I didn't quite understand before," he said, "but I understand now. It's pretty funny."

"Do you think so?" said d'Artagnan. "All the better! But let's go quickly, and hope it stays funny to the end." And he leaped to the ground outside the wall.

Porthos followed him.

"Keep the cardinal between you, Messieurs," said d'Artagnan, "while I take the vanguard." And drawing his sword, he led them into the dark.

After a moment he paused and said, "Monseigneur, which way is the high road? Think carefully before replying, for if Your Eminence made a mistake, it could have serious consequences, not least for yourself."

"Follow the wall, Monsieur," said Mazarin, "and you can't go astray."

The three friends hastened forward, but soon had to slow their pace, for the cardinal, though he tried to keep up, couldn't manage it.

Suddenly d'Artagnan collided with something warm that trembled slightly. "Hey, a horse!" he said. "I just ran into a horse, Messieurs!"

"So did I!" said Athos.

"Me, too!" said Porthos, who, faithful to his orders, still had the cardinal by the arm.

"Now that's what I call a stroke of luck, Monseigneur," said d'Artagnan, "just when Your Eminence was complaining about having to walk. . . ."

But as he said these words he felt the barrel of a pistol prod his chest, and heard a grave voice say, "Hands up!"

"Grimaud!" he cried. "Grimaud! What are you doing here? Has heaven sent you to us?"

"No, Monsieur," said the loyal old servant. "It was Monsieur Aramis. He posted me here to guard the horses."

"Aramis is here, then?"

"Yes, Monsieur, since yesterday."

"And what are you doing?"

"We're watching."

"What! Aramis is here?" repeated Athos.

"At the rear gate of the château. That was his post."

"How many men does he have?"

"Sixty."

"Send to warn him."

"Right away, Monsieur." And thinking that no one could do a better job of it than he, Grimaud took off at full speed, while the three friends gathered themselves and waited. The only unhappy member of the group was Monsieur de Mazarin.

XLV

In Which We Finally Begin to Believe that Porthos Will Become a Baron and d'Artagnan a Captain

Ten minutes later Aramis arrived, accompanied by Grimaud and eight or ten gentlemen. He was radiant and threw his arms around his friends' necks. "You're free then, Brothers! Free without my help! You didn't need a thing from me despite my best efforts!"

"Don't worry about that, dear friend," said d'Artagnan. "Your efforts weren't unneeded, just deferred—because this business is far from over."

"I'd laid my plans well, though," said Aramis. "I got sixty men from the coadjutor, and posted twenty around the walls of the park, twenty on the road from Rueil to Saint-Germain, and twenty scattered through the woods. Thanks to this strategy, I've intercepted two letters from Mazarin to the queen."

Mazarin perked up his ears.

"Letters which you've honestly, I hope, returned to the cardinal," said d'Artagnan.

"If only I thought treating him with such forthright chivalry would shame him!" said Aramis. "In one of these dispatches the cardinal complains that the coffers are empty and that Her Majesty has no more money, while the other announces his plan to transport his prisoners to Melun, since Rueil didn't seem safe enough to him. You'll understand, *cher ami,* what hope I derived from the second letter! I planted my ambuscades around the château, placed my men, kept a supply of horses at hand, overseen by the intelligent Grimaud, and waited for them to bring you out. I hoped to be able to do it without even a skirmish but hadn't really expected to see any action before tomorrow morning. And now tonight you're free, with all combat avoided, and so much the better! How did you manage to escape that weasel of a Mazarin? You must have plenty to complain about his treatment of you."

"Not too much," said d'Artagnan.

"Really!"

"More than that, I'll actually praise him."

"Impossible!"

"Not at all, for it's thanks to him that we're free."

"Thanks to him?"

"Yes, he had us led to the orangery by Monsieur Bernouin, his valet, and then he himself escorted us to the Comte de La Fère. Then he offered to grant us our freedom, which we accepted, and more than that he was so kind as to lead us to the wall of the park, which we climbed over, and outside of which we had the great good fortune to encounter Grimaud."

"*Bien*," said Aramis, "you're the only one who could reconcile me to him, and I just wish he were here so I could tell him I hadn't thought him capable of such fine behavior."

"Monseigneur," said d'Artagnan, unable to contain himself any longer, "permit me to introduce you to Monsieur le Chevalier d'Herblay, who wishes to offer, as you've heard, his respectful compliments to Your Eminence."

And he stepped aside, revealing Mazarin, looking confused and apprehensive, to the bewildered gaze of Aramis.

Then Aramis grinned. "Oh ho! What have we here? The cardinal himself—a fine catch indeed! *Holà!* Comrades! Bring the horses!"

Several cavaliers came running. "*Pardieu!*" said Aramis. "I think I'll be useful after all. Monseigneur, I hope Your Eminence will deign to receive my respects. I'll wager it was this Saint Christopher of a Porthos who transported you! By the way, I forgot . . ." And he gave an order in a low voice to one of the cavaliers.

"I think it would be a good idea to get moving," said d'Artagnan.

"Yes, I'm just waiting for someone . . . a friend of Athos."

"A friend of mine?" said the count.

"And here he comes, galloping through the underbrush."

"Monsieur le Comte! Monsieur le Comte!" called a young voice that made Athos tremble.

"Raoul!" the count cried.

The young man momentarily forgot his usual respect and threw his arms around the count.

"You see, Monsieur le Cardinal, what a shame it was to keep separated folk who love each other like we do?" said Aramis. "Messieurs," he continued, addressing the gathering cavaliers, "surround yourselves carefully around His Eminence to make sure we do him appropriate honor, since he deigns to grant us the favor of his company. I'm sure he'll be grateful. Porthos, never lose sight of His Eminence."

Then Aramis put his head together with those of d'Artagnan and Athos for a brief conference. "Come," said d'Artagnan, after five minutes' discussion. "We're off!"

"But where are we going?" asked Porthos.

"To your place, old friend—to Pierrefonds! Your lovely château is quite worthy enough to offer its noble hospitality to His Eminence. Besides, it's perfectly situated, neither too near nor too far from Paris, enabling easy communication with the capital. Come, Monseigneur, you'll be treated there like the prince that you are."

"A fallen prince," said Mazarin, piteously.

"We all take risks in war, Monseigneur," replied Athos, "but rest assured we won't abuse our advantage."

"No, but we'll certainly use it," said d'Artagnan.

For the rest of the night, the victors rode with the untiring speed of old, with Mazarin, gloomy and pensive, bouncing along in the middle of that troop of racing phantoms. By dawn they had made twelve leagues with barely a pause; half the escort was exhausted, and some of the horses fell to their knees. "The horses of today are not like those of the old days," said Porthos. "Everything decays."

"I've sent Grimaud over to Dammartin," said Aramis. "He's to return with five fresh horses: one for His Eminence and four for us. The critical thing is to keep Monseigneur close to us; the rest of the escort can rejoin us later. Once we get past Saint-Denis, we've nothing more to fear."

Grimaud in fact returned with five good horses; the local lord he'd gotten them from, being a friend of Porthos, had refused to sell them and had given them as a gift. Ten minutes later they reached Ermenonville, where most of the escort stopped. But the four friends, with renewed spirits, continued on with Monsieur de Mazarin.

At noon they entered the broad drive that led to Porthos's Château de Pierrefonds, where they were met by Mousqueton. "Ah!" he said. "Believe me, Monsieur, this is the first time I've breathed easily since your departure from Pierrefonds." And he ran off to announce to the other servants the arrival of Monsieur du Vallon and his friends.

"We are four," said d'Artagnan, "so we'll watch Monseigneur in relays, each three hours long. Athos will inspect the château's defenses, with an eye to making them impregnable in the event of a siege, Porthos will attend to the provisions, and Aramis to the barracking of the garrison. In other words, Athos will be chief military engineer, Porthos the quartermaster general, and Aramis personnel officer."

Meanwhile, Mazarin was installed in the most elegant suite in the château. "Messieurs," he said, once he was settled in his quarters, "you don't expect, I imagine, to keep me here incognito for long?"

"No, Monseigneur," d'Artagnan replied, "on the contrary, we'll soon publicize the fact that we're holding you."

"Then you'll be besieged."

"We're counting on it."

"And what will you do?"

"We'll defend ourselves. If the late Cardinal Richelieu was still among us, he'd tell you the story of the bastion of Saint-Gervais, where the four of us, with one lackey and twelve dead bodies, held out against an army."

"Such feats may occur once, Monsieur, and then never recur again."

"But today we have no need to repeat such heroics—for tomorrow the Parisian army will be alerted, and the next day it will be here. The decisive battle will take place, not at Saint-Denis or Charenton, but at Compiègne or Villers-Cotterêts."

"Monsieur le Prince will beat you, as he always has."

"It's possible, Monseigneur—but before the battle we'll send Your Eminence on to another of our friend du Vallon's châteaux, as he has three like this one. We don't want to expose Your Eminence to the hazards of war."

"Come," said Mazarin, "I see that I must capitulate."

"What, before the siege?"

"Yes, the conditions will probably be better."

"Monseigneur, as far as conditions are concerned, you'll see how reasonable we can be."

"What, then, are your conditions?"

"Let's sleep on it, Monseigneur, to give us all time to reflect."

"I need no rest, Messieurs—I need to know whether I'm in the hands of enemies or friends."

"Friends, Monseigneur, friends!"

"Well, then, tell me right now what you want, so I can see if we can find an agreement. Speak, Monsieur le Comte de La Fère."

"Monseigneur," said Athos, "I have nothing to ask for myself, and too much to ask for France. I will therefore defer to Monsieur le Chevalier d'Herblay." And Athos bowed, took a step back, and leaned against the mantel, clearly determined to be no more than a spectator at this negotiation.

"Speak, then, Monsieur d'Herblay," said the cardinal. "No evasions or ambiguities, please: be brief, clear, and precise."

"Very well, Monseigneur, I'll lay my cards on the table."

"Let's see them."

"I have in my saddlebag," said Aramis, "the list of concessions proposed to you the day before yesterday at Saint-Germain, by the deputation of which I was a part. Let's first address the restoration of ancient rights—the articles on this list shall be accepted."

"We were close to agreeing to those anyway," said Mazarin. "Let's pass on to the . . . special conditions."

"Do you think we have some?" said Aramis, smiling.

"I think you're not all as selfless as the Comte de La Fère," said Mazarin, turning toward Athos and saluting him.

"Really? Well, Monseigneur, you're right," said Aramis, "though I'm glad to see you recognizing the count's true worth. Monsieur de La Fère's spirit is a cut above, beyond vulgar desires and human passions; his is an ancient soul, and proud. You're quite right, Monseigneur, that the rest of us are not of his quality, as we're the first to admit."

"Aramis," said Athos, "is this mockery?"

"No, *mon cher* Count, no, I only say what all of us think, and all who truly know you. But you're right, it wasn't of you we were talking, but of Monseigneur and his unworthy servant the Chevalier d'Herblay."

"Well! What do you desire, Monsieur, beyond those general conditions which we'll get back to later?"

"I desire, Monseigneur, that Normandy be officially granted to Madame de Longueville, with full amnesty and five hundred thousand livres. I desire His Majesty the King to stand as godfather to the son to which she's just given birth[56]—and that Monseigneur, after attending his baptism, shall go and pay his respects to our Holy Father the Pope."

"That is to say, you wish me to relinquish my office as minister, to leave France in self-imposed exile?"

"I wish Monseigneur to assume the office of pope at the first available vacancy, upon which I reserve the right to ask him for plenary indulgences for myself and my friends."

Mazarin made an indescribable grimace. "And you, Monsieur?" he asked d'Artagnan.

"I, Monseigneur," said the Gascon, "am in every respect of the same opinion as Monsieur le Chevalier d'Herblay—except for the final article, on which I entirely differ. Far from wishing that Monseigneur should leave France, I want him to continue as prime minister, for Monseigneur is a great politician. I'll even do my best, as much as it depends upon me, to help him settle his differences with the Frondeurs, but only on condition that he remember the king's faithful servants, and that he will give command of the first company of the musketeers to someone I shall designate. And you, du Vallon?"

"Yes, Monsieur, speak on your own account," said Mazarin.

"I wish," said Porthos, "that Monsieur le Cardinal, to honor the house which has given him asylum, shall, in remembrance of this adventure, elevate my estate to a barony. I also wish the promise of a Knightly Order for one of my friends at Her Majesty's next bestowal."

"You know, Monsieur, that only those who've proven themselves are eligible for such an Order."

"This friend has been so proven. Besides, if it came to it, Monseigneur would know how to avoid such formalities."

Mazarin bit his lip; the blow was direct, and he drily replied, "It seems to me these things are hard to reconcile, Messieurs—if I satisfy some of them, I dissatisfy others. If I stay in Paris I can't go to Rome, and if I become pope I can't remain prime minister—and if I'm not a minister, I can't make Monsieur d'Artagnan a captain and Monsieur du Vallon a baron."

"That's true," said Aramis. "Therefore, since I'm in the minority, I hereby withdraw my proposals regarding the trip to Rome and Monseigneur's resignation."

"I can remain a minister?" said Mazarin.

"You remain a minister; that's agreed, Monseigneur," said d'Artagnan. "France has need of you."

"Those proposals are withdrawn," said Aramis. "His Eminence will remain prime minister, and even the favorite of Her Majesty, if he deigns to grant me and my friends what we ask for France . . . and for ourselves."

"Attend to yourselves, Messieurs, and let France settle with me as she thinks best," said Mazarin.

"No, that won't do," replied Aramis. "There must be a treaty with the Frondeurs, and Your Eminence will sign it in front of us, while also committing to obtain the queen's ratification of it in every detail."

"I can answer only for myself, I can't answer for the queen," said Mazarin. "What if Her Majesty refuses?"

"Oh," said d'Artagnan, "Monseigneur knows very well that Her Majesty can refuse him nothing."

"Here, Monseigneur," said Aramis. "This is the treaty proposed by the deputation of the Fronde; Your Eminence may read and examine it."

"I already know it," said Mazarin.

"Then it only remains to sign it."

"You must realize, Messieurs, that a signature obtained under these circumstances will be regarded as given under duress."

"Monseigneur will be available to attest that it was given voluntarily."

"But what, then, if I refuse?"

"Then, Monseigneur," said d'Artagnan, "Your Eminence will have no one to blame but himself for the consequences of that refusal."

"You would dare to lay hands on a cardinal?"

"You've done no less against His Majesty's Musketeers!"

"The queen will avenge me, Messieurs!"

"I doubt that she could, though she might have the will to try. But we'll take Your Eminence to Paris, and the Parisians will rally to our defense."

"How worried they must be right now in Rueil and at Saint-Germain!" said Aramis. "Everyone must be asking where the cardinal has gone, what's become of the minister, what's happened to the favorite! They must be seeking Monseigneur in every nook and cranny! And if the Fronde is aware of Monseigneur's disappearance, how they must be rejoicing!"

"It's appalling," murmured Mazarin.

"Then sign the treaty, Monseigneur," said Aramis.

"But what if I sign it and the queen refuses to ratify it?"

"I'll undertake to go see Her Majesty and obtain her signature," said d'Artagnan.

"Take care," said Mazarin. "You might not get the reception at Saint-Germain that you hope for."

"Ah, bah!" said d'Artagnan. "I can arrange things to make sure I'm welcomed; I have a means to do that."

"What?"

"I'll bring Her Majesty that letter in which Monseigneur announces the complete depletion of the treasury."

"And then?" said Mazarin, turning pale.

"And then, when Her Majesty is at the height of her dismay, I'll escort her to Rueil, lead her to the orangery, and show her a certain lever that moves a certain slab."

"Enough, Monsieur, enough!" murmured the cardinal. "Where is that treaty?"

"Here it is," said Aramis.

"You see how generous we are," said d'Artagnan, "for we could do many things with such a secret."

"Sign here," said Aramis, handing the cardinal a pen.

Mazarin stood and paced back and forth for a minute, more in distraction than dejection. Then suddenly he stopped and said, "And when I've signed, Messieurs, what will be my guarantee?"

"My word of honor, Monsieur," said Athos.

Mazarin trembled, examining for a moment that noble and loyal face, and then taking the pen, he said, "That's good enough for me, Monsieur le Comte."

And he signed.

"And now, Monsieur d'Artagnan," he added, "prepare to leave at once for Saint-Germain to carry a letter from me to the queen."

XLVI

In Which More Is Accomplished with a Pen and a Threat than with a Sword and Devotion

D'Artagnan knew at least this much of mythology, that Opportunity has only a tuft of hair to seize it by, and he wasn't a man to let it go by without seizing it. He arranged a means of quick and reliable travel by sending relay horses to Chantilly in advance, so that he could be in Paris in five or six hours. But before leaving he thought about the fact that he, though a man of wit and experience, was about to charge into uncertainty, leaving certainty behind.

But was it certainty? "In fact," he said to himself before mounting his horse, "Athos is a hero from romance blinded by his own generosity, Porthos is good-natured but easy to influence, and Aramis is a complete hieroglyphic, impossible to read, capable of anything. What will these three elements produce when I'm not there to regulate them? The release of the cardinal, perhaps. Now, the release of the cardinal would be the ruin of our hopes, and so far, hopes are all we have to show for twenty years of labors compared to which those of Hercules were the work of a pygmy."

He went and found Aramis. "You, my dear Chevalier d'Herblay," he said, "are the Fronde incarnate. Beware of Athos, who won't stoop to soil his hands with business, not even his own. Be even more wary of Porthos, who, to impress the count, whom he regards as a divinity on earth, would even help Mazarin to escape, if Mazarin cries tears of distress or thinks to appeal to his chivalry."

Aramis smiled a smile that was both shrewd and resolute. "Never fear," he said, "I have my conditions to protect—though I'm working less for myself than for others. For the sake of everyone's rights, I'll make sure that those who are entitled to it reap the profit of this affair."

Good, thought d'Artagnan. *I'm not worried about this flank.* He shook hands with Aramis and went to seek Porthos.

"Old friend," he said, "you and I have worked hard to build our fortunes, and it would be ridiculous if, just when we're about to reap our rewards, you were tricked out of them by Aramis, who is not without cunning, and who, just between the two of us, sometimes plays his own game. Or to have them slip through our fingers because Athos, though noble and unselfish, can also be careless, because as one who desires nothing for himself, he doesn't weigh the desires of others. What would you say if one of our two friends proposed liberating Mazarin?"

"I'd say we had too much trouble getting him to think of letting him go."

"Bravo, Porthos! And you would be right, my friend, for with him would go your barony, which is practically in your hands—not to mention the fact that once free, Mazarin would turn around and sentence you to hang."

"Really! You think so?"

"I'm sure of it."

"Then I'll see him dead before I allow him to escape."

"Good thinking. After all, when we made our original bargain, we weren't beholden to the Frondeurs, who anyway are a bunch of politicians who don't see things like we old soldiers do."

"Don't worry, dear friend," said Porthos. "I'll watch you from the window as you ride away until you've disappeared, and then go and station myself outside the cardinal's door, which has a glass pane so I can see everything inside. One false move, and I'll exterminate him."

Bravo! thought d'Artagnan. *On this flank, at least, the cardinal is well guarded.* And he shook hands with the master of Pierrefonds and went looking for Athos.

When he found him, he said, "My dear Athos, I'm leaving. I have only one thing to say to you: you know Anne of Austria, and you know the continued captivity of Monsieur de Mazarin is my only guarantee of survival. If you let him get away, I'm a dead man."

"It is only that consideration, my dear d'Artagnan, that induces me to stoop to the job of jailer. I give you my word that upon your return, you'll find the cardinal where you left him."

That reassures me more than any number of royal signatures, thought d'Artagnan. *Now that I have the oath of Athos, I can go.*

D'Artagnan rode off alone, with no escort but his sword, and with nothing but a pass from Mazarin ordering his admittance to the presence of the queen.

Six hours after leaving Pierrefonds, he arrived at Saint-Germain. Mazarin's disappearance was still unknown to anyone but Anne of Austria, who hid her anxiety from even her most intimate friends. The two Swiss had been discovered bound and gagged in the quarters of d'Artagnan and Porthos, but after the use of their limbs and tongues had been restored to them, they could tell only what they knew, which was that they'd been jumped, stripped, and tied up. But as to what Porthos and d'Artagnan had done after they'd gotten out, they had no more idea than the other inhabitants of the château.

Except for Bernouin, who knew a bit more than the others. Bernouin, not seeing his master return by the time midnight was striking, had taken it upon himself to search the orangery. The furniture barricading the outer door had filled him with suspicions, but he kept them to himself and instead undertook patiently to clear the passage. Once he'd reached the inner corridor, he found a whole series of doors standing open. Passing through them and out into the park, it was easy to follow the footprints in the snow to the outer wall. They continued on the other side until they mingled with a trampling of horses' hooves, indicating practically a whole troop of cavalry had ridden off in the direction of Enghien. From that moment he had no doubt but that the cardinal had been abducted by the three prisoners, since they had disappeared with him, and he had ridden to Saint-Germain at once to warn the queen of the cardinal's capture.

Anne of Austria had commanded Bernouin to tell no one, and he'd obeyed her scrupulously. She informed only Monsieur le Prince, to whom she told everything, and the Prince had immediately put five or six hundred riders into the environs of Rueil, ordered to detain any suspicious group riding away from the château and bring them at once to Saint-Germain.

Now, d'Artagnan wasn't a group, as he was alone, and since he wasn't riding away from Rueil but rather toward Saint-Germain, no one paid any attention to him, so he didn't run into any trouble. Upon entering the courtyard of the Château de Saint-Germain, the first person our ambassador saw was Bernouin himself, who was loitering at the gates, waiting for word of his missing master.

At the sight of d'Artagnan riding into the *cour d'honneur*, Bernouin rubbed his eyes, thinking he must be mistaken. But d'Artagnan gave him a friendly salute, dismounted, and, tossing the bridle into the hands of a footman, advanced smiling toward the minister's valet. "Monsieur d'Artagnan!" cried Bernouin, like a man having a nightmare and calling out in his sleep. "Monsieur d'Artagnan!"

"Himself, Monsieur Bernouin."

"But what are you doing here?"

"Bringing you news of Monsieur de Mazarin, news piping hot."

"And what has become of him?"

"He's as well as you or I."

"He's come to no harm, then?"

"None whatsoever. He just felt the need to take a tour of the Île-de-France, and begged Monsieur le Comte de La Fère, Monsieur du Vallon, and myself to accompany him. We're too much his humble servants to refuse such a request. We left last night, and here we are."

". . . And here you are?"

"His Eminence had something to convey to Her Majesty, something private and intimate, a mission that could be entrusted only to a proven man, so he sent me to Saint-Germain. So, my dear Monsieur Bernouin, if you wish to serve your master well, please inform Her Majesty that I'm coming to see her, and for what purpose."

Whether he was speaking seriously or whether these remarks were some sort of jest, it was nonetheless clear that under the circumstances d'Artagnan was the only man able to put Anne of Austria's mind at rest, so Bernouin didn't hesitate about going to inform her of his unusual request. And as he'd foreseen, the queen ordered him to admit d'Artagnan at once.

D'Artagnan approached his sovereign with all the signs of deepest respect. Arriving three paces in front of her, he went down on one knee and presented his letter. This, as we've said, was a simple note, half of introduction, half a request for an audience. The queen, reading it, recognized the cardinal's handwriting, though her own hand trembled slightly. But as the note said nothing of what had happened, she asked for details.

D'Artagnan told her everything with that simple, forthright air he could employ so well in the right circumstances. The queen, as he spoke, regarded him with increasing astonishment; she couldn't understand how a man could dare to conceive such an undertaking, let alone have the audacity to recount it to one who had almost a duty to punish him for it. "What, Monsieur!" the queen cried, red with indignation, when he'd finished his account. "You dare to confess such a crime to me! To tell me of your treason!"

"Your pardon, Madame, but I must have explained things poorly, or Your Majesty has misunderstood, for there's neither crime nor treason in this. Monsieur de Mazarin put Monsieur du Vallon and myself in prison because we couldn't believe he'd sent us to England to stand quietly aside while they cut off the head of King Charles I, the brother-in-law of your husband the late king and the spouse of Madame Henriette your sister, so we did all we could to save the life of the royal martyr. We were therefore certain, my friend and I, that there'd been some sort of mistake, and an explanation of some sort was needed between ourselves and His Eminence. Now, an explanation touching on such matters must be conducted in security and privacy, away from the eyes and ears of meddling subordinates. And so, we escorted the cardinal to my friend's château, where we had our explanation. And, well, Madame! As we'd foreseen, there *had* been a mistake. Monsieur de Mazarin had been under the impression we'd served

General Cromwell instead of King Charles, a thing that would have been a disgrace that stained us, the cardinal, and even Your Majesty, an act of cowardice that might have cast a shadow even upon the royalty of your illustrious son. Now that we've provided him with proof to the contrary, we're ready to give it as well to Your Majesty herself, by appealing to the august widow who weeps in the Louvre, where your royal munificence has granted her hospitality. This proof has so thoroughly satisfied the cardinal that, as evidence of his satisfaction, he's sent me, as Your Majesty can see, to talk with Madame about what reparations are due to gentlemen so poorly appreciated and wrongly persecuted."

"I hear you and must say I admire you, Monsieur," said Anne of Austria. "In truth, I've rarely seen such boundless impudence."

"Come," said d'Artagnan. "I see that Her Majesty is, in her turn, as deceived about our intentions as Monsieur de Mazarin was."

"You are mistaken, Monsieur," said the queen. "In fact, I am so little deceived that, within ten minutes, you will be under arrest, and in an hour I'll leave at the head of my army to go rescue my minister."

"I'm sure Your Majesty will commit no such imprudence," said d'Artagnan, "because it would be useless and would result in serious consequences. Before he could be rescued Monsieur le Cardinal would be dead, and His Eminence is so entirely convinced of the truth of what I say that on the contrary he asked me, in case Your Majesty should be inclined to make such a decision, to do everything I could to get her to reconsider."

"Well! I can at least be satisfied by having you arrested."

"Not really, Madame, for precautions have also been taken for that contingency, as well as for attempts to rescue the cardinal. If I haven't returned by a certain time tomorrow, the following day the cardinal will be taken to Paris."

"You will find, Monsieur, that in your situation you've been out of touch with people and events, or you'd know that the cardinal has already visited Paris five or six times since we left it, and that he saw Monsieur de Beaufort, Monsieur de Bouillon, Monsieur le Coadjuteur, and Monsieur d'Elbeuf, and that not one of them even considered having him arrested."

"Your pardon, Madame, but I know all that, so it's not to Monsieur de Beaufort, Monsieur de Bouillon, Monsieur le Coadjuteur, or Monsieur d'Elbeuf that the cardinal would be brought, because those gentlemen make war on their own accounts, and can therefore be bought cheaply. Instead he'd be taken to parliament, which can be purchased piecemeal, but not even Monsieur de Mazarin himself is wealthy enough to buy it en masse."

"I believe," said Anne of Austria, glaring at him, a look that would have been contemptuous in a woman but was terrible in a queen, "that you are threatening the mother of your king."

"Madame," said d'Artagnan, "I threaten only because I must. I speak above my station only because I must place myself on the level of people and events. But believe one thing above all, Madame, the truth that the heart in my breast beats for you, and that you have been the constant idol of our lives, which we have, as you well know, risked many times for Your Majesty. Come, Madame, won't Your Majesty have pity on her servants, who've been laboring for twenty years in the shade, without uttering a single syllable about the solemn and sacred secrets they had the honor to learn on your behalf? Look at me, who is speaking to you now, Madame, and whom you accuse of raising my voice and taking a threatening tone. Who am I? A poor officer without fortune, without family, and without a future if the regard of my queen, which I've sought for so long, doesn't fall on me for a moment. Look at Monsieur le Comte de La Fère, a paragon of the nobility, who took sides with those opposing his queen—or rather, her minister—and yet makes no demands. Look, at last, at Monsieur du Vallon, that loyal soul, that iron arm, who's been waiting twenty years for the word from your lips that will make him, by a coat of arms, what he is already in courage and in heart. And consider your people, who are certainly the care of a queen—your people, who love you but are starving, who ask no better than to bless you but who . . . no, I'm wrong, your people will never curse you, Madame. Well! Say the word, and all is over: war gives way to peace, tears to joy, calamity to happiness."

Anne of Austria looked with some astonishment at the martial face of d'Artagnan, which showed an unexpected look of tenderness. "Why didn't you say all this before acting?" she said.

"Because action, it seems to me, was needed to prove to Your Majesty something which she doubted: that we still have courage and worth, and that those qualities should be valued."

"And that courage will face any threat, from what I've seen," said Anne of Austria.

"It's never retreated from anything in the past," said d'Artagnan. "Why should it do less in the future?"

"And this courage, in the event of a refusal, and consequently a struggle, would it go so far as to take me from the midst of my Court and give me up to the Fronde, as you threaten to do with my minister?"

"That thought never occurred to us, Madame," said d'Artagnan with the Gascon bombast that in him was mere candor. "But if the four of us resolved to do it, we'd certainly succeed."

"I ought to have known that," murmured Anne of Austria. "They are men of iron."

"Alas, Madame!" said d'Artagnan. "That proves my point, for it's only now that Your Majesty sees us as we truly are."

"But now," said Anne, "if I see it at last . . ."

"Your Majesty will do us justice. When she does us justice, she will no longer treat us as common men—she'll see me as an ambassador worthy to discuss the high matters he's been entrusted with."

"Where is the treaty?"

"Here."

Anne of Austria cast her eyes over the treaty d'Artagnan had presented to her. "I see nothing but general conditions," she said. "The interests of Messieurs de Conti, de Beaufort, de Bouillon, d'Elbeuf, and the coadjutor are all addressed. But yours?"

"We render ourselves justice, Madame, without presuming to undue status. Our names aren't worthy of appearing next to these."

"But you've not, I presume, renounced your pretensions in person?"

"I believe you're a great and powerful queen, Madame, and it would be beneath your greatness and your power not to reward properly those arms that will bring back His Eminence to Saint-Germain."

"Such is my intention," said the queen. "Come, speak."

"Forgive me if I begin with myself, but I must assume a priority, not that I've taken, but was given to me: he who has negotiated the redemption of the cardinal ought to be, for the reward to be worthy of Your Majesty, appointed a chief of the royal guards, probably the Captain of the King's Musketeers."

"You're asking me for Monsieur de Tréville's position!"

"That position is vacant, Madame, since Monsieur de Tréville's retirement last year, and hasn't been filled."

"But that's one of the premier military offices in the king's household!"

"Monsieur de Tréville was a simple cadet from Gascony like me, Madame, and he held that office for twenty years."

"You have an answer for everything, Monsieur," said Anne of Austria. And she took from a desk an order of brevet, filled it out, and signed it.

"Certainly, Madame," said d'Artagnan, taking the order and bowing, "this is a fine and noble reward—but the world is full of uncertainty, and a man who fell from Your Majesty's favor one day would lose this office the next."

"What do you want, then?" said the queen, blushing at the way this man's subtle mind had read her own.

"A payment of a hundred thousand livres to the poor Captain of the Musketeers on the day when his services are no longer agreeable to Your Majesty."

Anne hesitated.

"I must point out that the Parisians, just the other day," continued d'Artagnan, "offered, by decree of parliament, six hundred thousand livres to anyone who would deliver them the cardinal, dead or alive—to hang him if alive, and drag him through the streets if dead."

"I suppose, then," said Anne of Austria, "that your request is reasonable, since you ask for only one-sixth what the Parliament proposed to pay." And she signed a note promising a hundred thousand livres.

"What next?" she said.

"Madame, my friend du Vallon is rich, and therefore seeks no monetary reward, but I seem to recall that there was a discussion between him and Monsieur de Mazarin about elevating his domain to the status of a barony. In fact, it was a promise."

"A country bumpkin!" said Anne of Austria. "People will laugh."

"Let them," said d'Artagnan. "But there's one thing I'm sure of: no one who laughs at him will do so more than once."

"Approval for the barony," said Anne of Austria, and she signed.

"Now there just remains the Chevalier, or the Abbé d'Herblay, as Your Majesty prefers."

"He wants to be a bishop?"

"No, Madame, he requests nothing so high or so difficult."

"What, then?"

"For the king to stand as godfather to the son of Madame de Longueville."

The queen smiled mockingly.

"Monsieur de Longueville is of royal blood, Madame," said d'Artagnan.

"Yes," said the queen, "but is his son?"

"His son should be, Madame, since his mother's husband is."

"And your friend has nothing more to ask for . . . Madame de Longueville?"

"No, Madame—for he presumes that His Majesty the King, deigning to stand as the child's godfather, can't possibly present his mother a gift of less than five hundred thousand livres, as well as preserving his father's status as governor of Normandy."

"I think I can commit to the government of Normandy," said the queen, "but as to the five hundred thousand livres, the cardinal never ceases to tell me that the coffers of State are empty."

"We shall search the coffers ourselves, Madame, if Your Majesty will allow it, and I'm sure we'll find it."

"What else?"

"Else, Madame?"

"Yes."

"That's everything."

"Don't you have a fourth companion?"

"True, Madame, the Comte de La Fère."

"What does he ask for?"

"He asks for nothing."

"Nothing?"

"Yes."

"Is there a man in the world who, when in a position to ask, asks for nothing?"

"There is the Comte de La Fère, Madame—but the Comte de La Fère isn't a man."

"What is he, then?"

"The Comte de La Fère is a demigod."

"Has he not a son or a nephew, a young man whom Comminges spoke of as a brave lad, who brought the battle flags from Lens with Monsieur de Châtillon?"

"He has, as Your Majesty says, a ward called the Vicomte de Bragelonne."

"If we offered this young man a regiment, what would his guardian say?"

"He might, perhaps, accept it."

"Perhaps!"

"Yes, if Your Majesty asked him to do so."

"He's an unusual man, Monsieur, as you yourself said. Well, we'll think about it, and we may perhaps ask him to take it. Are you satisfied, Monsieur?"

"Yes, Your Majesty. But there is one thing the queen hasn't yet signed."

"What's that?"

"The most important thing of all."

"My acceptance of the treaty?"

"Yes."

"No hurry. I'll sign the treaty tomorrow."

"The one thing I can definitely say to Your Majesty," said d'Artagnan, "is that if Your Majesty doesn't sign the treaty today, she'll never find the time to sign it later. Be so good, I beg of you, as to write at the bottom of this summary, which as you can see is entirely in the handwriting of Monsieur de Mazarin, 'I consent to ratify the treaty proposed by the Parisians.'"

Anne was caught; there was no way to back down, she had to sign it. But scarcely had she put down the plume before pride burst forth in her like a tempest, and she began to weep helplessly—for at that time queens wept like ordinary women.

D'Artagnan was taken aback by these tears. The Gascon shook his head—for these royal tears burned his heart. "Madame," he said, kneeling, "behold this unhappy gentleman prostrate at your feet. He begs you to believe that at a single gesture from Your Majesty, he would be capable of anything. He has faith in himself, he has faith in his friends, all he wants is to have faith in his queen. And as proof that he fears nothing, that he threatens nothing, he will bring back Monsieur de Mazarin without conditions. Here, Madame, take back Your Majesty's sacred signatures; if you think I should have them back again, that's up to you. But from this moment on, you're committed to nothing."

And d'Artagnan, still on his knees, his eyes flashing with pride and courage, returned to Anne of Austria that stack of papers which he had won from her one by one, and with such effort.

There are moments—for if all is not good in this world, neither is all bad—when in the hardest and coldest heart there springs, watered by the tears of great emotion, a generous upwelling of feeling, which calculation and pride would stifle if there was nothing noble to counter them. Anne was caught in one of those moments. D'Artagnan, by yielding to the urging of his own heart, which beat in harmony with that of the queen, accomplished a great feat of diplomacy. And he was immediately rewarded for his devotion—or his wisdom, depending on whether one wishes to honor his heart or his mind.

"You were right, Monsieur," said Anne. "I had misjudged you. Here are the signed orders, which I freely return to you. Go, and as soon as you can, bring the cardinal back to me."

"Madame," said d'Artagnan, "twenty years ago—for I have a good memory—I had the honor, from behind a tapestry at the Hôtel de Ville, to kiss one of your beautiful hands."

"Here is the other," said the queen, "and that the left should be no less generous than the right"—she drew from her finger a diamond nearly as fine as the original—"take and keep this ring in memory of me."

"Madame," said d'Artagnan, rising, "I have but one desire, which is that the first thing you'll ask of me is my life." And then, with that stride that belonged to him alone, he turned and went out.

"I've badly misjudged those men," said Anne of Austria, following d'Artagnan with her eyes, "and now it's too late for me to use them, for in a year the king will be old enough to rule!"[57]

Fifteen hours later, d'Artagnan and Porthos brought Mazarin back to the queen, and received, the one his promotion to the rank of Captain-Lieutenant of the Musketeers, and the other, his elevation to the baronetcy.

"Well! Are you satisfied?" asked Anne of Austria.

D'Artagnan bowed. But Porthos turned his letter patent over and over in his hands, and looked at Mazarin.

"What is it, then?" asked the minister.

"It's just that, Monseigneur, there was talk of the promise of a knightly order at the first promotion."

"But you know, Monsieur le Baron," said Mazarin, "that one can't become a Knight of the Order without proof of valor."

"Oh!" said Porthos. "It wasn't for me, Monseigneur, that I requested the cordon bleu."

"For who, then?" asked Mazarin.

"For my friend, Monsieur le Comte de La Fère."

"Oh!" said the queen. "That's another thing entirely. His valor is proven."

"He'll have it?"

"It is done."

That very day the Treaty of Paris was signed,[58] and it was proclaimed everywhere that the cardinal had sequestered himself for three days while he worked out the details.

Here's what was gained by this famous treaty:

Monsieur de Conti got Damvilliers, and, having proven himself as a general, obtained the right to remain a Man of the Sword and not have to become a cardinal. Furthermore, there was some talk of his marrying one of Mazarin's nieces, talk that was heard with favor by the prince, since, after all, he had to marry someone.

Monsieur le Duc de Beaufort returned to Court with reparations for all the injuries he'd suffered, and with all the honors due to his rank. He was granted full amnesty for all those who'd helped him to escape, the return of the admiralty once held by his father the Duc de Vendôme, and an indemnity for those houses and châteaux which had been demolished by the Parliament of Brittany.

The Duc de Bouillon received domains equal in value to his lost principality of Sedan, an indemnity for eight years of his non-enjoyment of said principality, and the title of *prince* thereafter accorded to him and the descendants of his house.

The Duc de Longueville was made governor of Pont-de-l'Arche in Normandy, received five hundred thousand livres for his wife, and the honor of seeing his son held at the baptismal font by the young king and young Henrietta of England.[59] (Aramis had stipulated that Bazin would officiate at this rite, and Planchet would cater the reception.)

The Duc d'Elbeuf obtained the payment of certain sums due to his wife, one hundred thousand livres for his eldest son, and twenty-five thousand for each of his other three.

Only the coadjutor had been given nothing. It was promised that negotiations would be opened with the pope to get him a cardinal's hat, but he knew not to depend on such promises from the queen and Mazarin. Unlike

Monsieur de Conti, who had won the right not to become a cardinal, he was obliged to remain a Man of the Sword.

So, while all Paris rejoiced in anticipation of the return of the king, set for the following day, Gondy alone, left out of the general joy, sent for the two men he usually called upon when in a dark frame of mind.

These two men were the Comte de Rochefort and the beggar of Saint-Eustache. Both arrived with their usual punctuality, and the coadjutor spent most of the night talking with them.

XLVII

In Which It Is Shown that It Can Be Harder for a King to Return to His Capital than to Leave It

While d'Artagnan and Porthos were returning the cardinal to Saint-Germain, Athos and Aramis, who had parted from them at Saint-Denis, had returned to Paris, where each of them had a visit to make. Aramis went without delay straight to the Hôtel de Ville, where Madame de Longueville held court. When she was first told of the peace the lovely duchess responded with anger and dismay. War had made her a queen, and peace would mean an abdication; she declared she'd never accept the treaty and vowed eternal conflict. But when Aramis painted this peace in its true light, pointing out its advantages, such as trading a precarious royalty in war-torn Paris for the secure viceroyalty of Pont-de-l'Arche—in other words, all of Normandy—when she thought of what she could do with the five hundred thousand livres promised by the cardinal, and when she considered the honor the king would do her child by holding him at the baptismal font, she stopped being serious in her complaints, though she continued her protests in that way that pretty women have, defending herself only to make her surrender worthwhile.

Aramis pretended to believe in her protests, not wanting to deny himself the merit of having won her over. "Madame," he said to her, "you were seeking a way to defeat your brother, Monsieur le Prince, that is, the greatest commander of our age, and when women of genius want something, they always succeed. And you *have* succeeded: Monsieur le Prince is beaten, since he can no longer wage war. Now, begin to draw him to our party. Gently detach him from the queen, whom he dislikes, and Monsieur de Mazarin, whom he despises. The Fronde is a comedy of which we've played only the first act.⁶⁰ We'll have our reckoning with Monsieur de Mazarin in the finale, on that day when, thanks to you, Monsieur le Prince turns against the Court."

Madame de Longueville was persuaded. The duchess had so much faith in the power of her beautiful eyes that she had no doubt they could influence even Monsieur de Condé—and rightfully so, according to the scandalous accounts of the time.

Athos, on leaving Aramis at the Place Royale, had gone to see Madame de Chevreuse. Here was another leading Frondeuse to win over, but she was more difficult to convince than her younger rival, as no conditions had been stipulated in her favor. Monsieur de Chevreuse was not to be appointed any province's governor, and if the queen agreed to be a godmother it could be only to a grandchild. Thus, at the first words of peace, Madame de Chevreuse frowned fiercely, and despite all Athos's logical arguments that to continue the war was impossible, she insisted on further hostilities.

"My lovely friend," said Athos, "please hear me when I tell you everyone is sick of the war, that everyone, except perhaps you and the coadjutor, are ready for peace. You will get yourself exiled as in the time of King Louis XIII. Believe me, we're beyond the age of cabals and intrigues, and your beautiful eyes weren't made to be reddened by weeping for Paris, where there will always be two queens so long as you are here."

"Oh!" said the duchess. "I can't make war by myself, but I can avenge myself on this ingrate of a queen and this upstart of a favorite . . . and, faith of a duchess, I will be avenged!"

"Madame," said Athos, "I implore you, do nothing to endanger Monsieur de Bragelonne's future. His career is launched, Monsieur le Prince is fond of him, and he is young—let him find his footing alongside his young king. *Hélas!* Excuse my weakness, Madame, there comes a time when a man sees himself born again in his children."

The duchess smiled, half tenderly, half ironically. "Count," she said, "you've been won over, I fear, to the party of the Court. Is that the cordon bleu of a knightly order I see there in your pocket?"

"Yes, Madame," said Athos, "I have the Order of the Garter, which King Charles presented to me a few days before his death." The count spoke the truth: he was unaware of Porthos's request on his behalf and knew of no other order.

"*Allons!* Then I suppose I must become an old woman," said the duchess, rueful.

Athos took up her hand and kissed it. She looked at him and sighed. "Count," she said, "it must be a charming locale, your Bragelonne. You're a man of exquisite taste: you must have water, and woods, and gardens." She sighed anew and rested her lovely head on her coquettishly curved hand, admirable as ever in contour and color.

"Madame," replied the count, "I was lost—what did you say just now? Never have you been more youthful and more beautiful."

The duchess shook her head. "Will Monsieur de Bragelonne stay in Paris?" she said.

"Do you think he should?" asked Athos.

"Leave him to me," replied the duchess.

"No, Madame—perhaps you've forgotten the story of Oedipus, but I haven't."

"How charming you are, Count. In truth, I believe I'd like to spend a month at this Bragelonne of yours."

"But wouldn't that make me too great an object of envy, Duchess?" Athos replied gallantly.

"No, I'd go incognito, under the name of Marie Michon."

"You are adorable, Madame."

"But as to Raoul, don't let him stay there."

"Why not?"

"Because he's in love."

"He, a child!"

"But it's a child whom he loves."

That made Athos thoughtful. "You're right, Duchess—this intense love for a child of seven will break his heart someday. There will be fighting in Flanders; he shall go."

"Then, when the time comes, you'll send him to me, and I'll armor him against love."

"Alas, Madame!" said Athos. "These days love is like war, and armor has become useless."

At that moment Raoul entered; he'd come to announce to the count and the duchess that he'd heard from his friend, the Comte de Guiche, that the solemn return to Paris of the king, the queen, and her minister was to take place the following day.

The next day, at dawn, the Court made its preparations to leave Saint-Germain. The queen, on the previous evening, had sent for d'Artagnan. "Monsieur," she had said to him, "I've been told that Paris is still unsettled, and I fear for the king. Stay near the carriage's right door, where he will sit."

"Your Majesty can rest easy," said d'Artagnan. "I'll answer for the king." And saluting the queen, he went out.

Upon leaving the queen's quarters, Bernouin informed d'Artagnan that the cardinal awaited him on a matter of importance. He went straight to the cardinal's study.

"Monsieur," said the cardinal, "there's talk there may be a riot in Paris. I shall be sitting to the left of the king, and as I'm the main one who's threatened, prepare to guard the carriage's left door."

"Your Eminence can rest easy," said d'Artagnan. "They won't touch a hair of your head."

"The devil!" he said, once outside in the antechamber. "How do I get out of this one? I can't be at both doors of the carriage at the same time. Ah, bah! I'll guard the king, and Porthos will guard the cardinal."

This arrangement suited everyone, a thing almost unprecedented. The queen had confidence in the courage of d'Artagnan, whom she knew, and the cardinal in the strength of Porthos, which he'd felt personally.

The procession set out for Paris in a prearranged order: Guitaut and Comminges marched in advance at the head of the guards, then came the royal carriage, with d'Artagnan at one door and Porthos at the other, and then the King's Musketeers, for twenty-two years the comrades of d'Artagnan, who'd been their lieutenant for twenty, and their captain since yesterday.

On arriving at the city gate, the carriage was greeted by loud cries of *"Vive le roi!"* and *"Vive la reine!"* There were even a few lone cries of *"Vive* Mazarin!*"* but no one else took them up.

They were headed for Notre-Dame, where a *Te Deum* was to be sung. The entire population of Paris was in the streets; the Swiss Guards lined both sides of the route, but as the route was long, the line was only one man deep, with a soldier every six or eight paces. This barrier was quite insufficient; from time to time the dyke broke under the flood of people, and it took forever to reform it.

At every rupture, however benevolent, since the Parisians just wanted to see their king and their queen, of whom they'd been deprived for a year, Anne of Austria glanced anxiously at d'Artagnan, who reassured her with a smile.

Mazarin, who'd spent a thousand louis for the cries of *"Vive* Mazarin!*"*, and who hadn't thought the shouts he'd heard worth twenty pistoles, was also looking anxiously at Porthos. But his gigantic bodyguard replied to these looks in his sonorous bass voice with, "Never fear, Monseigneur," so Mazarin was less and less worried.

When they reached the Palais Royal, the crowd was even thicker; it flowed toward that spot from every adjacent street, and one could see, like a cresting river, the flood of the populace surging toward the carriage, and roaring loudly down the Rue Saint-Honoré.

When they reached the palace square, it resounded with loud cries of "Long live Their Majesties!" Mazarin leaned out his door, and two or three shouts of "Long live the cardinal!" greeted his appearance, but they were followed by a storm of whistles and boos. Mazarin turned pale and fell back inside.

"Rabble!" muttered Porthos.

D'Artagnan said nothing, but twisted his mustache with a gesture that indicated his Gascon good humor was giving way to irritation.

Anne of Austria leaned toward the ear of the young king and said, in a low voice, "Salute Monsieur d'Artagnan graciously, my son, and say a few words to him."

The young king leaned out the window of his door. "I've not yet wished you bonjour today, Monsieur d'Artagnan," he said, "but you should know that I recognize you—it was you behind the curtains of my bed, that night when the Parisians wanted to see me sleeping."

"And if the king will permit it," said d'Artagnan, "it will always be me who's near him whenever danger threatens."

"Monsieur," said Mazarin to Porthos, "what would you do if the entire mob rushed us?"

"I'd kill as many of them as I could, Monseigneur," said Porthos.

"Hmm!" said Mazarin. "No matter how brave and strong you are, you couldn't kill them all."

"You may be right," said Porthos, standing in his stirrups to survey the immense crowd. "It's true, there are a lot of them."

"I think I'd rather have the other bodyguard," muttered Mazarin. And he sat farther back in the carriage.

The queen and her minister were right to be worried, or at least the latter was. The crowd, while continuing to show respect and even affection for the king and the queen regent, began to grow more agitated. The procession heard a rising sound that, when heard above the sea's waves, indicated the onslaught of a tempest, and when heard above a multitude, indicated an oncoming riot.

D'Artagnan turned toward the musketeers and made a small but significant nod toward the crowd, a gesture understood by his brave elite guards. The ranks of the riders tightened up, and a shudder ran through the men.

At the Barrière des Sergents the procession ground to a halt. Comminges left the head of the escort and came back to the royal carriage. The queen questioned d'Artagnan with a look, and he replied the same way. "Onward. Push forward," said the queen.

Comminges returned to his post. With an effort, the vanguard pushed through the human wall, though not without some violence. Ugly shouts rose from the crowd, this time aimed not just at the minister, but at the king.

"Forward!" D'Artagnan loudly cried.

"Forward!" repeated Porthos.

But, as if the multitude had only waited for a single incident to change its nature, all the hostility that had formerly been restrained suddenly burst forth.[61] Shouts of "Down with Mazarin! Death to the cardinal!" came from all sides.

At the same time, from the Rue de Grenelle-Saint-Honoré and the Rue du Coq came a double surge that broke though the thin line of Swiss Guards, two fierce currents that swirled right up to the sides of the horses of d'Artagnan and Porthos. This new irruption was more dangerous than anything before, for it consisted of armed men, with weapons better than those the common people usually bore. It was easy to see that this was no random movement of malcontents but rather a deliberate attack, organized by someone with a grasp of command. Each attacking column was led by a chief, one of whom seemed to be, not one of the common people, but instead a ragged beggar, whereas the other, though dressed as a bourgeois, couldn't conceal the demeanor of a gentleman. The two were evidently allies.

As the streams converged the royal carriage felt a tremendous jolt. Then thousands of cries were heard, the genuine clamor of a riot, punctuated by two or three gunshots.

"Musketeers, to me!" cried d'Artagnan.

The troop of musketeers advanced in two lines, one to the right of the carriage, the other to the left: one to the aid of d'Artagnan, the other to the aid of Porthos.

Then a pitched mêlée ensued, all the more terrible as it seemed to have no purpose, all the more desperate as it seemed no one knew whom they were fighting or why.

Like all such mad movements of crowds, the shock of this savage charge was terrible. The musketeers, badly outnumbered, unable in the press to move or turn their mounts, began to get separated.

D'Artagnan moved to lower the carriage's shutters, but the young king waved him away, saying, "No, Monsieur d'Artagnan, I want to see."

"If Your Majesty wants to see, then let him look!" said d'Artagnan. And turning around with that fury that made him so terrible in battle, he spurred toward the leader of the rioters, who, with a pistol in one hand and a long sword in the other, was fighting his way toward the carriage, engaging two musketeers at once.

"Give way, *mordioux!*" shouted d'Artagnan. "Give way!"

At this voice, the man with the pistol and the long sword looked up, but too late: d'Artagnan's rapier thrust took him through the chest. "Ah! *Ventre-saint-gris!*" cried d'Artagnan, withdrawing his sword too late. "Why the devil did it have to be you, Count?"

"To fulfill my destiny," said Rochefort, falling to one knee. "Ah! I've recovered from three of your sword-thrusts—but I won't recover from the fourth."

"Count," said d'Artagnan, voice choking, "I struck without knowing it was you. I'd be forever sorry if I sent you to your death, and you died hating me for it."

Rochefort extended a hand to d'Artagnan, and d'Artagnan took it. The count tried to speak, but a gush of blood filled his mouth, he stiffened in a final convulsion, and died.

"Back, you rabble!" snarled d'Artagnan. "Your chief is dead, and you have no more business here."

In fact, as if the Comte de Rochefort had been the soul of the attack on the king's side of the carriage, the mob that had followed and obeyed him turned and ran when they saw him fall. D'Artagnan led a charge of twenty musketeers up the Rue du Coq and that side of the riot blew away like smoke, scattering across the Place de Saint-Germain-l'Auxerrois and toward the quays.

D'Artagnan turned back to assist Porthos, in case he needed it, but Porthos, on his side, had done his work with the same thoroughness as d'Artagnan. The left side of the coach was cleared, and its shutter was slowly raising, as Mazarin, less bellicose than the king, tentatively took a look outside.

Porthos seemed melancholy. "Why the devil do you look so glum, Porthos?" said d'Artagnan. "That's a strange attitude for a victor."

"But you yourself seem more than a little upset," said Porthos.

"And I have cause, *mordioux!* I just killed an old friend."

"Really?" said Porthos. "Who?"

"That poor Comte de Rochefort. . . ."

"Well, I'm in the same boat! I just killed someone whose face I thought I recognized. Unfortunately, I struck him in the head, and in a moment his face was covered with blood."

"Did he say anything as he fell?"

"He did! He said, 'Oof!'"

"I see," said d'Artagnan, unable to contain a laugh. "If that's all he said, that didn't tell you much about him."

"*Eh bien*, Monsieur?" asked the queen.

"Madame," said d'Artagnan, "the road is perfectly free, and Your Majesty can continue on her way."

In fact, the entire procession arrived without accident at the Cathedral of Notre-Dame, on the steps of which all the clergy, the coadjutor at their head, awaited the king, the queen, and the minister, for whose blessed return they were to sing the *Te Deum*.

During the service, as it was approaching its end, a frightened young gamin entered the church, ran to the sacristy, quickly donned the robe of a choirboy, and, slipping through the crowded church thanks to the sacred vestments he wore, approached Bazin, where the beadle, clothed in his blue robe and holding his silver-crowned staff, stood gravely across from the Swiss Guard at the entrance to the choir.

Bazin felt a furtive tug at his sleeve. His eyes, beatifically raised toward heaven, slowly descended toward earth until he recognized Friquet. "What is it, little clown?" asked the beadle. "How dare you disturb me in the exercise of my holy duties?"

"Do you remember, Monsieur Bazin," said Friquet, "that Monsieur Maillard, the holy water dispenser at Saint-Eustache?"

"Yes. What of him?"

"Well, in the riot he got hit in the head by a big sword, swung by a great giant wearing gold lace on every seam."

"Indeed?" said Bazin. "In that case, he must be badly injured."

"So badly injured that he's dying, and says he wants to confess to Monsieur le Coadjuteur, who has the power, he says, to forgive even the greatest sins."

"And does he imagine that Monsieur le Coadjuteur will take the trouble to see him?"

"Yes, because it seems Monsieur le Coadjuteur promised to do just that."

"And who told you that?"

"Monsieur Maillard himself."

"Then you've seen him?"

"Certainly, I was there when he was struck down."

"And what were you doing there?"

"Doing? I was shouting, 'Down with Mazarin! Death to the cardinal! Hang the Italian!' Isn't that what you told me to shout?"

"Not so loud, little clown!" said Bazin, looking anxiously around him.

"So, he said to me, this poor Monsieur Maillard, 'Go and fetch Monsieur le Coadjuteur, Friquet—and if you do, I'll make you my heir.' He said that, Père Bazin, the heir of Monsieur Maillard, holy water dispenser of Saint-Eustache! I'll be set for life! I'd really like to do this for him, what do you say?"

"I'll go and inform Monsieur le Coadjuteur," said Bazin. In fact, he slowly and respectfully approached the prelate, whispered a few words in his ear, received as reply an affirmative gesture, and then backed away with the same care and respect. "Go and tell the dying man to be patient," he said to Friquet. "Monseigneur will be there within the hour."

"Good," said Friquet. "My fortune is made."

"By the way," said Bazin, "where did they take him?"

"To the tower of Saint-Jacques-la-Boucherie."

And, enchanted with the success of his diplomatic mission, Friquet, without removing his choirboy robes, which after all made his journey that much easier, left the basilica and ran off, as quickly as he could, to the tower of Saint-Jacques-la-Boucherie.

In the same manner, as soon as the *Te Deum* was finished, the coadjutor, as he'd promised, and also without removing his priestly vestments, made his own way toward the old tower he knew so well.

He arrived in time: though fading fast, the wounded man wasn't yet dead.

They entered the room where the dying beggar lay. A moment later Friquet came back out, holding in his hands a bulging leather sack, which he opened as soon as he was out of sight, and found to his astonishment was filled with gold coins. The beggar had kept his word and made him his heir. "Oh, Mother Nanette!" Friquet cried, and then choked up, unable to say another word. But his strength otherwise hadn't left him, and he ran desperately through the streets. Then, like the Greek from Marathon falling down in the market of Athens with the laurel in his hand, Friquet tripped as he arrived at Councilor Broussel's door and fell into the foyer, scattering gold everywhere as it poured from the sack.

Mother Nanette started by picking up the coins and ended by picking up and hugging Friquet.

Meanwhile, the procession returned to the Palais Royal. "Ma Mère, he's a very valiant man, that Monsieur d'Artagnan," said the young king.

"Yes, my son, and he did great service for your father. Manage him well and he'll do the same for you."

"Monsieur le Capitaine," said the young king as he was descending from the carriage, "Madame the queen has desired me to invite you to dine with us this evening, you and your friend the Baron du Vallon."

This was a great honor for d'Artagnan and for Porthos, who lit up with delight. However, throughout the meal, the worthy baron seemed preoccupied. "What's eating you, Baron?" d'Artagnan asked him as they descended the Palais Royal's grand staircase. "You seemed anxious during dinner."

"I was racking my brains," said Porthos, "trying to remember when it was that I'd seen that beggar chief I must have killed."

"And could you recall?"

"No."

"Ah, well! Keep at it, my friend. And when you remember, you'll tell me about it, won't you?"

"*Pardieu!* I should say so," said Porthos.

XLVIII

Conclusion

Upon returning home, the two friends found a letter from Athos inviting them to meet him at the Grand Charlemagne the next morning.

They both went to bed at an early hour, but though tired, neither slept. One doesn't achieve all one's earthly desires and then simply fall asleep—at least not the first night.

The next day, at the appointed hour, they went to visit Athos. They found the count and Aramis dressed in traveling clothes. "Oh ho!" said Porthos. "Then we're all leaving? I also made my preparations to go this morning."

"My God, yes," said Aramis. "With the Fronde over, there's nothing left to do in Paris. Madame de Longueville has invited me to go and spend a few days in Normandy, and has charged me, while her son is getting baptized, to go and find suitable lodgings for them in Rouen. I shall fulfill this commission, and then, if nothing else comes up, I'll go back and bury myself in my monastery at Noisy-le-Sec."

"And I shall take myself back to Bragelonne," said Athos. "You know, my dear d'Artagnan, that I'm really nothing more these days than a provincial country gentleman. Raoul has no other fortune than my own, poor lad, so I must husband it as well as I can, as I'm really little more than its trustee."

"And Raoul, what will he do?"

"I leave him to you, my friend. You'll be off to make war in Flanders, so take him with you; I fear a prolonged stay in Blois will only ruin him. Take him with you and teach him to be brave and forthright, as you are."

"And I," said d'Artagnan, "though I won't have you, Athos, at least I'll have Raoul's sweet blond head around. He may be just a child, but your entire soul is reborn in him, dear Athos, and when he's with me, I can almost believe I have you yourself by my side."

The four friends embraced each other with tears in their eyes. Then they parted, not knowing whether they would ever meet again.

D'Artagnan returned to Rue Tiquetonne with Porthos, who was still preoccupied with trying to place the features of the man he'd killed. On arriving in front of the Hôtel de La Chevrette, they found the baron's equipage ready to go, with Mousqueton already in the saddle.

"See here, d'Artagnan," said Porthos, "put away the sword and come with me to Pierrefonds, or Bracieux, or Vallon, and we'll grow old together talking about our adventures with our comrades."

"Not me!" said d'Artagnan. "*Peste!* They're about to open a new campaign, and I want to get in on it—I still have some ambitions!"

"What more could you possibly want?"

"To be a Marshal of France, *pardieu!*"

"Really?" said Porthos, who was never sure when to take d'Artagnan's Gasconades seriously.

"Come with me, Porthos, and we'll make a duke of you yet," said d'Artagnan.

"No," said Porthos. "Mouston has lost his taste for war. Besides, they've arranged for me a solemn and triumphal entry to my château, which will make my neighbors die of envy."

"I can't offer anything better than that," said d'Artagnan, who well understood the vanity of the new baron. "Au revoir, then, my friend."

"Au revoir, friend Captain," said Porthos. "You know that whenever you want to see me, you'll always be welcome in my barony."

"Yes," said d'Artagnan. "When I return from the campaign, I'll come visit you."

"Monsieur le Baron's equipages are waiting," said Mousqueton.

And the two friends parted after shaking hands. D'Artagnan remained at the gate, watching with a melancholy eye as Porthos rode away.

But after about twenty paces, Porthos stopped short, smacked his forehead with his great hand, and returned. "I remembered," he said.

"What?" asked d'Artagnan.

"Who that beggar was that I killed."

"Really? Who was it?"

"It was that scoundrel Bonacieux!"[62]

And Porthos, delighted at having his mind empty again, caught up with Mousqueton and disappeared around the corner of the street.

D'Artagnan stood motionless for a minute, thinking to himself, then, turning, he saw the beautiful Madeleine who stood worried on the threshold, uncertain at seeing d'Artagnan in his new grandeur.

"Madeleine," said the Gascon, "I shall be moving into your best apartments on the first floor; I'm obliged to maintain a certain dignity now that I'm Captain of the Musketeers. But," he added, "just keep that room on the fifth floor for me as well. One never knows what might happen."

THE END

~The Musketeers Cycle continues in Book 5, *Between Two Kings*~

Historical Characters

ANNE: *Anne of Austria, "Anne d'Autriche," Queen of France* (1601–66). Eldest daughter of King Philip III of Spain and sister to King Philip IV, Anne was wed to King Louis XIII of France in a political marriage at the age of fourteen. A Spaniard among the French, unloved by the king, proud but intimidated, and vulnerable to manipulation by her friends, she wielded very little influence until she finally gave birth to a royal heir, the future Louis XIV, in 1638. After Louis XIII died in 1643, with his heir still a child, Anne was declared Queen Regent, and thereafter came into her own, holding France together against threats both internal and external until Louis XIV was old enough to rule. Anne was intelligent and strong-willed but not a skilled politician; in that she was aided by her close association with her prime minister, Cardinal Mazarin. Were they lovers? Anne's exact level of intimacy with Mazarin is a matter of conjecture; Dumas the novelist prefers the juiciest possible interpretation.

ARAMIS: *Aramis, Chevalier/Abbé René d'Herblay,* is based loosely on Henri, Seigneur d'Aramitz (1620?–1655 or 1674), as filtered through Courtilz de Sandras's fictionalized *Memoirs of Monsieur d'Artagnan.* Though Sandras had made Aramis the brother of Athos and Porthos, the historical d'Aramitz was a Gascon petty nobleman, an abbot who spent at least the first half of the 1640s serving under his uncle, Captain de Tréville, in the King's Musketeers. Sources disagree as to the date of his death.

Artagnan see D'ARTAGNAN

ATHOS: *Athos, Comte de La Fère,* is based loosely on Armand, Seigneur de Sillègue, d'Athos, et d'Autevielle (c. 1615–1643), as filtered through Courtilz de Sandras's fictionalized *Memoirs of Monsieur d'Artagnan.* Though Sandras had made Athos the brother of Aramis and Porthos, the historical d'Athos was a Gascon petty nobleman who joined his cousins, Captain de Tréville and Isaac de Portau (Porthos) in the King's Musketeers in 1640. Little is known of his life; he was killed in a duel in December 1643.

BEAUFORT: *François de Vendôme, Duc de Beaufort* (1616–69). Beaufort was the grandson of King Henri IV and his mistress Gabrielle d'Estrées, which made him a Prince of the Blood because his father, César de Vendôme, though illegitimate, was an acknowledged royal bastard. After the death of Louis XIII, the popular Beaufort expected to be a leading member of the Regent's Court, but when his rivalry with Mazarin came to a head the queen sided with the cardinal, and Beaufort was imprisoned in the royal Château de Vincennes. After his dramatic escape from Vincennes in 1648, he cast his lot with the Fronde, but rejoined the Court in 1653 after the Fronde sputtered out, and thereafter behaved as a loyal subject of Louis XIV.

BERNOUIN: *Monsieur Bernouin* or *Barnouin.* Little is known about Mazarin's premier valet de chambre Bernouin, except that he may have been a Provençal who came north to Paris with his master when Mazarin became a protégé of Richelieu.

BRAGELONNE: *Raoul, Vicomte de Bragelonne.* The young viscount is almost entirely Dumas's invention, based solely on a single reference in Madame de La Fayette's memoir of *Henriette d'Angleterre,* which mentions that in Louise de La Vallière's youth in Blois she had once loved a young man named Bragelonne. Raoul's relationship with Louise—and her relationship with King Louis XIV—will be central to all the volumes of the Musketeers Cycle that follow *Blood Royal.*

BROUSSEL: *Councilor Pierre Broussel* (1575?–1654). A popular and influential councilor in the *Parlement de Paris* during the Fronde, Broussel was a persistent voice opposed to the steep rise in royal taxes, leading to his arrest on Mazarin's orders on August 26, 1648, an act that precipitated the Day of the Barricades. Released two days later, he was hailed as a hero by the Parisians, and continued to lead the anti-Mazarin faction in parliament as long as the Fronde continued. He was a canny politician, and if Dumas portrays him as a bit of a fool, this was probably due to Broussel's depiction in the memoirs of his rival Cardinal de Retz (the former coadjutor), who called him "senile."

Cardinal see MAZARIN or RICHELIEU

CHARLES I: *Charles Stuart, King Charles I of England* (1600–1649). Charles was a complex man who led an eventful life, not easily summarized. Born in Scotland, his father inherited the throne of England in 1603, and thereafter Charles was raised as an Englishman. But he wasn't trained to wear the crown, as he had an elder brother, Prince Henry, who was the heir to King James. When Charles was twelve Henry unexpectedly died, and suddenly Charles was the heir. He came under the influence of a royal favorite, the first Duke of Buckingham, who was an appalling role model, arrogant and authoritarian. By the time Charles assumed the throne in 1625 he was determined to rule by divine right, an attractive program to a monarch who just wasn't very good at politics. He was almost immediately married to the sister of Louis XIII, Princess Henriette of France, a controversial match because of her ardent Catholicism. It was a stormy marriage at first, but after Buckingham was assassinated in 1628 Charles seems to have reassigned his affections to his wife, who thereafter bore him nine children. Charles's preference for direct rule led him into protracted conflict with the English Parliament, which led to open warfare in 1642. The king was detained or placed under arrest several times, the last in November 1648; he was tried in January 1649, in London under Cromwell's military control, and beheaded on January 30. For the purposes of his novel Dumas depicts Charles as noble and sympathetic, even sentimental, but this is a grave oversimplification.

CHAVIGNY: *Leon Le Bouthillier, Comte de Chavigny* (1608–1652). Like Mazarin a protégé of Richelieu, and a minister of state for foreign diplomacy late in the reign of Louis XIII, when Louis died Chavigny, like Mazarin, continued as a member of the King's Council under the regency of Queen Anne. Chavigny and Mazarin were rivals on the council, but Chavigny was outmaneuvered by the cardinal and forced out, though he retained his role as the Governor of the Royal Château of Vincennes. Loyal to the Court during the first half of the Fronde, he later allied himself with the Prince de Condé and was himself arrested on the orders of Cardinal Mazarin.

CHEVREUSE: *Marie-Aimée de Rohan-Montbazon, Duchesse de Chevreuse, "Marie Michon"* (1600–79). One of the most remarkable French women in a century that abounded in remarkable French women, Marie de Rohan was a vector of chaos who challenged every social convention of her time with wit, cheer, charm, and unshakable self-confidence. Throughout the reign of Louis XIII, she was a steadfast friend and ally to Anne of Austria when the queen had few of either. Brilliant, beautiful, free-spirited, mischievous, adored, and adorable, she had a long list of lovers on both sides of the English Channel, many of whom ended up dead or in prison thanks to her habit of involving them in plots and conspiracies against the French Crown. She first came to prominence in 1617 when she married Albert de Luynes, Louis's former falconer and first favorite; when Luynes fell from favor in 1621 and almost immediately died, Marie avoided obscurity by marrying the Duc de Chevreuse, a wealthy Lorraine noble and perennial ornament of the French Court. Marie and her second husband had what nowadays would be called an "open marriage," leaving Madame de Chevreuse free to pursue her own interests, which were romance and treason in equal measure, mixing the two whenever possible. She was involved in every notable conspiracy of the reign of Louis XIII, was an inveterate enemy of Cardinal Richelieu, continued to make trouble for his successor Cardinal Mazarin during the Fronde, and will continue to play a prominent part in the rest of Dumas's Musketeers Cycle, including the next one, *Between Two Kings*.

COADJUTOR: *Jean-François Paul de Gondy* or *Gondi, Bishop Coadjutor of Paris* (and later *Cardinal de Retz*) (1613–1679). The Gondis were a family of Florentine bankers who were introduced to France in 1573 by Queen Catherine de Médicis and had quickly associated themselves with the high nobility. As a third son Jean-François was destined for the military, but the death of his elder brother meant he had to change gears and go into the Church to maintain the family's hold on their clerical appanages, which included part of the Bishopric of Paris. A thorough Parisian, Gondy was educated at the Sorbonne and tutored in religion by St. Vincent de Paul. During the reign of Louis XIII, he was ambitious for appointment to the position of Bishop Coadjutor of Paris, but in his youth, he had written some political essays with republican leanings that probably caused Cardinal Richelieu to suppress his advancement. After Louis XIII died, Queen Anne finally granted him the appointment; he immediately began currying favor with the citizens of Paris, speaking up on their behalf when it seemed in his interest to do so, and when the Fronde broke out in 1648 he seized the opportunity to put himself at its forefront. During the chaotic ending of the civil war in 1652 he was finally awarded a cardinal's hat, but then arrested shortly thereafter and imprisoned for two years before he escaped and left the country. In 1662 the young Louis XIV restored him to favor; he returned to France, where he was active in Church politics and diplomacy, and once more took up writing. His lively but not entirely dependable memoirs, which had been reprinted in France in 1837, were one of Dumas's primary sources. They're a good read, even today.

COMMINGES: *Gaston-Jean-Baptiste, Comte de Comminges, Lieutenant* (later *Captain*) *of the Queen's Guard* (1613–1670). Comminges was brought up at Court, and served in the Queen's Guard under his uncle, the Sieur de Guitaut (see below), eventually replacing him upon his retirement. He was far more loyal to Mazarin than Dumas makes out: it was Comminges who had arrested the Duc de Beaufort in 1643, he was named a Marshal of France in 1649, and Lieutenant-General of the King's Armies just two years after that. The wars over, he was appointed French ambassador to England after the Restoration of Charles II, serving in London from 1662–1665.

CONDÉ: *Louis de Bourbon, Prince de Condé, "Monsieur le Prince,"* later *"The Grand Condé"* (1621–1686). One of the most celebrated military commanders of his time, when he was still the Duc d'Enghien he won two signature victories in the long war against Spain, those of Rocroi in 1643 and Nördlingen in 1644. Upon the death of his father in 1646 Louis became Prince de Condé, First Prince of the Blood and third in line for the throne, but he continued his role as France's leading general, further cementing his military reputation with the victory of Lens in 1648. This was followed by his successful leadership of the royal troops in the first half of the Fronde, when he commanded at the Battle of Charenton. After that he appeared to resent deferring to Cardinal Mazarin, and in 1650 seemed to be preparing to claim a broader role in the government, possibly even the regency, when Mazarin had Condé, his brother Conti, and his sister the Duchesse de Longueville arrested, which triggered the Second Fronde. In the confusion that followed, Anne was forced to release Condé and his siblings, but Monsieur le Prince was now her sworn enemy, and after the Fronde ended he actually left France to fight for Spain. After the long Franco-Spanish war finally ended in 1659, Condé was rehabilitated by Louis XIV and welcomed back to France, where he served with distinction until his death.

CONTI: *Armand de Bourbon, Prince de Conti* (1629–1666). Younger brother of the Prince de Condé and the Duchesse de Longueville, the completely inexperienced Conti was named a leader of the Parisian forces in early 1649 solely because he was the ranking Prince of the Blood among the princes and peers supporting the Fronde. During the second Fronde he was briefly imprisoned by Mazarin along with his siblings, but Conti was more interested in religion than politics, and after the end of the Fronde he was reconciled with Cardinal Mazarin and ended up marrying one of his nieces.

CROMWELL: *Oliver Cromwell, Lord Protector of the Commonwealth* (1599–1658). A towering and divisive figure whose character and deeds are still controversial, Cromwell was a Puritan and Member of Parliament who rose to prominence as a commander of the parliamentary forces against King Charles's supporters early in the English Civil War. He gradually emerged as both a political and military leader, and used the power of his loyal soldiery to enforce the purge of Parliament that enabled the trial and execution of the king. Dumas depicts Cromwell as a calculating mastermind in the mold of Richelieu and Mazarin, but his success was probably due more to relentless determination and force of will than to wits and cunning. As Lord Protector he ruled England, Ireland, and Scotland for almost ten years, brutally crushing all opposition. He died of natural causes in 1658, and the Restoration of the monarchy came two (eventful) years later—as we'll see in *Between Two Kings,* the next book in the Musketeers Cycle.

D'ARTAGNAN: *Charles de Batz de Castelmore, Chevalier (later Comte) d'Artagnan* (c. 1611–1673). The historical d'Artagnan was a cadet (younger son) of a family of the minor nobility from the town of Lupiac in Gascony. Like so many other younger sons of Gascony, he followed his neighbor Monsieur de Tréville to Paris to make his fortune, and by 1633 was in the King's Musketeers at a time when Tréville was a lieutenant. D'Artagnan spent the rest of his life in the musketeers, except for the periods when the company was briefly disbanded and he soldiered with the Gardes Françaises. He gradually rose through the ranks until he became Captain-Lieutenant (in effect, Captain) of the Musketeers in 1667. During the Franco-Dutch War of 1673 he was killed at the Battle of Maastricht. Dumas, of course, borrowed d'Artagnan from Courtilz de Sandras's highly fictionalized biography, *The Memoirs of Monsieur d'Artagnan,* but his personality and character in the novels of the Musketeer Cycle are entirely the product of the genius of Dumas.

D'Orléans see GASTON

GASTON: *Prince Gaston de Bourbon, Duc d'Orléans, "Monsieur"* (1608–1660). Younger brother to Louis XIII and first heir to the throne, favorite son of Marie de Médicis, Gaston seems to have had no redeeming characteristics whatsoever. Proud, greedy, ambitious for the throne but an arrant coward, he was the figurehead in one conspiracy after another against the king and cardinal. These plots failed every time, after which Gaston invariably betrayed his co-conspirators in return for immunity from consequences—because as the healthy heir to a chronically unhealthy king, he knew his life was sacrosanct.

Gondy see COADJUTOR

GRAMMONT: *Antoine III, Duc de Gramont or Grammont, Marshal of France* (1604–1678). In 1640, when he was still just the Comte de Guiche, Antoine was the arrogant and lecherous villain of Rostand's *Cyrano de Bergerac.* A capable military commander, he was made a marshal in 1641, and for his victories—and because he was married to one of Richelieu's nieces—he was elevated to the peerage and became Duc de Gramont in 1643. He served Louis XIV as a diplomat.

GUICHE: *Guy Armand de Gramont, Comte de Guiche* (1637–1673). Armand de Guiche, son of the Duc de Gramont, was one of the leading playboys of the Court of Louis XIV; as Raoul de Bragelonne's closest friend, we'll be seeing a lot more of him in the subsequent novels in the Musketeers Cycle, starting with *Between Two Kings.*

GUITAUT: *François de Pechpeyroux de Comminges, Sieur de Guitaut, Captain of the Queen's Gaurds* (1581–1663). Guitaut, a crusty old relic of the Wars of Religion, was famously loyal to Anne of Austria, and served her for decades.

HARRISON: *Colonel* (later *Major-General*) *Thomas Harrison of the New Model Army* (1606–1660). Harrison was an attorney and parliamentarian who became an important military commander and ally of Cromwell during the English Civil War. A fervent anti-Royalist, he was one of the captors of Charles I, sat as a commissioner (judge) at his trial, and signed his condemnation. He never repudiated the execution of King Charles, and after the Restoration he was tried as a regicide, condemned, and drawn and quartered.

HENRIETTE: *Henriette Marie de Bourbon, Queen of England* (1609–1669). Daughter of Henri IV and sister of Louis XIII, Henriette was married by proxy to England's Charles I shortly after he assumed the throne in 1625. Haughty, entitled, and fiercely Catholic when to be Catholic in England was a major liability, Henriette's relationship with Charles was stormy at first, but eventually they proved to be well matched, and she bore him nine children. (The youngest, named after her mother, this editor has chosen to call *Henrietta* in order to differentiate the two.) During the English Civil War, she was forced to flee to France, where she lived in poverty until the Restoration.

Herblay see ARAMIS

King see CHARLES I or LOUIS XIII or LOUIS XIV

La Fère see ATHOS

LA PORTE: *Pierre de La Porte, Cloak-Bearer to the Queen* (1603–1680). La Porte entered Queen Anne's service in 1621 and became one of her most trusted confidential servants, assisting the queen in her petty intrigues and conducting her correspondence with the Duchesse de Chevreuse. Richelieu finally had him thrown in prison in 1637, though he was freed in 1643 after both king and cardinal had died. The 1839 edition of La Porte's *Memoirs* was one of Dumas's primary sources. La Porte will reappear in an important (albeit non-historical) role in the final book in the Musketeers Cycle, *The Man in the Iron Mask*.

LONGUEVILLE: *Anne-Geneviève de Bourbon Condé, Duchesse de Longueville* (1619–1679). Though mostly offstage in *Twenty Years After,* the sister of the Grand Condé was a key player in the politics of the Fronde, and one of Mazarin's most determined foes. A child of rebellion, she was born in the dungeon at Vincennes during the imprisonment of her parents, the elder Prince de Condé and Charlotte de Montmorency, who'd been jailed by Queen Marie de Médicis for opposition to her regency during the youth of Louis XIII. Lively, witty, and beautiful, she was an ornament of the salons of Madame de Rambouillet in the 1630s, until she was married in 1642 to the Duc de Longueville, a widower twice her age. It was not a happy marriage, and she turned her energy to love affairs and politics. A friend and ally of Coadjutor de Gondy, she threw herself into the turmoil of the first Fronde, attracting to the cause her younger brother de Conti and even her husband, though she was conducting an open affair at the time with another noble Frondeur, the Prince de Marcillac. After the Parisian Frondeurs were defeated militarily by her other brother, the Prince de Condé, she persuaded him to conspire against Mazarin, and in 1650 the cardinal had all three siblings jailed in the prison where Madame de Longueville was born. After the Fronde came to a messy end, she retired from public life and devoted herself to religion, becoming an important patron of the Jansenist movement.

LOUIS XIII: *King Louis XIII, His Most Christian Majesty of France, "Louis the Just"* (1601–43). Dumas wrote a great deal about Louis XIII and his reign, most of it quite accurate, in part thanks to the research of his assistant Auguste Maquet. Dumas had a good grasp of the melancholy king's character and portrayed it well, especially in the second book in the Musketeers Cycle, *The Red Sphinx.*

LOUIS XIV: *Louis de Bourbon, King of France* (1638–1715): The only Frenchman of his century more important than Richelieu, the Sun King consolidated all power in France under royal control, thus ending centuries of civil strife, but creating a political structure so rigid it made the French Revolution almost inevitable. *Twenty Years After* and *Blood Royal* begin Louis's relationship with d'Artagnan, which will evolve for the rest of the Musketeers Cycle until it achieves resolution in *The Man in the Iron Mask*.

LOUVIÈRES: *Jérôme Broussel, Seigneur de Louvières.* The son of the Parliamentarian Frondeur (see above), Louvières was a lieutenant in the royal army who was denied advancement because of his father's opposition to the Court, and therefore joined the Fronde himself. When queen and Court abandoned Paris, parliamentary forces occupied the Bastille, old Governor du Tremblay retired, and Councilor Broussel was appointed to take his place. He delegated the position to his son, who held it until the Fronde ended in 1652.

MAZARIN: *Cardinal Jules Mazarin,* born *Giulio Raimondo Mazzarino* or *Mazarini* (1602–1661). In 1634 the Italian-born diplomat became a protégé of Cardinal Richelieu and in 1639 was naturalized French and entered the king's service. Through Richelieu's influence he was made a cardinal in 1641 and brought onto the King's Council. After Richelieu and Louis XIII died, Mazarin made himself indispensable to the regent, Anne of Austria, and basically stepped into Richelieu's shoes to become France's prime minister. He was probably intimate with Queen Anne and functioned as her co-ruler until Louis XIV attained his majority. He was an extremely able diplomat, negotiating an end to the Thirty Years' War, maintaining royal authority through the chaotic years of the Fronde, striking an alliance with Cromwell, and maneuvering the fractious French nobility back into compliance with the crown in time to hand an intact and flourishing state over to King Louis XIV. He was widely disliked for being a foreigner and *arriviste* who presumed to place himself above the native nobility, feelings basically endorsed by Dumas, who preferred men of heart to men of mind. We saw the beginning of his career in *The Red Sphinx* and will see the end of it in *Between Two Kings*.

PORTHOS: *Porthos, Baron du Vallon,* based loosely on Isaac de Porthau (1617–1712), as filtered through Courtilz de Sandras's fictionalized *Memoirs of Monsieur d'Artagnan.* Though Sandras had made Porthos the brother of Aramis and Athos, the historical de Porthau was a minor Gascon nobleman who joined his cousins, Captain de Tréville and Armand d'Athos, in the King's Musketeers in 1642. When his father died in 1654 he left the musketeers and returned to Béarn, where he served as a parliamentarian and local magistrate until his death in 1712. His character and personality in the Musketeers novels are entirely the invention of Dumas.

Retz see COADJUTOR

RICHELIEU: *Armand-Jean du Plessis, Cardinal de Richelieu* (1585–1642), Louis XIII's incomparable prime minister. One of the two most important Frenchmen of the 17th century, exceeded only by Louis XIV, Richelieu has been the subject of scores of biographies (including one by Dumas), and his life and works have been analyzed in excruciating detail, starting with his own *Memoirs.* His deeds were momentous, but it was his character and personality that interested Dumas, who loved historical figures who were great but also greatly flawed. After deploying Richelieu in *The Three Musketeers* as the worthy antagonist of his most enduring heroes, Dumas couldn't resist revisiting him as a protagonist for *The Red Sphinx.* Though gone from the Musketeers Cycle after *The Red Sphinx,* Richelieu nonetheless casts a long shadow over the rest of the series, all the way through *The Man in the Iron Mask.*

ROCHEFORT: *Comte Charles-César de Rochefort.* The dangerous intriguer who appears in *The Three Musketeers, Twenty Years After,* and *Blood Royal* is a composite of two of Courtilz de Sandras's characters, the Comte de Rochefort from the 1689 pseudo-biography *Les Mémoires de M.L.C.D.R.* (1689), where M.L.C.D.R. stands for Monsieur le Comte de Rochefort, and the villain Rosnay from *The Memoirs of Monsieur d'Artagnan*, the result then brought to vivid life by Dumas. It's difficult to identify Dumas's amoral adventurer with a single historical figure; for one thing, *Rochefort* is a common place-name in France, and a Comte de Rochefort could have come from any of several noble French families. The agent of Richelieu in Sandras's story has been speculated to be from the Rocheforts of Saint-Point in Burgundy, and might have been based on Claude de Rochefort d'Ailly, Comte de Saint-Point, who was active in the first half of the 17th century. Another nominee is Henri-Louis d'Aloigny, Marquis de Rochefort (born 1625), who was one of the lieutenants of Marshal Turenne. At this remove, it seems impossible to be sure who he was.

TRÉVILLE: *Jean-Arnaud de Peyrer, Comte de Troisville or Tréville, Captain of the King's Musketeers* (1598–1672). The archetypal poor Gascon who came to Paris to find success by joining the King's Musketeers, he worked his way up through the ranks, finally becoming Captain-Lieutenant in 1634. He was certainly present at both the Siege of La Rochelle, depicted in *The Three Musketeers,* and the Battle of Susa Pass recounted in *The Red Sphinx.* He was associated with (but not complicit in) the Cinq-Mars conspiracy of 1642 and was briefly exiled, and then restored to favor when Queen Anne assumed the regency. She elevated him to the rank of count in 1643, but he didn't get along with Mazarin, who forced his retirement in 1646 by temporarily disbanding his company of musketeers. He was reconciled to the Court in the 1660s, possibly due to the influence of the historical d'Artagnan with the young Louis XIV.

Vallon see PORTHOS

Notes on the Text of *Blood Royal*

1. The tower of Saint-Jacques-la-Boucherie: A beautiful sixteenth-century High Gothic church that would have been, in 1648, almost dead center in Paris. The church was destroyed in the French Revolution except for its extravagant bell tower, which still stands. Dumas loved the tower, and even wrote a melodrama, *La Tour Saint-Jacques* (1856), set in it.

2. The Court of Miracles: The legendary "Beggars' Court" of Paris, where every night miracles occurred as the lame revealed they could walk and the blind showed they could see. The *Cour des Miracles* has appeared in countless works of fiction, most famously Victor Hugo's *The Hunchback of Notre-Dame* (1831).

3. Preparing the barricades for the following day: That day would be August 26, 1648, known thereafter in French history as The Day of the Barricades. It was the first major outbreak of violence in the Fronde, and the first major setback for the Court.

4. The Tour de Nesle: A medieval guard tower on the Seine at the western end of the old walls around the Left Bank districts, just across from the Louvre. It was the titular location of one of Dumas's most successful (and lurid) early melodramas, *La Tour de Nesle* (1832).

5. Maréchal de La Meilleraie: Charles de La Porte, Duc de La Meilleraie (1602–1664) had been a Marshal of France since 1639. D'Artagnan served under him at the Siege of Perpignan in 1642.

6. Someone like Vitry: The Marquis de Vitry, Louis XIII's guard captain, who in 1617 had killed the queen mother's favorite Concino Concini at the behest of the king and his falconer, Luynes. (See note 2.)

7. Like Diane de Poitiers and Ninon de Lenclos: Famous beauties: Diane de Poitiers (1499–1566) was the leading mistress of both King François I and his son, Henri II; Ninon de Lenclos or l'Enclos (1620–1705) was a celebrated courtesan who was also a writer and patron of the arts.

8. Malatesta and Castruccio Castracani: Dumas refers here to the notorious late-medieval Italian feud between the families of the Ghibellines (including the Malatesta) and the Guelphs (such as Castracani).

9. A short trip to Saint-Germain: Not to the Faubourg Saint-Germain, the Left Bank district of Paris just outside the city walls to the west that was the site of much of the action of *The Three Musketeers,* but rather to the town of Saint-Germain-en-Laye ten miles northwest of the city, a suburb dominated by the old royal Château de Saint-Germain.

10. Revenge for the Sicilian Vespers: In 1282, Charles, the Duc d'Anjou, who had ruled the Kingdom of Sicily brutally for almost twenty years, suffered an insurrection: starting at Vespers on Easter Monday, the Sicilians rose up and started killing the ruling Angevins, and in the following six weeks thousands of them were slaughtered.

11. The Cours-la-Reine: A tree-lined promenade outside the walls of Paris that extended west from the Tuileries along the Right Bank of the Seine.

12. Monsieur, his brother: Not Louis XIII's younger brother Prince Gaston, but rather Louis XIV's younger brother Philippe, the Duc d'Anjou (1640–1701). We'll see a lot more of him in the later books in the Musketeers Cycle.

13. Val-de-Grâce: A church and royal abbey founded in 1621 by Anne of Austria and expanded over the years by the queen's continuing donations. Situated on Rue Saint-Jacques on the Left Bank, during the reign of Louis XIII Anne used it as a refuge from the Court when she felt ignored or persecuted.

14. I'm called Dulaurier: According to Madame de Motteville, this incident of the Parisians viewing the sleeping king did take place, but in 1651 rather than 1648, and it was masterminded by Queen Anne herself. The leader of the Parisian delegation was a Monsieur de Laurier.

15. Madame la Princesse, and Madame the Princess Dowager: That is, Claire-Clémence de Maille-Brézé, Princesse de Condé, and her mother-in-law Charlotte de Montmorency, the Dowager Princess of Condé.

16. Monsieur le Duc d'Orléans, Madame la Duchesse, la Grande Mademoiselle: That is, Prince Gaston, his wife the Duchesse d'Orleans, and their daughter Anne Marie d'Orléans, Duchesse de Montpensier.

17. A full *louis*: The *louis d'or* was a French gold coin introduced into circulation in 1640 by Louis XIII (who put his face and name on it). In size and weight it was an imitation of the Spanish double *escudo* (or "doubloon"), which was also the pistole so frequently

mentioned in the Musketeer novels and the most common gold currency in Europe. A pistole was worth ten or eleven livres, or about three crowns (*écus*); the *louis d'or* was worth the same or slightly more.

18. The sweet dreams that came after collecting two hundred and nineteen louis in an hour: In one chapter, d'Artagnan saves the French monarchy by masterminding the escape of the king and queen from a Paris in revolt, an extended exploit requiring brains, boldness, insight, and physical courage. In the next chapter, in the empty château to which he'd led them, d'Artagnan makes several hundred pistoles from the French Court by selling them overpriced pallets of straw on which to bed down—and it's clear that he savors fleecing the aristocrats as much as he did saving them.

19. The town that Charles I has just turned over to the parliamentary forces: Well, not exactly: King Charles's stint at Newcastle took place in 1644, over four years earlier. Dumas drastically abridges Charles's final conflicts with the English Parliament.

20. Order of Saint-Esprit: The Ordre du Saint-Esprit, Order of the Holy Spirit, was a knightly order established by King Henri III in 1578 during the Wars of Religion as a counterweight to the Order of the Golden Fleece, whose members largely supported the fractious nobility of the Catholic League.

21. Orders of the Garter: The Most Noble Order of the Garter was an English knightly order founded in 1348 by Edward III; it was highly prestigious, and only the monarch could induct new members into its ranks.

22. Nebuchadnezzar: The Puritans had a way of relating everything and everybody to stories and personages in the Bible, and frequently compared Charles I to the wicked king of Babylon.

23. Brought Colonel Tomlinson an order to escort the king to Holdenby Castle: In 1647 Charles was briefly held at Holdenby Castle by Tomlinson, but Dumas forgot about establishing this point here and two chapters later has the king conducted to London by Colonel Harrison.

24. Philiphaugh: In September 1645, at Philiphaugh just north of the Scottish border, the Royalist army under Montrose was crushed by Leslie's force of Covenanters allied with parliament. Afterward four hundred prisoners and camp followers, many women and children, were murdered in cold blood.

25. His Majesty's trial will take place as soon as they arrive in London: Dumas once again compresses time: when Charles's trial began on January 20, 1649, he'd already been jailed in London for about five weeks.

26. A few hands of lansquenet: Lansquenet was a gambling card game of almost pure luck in which players bet as to whether their card would beat the dealer's as cards were turned up from the deck. Invented in the 16th century, it was popular for about 150 years, and was simple enough that it could be played even by drunken soldiers—indeed, its name derives from *Landsknecht*, a name for German mercenary troops.

27. A Knight of Malta: In 1649 the Knights Hospitaller, or Knights of Malta (full name: Order of Knights of the Hospital of Saint John of Jerusalem) were the last surviving Catholic military order from the time of the Crusades, and had been fighting militant Islam in the Mediterranean for over five hundred years. After having been driven back from Jerusalem, Cyprus, and Rhodes, in 1530 the knights had been granted the island of Malta by the King of Spain, and after that were known by the name of their last refuge. Membership in the order was prestigious, and though by the 17th century some French Knights of Malta still fought from the decks of galleys in the Middle Sea, many more enjoyed the status of knight without the risk of actual combat.

28. He plays biribi?: More popular gambling games: basset was an early beat-the-dealer card game that was slanted toward the bank but had attractively high payouts for certain combinations, while biribi, or cavagnole, was a lotto-style game in which players placed bets on squares from 1 to 70 while a dealer drew matching tiles from a bag.

29. His colleague Colonel Pride: Thomas Pride (?–1658) was one of Cromwell's loyal officers, and the man who executed the purge of Parliament in December 1648 that removed every member suspected of Royalist sentiments. He was also one of the king's judges at his trial.

30. Westminster Hall: The Palace of Westminster, on the Thames in central London, housed both the Parliament of England and the Royal Courts of Justice. The old medieval structure had been rebuilt and expanded in the 16TH century.

31. Colonel Fairfax: Sir Thomas Fairfax (1612–1671) had been appointed overall commander of the Parliamentary forces in 1645, but by 1648 he'd been completely superseded by Cromwell. After 1650 he retired from public life and began working in the background to support the Restoration.

32. The palace of Whitehall: Since 1530 the Palace of Whitehall had been the London residence of the English monarchy, and would continue so until it burned down in 1698. It wasn't far from Westminster.

33. As was done with poor Chalais: Henri de Talleyrand-Périgord, Comte de Chalais (1599–1626) was one of King Louis XIII's handsome young favorites, until he was arrested for complicity in a planned coup by Prince Gaston. Chalais, though the least of the conspirators, was made the scapegoat and condemned; he was executed in a spectacularly bungled beheading that took the amateur headsman hired for the job over thirty blows to complete. On the other hand, the exact identity of the masked executioner who beheaded Charles I is unknown to this day; it might have been Richard Brandon, the official London hangman, but he is also said to have refused the job.

34. The *Thousand and One Nights* had just been translated: Dumas is about sixty years too early on this one: Antoine Galland's multi-volume French translation of *The Thousand and One Nights* was published between 1704 and 1717.

35. The giant Adamastor: In *The Lusiads* (1572), an epic in verse by the Portuguese poet Luís Vaz de Camões that celebrates the circumnavigation of the globe by Vasco de Gama, the giant Adamastor rises from the sea to block the great navigator when he tries to round the Cape of Good Hope. Adamastor was a creation of de Camões and not a figure from Greek myth, the poet's claims to the contrary.

36. There's the Plough: To the British and French, the Plough is the constellation that Americans call the Big Dipper and was known to the Ancients as the Great Bear.

37. The accounts of Jean Mocquet: A celebrated French explorer and trader, Mocquet (1575–1617) wrote a six-volume account of his travels and adventures in Africa and the Near East that was published in 1617; Dumas read the edition reprinted in 1831.

38. The Place de Grève: The broad plaza in front of the Hôtel de Ville (see note 45) was a public gathering-place most famously used for public executions—nobles were beheaded, commoners hanged. Since 1802 it's been called the Place de l'Hôtel de Ville.

39. The Ducs d'Elbeuf and de Bouillon: Two lower-ranking Princes of the Blood: Charles de Lorraine, Duc d'Elbeuf (1596–1657), Beaufort's uncle, was a blustering loudmouth, while Frédéric-Maurice de la Tour d'Auvergne, Duc de Bouillon (1605–1652)

was an inveterate conspirator; before joining the Fronde, under the previous reign he'd gotten practice by plotting against Louis XIII and Richelieu.

40. We Seek our King: Throughout the Fronde the rebels maintained the conceit that they were actually rising up on the king's behalf, to free the young Louis XIV from the malign influence of Mazarin and other evil counselors.

41. De Flamarens: Antoine-Agesilan de Grossolles, Marquis de Flamarens (?–1652), a patron of the writer Chapelain, supported the Court and was killed in the last major battle of the Fronde, at Porte Saint-Antoine on July 2, 1652.

42. De Châtillon: Gaspard de Coligny, Duc de Châtillon (1620–1649) served in various command roles in the royal army from 1640 on, under the Maréchal de Gramont and the Prince de Condé, before meeting his death at Charenton, the first major battle of the Fronde.

43. The river had invaded half of the capital: Heavy rains in December 1648 had continued into January, 1649, causing the swollen Seine to overtop its banks and flood the low-lying areas of Paris. This made it even harder for the desperate capital, already under blockade by the Prince de Condé's troops, to receive food and supplies.

44. A regiment he's named the Corinthian after his archbishopric: Gondy, Bishop of Corinthe since 1644, did in fact name the regiment he raised "the Corinthian," in line with his pretensions both military and ecclesiastic.

45. The Hôtel de Ville: The Hôtel de Ville is the municipal building Americans would call City Hall; Paris's Hôtel de Ville stands on the Right Bank in central Paris facing a large riverfront plaza, the Place de Grève. A grand and imposing edifice, it wasn't fully finished until 1628.

46. He was cruelly punished for his audacity: A reference to Coligny's duel with the Duc de Guise over Madame de Longueville.

47. Monsieur de Clanleu, who commands your troops at Charenton: Bertrand d'Ostove, Marquis de Clanleu, Parisian commander for the Parliament, was killed while bravely trying to rally his troops at the Battle of Charenton.

48. They couldn't agree on a new color for the coadjutor's hat: That is, the queen and cardinal had not agreed to elevate the coadjutor to wear the red biretta of a cardinal.

49. They would have been brought before Monsieur de Longueville, who would then decide whether they should be treated as friends or enemies: Something Aramis in particular would be keen to avoid, since he'd been carrying on an affair with Madame de Longueville.

50. A giant like Enceladus or Briareus: Giants of Greek myth: Enceladus was one of the Titans who battled the gods, while Briareus fought against the Titans on the side of the divines.

51. Ratafia, that famous local liqueur: The French version of ratafia is a liqueur made from fortified wine flavored with lemon peel, almonds, cherries, and peaches.

52. Those famous conferences that were to last for three weeks, resulting in the "Lame Peace": The peace negotiated between the Parliament and Court in March 1649 lasted less than a year, until the queen's arrest of the Prince de Condé and his siblings in January, 1650 kicked off the Second, or Princely Fronde.

53. I sent them to aid King Charles: Mazarin tells Comminges a bald-faced lie, aware that d'Artagnan is unlikely to contradict him.

54. The sky of Tarbes: That is, over Gascony.

55. Milo of Croton: Legendary Greek wrestler from the 6th century B.C.E. whose feats of strength and larger-than-life personality make him almost a template for Porthos. Milo was the champion wrestler of the original Olympics six times in a row, only losing on his seventh attempt to a younger wrestler from his own town of Croton.

56. The son to which she's just given birth: Madame de Longueville's son, Charles Paris d'Orléans, was in fact born at the Hôtel de Ville in 1649 during the First Fronde, but the Prince de Marcillac was his father, not Aramis. (See note 59.)

57. And now it's too late for me to use them, for in a year the king will be old enough to rule: We will see, in the later volumes in Dumas's Musketeers Cycle, how King Louis XIV will learn from the four musketeers—and become greater than them as a result.

58. That very day the Treaty of Paris was signed: The Peace of Rueil was signed on March 11, 1649, effectively ending the First, or Parliamentary Fronde.

59. The honor of seeing his son held at the baptismal font by the young king and young Henrietta of England: This is the one provision entirely invented by Dumas: King Louis did not stand as godfather to Madame de Longueville's son. Indeed, she named as his godfather the entire City of Paris. (See note 56.)

60. The Fronde is a comedy of which we've played only the first act: Aramis is quite correct: the fundamental issues that drove the unrest have not been fully addressed, the Prince de Condé will join his siblings and turn against the Court, and the Fronde will resume the following January and continue to sputter for another two years.

61. The hostility that had formerly been restrained suddenly burst forth: Up till this point, Dumas's accounts of the unrest in Paris have been quite accurate, but this final riot is an invention to pin a climax on the novel.

62. That scoundrel Bonacieux: That is, the Parisian mercer Bonacieux, whose wife Constance fell in love with d'Artagnan in *The Three Musketeers*; Bonacieux betrayed Constance into the hands of the allies of Milady de Winter, who murdered her to get revenge on d'Artagnan. The sin that required the coadjutor's absolution is finally revealed.

Acknowledgments

The cover painting, titled *The Wounded Cavalier*, is by the Pre-Raphaelite artist William Shakespeare Burton. The interior illustrations are by Louis Marckl, Frank T. Merrill, and Eugène Courboin; many thanks to John Armstrong for digitizing and formatting these old engravings.

Thanks also to my literary agent Philip Turner, the good shepherd who has guided this series to publication.

And many thanks, as ever, to Claiborne Hancock, Sabrina Plomitallo-González, and Maria Fernandez at Pegasus Books for another handsome edition in the Musketeers Cycle. Every book looks better than the previous.

For your benefit, reader, I'd like to welcome you to my website, Swashbucklingadventure.net, where you'll find news and information about this book and others, plus additional related matters of interest. I hope to see you there!

Lawrence Ellsworth,
May 2020